T0247133

Extracted

THE LOST IMPERIALS
BOOK ONE

TYLER H. JOLLEY
&
SHERRY D. FICKLIN

EXTRACTED
Copyright ©2016 Tyler H. Jolley & Sherry D. Ficklin
All rights reserved.
Cover Design by: Whit & Ware Design
Typography by: Courtney Knight

ISBN 978-1-63422-207-5(paperback)
ISBN 978-1-63422-208-2 (e-book)

Printed in the United States of America

content disclosure

For more information about our content disclosure,
please utilize the QR code above with your smart phone
or visit us at www.CleanTeenPublishing.com

EMBER
Prologue

I don't feel the needle slide beneath my skin. It's nothing, not even a whisper compared to the other pain. Above me, some kind of human-machine hybrid presses down on my shoulders, holding me to the gurney. Its face is a mask of brass, tinted glass, and pieces of leather. Tufts of hair poke out from around the top and sides. I want to scream, but I can't. The pain has me in its grasp, like a hand around my throat, constricting until I have to fight for each breath.

At my left is a man who is, I assume, a doctor. The pocket of his white lab coat is stuffed with syringes, which he keeps plunging into my arm. He pulls out another one, bites the cap off, and spits it aside before stabbing me again. I have to look away. There is only one familiar face in the room. He's on my right, clenching my uninjured hand in his, murmuring softly and stroking my hair.

"It's all right. Everything's going to be okay."

I writhe. Whatever was in that last needle is

burning through my veins. My eyes water, but I can't move to wipe the tears away. Soon, the pain begins to fade. In the corner of the room, a man speaks. He's looking at me with distaste.

"And the other one?" the man in the corner asks.

"Gone," the one holding my hand responds, his eyes never leaving mine. Behind his glasses, his eyes are green. The greenest things I've ever seen. I focus on them, using them to clear away the fog inside my mind. He continues to speak, not looking away from me. "It was all I could do to get her out before the whole thing went up in flames."

"Then we will make do," the man in the corner says curtly before vanishing into thin air.

I open my mouth to speak, but even with the pain subsiding, no sound escapes.

"Shh," he coos. "It's all right. You're safe now."

LEX
One

We've never formally been introduced to the students from the Tesla Institute, mostly because every time we meet, things go from zero to face punch too quickly for small talk. I scan the crowd below for any hint that the Tesla kids are around, but all is clear. Hopefully, they show. I have to admit, I enjoy the excitement. And this World's Fair thing is the dullest mission I've ever done.

I look back down at the wrinkled photo of VonWeitter, the designer of the solar panel device Claymore sent us here to steal. Hopefully, we can use it to keep the lights on at the Tower. The constantly flickering gas lamps are a pretty big fire hazard, as it turns out.

Out the corner of my eye, I see Stein lean forward and shift closer to me. She's so close I can smell her; the scent is like rain and fresh cotton. It's distracting. Just like her. I smirk, shove the photo in my vest pocket, and retrieve the candy bar I'd gotten for her. She smiles when she sees it, and my heart goes double-time.

"What are you thinking about, Stein?" I ask, breaking off a chunk of chocolate and offering it to her. After bending forward, she takes it with her teeth.

She tips back her black satin top hat, a look in her eye—challenging me. I can almost read her mind. Do I really want to sit here and talk about our *feelings*? Dude, she is turning me into such a chick. I decide to let it drop.

Stein leans back on her hands. "This is so good. Where did you get it?"

I swing my legs over the rafter. "There's a clown selling it outside the exhibit hall. I got a five-finger discount."

She looks pleased, which makes me glad I risked the lift. We don't get a lot of small indulgences like chocolate back home, so whenever I have the chance to get her something, I take it. I break off a square and take a bite.

I wish we kept some chocolate back at the *Hollows*, but most of us can't sit still for three seconds—I can't imagine how bad it would be if we were hyped up on sugar all the time. I get this image of my best friend, Nobel, in my mind, vibrating across the floor like a belt sander, candy bar in one hand, soda in the other. It makes me snicker, and Stein shoots me a confused look. I just grin and ease to my feet. Handing the rest of the candy over to her, I sit back down.

The metal crossbeams of the ceiling are even less comfortable than they look. Of course, I doubt the designers imagined people would be squatting up in the rafters. I fidget every so often, trying to prevent permanent rivet dents from forming on my butt, and keep my mind off my cramped position and on the mission. Below us, Nobel fights with a huge spool of pink cotton candy. He's desperately trying to get a bite without the fluff sticking to his face—and he's failing miserably.

I chuckle, wad up the empty chocolate wrapper, and chuck it, nailing him right in the temple. He looks up. I wave.

He flips me off.

"Did you dip this in gear oil or did you just forget to wash the grease off your fingers first?" Stein asks around the last bite of candy.

"Wash? No. Wipe on pants? Yes."

Most girls might be grossed out, but she just smirks. I look down at my hands. They are dirty enough that I can make out the dark impressions of my fingerprints. Guess just wiping them off didn't get them as clean as I thought. Not really my fault, considering Nobel's device, the one that will lower me to the floor, is leaking oil.

I run my already-messy hands over the machine again. Two pressure gauges are set between three large pistons with a couple of hydraulic hoses crawling out the sides. It looks like it's made of old car parts. Knowing Nobel, that's exactly the case. But Stein isn't great with mechanical things, and I can tell from her expression that she doesn't quite trust the device.

Stein sighs. She looks half-bored, half-nervous.

I stare at her for a second, struck by how pretty she looks in the dim glow of the lights beneath us. Most of us are scarred and worn. Not Stein, though. She's always flawless. She smiles at me as if she can read my mind, so I reach over and tug on a loose strand of her dark hair.

Turning away, I sweep a glance over the massive room. Half an hour ago, it was filled with people listening to the lectures and viewing gizmos, but now it's waned to a handful of people milling about. Most of them are part of my crew.

Where would I be right now if Claymore hadn't found me? I might have been one of those men down there in a fancy suit. Or maybe I would have been a scientist or an inventor. I'm not a brain like Nobel, but I'm good with my hands, and I'm quick on my feet. Whatever I could have been would never make me as happy as I am right now as a Hollow. I really can't remember my past—none of us can—so all we have is the present.

And the present doesn't suck.

The first trip through the *time stream* is like being born again, or at least that's the sales pitch. Not sure if I buy it. Gloves says it's the stream's way of washing us clean, of transitioning us into our new lives. It feels more like a cost—the price we have to pay for our abilities. I have a scar on my neck and jawbone, probably from some kind of tragedy or abuse in my old life. Sometimes, I'm curious about it. I even asked Gloves a couple of times, but he always brushed it off. Eventually, I gave up asking. I haven't thought about it in a long time; I'm not sure why I'm thinking about it now except something is stirring in my gut, a feeling that something is about to go very wrong.

Next to me, Stein is frozen and silent, breathing in the noisy air and the rush of people below us. I can't help wondering if she feels it too, this unease, although I'd never ask and she'd never admit it.

Nobel whistles, and my eyes shoot down. After

he tosses the remnants of his cotton candy into the trash, he slides his grimy surgeon's mask over his nose and mouth. He whistles again, this time a sharp, quick noise. I follow his motions to a man carrying a large roll of papers through the dwindling crowd. VonWeitter.

With a nod to Stein, I lower myself into position and scan the crowd. Sweat drips from my eyebrow into my eye, and I blink. I can see my fellow Hollows close in like the pulling on a purse string.

I get into position, and Stein yanks on the start cord. The machine lets out a quiet belch and dies. She tries again while I stare at her with furrowed eyebrows. This has to work or we're screwed. She pulls the cord again. The machine finally coughs grey smoke and purrs to life.

Below us, the other Hollows quickly usher the bystanders to the exits. Within minutes, only Nobel and VonWeitter remain in the exhibit hall.

"Ready," Stein whispers.

I nod. Handing her my ratty old jester's hat, I hook the end of the cable to my harness. When I lean forward, I descend to the floor like a giant spider going after a meal, the machine slowly unspooling above me. VonWeitter is right below me. I land behind him, knocking him out cold. Nobel darts over and grabs the plans. Slipping out of the harness, I attach it to VonWeitter, and then give Stein a thumbs-up. She puts the machine in reverse. I bear hug the unconscious man, and then we rise to the ceiling.

Stein is ready on the rafters with an ether-soaked rag in her hand as his eyes begin to flutter open. He doesn't even get out a confused word before she's on him.

Pressing the rag to his face, Stein smiles. "Do you believe in the Ether Bunny?"

In seconds, he's out again, lolling like a rag doll and heavy as sin. We tie him to one of the steel crossbeams. Grabbing an ace of spades playing card from my pocket, I tuck it in the pocket of his wool jacket. I have to leave my calling card just in case the Tesla crowd shows up.

Stein winks, tucks her hair into her top hat, and takes off like a squirrel along the beam. I don't have to ask where she's going. Her job now is to secure the meeting place so we can *rift* out unnoticed. We picked a theater in the heart of the Fair as our exit point. It should be emptying out after the last show, and it will be the perfect place to take a head count and then get back to base.

I unclamp Nobel's machine and scale along the beams until I make it to the edge of the building. Nobel reaches a hand up, helping me down the last few feet. After a quick glance over the plans to make sure we have the right blueprints, Nobel motions to the others to join us. Once we're all together, he throws an arm around my shoulders. We head for the vestibule in front of the exhibit hall. Posters cover the walls. Flyers and trash litter the ground.

"Not bad, Lex," Nobel says. "Maybe next time, you could move a little slower."

I shrug him off. "Whatever, dude. Your machine decided to take a lunch break. I thought Stein was going to have to punch it."

"Was it my machine?" Nobel asks in a high-pitched voice. "Or were you just distracted by your girlfriend's assets?"

Now, I just roll my eyes, partly proud and partly irritated that he was mostly right. "I dare you to say that to her face."

He holds up his hands in surrender. "Let's blow this joint before VonWeitter wakes up."

We are halfway to the theater when a familiar sound makes me pause. It's a sound I recognize from too many sparring sessions with Stein—the sound of a body being hurled through wood.

Without a word, we break into a run. My pulse races as we head for the fight, cutting through the crowd of people.

That sound can only mean one thing.

The Tesla brats are here.

Nobel trips over some kid's toy and stumbles. The gnawing feeling in my stomach is getting worse. It's the unsettling mix of nerves and excitement. The cold air rushes over me as we reach the docks just in time to see a redheaded girl throw Stein into a snack shack. I don't have time to wonder why she's on the wharf—I just run for her. She's still on her back as the Tesla girl reaches down and picks up a large chunk of door, hoisting it over one shoulder like a baseball bat.

"Stein!" I yell, ready to lunge, but before the girl can take a swing, Stein rears up and kicks out, catching her in the knee and sending her rolling across the dock.

"The theater is compromised," Stein gasps, holding her chest as she climbs out of the splintered wall. She's moving slowly, hurt, but not too badly from the looks of it. I want to rush to her side, but she levels a gaze at me and points toward the theater. People are screaming, and in the distance, the whistle of a fire truck cuts through the frenzy. I turn toward the theater, realizing that the smoke billowing up from the building is our signal the fight has begun.

Stein screams behind me. Before I can turn around, someone has me in a sleeper hold and drags me to the end of the dock. I see Nobel as a Tesla kid pushes him to the ground. Whoever has me flips me over, feet pressing into my ribs. I'll say this about the Tesla kids—they can fight. Though not as scrappy as we are, they're obviously trained. But we aren't above cheating.

I grab his foot as he tries to kick me again, using the force of his weight against him. He slams into the ground. He's down long enough for me to get up— mistake number one. Me on my feet isn't something he wants to mess with. I lunge toward him, and he counters, punching me so hard I stumble. Footsteps pound against the wharf, and he looks away—mistake number two. I use the small lapse in his concentration to my advantage. Head-butt to the nose. Judging by the loud crack and the expletive that follows, I must have broken something. While the guy is disorientated, I uppercut him.

When he hits the ground, I run toward the center so I can see all the other Hollows. "Come on, guys. New plan. Smoke 'em if you got 'em," I yell. It's our code for *this mission has gone to hell in a handbasket, so break off and rift out as soon as you can from wherever you can.* A few of them nod and reach into their pockets to grab the green Contra.

I run toward the shore where the redheaded girl sits on top of Stein, laying down blow after blow, when out of nowhere, a right hook catches me unexpectedly, laying me out flat. Groaning, I roll over, attempting to push myself up, but a boot between my shoulder blades takes me back to the ground.

"When did this become a two-on-one fight?" I ask, looking over my shoulder. A big guy, his ugly face smiling and dripping with blood, is looking down at me. A blond boy comes over and leans down.

"We gotcha," he whispers as they pull me from the ground.

I kick to no avail. The older guy, the only one I recognize, has grabbed one of my legs.

Blondie has the other and they are pulling me to the end of the dock. I keep kicking and dig my fingernails into the wooden dock, but I'm stuck. There's no way to stop them. Desperate now, I look for Nobel, but he's holding his own against another new face.

I flip over on my back. The maneuver makes the older guy drop my leg. It's just enough to help me, and I squirm free and jump to my feet. My shirt is soaked with my blood, and I start to move, but I see a girl. She's running toward us, and the closer she gets...

I want to look away, but I'm frozen. The blond boy finds me again, holding me tightly. But I can't make myself move.

In the back of my head, I hear sounds. A girl laughing. Gunfire. Screaming. Bright speckles explode like grenades in my vision. For a minute, everything is white, but the color fades fast. It's replaced by a wave of calm emptiness. The blackness creeps slowly into the periphery of my vision and flows like black ink across my pupils. Fighting against the darkness, I blink, shaking my head until I'm dizzy.

Someone's on the two guys, pounding the one I tripped earlier and pulling the blond one off me. I know it's my people—know I'm supposed to rift out after everyone else—but my head is swimming. I reach for the *Contra* in my pocket, feel it in my fingers, but then it slips from my grasp and falls between the slats in the dock.

I look over just before everything goes dark. Stein rolls away from her attacker—the blond boy she pulled off me. She quickly reaches into her pocket and swallows her green Contra. When she vanishes, I feel only relief. I might die here, and it's good she won't be here to see it.

I fall to my knees. My mind is going blank. Nobel's masked face is close to mine. He slaps me. I think he calls my name. His greasy fingers shove the smooth Contra pill far into my throat. My eyes close, and all I have to do is swallow.

Tesla Journal Entry: June 16ᵀᴴ, 1892

I begin this entry with both humility and lingering disbelief in what I have witnessed with my own eyes this day.

The experiment seemed simple in theory. Matter at rest, if such a thing could exist, would be matter dead. Death of matter! Never has a sentence of deeper philosophical meaning been uttered. This is the way in which Prof. Dewar forcibly expresses it in the description of his admirable experiments, in which liquid oxygen is handled as one handles water, and air at ordinary pressure is made to condense and even to solidify by the intense cold. Experiments, which serve to illustrate, in his language, the last feeble manifestations of life, the last quiverings of matter about to die. But human eyes shall not witness such death. There is no death of matter, for throughout the infinite universe, all has to move, to vibrate, that is, to live.

So to regenerate life in seemingly dead matter should be a small thing—to return it to its natural state of unrest. Electricity, ah, that is the key. I am still assured of it. But today's results were shocking, so much so that I dare not speak the truth of it but here in my private journal.

My dear assistant Helena, a drab but intelligent woman by any standards, has been by and by contributing to these experiments.

The general plan was to charge condensers, from an alternate-current source of high tension, and to discharge them disruptively while observing well-known conditions necessary to maintain the oscillations of the current as it passed through 'dead' matter. In this case, a rat euthanized for this specific trial.

The energy, however, refracted off a coil of copper wire behind the target and was sent directly into Helena, who immediately vanished before my eyes.

Bah, impossible!

Yet, my mind could not ignore what my eyes showed me. I searched the area for some time for some clue as to what had happened only to have Helena reappear in the exact spot some four hours later, though she says it felt to her as if only moments had passed, unharmed, though with large portions of her memory fragmented.

After several cups of tea, Helena, visibly shaken, was able to recount the experience from her own perspective. She described a sensation of being torn apart by wind, though no damage was visible to herself, her clothing, or her hair. She spoke of being lost, unable to control her movements, like a rudderless ship blown about in this alternate place. Understandably in a state of panic, she lunged to escape and was returned to the lab.

I must admit the idea intrigues me. Where did she travel to? Was it, as some notable scientists have postulated, a dimensional tunnel in space and time? I must think further on these events and decide how to move forward.

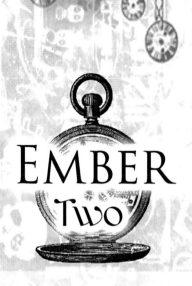

EMBER
Two

I will not die in this hideous dress. That's my only desire today. Everything else is negotiable—icing on the cake.

Ignoring the too-tight bodice and itchy lace hem, I take a deep breath, drawing my focus inward until I feel razor sharp. Now, I'm no longer part of the crowd milling through the Fair, but above it, outside it. The faces spin around me, but I'm disconnected from them. Searching. Slowly, the hyperawareness fades as my heartbeat calms and my breathing regulates.

"Tesla," Ethan calls out. "Time and date verification."

The thick, not-quite-mechanical voice of our leader responds through the communication devices in each of our ears, "Location verified. Six point nineteen, eighteen and ninety-three, nine hundred hours."

"Target verification?" Kara asks, wiggling her pinky in her ear like there's water in it before shaking out her auburn hair.

"Target verified," he answers. "Dr. Klaus Von Weitter. Assignment: prevent theft of Solara Project designs."

"Tesla, are you sure about this?" Ethan asks, scanning the crowds around us. "I don't see any Hollows here."

"Confirmed. The timeline alteration algorithm has traced the ripples back to this event. They are here, somewhere. The timeline has been altered."

Ethan nods, looking over at me. I have to admit, he looks ridiculously handsome in his costume today. The black-striped slacks and the long grey jacket that trails down his back make him look older than usual. The grey is drab, but his blue eyes are startlingly bright. He's also wearing a matching bowler hat and carrying a cane, which is the only accessory I've ever seen him demand. I reach up to adjust his bone-white bowtie.

"Bowties are sexy," he says with a wicked grin.

"Just because you keep saying it doesn't make it true," I respond, no humor in my voice. Normally, his quips make me smile, but not today. I'm on edge, though I'm not entirely sure why. Maybe my historically accurate panties are in a bunch.

This isn't my first mission. In fact, it's not even a particularly difficult one. The Solara plans aren't exactly nuclear launch codes. I'm not sure why the Hollows want them so badly, except to create chaos. What could be so special about a rough solar collector? Nothing—it's the rush, the thrill of the chase. They're little better than feral cats. Still, if they want it, we can't let them have it. Our job is as simple as that. But the tiny hairs on the back of my neck are standing up. The air around me feels thick, as if the world is holding its breath. Glancing over at Kara, I wonder if she feels it too. Her expression is serene, if a little pale. The light dusting of freckles over her nose is more noticeable than normal, and her eyes are rimmed with red. Late night training again, no doubt.

Somewhere in the back of my head, a version of my own voice reminds me that this might very well be my last mission. The Trial is coming up, and it's either pass or die. We've all been logging extra time in the gym and on the books. Well, everyone but Ethan. I wish I had half of his confidence. He'll pass even if none of the rest of us do. I'm sure of that, although not fully comforted by it somehow.

I shove the thought away, fighting to stay focused. Doubt never accomplishes anything, as Mistress Catherine likes to say. Draping one arm over my shoulder, Ethan gives me a quick, reassuring hug. "Relax, Ember. We aren't defusing a nuclear bomb. We're just here to keep one nerdy scientist safe. How hard can it possibly be?"

I sigh. "I really hate it when you do that."

"Do what?" he asks innocently.

Read my mind. "Beg for trouble."

He grins widely as a pair of elderly gentlemen brush past us and shoot Ethan a glance that clearly screams "inappropriate behavior." For a moment, even I'd forgotten how far back we'd traveled—how far away from our home back at the Tesla Institute. No, in this time, people simply didn't show amusement or familiarity. It was rude. The way Ethan steps back from me, cooling his expression, makes me eager to leave 1893 in the rearview mirror.

He shakes his head, falling back into mission mode. "We're only going to get one shot at this. Are you ready, Kara?"

"I think this dress is trying to kill me," Kara

complains, tripping forward as she steps on the long skirt.

I can't help smirking. "Be thankful they aren't wearing the bustles anymore. Good luck getting off a decent roundhouse kick in one of those."

She smooths her hands down the front of her pink-and-brown dress, then smacks at the puffy sleeves. I withhold a snicker.

Squaring my shoulders, I raise my chin to the bright midday sun. It's cool today for mid-June, and a light breeze caresses my face. That's a good thing. These dresses are heavy, tight, and not at all like our usual clothes. Beside me, Kara curses and fights to tuck stray wisps of hair back into its coil at the back of her neck.

"So, where do we find this guy?" Kara asks, glancing around.

"Current location unknown," Tesla's voice cuts in again.

"Oh, great. Some super computer you are," she mumbles under her breath. Then, louder, she asks, "Where's Flynn? I feel the need for some serious adult supervision."

I couldn't agree more.

Ethan takes a deep breath. "I don't know. Something's wrong. I can feel it in my gut."

"Is that intuition or heartburn? You did just eat your weight in chili dogs," I say, though I know better than to question his gut. It tends to be dead right.

"Chicago Dogs," Kara corrects me.

Yes. The taste of peppers lingers somewhere in the back of my mouth, making me wish I'd smuggled in some gum. Still, it's probably the most delicious thing I've ever eaten. The Institute has us on strict diets of protein powder and gross, organic, tofu-based foods. Various food vendors lined the entrance to the Fair, so when we saw the dog cart, no way were any of us going to pass them up. The fact we aren't still glutting ourselves is a testament to our self-control. If everything goes well, we might just make a pit stop before we rift back home.

"Focus. Get on point," Tesla commands through the earbuds.

Kara and I exchange a frown before the three of us shift to stand back to back and scan the crowd. Beside me, I feel Ethan tense. The way he can transition from lighthearted, playful Ethan into *leader* Ethan is unsettling and as quick as snapping your fingers. His entire demeanor changes when he's on point—even his voice, which drops to a deep monotone.

"Let's split up," Ethan decides, pointing. "Kara, you head over to his booth at the main convention center. I'll take the east side. Ember, you take the west. We'll meet up by the pier. Anyone runs into trouble, have Tesla put out a call to the rest of the team."

I don't like it. I'm feeling jumpy, which isn't like me at all. Maybe it's just nerves, or maybe I just don't like the idea of being separated from them. Either way, I don't say anything. Ethan and Kara have been with me over a year—since the day I was recruited—and I trust them with my life a hundred times over.

Without a word, we go our separate ways. I'm weaving through the crowd when I spot something—a girl about my age in a tall, black top hat and a long leather trench coat. I catch a glimpse of her as she moves past the Zoopraxographical Hall. Her dark hair is tucked up into the hat, exposing a trail of green tattoos down the back of her neck. I bite my lip.

She's one of them. A Hollow.

The man at the ticket booth, next to the theater entrance, can't take his eyes off her. Staring, he continues to issue tickets from behind a glass window to the showing on the small screen. Glue-plastered announcements on the exterior brick walls advertise the moving picture as *The Science of Animal Locomotion*. The top hat girl has her back to me and is leaning against the doorjamb, her arms folded across her chest.

She's pretty, if not a bit overdone. Her eyes are ringed in dark kohl liner, and her lips are a deep red. She has tight black pants on under the jacket, and there are belts and straps around her waist and down her thighs. She's out of place, and people whisper behind her back. Most of the women in this time are wearing floor-length, high-necked day dresses and corsets. This girl looks like Goth Barbie. She didn't even bother to remove the silver hoop from her eyebrow.

I glance around, looking for more Hollows, but I don't see any. That's strange. They normally travel in packs. Maybe, if she hasn't made me out as a *Rifter*, I can just follow her and she'll lead me to the others. It seems like the smartest plan. All I have to do is keep my mouth shut.

"Nice costume," she mutters, not looking at me.

So much for being stealthy.

"Thanks," I say.

"I hope it's not a rental."

Before I can react, she's spinning. The heel of her boot connects with my lower back and sends me sprawling to the earth. She's on top of me in a heartbeat, pressing my face to the ground.

She leans forward and whispers, "Tesla is here, did you know that? Not *your* Tesla, of course, but the Tesla from this time. He's fifty yards away, giving a demonstration of his brilliant little coils. It would be so easy for me. The flip of a switch, a misplaced bucket of water. I could end this whole thing right now."

I can hear the smile in her voice as she grinds my face in the dirt. "Oh. But don't worry. I won't. Not this time. That's not what we're here for."

She is quick to her feet. Lifting me up by my hair, she hurls me forward into the theater. We surge through the doors to a chorus of shushing. But, as soon as the people turn to see the commotion, they are fixated on her. It's not just the strange wardrobe that has people spellbound. She is radiating power and deadly beauty. It's almost hypnotic. Even I can feel it.

I am so out of my league.

Standing in the aisle, I spit out the blood pooling in my mouth. I look at our audience and wipe my mouth on my sleeve, earning me a look of disgust from the people who are staring.

The crowd lets out a gasp.

"You mean you *can't* kill Tesla," I counter, my voice barely more than a whisper. "You

can't because you'd risk unraveling your own timeline." I crouch down. She kicks me and I manage to block the blow, but the momentum sends me back to the ground with a sharp pain in my forearm.

"Sometimes, I think it might be worth it," she says, her voice dripping with bitterness as she makes her way over to me. People are standing now, demanding she stop. The women are ushering the children to the opposite exit. One man puts a hand on her shoulder, but she grabs his arm, twisting it behind his back with a loud snap before tossing him aside. "So, are we going to do this the hard way, or—who am I kidding? There's really just the hard way."

I leap forward, catching her off guard with a punch to the face. A satisfying crunch tells me I've broken her nose. She stumbles backward but doesn't fall. The back few rows of people are abandoning their seats and running past us.

She smiles, and the blood runs down her lip into her mouth, turning her teeth pink.

She lunges. This time, I'm better prepared for it and manage to duck the blow while coming up and landing a blow of my own to her ribs. She gasps, but she spins again and kicks out at me. I roll backward and spring to my feet.

"You've got some moves. I'll give you that, Tesla Girl," she says, readjusting her hat.

"How is that thing still on your head?" I blurt out, gasping for breath.

She lifts the hat off her head and brings it to her chest with a sarcastic bow before stuffing it back on.

Okay. That's kind of impressive, I admit to myself.

Nearly everyone is staring at us now. Some are wondering aloud if it's part of the show, while others are threatening to get the police.

She grabs an oil lamp from the wall and hurls it at me. I duck, and it hits the wall behind

me in an explosion of light that catches the rug and the bottom of the white screen. The crowd that had been watching us runs wildly out of the theater.

Turning to look at the flames is my mistake, but I can't help it—the urge to look is impossible to resist.

As soon as the flames register in my brain, my legs turn to mush. The Hollows girl is on me again before I can move, her fist meeting my jaw with the force of a freight train.

I fall to my hands and knees. Grasping her ankle, I pull. She falls onto her backside. I roll on top of her and draw back to punch, but before I can, she wraps her leg around my neck and pulls me off her. She twists, and lightning pain shoots up my neck.

For a few breaths, I can't move. Slowly, the feeling returns to my fingertips. When I can sit up, she's gone, and the room around me is full of rolling smoke. I cough. My chest constricts, refusing to take in air.

I can see the door and the daylight beyond even through the dense, black clouds. I want to run. Every nerve in my body is an electric current, driving me out of the path of the flames. My insides are screaming. Behind me, the screen falls in ragged sheets, sending embers and smoke into the air.

Then, I hear the scream.

I follow the sound, pressing myself as close to the ground as I can manage. In the far corner, a boy is curled into a ball with tears rolling down his cheeks.

Beside me, a piece of ceiling falls, fraying my nerves. I can't breathe. Can't move. The fear is paralyzing, spreading, and it clogs my veins like concrete. My body and mind are at war. Suddenly, I'm back in my nightmare. I'm in a bedroom, but not mine. There's someone there with me—a boy whose face I can't quite see. He's yelling something. I'm trying to run to him, but my legs are weak. It feels like running through quicksand. I scream, cry, and pound the ground with my fists, but it's no use.

"Help, please!"

I open my eyes, and I'm back in the theater. The little boy is right in front of me. I can hear and see him. When I scream against the fear, it shatters like glass. I can move again. Relief floods me, driving me forward. *I'm not going to die here,* my mind tells me. As I crawl toward the boy, another voice echoes in my head.

"Ember. Leave the boy," Tesla demands.

I shake my head and cough. "I can't."

"Ember. Leave the boy. That's an order."

I'm still coughing, my body doubled over in convulsions. I don't have much time before the smoke and flames eat me alive, but I know I can't leave him. My body is moving on its own now.

"I can save him! I can save him this time!" *This time.* I've had this dream before with another boy. In my dreams, he dies—or maybe we both die in the end—but they never seem to get that far. I know the outcome, though, even if I've never made it that far in the dream. This isn't a dream—this is real. And today, here, now, I can save us both.

Tesla's voice echoes again, louder now. "That is an order. Leave the boy and get to your team now. They are engaged at the wharf."

The order makes me pause. I'm so used to following every order Tesla gives me that it's as natural as breathing. But this feels wrong. "I can't," I whisper hoarsely.

"It's not your job to interfere with this. Get to your team now. Leave the boy."

I can't pry my eyes off the boy. He can't be a day over eight years old, I decide as he

reaches up, clutches the collar of his shirt, and

begins to chew on the lapel.

The gesture is familiar. Not the same exactly, but something in the back of my mind makes enough of a connection that my hesitation snaps like an overstretched rubber band.

"I'm going to be in so much trouble for this," I say to myself as I lunge for the boy, wrap my arms around him, and press his face into my neck.

"Can you climb onto my back?" I ask. He nods limply. I wrap his arms around my neck and crawl for the door.

It feels like hours before a dozen pairs of hands grab us, some pulling the boy away from me, some dragging me forward. The hem of my dress is on fire. Someone stomps on it. I hear a loud, piercing whistle. The fire department.

Looking over, I see the boy clinging to his mother's skirt as she holds him, tears of relief running down both their faces. My eyes lock onto his. The look he gives me isn't one of relief or thanks. It's fear. As if, somewhere in his small mind, he knows I'm different. Not right. I look away because it's true. Even among freaks, I'm a freak.

I struggle to my feet, pushing away the hands trying to help me. Anger boils inside me. Memories of the nightmares hover like ghosts on the edges of my mind, struggling to make themselves clear. But I don't have time for that now, so I let them fade away. My team needs me. I stumble into a run toward the expo hall, praying my legs won't give out on me before I get there.

I tap my ear. "Which way?"

"Left," Tesla responds.

Ethan's voice breaks in. "Ember? If you aren't too busy, we could really use a hand here."

He sounds winded and hurt. I wince. My concern for my friends—my family—overwhelms everything else. There's no such thing as pain now. I'm light on the balls of my feet. Around me, the air thins, faces blur, and noises blend into one, indistinguishable cry.

I run for them, praying I'm not too late.

LEX
Three

The common room in Wardenclyffe Tower isn't the cleanest place on the planet, but I've come to appreciate the dirt-stained rugs and the ugly, mustard-colored walls. Today is a good day. There's no sight of any resident rodents slinking across the floor, nobody is bleeding too badly, and there's a general tone of relaxation in the air.

I sit at a table with Nobel as he tinkers with his latest experiment. Across the room, Stein polishes a battle-axe. I take a copper spring from the table of *tech* and fling it across the room. She doesn't look up as it bounces off the wall behind her. Grabbing another, I stretch it a little more so that it will make it the distance. I get her right in the shoulder. Perfect shot. She looks up, rubbing her arm, and I flash a wide, cheesy smile. Stein puts the rag down and heaves the battle-axe over her shoulder.

"You sure you're up for this?" Stein asks.

I crack my neck. "I'm sure. It'll get the blood pumping. Help me think."

She grins. "Your funeral."

With a wave, she's off, sprinting toward the other side of the common area.

I chase after her, stopping to grab an axe of my own, and find her waiting for me, perched in a crouch at the lip of the half-pipe. The skaters grab their boards and gravitate toward where a small crowd is forming, and I know why. Stein has stripped off the long trench coat she normally wears, leaving only her black leather pants and tank top. She tips her top hat to me before tossing it aside as well. She looks alert, dangerous, and smoking hot. I adjust my grip and slowly swing the axe. She pounces onto the back of an old tattered couch.

All in the common room have now abandoned their activities to come watch us practice. We don't have any specific room we practice in—it's kind of a move or be moved situation whenever someone is sparring. The common room wears scars from many such matches. Once-heavy damask drapes are now moth-eaten and threadbare. Even the steel plates covering the windows are scratched and scuffed, bits rusted and falling away, and the armchair has a gaping hole down the back from the last time we practiced. Around me, familiar faces watch with excitement.

Their eyes don't bother me—they only fuel me, make me burn hotter. It must be how rock stars feel on stage. Everyone wishing they could be you, just for a moment. I twirl the axe again, drawing whistles and applause from my audience. It's almost enough to take my mind off the events of the wharf. Some poetic wise guy hits the old CD player and "Thunderstruck" by AC/DC blares through the ancient speakers.

Stein blows me a kiss from her perched position.

I pretend to grab it out of the air and stuff it in my pocket near a handful of bottle caps. Some couples snuggle or hold hands and take long walks. Not us. This is how we dance.

A cloud of dust rises from the couch as Stein lunges off the edge and runs at me. I swing the axe, knowing it won't connect. She drops to her knees at the last second and uses a worn Oriental rug to slide past me, the blade narrowly missing the top of her head. On her knees, she punches me in the side of the leg, knocking me off balance just long enough for her to tuck and roll away.

The crowd stamps their boots to the beat. Some of the kids are slapping their knees and singing along. Somewhere behind me is a shrill whistle, the release of steam pressure from a prosthetic appendage.

"How did that redhead at the Fair ever get a piece of you?" I ask as we begin to exchange blows.

"Please. That chick had zero skills. She just got lucky."

"I wish I could get that lucky with you sometimes," I grumble.

That pulls Stein to a stop, and I'm able to kick her in the stomach and send her tumbling backward. For a split second, I'm afraid I might have really hurt her. But when she looks up at me, she's all smiles. "Is that so?"

Now I stop. "That's not quite what I meant."

"Oh, I know what you meant." She lunges again and kicks the axe out of my hands. It lands with a clang and skids across the floor. "You know, you're lucky Nobel shoved that contra down your throat, or you never would have made it back to the Tower."

"Your point is?"

"My point is, be more careful, you stupid dillweed."

I look around at my friends. They're all cheering, and all eyes are on us. I love this moment.

"Aww, shucks. You really do care."

Stein turns her back to me, wraps her arm around the long, golden rope attached to the drapes, and uses it to climb her way up the window covering until she is balancing on a thick ledge of crown molding above the main window.

"What are you planning to do from way up there?" I call, unable to keep the amusement out of my voice. "You getting tired already?"

"You wish. I'm just giving you a breather. I'm not even breaking a sweat here."

"You don't sweat."

She laughs, and the sound is smooth and deep, like honey. "True. I *glisten*. You, on the other hand, you look a bit peaked. You sure you aren't going to pass out again?"

I sigh. "I'm never living that down, am I?"

She makes a face like she's thinking about it before brushing her dark hair out of her eyes and winking at me.

I reach over to retrieve the axe and pitch it toward the plaster ceiling above her. A light dusting of white powder rains down on her, making her cough and release one hand from the rod to cover her mouth. I yank the curtain. She falls, landing right in my arms. I've almost forgotten the crowd is there until they start cheering and clapping again.

"Nice catch," she whispers, her face so close to mine I'm sure no one else can hear. I relish in the moment even though we have an audience. She gently touches the scarred side of my face and neck.

Her fingers take me back to the first time I lay in Stein's lap and let her give me my first rifting tattoo. We all get chevrons for each mission. Most of us put them down our spine, but Stein convinced me to tattoo my scar—to change it—so that it looks like a hand made out of smoke. Its inky fingers crawl along my jawline, as if cradling the side of my face. It's a piece of her that's always holding on to a piece of me.

I lower my face to hers, and we touch noses. But when I tilt my head to steal a kiss, she wriggles free and runs into the crowd. Soon enough, she emerges from our cheering fans, wielding a blunt-edged broadsword.

"No fair," I grumble. Something hits me in the foot. I look down to see that someone has slid me a flail. Standing with one hand on her hip, the other holding the sword like a cane, Stein grins. Behind her, the crowd thrusts fistfuls of money into the air as Nobel scrambles to collect the bets.

"Five to one on Stein," he shouts, winking at me over his shoulder.

Stein lunges, slicing wildly at me. She's not used to fighting with such a heavy weapon, and the weight of it is throwing her off balance. I take advantage and press forward. She holds the sword like a baseball player, and I manage to wrap the ball and chain around the blade. Both flail and sword fall to the floor.

"No cheating!" she yells, backing up slowly.

"If you aren't cheating, you aren't trying," I say.

Stein backs away, and another weapon slides from the crowd of Hollows in her direction. She picks up the sickle.

31

"Guys! Quit being so helpful, okay?" she says with a grin as she takes a step forward.

I expect her to force the advantage, but instead, she blows past me and runs down the stairs toward Nobel's workshop.

"Oh man. I hope you don't have anything important in there." The last time we sparred in the lab, we almost destroyed a cabinet full of *rifting tech*. I cringe at the memory of the three-day clean-up duty.

A look of near panic crosses Nobel's face, and he jerks his head. "Go get her."

I chase her, grabbing two sai from the crowd like a marathon runner grabbing a baton.

"Really, guys?" I say, blowing past them. "Sai against a sickle? Thanks."

The stairwell is narrow, steep, and empty all the way down. I look back as the mass of Hollows begin pressing themselves into the stairwell.

Slowly, slinking down the spiral stairway, I take one step at a time with my back to the outer wall. Stein likes to scale things, so I scan the rafters as I go. Walking down these steps is like entering a tomb that's been sealed for thousands of years. Why Nobel keeps his lab down here is beyond me.

"Stein, where are you?" I call out.

I kick a small rock down the stairs to see if I can draw her out. No luck. I hold the sai out in a defensive position and keep descending.

Once I clear the stairs, I enter the short hallway that leads to Nobel's lab. Fortunately, he leaves a light on outside the doorway. With a quick hand in the air, I stop the crowd following behind me. A soft chorus of disappointed groans follows me as I inch forward.

"Stein?"

I creep along the hallway, expecting Stein to drop down on me any minute. There's no place to hide in the hallway except the rafters. I reach the end, where Nobel's lab door is normally locked. It's made out of ornate wood with a brass owl perched on the top of the door's molding. The door is ajar. I give it a gentle push and carefully step inside. The room is mostly dark, the only glow coming from a Bunsen burner on the corner table. The dark blue bubbling liquid suspended above it stinks of rotten eggs. Not exactly romantic candlelight, but it'll do.

"Stein? You can't hide from me forever, you know?"

"I'm not hiding," she says. I follow the sound of her voice to a large cabinet full of chemistry glassware in the corner of the room. Just as I fling the doors open, rattling the jars, I hear her add, "I just wanted to get you away from the crowd, so I could do this—"

Too late, I see that she's standing on top of the cabinet. She drops, taking me by surprise as she knocks me to the ground and pins me to the floor. The sickle is gone, but she's pressing her forearm into my throat. Just when I think I'm going to have to tap out, she leans forward and kisses me. Relaxing, I let the sai drop to the floor and wrap my arms around her. She smells like flowers, grease, and metal, and even though we've been sparring, her bare skin is cool to the touch. When she pulls away, I sigh.

"Do you submit?" Stein asks with a huge grin.

"Um, no," I say and rear up, flipping us over so she's pinned beneath me. After a short struggle, I have both of her hands pinned over her head. As strong as she is, my weight is too much for her. Leaning forward,

I press a kiss to the hollow of her neck. "You give?"

"Never," she says, squirming. I bring one hand down and hold her by the neck. She squeezes her eyes closed, her body tensing beneath me. It only takes me a second to realize something is wrong. I withdraw my hand.

"Hey, are you okay?" I ask, rocking back on my feet so I'm perched over her legs but no longer touching her.

She shakes her head and blows out a long breath. Slowly, she rises up so she's on her elbows, half sitting.

"Stein? What's wrong?"

"Nothing. I'm fine."

I stroke her hair and tuck the strands behind her ear. "You're lying."

She finally reopens her eyes. "No really, I'm okay. Just forgot how to breathe for a second. What can I say? You have that effect on me."

I notice that her shirt has crept up enough to reveal the small, sun-shaped birthmark around her belly button. I trace it with my finger. It's perfectly symmetrical, and it's only a few shades pinker than her skin. I know how she wonders about that mark— where it came from, what it means. We're both only half of a timeline, our pasts missing.

"You know you can tell me anything," I say gently, looking her in the eye as I tug the lace of her shirt back down over the mark.

Sitting up the rest of the way, she looks away from me. I reach out and take hold of her chin, turning her face back to mine.

"I mean it, Stein."

At first, I think she's going to say something, but

the mask of fierceness returns, and she throws me off instead. For a second, I'm lying on my back, stunned. Then I look up and see faces watching us from the doorway.

"Looks like my adoring fans have found us." I snicker and roll to my feet.

I look back at Stein. She pulls her hair into a ponytail using some surgical tubing she found on a lab bench, and her expression is sour. I can't blame her. We get so little time to ourselves here. But that's what happens when the two strongest Rifters get together. We tend to draw a crowd. Normally, it's fun. But I would have liked a few more minutes alone with her.

Stein drops her hands to her sides and takes a step toward me. "Yeah, well, your adoring fans can kiss my—"

She kicks me, and I fly out the door into the short hallway. My face stings from hitting the ground and my fingers come away bloody.

A mix of cheers and taunts ring out above me as I look up at the water-stained ceiling. Nobel leans over me, the goggles over his eyes making him look even more manic and bug-like than usual.

"Thanks for keeping the damage to a minimum this time," he says. He offers me a hand up, which I gratefully accept. "Oh, by the way, Gloves wants to see you."

I look around as the crowd disperses, but Stein is nowhere to be seen. "Where'd Stein go?"

Nobel points into the crowd at the bottom of the stairs. "I think she went that way."

The crowd parts, and she looks over her shoulder.

"So I guess we'll finish this later?" I say as I walk

up to her.

She smiles, and it's satisfied, but not happy. "First blood wins, Lex." She takes her free hand and rubs her thumb over my top lip, holding it up so I can see the blood.

I can't help grinning. "Can you keep a secret?"

Stein frowns and slips a finger into my belt loop. "I suppose."

"I like it when you win."

* * *

The hallway to Gloves' office always smells like beef stew or some other thick, spicy meal. The kitchen is just at the other end of the hall, and I'm sorely tempted to keep walking. An ache in my stomach reminds me I haven't eaten yet today. I take a deep whiff of it. Instantly, I'm almost drooling.

Only Stein pulling me to a stop outside the gloomy office keeps me from walking past.

"Come in," Gloves says after Stein's knock. A rush of hot steam and smoke billows out the door into the hall, overtaking the other, more pleasant smells.

"I always feel like we're walking around in a smoker's lung," Stein says, motioning for me to go in first.

Gloves' office is filled floor to ceiling with toy trains that run off coal. There are stacks of black rock scattered around, and it just happens to be Gloves' favorite interior design element.

"Sir?" I call out to get his attention. It's almost impossible to see anything other than the smoke. Beside me, Stein coughs and pulls her shirt over her nose and mouth.

"I'm here," Gloves says. "Follow the red locomotive."

Taking Stein's hand, I lead her through the maze of coal piles behind the red toy train.

When we complete our journey through the "Land of the Locomotives," Gloves is in the back of the room, polishing one of his toy engines.

"I need you to go to the Amber Room again," Gloves says matter-of-factly, rolling his wheelchair closer to where we are standing.

"Why?" Stein demands. The Amber Room isn't her favorite place. Actually, though she'd probably never admit it, the place creeps her out. The Amber Room is a chunk of an 18th century Russian royal palace. It's beautiful, all covered in gold leafing and mirrors. But every time we go there for something, she gets tense and jumpy. I'm not sure even she knows why. When I ask, she waves it off, but I can see the change in her expression. How she clenches her teeth and cracks her knuckles just talking about it. Her annoyance radiates off her like heat waves.

"This time, you need to retrieve the hairbrush from the vanity in the northeast corner."

I can see Stein is about to protest, but I interrupt her. "Sir? With all due respect, this is our third trip to the Amber Room. Even if we manage not to overlap ourselves, the stream around it is already weak. Is it worth the risk?"

He glares at me. His normally white muttonchops are black with soot and his face is etched with grime. I fold my arms over my chest. It's a valid question. Risking a paradox by going back to a place and time we've already been is just stupid. All it takes is one touch, one second of physical contact, to unravel the time stream. Granted, there are precautions we can take to prevent it, but it's a bit like Russian roulette. Eventually, someone's going to bite the bullet.

"If you must know," Gloves says, "we've stolen it."

It takes me a second to process that. I look at Stein. Her face is neutral, although her voice is edged with disbelief.

"What do you mean—you stole it? You stole a whole room?"

Gloves nods.

I hold up a hand. "Wait a second. Why steal the whole room? Why not just take whatever you wanted to begin with?"

Gloves sighs. Turning his back to us, he picks up an old pocket watch and begins dismantling it as he speaks. "It's a very long story. Suffice it to say that there is an object inside that Tesla wants. And he wants it so badly that Helena—the woman who discovered the object—stole it from Tesla and hid it somewhere inside. The problem is that she was never able to tell us what it was or where in the room she hid it. But make no mistake, whatever it is, it's dangerous. That's why we stole the Amber Room and hid it in time so Tesla will never find it. We are taking it apart piece by piece to find what we are looking for, testing everything as we go."

"Why not just take a big group and clear the whole room?" I ask.

Pocket watch innards fly through the air as he jams the screwdriver in too far. "The *time bubble* holding it is fragile. Too many Rifters coming through at once might damage it. Stewart Stills created it, much like the bubble that surrounds the Hollow Tower now, but because it exists out of its original time, it must be explored carefully."

Stein cocks her head to the side. "Why don't you just ask Helena about it?"

Gloves slams his fists into the workbench, sending tools and tiny pieces of trains flying. I'm so caught off guard by his response that I take an involuntary step back. I don't think I've ever seen Gloves lose his temper. Ever.

"Because she's dead," he says through clenched teeth. "And traveling back into her timeline isn't an option." Dropping the remnants of the watch, he turns back to us. "Do you really think you're the first team we've sent in there? We've all done missions to the Amber Room. Some of us more than once. We stagger the rifts out as much as possible, but our repeated visits are weakening the time bubble Stills placed it in. It's collapsing. Our time to find the object is running out."

He lowers his head, glaring at us, daring us to defy him.

It's all I can do not to cough my response. "Yes, sir."

"Have you had the beef stew?" Gloves asks out of nowhere. He is always distracted with weird stuff like that. It's one of the reasons we aren't supposed to have sugary sweets in the Tower. He says it rots our minds and bodies, makes us lose focus. We have a running bet that he knows firsthand.

I shake my head.

"Not yet, sir," Stein says. She looks at me with a worried look.

I shrug my shoulders.

"You need to go eat," Gloves says. "But let me

make your Contra before you go."

He putts over to a fish tank that is illuminated by a wall of small, cast-iron furnaces. Snails with geared-shells hold tightly to the inner wall. He reaches over the side of the reservoir like a kid reaching into a cookie jar and pulls four snails from their home, bringing them over to us. Twisting the gears on the shell, he removes the slimy bodies and tosses the slick creatures back into the tank.

"I've never seen him actually make the Contra," Stein whispers out of the side of her mouth while watching him intently.

"The time stream is a very unique organism. Every time that exists in the past, present, and future, and every event in it, has a unique frequency." One by one, he cracks open the geared-shell until he holds four pieces in his hand.

"These snails are a very unique hybrid of mollusk. Part invertebrate, part machine," Gloves explains. "They secrete a neural stimulant that attaches to the basal ganglia at the base of the brain. This neural stimulant is what fires a specific neural pathway in your brain that resonates at the same frequency to the specific time you are traveling to."

"So those shells have the chemical in them that makes Contra?" Stein asks.

"Correct. After I finish cooking these shells, the chemical with the correct time frequency will be contained in the little green pill you have all learned to rely on."

Gloves takes the shells over to one of the small furnaces on the back wall of his office. This particular cast-iron furnace door has a dial on it. He removes a steel tray and sets the shells on it.

"Consider this oven the tuning fork for the time stream resonations. When the Contra is done, it will have the exact date and time to the Amber Room and the exact date and time for you to get back to the Tower. The chemical inside will stimulate a neural pathway in your brain with the same frequency so you can make it there and back safely."

He slides the tray with the geared-shells inside. With a small click, the door latches closed. Turning the dial as if he were opening a safe, Gloves puts the Amber Room time in for us so we don't overlap ourselves. After unlatching the small furnace door, he removes the tray, discards the shells, and hands us four small green pills. "You will leave first thing tomorrow."

Stein and I take our Contra and follow the red locomotive back to the door of his office. Relieved to be out of the hot, smoke-filled office, I wipe my brow.

"What was that about?" Stein asks, pocketing her pills.

I shake my head, mostly because I have no idea. "I wonder what's so important?"

She doesn't answer as we walk down the hall, and I know she's doing the same thing I am—racking her brain, trying to remember everything in the room. It's all such benign stuff. Nothing that screams "dangerous object," at least.

We reach the door to her room, and I pause as she pushes it open and steps inside. I'm not sure why I hesitate. I've been in her room a hundred times before, but something about it still feels strange, like entering a foreign country. She turns, grabs me by the wrist, and pulls me inside. I lean against her dresser as she flops on her bed and pulls a pillow onto her lap.

"It'll be fine," I tell her. I hate seeing her look so worried, but I don't want to press her about it either. "We'll just be really careful. Gloves is sending us there a few hours after our last rift in, so there's no risk of running into our alternate selves. We just need to get in, get the object, and get out."

She shakes her head, her face more pale than usual. "I know. It's just—I have a weird feeling about that place. Like something really bad happened there. Or will. I know. It's stupid."

"It's not stupid, Stein." I take a deep breath, choosing my next words carefully. "You have good instincts. I trust them, and I trust you. But you have to know, I will always come back for you."

Her face softens, and the tension slips from her shoulders.

I reach behind me and pick up a piece of paper from her dresser. It's a picture she drew of Nobel. It's so lifelike I can almost hear him laughing. She captured him in a rare mood that day. We'd been working on some new weapon designs, and he'd accidentally shot me with a Taser bolt. He laughed so hard I thought he was going to wet himself.

I'm so focused on the drawing I don't even hear Stein get up and cross the room, but in an instant, she's here, plucking the picture from my hands and tossing it aside.

"It's really good," I say, a slight squeak in my voice. I blush. How does she do that to me?

Stein just nods and leans into me. I wrap my arms around her tightly. She usually doesn't like to be held like this. I think it might be some kind of residual claustrophobia or something from her past life that she can't remember. I have little things like that—small triggers that set off weird feelings or make me hesitate. But now she's clutching me like I'm the last solid thing in the world, and it feels really good. She buries her face into my neck, and I can feel the heat of her breath. When she finally turns her head up, I lean down and press my lips against hers. She's so impossibly soft I forget to breathe. My mind goes blank. It's just Stein and me.

When she pulls back, I let her go even though I really just want to hold on. She sighs, grabs her long, black leather jacket from the closet, and tosses it over her shoulder.

"We should go eat. I'm starving," Stein says.

The door squeaks, and Nobel pops his head inside. "Did someone say dinner?"

I push myself off the desk, trying to hide my disappointment. "Yep. Let's go get some grub."

As we walk, I fill Nobel in on what Gloves told us about the Amber Room. I expect him to be surprised or at least curious, but he's neither. All he says is, "How is it that everything else in that room is filthy, but somehow, those gloves are always clean?"

I shrug. "No idea. Maybe he uses a really good stain repellant?"

"If so, I want some. I'm tired of trying to wash blood out of my jacket," Stein chimes in.

Nobel and I exchange a smile as she lovingly pets her coat.

"Then stop making people bleed on you," I say, putting my arm around Stein's waist as we enter the kitchen.

She looks up at me, and all traces of her earlier uncertainty are gone. "Now where's the fun in that?"

TESLA JOURNAL ENTRY: SEPTEMBER 9TH, 1892

We have witnessed the great strides that have been made in all departments of science in recent years. So great have been the advances that we cannot refrain from asking ourselves, is this all true, or is it but a dream?

After much theory and experimentation, I have come to the root of Helena's travels. She is, in fact, capable of traversing time itself. The way a normal man might cross the street! Ah, what a grand notion! So far as I can tell, it seems to be a gift quite specific to her, as I have tried to recreate the experiment on both myself and her husband Leonard with no success. I have successfully moved her through time twice, using the same principal that is by passing an electromagnetic wave through her directly. The first time she traveled for only an hour. After adjusting the voltage, I was able to send her forward an entire day! Success!

Though I am loathe to admit it, the process seems to be a biological one. I have asked her to invite her brother, a young man by the name of Garrison, here to assist in further experimentation. My hope is that the boy will be biologically similar enough to replicate the process.

A problem we have faced is that since her first accidental traveling, Helena has suffered some significant long-term memory loss. Her husband has been quite dutiful in helping her recover what was lost, but much of her own life history still eludes her. Small things sometimes trigger memory return. At Leonard's request, I have sent Helena to a doctor who claims to be able to restore her memory fully using hypnosis. I can only hope he succeeds. Though, I will add that the memory loss has made her more timid and easy to influence. Where often she would set her mind stubbornly on an idea, she has been much more receptive to accepting what I say. While this disturbs Leonard, I see it only as a benefit.

EMBER
Four

The scream builds like an explosion in my throat, only no sound erupts. The smoke is thick and black, and I can't draw a breath. My lungs burn. I blink, wiping the smoke-induced tears from my eyes with my sleeve. Above me, Ethan smiles. He's calling my name. I reach for him, desperate to escape the heat before I melt. But his face changes. He's yelling now, and his eyes are angry.

"Ember. Open up."

I jolt upright in bed, gasping. Along the walls, the gaslights flicker to life.

"Ember!" Ethan calls from the other side of my door.

Moaning, I throw back my wool blanket, stumbling forward to the brass keypad next to the door. I punch it with the side of my fist, and the door slides open with a rusty groan. On the other side, leaning casually against the doorjamb, is Ethan. His smile is bright, but the mischievous lift of his brow betrays his true colors. Only the barest hint of the bruises from our last mission remains along his square jaw. I sigh, wondering how he manages it. He looks perfect, whereas I look like I've been hit by a train. My hand immediately flies to my hair, fighting to smooth the unruly strands.

"Are you going to invite me in?" he asks nonchalantly. As if I should have been expecting him to be at my door, as if it were totally commonplace. I lean past him, glancing down the hallway in both directions. Finally, I shrug and motion for him to come in. Why not? What's one more rule broken today?

"I just wanted to check in and make sure you're all right. The fire—"

He doesn't have to finish. Without thinking, my hand goes to the inside of my arm, to the lumpy flesh there. My scars are old—healed—but the pain is still fresh. I don't remember the fire, not really. Every so often, I get a glimpse, a whiff of smoke or a flash of flame, and it drills into my head like a corkscrew. Something about the first trip through time erases the mind, wiping the memory slate clean. All I remember is Flynn carrying me through the doors of the infirmary. I remember the blistering pain and wishing they would just let me die.

But it healed. I lived, thanks to Flynn. The only reason Ethan knows about it is because once, during a random practice drill, the teachers thought they'd see how we'd handle being thrown into the fire, literally. I'd fallen into a panic and frozen up. I never told him the whole story, never mentioned the nightmares, and he didn't ask. He just sort of knew.

I shake my head and try for a reassuring smile. Judging by his arched eyebrow, he doesn't buy it for a second.

"I'm fine. It's just…" The words are replaced by a rush of emotion like a dam bursting inside my heart. Before I can process what's happening, Ethan is holding me tightly to his chest, and I'm heaving with silent sobs as tears roll down my face.

"I'm sorry," I say, shaking my head and wiping my face on my sleeve. "I was having a bad dream, and you were there, and—"

"Oh. Dreaming about me again, eh?" he asks, making my head snap up. I lean back, pushing him away.

"No, not like that."

He holds up a hand. "No. No. I understand. It's all right. Lots of girls dream about me, Ember. After all," he begins, walking around my room and running his hand over the collection of old skeleton keys hanging on my wall, making them chime like bells, "I am incredibly handsome. And strong. And brave." He walks his fingers across the stack of books on my desk. "It's only natural you'd dream about me. I'm practically Prince Charming."

I snatch my books out from under his hand as he smirks. "And humble too. Don't forget humble."

He holds his hands out in front of him. "And that, of course."

My mouth twitches. I know he's joking to make me feel better, but those things are all true, too. Not that I'd ever admit that to his face.

"Whatever you say, Ethan. Just keep in mind it was a *nightmare*," I say before carefully putting my books back on the massive wall shelf.

I can feel him walk up behind me, and a tingle

shoots up my back. "That's a lot of old, boring books."

I stuff the last book in its place on the top shelf and fold my arms across my chest, admiring the books. "Not boring." Reaching out, I run my fingers down the worn spine of *The Picture of Dorian Grey*. "These are just my favorites. I've read most of the ones in the library."

Ethan has a look of mock surprise on his face when I turn around, and his hand is over his heart. "We have a library? How did I not know this? I've been here for three years. Surely, I would have at least accidentally stumbled upon it looking for the bathroom or something."

I'm staring at him as he talks, but I'm not really hearing what he's saying. I'm too busy noticing something else.

"Your eyes are really blue," I blurt out like an idiot.

He looks stunned, and then flattered. "Yes, they are. A handsome, manly blue."

I can't suppress the snort. "No. I mean most of the time they're kind of light. But they aren't now. They're like midnight-blue."

"Yes," he agrees, wagging his eyebrows. "You can go write a girly poem about them if you'd like. Be sure you mention my rugged jaw, too."

I roll my eyes and step past him, sorry I said anything. "I'll call it *Ode to an Egotistical Tool*. Now, if you don't mind." I point to the door. "Get out."

He grabs my arm, turning me to face him. The humor in his face is gone, replaced by an intensity I rarely see when we aren't on an assignment. He pulls me close, clasping my hands in his. I have to hold in a shudder, which is odd because I'm warm. Like really warm all of a sudden. Maybe it has something to do with the way Ethan is staring at me with those dark blue eyes. How have I never noticed the subtle change of color before? And why is it getting hard to breathe?

"Before I go, I wanted to give you this." He stuffs his hand in the pocket of his vest and pulls out a silver chain with a heavy pendant hanging off the end. I hold out my hand, and he drops it into my palm. It's an ebony-and-ivory cameo on a chain. Only instead of a silhouette of a person, it's an image of an hourglass.

I'm too stunned to form words. It's so beautiful. I close my fingers around it and clutch it to my chest.

"I came across it a few months ago in wardrobe," he says, "and it made me think of you."

"You stole it," I finish for him.

He shakes his head. "You could just say thank you."

"It's beautiful. Thank you," I say, my heart dancing its way into my throat.

"It'll be all right, Ember. I promise. Whatever the nightmares are about, whatever's bothering you. It'll be all right."

He's so confident, so sure, that it's impossible not to believe him. I smile and nod once. He steps back and looks me over. "Now go get changed. You look like crap. And it wouldn't kill you to run a comb through that hair either. Seriously. Have a little pride."

Well, that didn't last long. I sigh and roll my eyes.

He just blows me a kiss. "Go talk to Flynn, and I'll meet up with you after, okay?"

"Sure. Whatever." I move to flip my hair back, but it's too matted, and my hand just sort of sticks in it. So I settle for an awkward head scratch.

He walks toward the door, looking back over his

shoulder at me for a second like he might have more to say, then turns and leaves the room.

As soon as he's gone, I can breathe again. I feel flustered and uncomfortable, but mostly, there's a deep sense of dread in the pit of my stomach at the idea of facing Flynn. For a minute, I debate just crawling back into bed. Yeah, right. If I don't go to Flynn, he'll no doubt come looking for me. And I'd rather be dressed for that particular conversation.

* * *

The Control Room has to be my least favorite place in the whole building. It's the central hub of the Tesla Institute, and is filled, floor to ceiling, with computers and monitors. Unfortunately, it's also about six stories underground and built like an old bomb shelter. The concrete walls are stained with ugly brown streaks dripping down from metal gas lamps screwed into the surface. The door itself might have been taken from an old bank vault—it's the ultimate padlock, easily three feet thick with brass beams that, when closed, fill holes in the walls themselves. At least the upper levels try to give the illusion of being outside. Not this room. Everything about it makes me feel like I'm walking into a dungeon. I slip through and make my way beyond the workbenches in the outer room. Passing one, I'm drawn to a small, metal spider-looking creature. Its bulbous head is full of red liquid. One sharp pincer is attached to the front, while a tiny chainsaw-looking limb sits next to it on the table. Reaching down, I poke at the machine.

"In here, Ember," Flynn calls from the next room.

"And don't touch the Peacekeeper."

Inside, moisture clings to every surface, and it's almost unbearably hot despite the many churning fans. The low hum from the computers mix with the occasional burst of steam from the more antique components. I break out into a sweat almost immediately.

Swallowing hard, I make my way toward the man at the main interface in the center of the room. Sitting in a high-backed, brown leather chair is Flynn. Only a small scratch on his chin mars his long face. He adjusts his glasses and waves me in. Beside him, in the interface panel, resides what's left of Nicola Tesla. A round window, built into copper paneling and filled with green, glowing liquid, houses the last remains of our leader. His brain floats there, suspended from tubes and wires hanging in the tank. To the right of the brain, in a box, a life-sized copy of Tesla is projected onto a wall of thick steam. He's like a ghost, glaring at me.

"Ember. You owe us an explanation," the projection demands. Its voice doesn't come from its mouth, but from tiny speakers hidden high in the ceiling.

"Yes, sir." I take a deep breath. "I know you ordered me not to go after the boy, but I had to. It was instinct."

It's Flynn who responds. "Ember, I understand the urge to save another's life. But you have to remember that Tesla gives you orders for a reason."

"Those plans weren't worth that little boy's life," I say so defiantly it surprises me. Flynn snaps his mouth closed and stares at me as if he's trying to decide what to say.

"Of course they were," Tesla breaks in. "The needs

of the many outweigh the needs of one."

On the interface to my left, a screen flickers to life. It's a newspaper report: VonWeitter's obituary, dated nine months after the Fair. He killed himself after having his research funding pulled.

"And as for the boy you pulled from the flames…" Tesla says with a pause. An image flashes onto the screen. This time, it's a police report. "The young man you saved lived only five more years. He was killed by police officers after robbing an elderly couple on the street. As soon as the fire began, I was able to calculate the ripples it created in the timeline. If the boy's life had been important, then I would have seen it. But in the end, it was not."

I feel my mouth drop open. "How can you say that? Every life—every single one—is important. Maybe not to you, but to someone." My hands ball into fists at my side. I know I shouldn't speak to him like this, but I can't help it. A cold fury is building inside me. Suddenly, the room doesn't seem so hot after all.

Even though his tone is still neutral, I can feel the sting of his words. "I can see beyond your tiny scope. I can see all that would have happened if the plans had been salvaged. The lives they would have changed, the discoveries they would have led to. They would have helped people in ways you cannot hope to fathom. Are those lives less important to you because you have not seen them for yourself?"

I look to Flynn, not knowing what to say. How could doing something that felt so right be so wrong? His face is sympathetic as he walks over and drops his arm across my shoulders. "I know it's hard, Ember.

But you have to learn to have absolute trust in Tesla. He knows what he's doing."

I look at the steamy ghost of Tesla. For all that he is, I know he's doing what's right for all of us. He's trying to make the world a better place. I get that. I respect that. It's what we all want, the whole reason we're here. It's why we train and use our abilities. Still, I can't get that boy's face out of my mind. In saving one, I failed so many others. My friends, my team, and countless faceless people I will never know. My stomach churns at the thought.

"I know. I'm sorry."

Tesla's voice never alters, nor does his expression change, but the threat still sends a shiver of dread up my back. "Your duty is to preserve the time stream at all costs. Sometimes, that cost is high. But you must not turn from it. If you ever again disregard my orders, I will cast you out. Is that clear?"

"I understand. It won't happen again," I say, glancing once more at the police report. But even as the words leave my mouth, they feel like a lie.

They don't seem to notice my deception. The Tesla projection vanishes, and Flynn squeezes my arm. "Let's go get that bump on your head looked at, shall we?"

I nod and let him lead me out of the room.

"So, tomorrow is your final Trial. Are you excited?" Flynn asks.

"Nervous. Petrified, to be honest." I'm rambling now, but there's nothing I can do about it. "I mean, not scared or anything. Just, more like, you know. Anxious. Like before Christmas. If Christmas was terrible and possibly deadly. Like that kind of Christmas."

He grins and hits the keypad. The door to the

hospital slides open. The rest of the center is always a little cold, but this place is sterile. It looks more like a really clean mental institution than a hospital. I feel the goosebumps breaking out across my arms.

"Is that why you look like you haven't been sleeping?" he asks, his voice concerned.

I bite my lip. Did I dare tell him about the dreams? The truth is, I haven't slept a full cycle in months. I've been training for almost a year, and now it's time for the test that will either carry me from recruit to operative, or send me packing to whatever corner of the time stream they want to drop me in if I fail. Of course, those are the most optimistic outcomes. The odds are, if I wash out, I'll just die.

Then the dreams started. As time went on, the dreams grew more detailed, more intense, until I realized they weren't bad dreams at all. They are my memories surfacing.

Some deep sense of self-preservation keeps me from going to anyone about it. Mostly, I'm afraid they'll take them away again. I hear rumors of recruits who begin remembering things. Supposedly, the Institute has a way to fix that, though no one is exactly sure how.

And I want to remember so badly.

I didn't even know how badly until the dreams began, but now I cling to each new nugget of history like a lifeline. I mentally file the pieces away until the day I can put my old life together.

"Ember, relax. You're grinding your teeth so hard they're going to be stumps when you finally open your mouth again." Flynn smiles and pokes me in the cheek. "Oh, that reminds me. I have something for you."

From his pocket, he pulls out an old-fashioned

skeleton key. It has a brass-green patina with a small leaf design on the tip. The keys are sort of a thing between us. He gave me the first one when I woke up in the hospital right after I arrived. He's been bringing them to me ever since.

"Thanks," I say earnestly just as Doc arrives to bandage me up and send me on my way.

* * *

Back in my room, I'm still flustered. We have training today, and after the monumental beating I received yesterday, I'm not sure I can muster up the strength. I sigh, picking out one of my training outfits from my large closet—black sweatpants with a single red stripe up each side, a simple grey tank top, and a soft brown vest with lots of pockets and hooks for my various tools. I pull on a pair of black-and-gold-striped arm warmers and strap the brass cuffs on each arm. My stomach gives me an angry growl. I thought the pangs had just been guilt and nerves, but now I realize I'm hungry. Like, haven't eaten in a month hungry. Maybe I can grab a protein bar and a juice before class.

I button my vest, just about to sprint for the cafeteria, when a knock at my door makes me jump. The doors have a chime if someone is requesting access—the tap is metallic and hollow sounding by comparison. Ethan and Kara are standing there in full sparring gear—tight pants and loose grey T-shirts—ready to head to class. Kara looks almost as colorful as I do, and the bruises from our battle with the Hollows are in full bloom along her jaw.

"Hurry up, slacker. We're going to be late," Kara

chastises playfully. I know she'd just as soon miss class altogether. Today, I would be tempted to ditch too, but I'm already skating on thin ice.

I snort. "I thought we were beyond the reaches of time."

Ethan shakes his head. "Time moves everyone, Ember. Even us. Maybe especially us."

I can't argue with that.

* * *

My breath comes in short, shallow bursts. I can feel the warmth of Ethan's body radiating like a tuning fork against my back. In front of me, there is only darkness. I strain, listening, waiting for the next wave of attack. The leather straps holding up my suede harness dig into the skin of my shoulders, but the ache only sharpens my focus. The urge to turn around is strong, though I know better. Months of training have taught me exactly what happens when I turn my back to the darkness. So I listen, honing my senses until I catch the sound of Ethan taking a small step forward, away from me. My eyes are useless, so I close them. Knowing my attackers are well paid for their ability to move in silence, there is little hope that they will give themselves away. We need another strategy. As if reading my mind, Ethan picks up the conversation we were having earlier.

"All I'm saying is, maybe you need the extra practice," Ethan says, his tone mocking. Even without being able to see him, I can sense him moving, beginning to circle counterclockwise. I know he's trying to draw them out, to bring the fight to him. It seems like a sound strategy, so I jump on board.

"Oh, yes, because it isn't like she turned around and kicked the crap out of you, too." I'm mimicking his movements now. My voice is flat, free from emotion, and my words are empty. I can't see him moving, but I can feel him, as if we're connected by a million invisible threads.

"How am I supposed to just punch a girl?" Ethan asks. "And I was tired from taking the guy out like five seconds earlier."

"She isn't a girl. She's more like a pissed-off kangaroo in a top hat. She has a nasty right hook, I'll give you that."

I hear the sharp whip of air as a bamboo pole cuts through the darkness, headed toward my face. Even with our phony argument going on, I'm able to hear it coming before it lands. I bring up my hands and block the blow with my forearms. The impact stings, bruising the bones there, but better my arms than my face. With a movement perfected after one too many blows to the head, I grab the pole and pull it aside, dragging my attacker with it. As he closes in, I drop the pole and lock arms with Ethan. I flip over his back and kick out, knocking my attacker to the mat. As he struggles back to his feet, Ethan spins into my place, delivering a secondary kick that sends the man flying into the wall with a dull thud. "Yeah, but she's scrappy," he says.

"Scrappy? Is that boy code for you couldn't stop staring at her rack?"

Behind me, I feel Ethan duck a blow, and then land one of his own before pressing his back against mine. "I... that's not... I didn't even... I mean..." he sputters.

I smirk. *Busted.*

Footsteps approach, but we keep sparring. I bend over, using my attacker's own momentum against him as I put my shoulder into his gut and stand, propelling him over my head and onto his back on the mat. I don't need to see my victory to realize what the maneuver has cost me. A muscle in my lower back seizes, and it's all I can do not to drop to my knees in agony. I clench my fists until I feel my fingernails cut bloody crescents in my palms. There is no way I'm going to be the weak link—no way I'm going to let Ethan fight alone. Back to back, that's how Rifters are trained to fight. And Ethan always has my back.

"Don't feel too bad. She was pretty *scrappy* after all."

Ethan mumbles, "It's a girl thing."

"Hold up, what's that supposed to mean?" I ask, stiffly regaining my footing as my back screams in protest.

As usual, Ethan turns to check on me. "Nothing personal, Ember."

Not wanting him to get slammed for it again, I grab him by the shoulder and pull, revolving us to our starting positions just as the first attacker flips back onto his feet and lunges. He would have taken me in the stomach, but I bring up my knee just in time to block his advance before kicking him in the face. There is a loud crunch that sounds like breaking bone. I hear him hit the mat with a groan. The lights flick back on, and Mistress Catherine blows her whistle.

Normally we spar with off-duty guards, since most of them have military training of some kind. They know how to take a hit and how to deliver one without doing too much damage. We might be lowly recruits, but Rifters are rare, and our lives are precious.

But as the man whose nose I have just broken pulls off his black ski mask, my heart falls into my shoes. Flynn is staring up at me, and his face is covered in blood.

"Nice hit, Ember," he says as blood drips from his nose and onto his white shirt. Mistress Catherine hands him his horn-rimmed glasses and shoots me an amused smirk. Behind me, Ethan snickers.

Great. And here I was thinking this day couldn't get any worse.

Reaching down, I offer Flynn a hand up, which he accepts with a smile.

"I'm so sorry," I mutter, but he waves it off.

"Catherine told me you were really coming along. I wanted to see for myself."

The others are shuffling out, so I turn to grab a towel and follow them, but Mistress Catherine closes the door behind a worried-looking Ethan, presses her back against it, and narrows her eyes at me. I used to think it was hard to look menacing in a knee-length pencil skirt and beige brocade top, but she radiates power. It might be the stern pucker of her thin lips, or the way her graying hair is knotted tightly at the nape of her neck. She resembles a librarian except for the long, jagged scar that runs from her left temple to the cleft in her chin. Well, that and the spider-shaped, iron shoulder harness permanently affixed to her upper arm.

Not sure what's going on, I freeze, yellow towel in hand. Before I can say anything, I feel something moving behind me. I manage to move to the side just as a wooden staff comes slamming down against the spot where I'd stood a heartbeat earlier. I turn and see Flynn grinning, blood still dripping off his chin. He spits before whirling the staff like a windmill in front of him. "What I don't understand," he says, circling to my left, "is how that Hollow got the best of you. According to Ethan's report, Kara had no problem with her. And Catherine here tells me that you mat Kara at almost every practice now."

I have no idea what to say. Does he think I let her beat up on me? Just then, my legs are swept out from under me. I fall to the mat, but, rolling swiftly backward, I bounce up onto my feet. Catherine has a staff, too, and comes toward me from the right. I hold up my hands and back up slowly. In the corner of the room, a vent erupts in a cloud of steam, and Tesla's image appears but says nothing.

"Look, I didn't let her get away," I say. "If that's what you're implying. She was strong. And fast."

Catherine shakes her head. "You are strong. And fast. And clever."

"I'm sorry!" I blurt out when my back hits the corner and they are still coming at me.

I don't think Flynn would ever hurt me, not really, but Catherine, well…

Without another word, they both attack. I manage to duck one blow but take another in the ribs before I decide to make a break for it. Jumping as high as possible, I'm able to get a hand on the chain attaching one of the punching bags to the ceiling and hoist myself up. I leap over Flynn and roll as I hit the ground behind him. They're quick, though, and have me surrounded again in seconds.

It's easy to forget that they are trained Rifters, too. Catherine doesn't rift anymore, but Flynn is still active and in really good shape. They aren't holding anything back either. Flynn lands a blow to my lower back, but when Catherine moves in, I'm able to grab her staff and force it from her bad arm. Suddenly, time is moving in a blur. I'm not thinking about my next move anymore. My body is reacting of its own accord. I'm not sure how it happens, but I blink and Catherine is on her knees. Flynn is standing in front of me, and I have the two staffs crossed at his neck. He's holding up his hands and saying my name.

I drop the sticks and step back. The muscles in my arms and legs are twitching like I've just run ten miles.

"That's what we mean," Catherine says, climbing stiffly to her feet. "You could have taken the Hollow girl. So, why did you hesitate?"

I close my eyes, calling the fight to the front of my memory. There was something about the girl. She was beautiful, for sure, but that wasn't it. There was something else, too. Something I can't put into words. I look up to find they're staring at me, waiting for some kind of answer. I can feel Tesla glaring holes into my back, watching me like one of his little science experiments. "I don't know what you want me to say."

Flynn sighs and holds his hands out to me. I take them without hesitation. "Ember, I know it's hard. I know you don't like hurting people. It's against your very nature to harm someone or let someone suffer. But *you* are too important to risk losing. Understand? Sometimes, you have to put someone down, let someone get hurt or even die, to save yourself and your team. You can't hold anything back."

I take a deep breath. "And what if someone dies because of me? Because, for some reason, my life is worth more than theirs?"

Flynn lowers his head, looking me in the eye. "That is a burden you will have to learn to carry."

* * *

My stomach is revolting by the time I make it to my next lesson, which is already in full swing when I slide into my seat. After a few minutes, a wadded-up wrapper hits me in the side. I turn to see Ethan staring at me.

He mouths, "What happened?"

I roll my eyes and mouth, "Later."

Lucky for me, Kara has somehow managed to smuggle in a few pieces of chocolate from who knows where. She passes me a few while Professor Mortimer scribbles on an archaic chalkboard. Good thing chocolate works on hunger and nervousness.

Mortimer teaches time manipulation studies. Across the board, he has scribbled a list of names. One of them jumps out at me.

"Can anyone tell me who these people are?" he asks, tugging his striped vest down over his rotund belly.

I raise my hand. Kara and Ethan exchange bored looks. I swear I hear Ethan mutter, "Overachiever."

"Ember?"

I lean forward over my desk, swallowing the last of the chocolate quickly. "Survivors of the Titanic?" I say.

"Correct."

"So what?" Kara asks sarcastically, twirling her long, loose hair around her index finger.

Mortimer points to the third name on the list. Molly Brown.

"This name wasn't on this list last year." He lowers his chin, looking at us over the top of his bifocals. I'm about to ask how that's possible, but then it dawns on me.

The Hollows.

He must be able to read my face because he nods. *Point made.* In the back of the class, slacker-boy Roy raises his hand for the first time possibly ever. "So what happened? I mean, what changed?"

"Everything, according to Tesla. The ripples caused by the change in the event were far-reaching and unstoppable. That one minor change affected history for the next three hundred years. Can you imagine if they had done more?"

"More?" someone asks behind me.

"He means, like, what if they had prevented the ship from sinking altogether?" Kara answers, still managing to sound vaguely uninterested.

I consider her words. "It would have been like setting off a nuclear bomb in the time stream."

I don't realize I've said it out loud until Mortimer agrees.

"You are very close to being literally correct. The fabric of time is fragile. Every ripple is a small tear, if you will, that weakens the stream. That's why we are so careful with our assignments."

It's a lecture I'm all too familiar with. Behind me, others groan in unison. He turns back to the chalkboard, and a wad of paper whizzes past his head, bouncing off the wall and landing in the trash. Kara snickers and holds her arms up over her head mouthing, "Three points."

"So why don't we send a few Rifters back and stop the Hollows from saving her?" Marcia asks from the seat behind Ethan. I turn to look at her. Her gaze is hard. She's one of the kids we call *arcs*. They are more brawn, less brain—with quick tempers and fists to match. Marcia is one of the few Rifters taking the Trial this year besides Ethan, Kara and me, and she's the odds-on favorite to wash out.

Behind her, Liam is chewing his cuticles nervously. He falls into another group which Kara has affectionately dubbed *the nerdlings*. They are the polar opposites of the arcs—super smart and mostly unable to hurt a fly. Tech heads. We don't see them much. They tend to hang out down in the labs. They are nice enough, just not really my speed. No, I'm perfectly content with my little trio. Across from me, Ethan smiles.

"We did. They failed. It happens often, unfortunately." Mortimer sweeps his gaze my way, and I flush. Glad to know I'm not the only one who botches missions, but I still feel unbelievably guilty. He continues, "We only get one chance to set things right."

"Why is that?" Ethan asks. "I mean, why can't we go back and try again?"

"Good question," Mortimer says. "Does anyone know why we can't go back to the same time more than once?"

I raise my hand again. "Because you already exist there. If you come into physical contact with yourself, you create a paradox in the stream."

"So send in another group of Rifters," Kara offers

thoughtfully.

"Not a good idea either," a voice from the back of the class chimes in. I glance over my shoulder to see who it is, though I could have guessed. A shorter, dark-haired boy with glasses sits two rows back. Riley. He's one of the few people in the class who can give me a run for my money in the testing scores arena. If the nerdlings had a king, he would wear the crown. "With a team already in play, the stream is vulnerable. You risk other, unintended alterations to the timeline. It becomes almost impossible for Tesla to work out the calculations at that point."

"Correct, Riley," Mortimer says. "The Tesla computer can calculate millions of ripples—minor alterations in the time stream that don't change the overall course of history. But when you have multiple teams on the ground, those ripples become more like tidal waves. Even his system can't keep up. We risk serious timeline changes and the chance of creating a major paradox." Paradoxes aren't something we mess around with. We're not sure exactly what they do, and we've been very careful never to create a paradox in the time stream. At this point, the paradox is just a mathematical theory that has never been tested. To test it would mean creating a paradox intentionally, and the effects of doing so could be catastrophic.

Mortimer looks at me, and I realize I missed something he said. I play it off and tune back in as he goes on. "But consider this. Time is a living thing, and it will always try to heal itself. So in a scenario where two versions of a person exist in the same space and time, time would have to either eliminate one version or break the stream itself into two separate pieces."

He pauses, giving us a minute to absorb what he's saying before he continues. "Either way, the damage caused would be unthinkable. Our best way to prevent the Hollows from damaging the timeline is to stay one step ahead of them."

"How exactly are we supposed to do that?" I ask, almost growling in frustration.

"Their numbers are superior to ours, that's true. But you will always be vastly superior to them. Tesla selects only the brightest, strongest Rifters to bring here and train. Be assured, you were all chosen to be here for a purpose."

"How?" I ask before I can stop myself. "How are we chosen? How did Tesla know what we were—what we could become?"

Mortimer tugs at the collar of his shirt and stands, moving back to the old chalkboard. "I don't know how he finds you, but I do know that the key to your abilities is in your genetics. So the fact that you are here tells me your genes are very strong." He takes a deep breath and begins furiously erasing the notes from the board, creating a cloud of white dust. "In the end, I'm confident that we will prevail," Mortimer adds over his shoulder before turning back to the board. He finishes erasing the names on the board and turns back to us. Clapping his hands together, he creates a small cloud of chalk dust.

"When are we going to learn about something cool?" A voice I don't recognize floats up from the back of the class. One of the arcs, no doubt.

Mortimer sits on the edge of his desk, looking surprised by the question. "And what, pray tell, would you consider *cool*?"

In front of me, a hand shoots up. "What happened to the Lost City of Atlantis?"

Mortimer flicks his hand. "It never existed. It was a literary object lesson."

Another voice calls out from the back of the room, "Who was Jack the Ripper?"

"A woman named Christine Lafourche. Interesting story, that—" Mortimer begins, but he's cut off.

"What happened to the Lost Imperials of the Romanov Dynasty?" Riley shouts.

"How exactly is any of that *cool*?" Ethan asks, not bothering to raise his hand. "I mean, seriously. Who cares? About any of this." He makes a swirling motion with his finger in the air. "Shouldn't we be spending more time tracking down the Hollows?"

"Ethan has a point," Kara cuts in. "I mean, why all the history lessons? Everything we need to know… Tesla will tell us in the field."

"The story of the Romanovs is arguably the greatest mystery of all time." Riley's voice is shrill with excitement.

Mortimer clears his throat. "How did you hear about this story, Riley? I'm sure there are no references in the library."

A sudden flush rushes to my cheeks, making my ears and neck burn. I'm getting lightheaded. I grab my desk and hold it tightly, struggling against the waves of nausea threatening to bring up my chocolate. Out of the corner of my eye, I can see Ethan staring at me. He reaches over, but I shake him off.

"Yeah, and why is that anyway?" Riley asks, but doesn't wait for an answer, turning toward Ethan instead. "The Russian Tsar and his entire family were slaughtered by the Bolsheviks. Only the Tsar's daughter and son escaped. Supposedly, the family was told they were going to take a portrait, and then a bunch of gunmen opened fire on them. But the kids, they just vanished."

I can feel prickles of ice climbing up my back and shooting up my neck as he goes on. I'm struggling to breathe as my lungs constrict. "Wow, nerdling. Do you dream of books?" Kara scoffs.

"I came across it on one of my missions. They made like a dozen movies about it. Anyway, it got me curious, so I did a little digging. A few women surfaced after a while claiming to be the missing princess, but they were all phonies."

Mortimer interrupts, trying to regain the focus of the students. "Yes, thank you for that, Riley. Now, as I was saying—"

"But the real story is much more interesting," Riley interrupted. "Some people say the women didn't die from the gunfire because they were wearing jeweled corsets that kept deflecting the bullets. The Bolsheviks had to chase them down and cut their throats."

Every muscle in my body goes rigid. I blink, trying to focus on Ethan's face, but everything goes dark. In the darkness, I hear a scream.

I think it's mine.

LEX
Five

For Gloves to venture out of his office, something must be seriously wrong.

Stein and I share a worried look over the tech table before he gets to us.

"How did something this small do so much damage?" I ask Nobel, glancing over my shoulder to the gurney behind us where Bruce writhes as some of the Hollows hold him down. His arm has been partially chewed off.

"Are you going to be able to help him?" Stein wonders quietly, following my gaze.

Nobel wipes his forehead with the back of his arm. "I'm going to try." He rounds the table, holding a syringe, and heads for Bruce.

Stein shakes her head. "What is this thing?"

I poke the mutilated robot. Glass shards protrude from a hole in the head casing, which was probably once an intact dome. The joints are made with small gears and pistons. It has one arm affixed with a large pincher claw—the other must have been ripped off.

"I have no idea," I answer honestly. "But this is bad. Really bad."

I don't say the next thought that pops into my head, but from the way Stein is looking at me, her face pale and somber, I can tell she's thinking the same thing. There's only one place this could have come from. Only one person who could have sent it.

Tesla.

Gloves chugs across the room, stuffing small bits of coal into the furnace of his locomotive wheelchair as he makes his way to us. The look on his face is a combination of fear and worry that leaves deep lines around his eyes and across his forehead. I take a deep breath, preparing for bad news.

"Clear out!" Gloves commands, glaring at the others. He points to Nobel, Stein, and me. "Not you three. You stay."

Nobel nods to Journey. "Take Bruce to my lab. He's stable for now. I'll be there shortly." She nods, and the group of Hollows who've been helping quickly wheel the gurney from the room.

Gloves slumps in his locomotive chair as he delivers the verbal blow. "We have a lost Hollow. Sisson."

The air goes out of the room like a crashing hot-air balloon. For a minute, I'm mute, trying to convince myself I somehow heard wrong. It's Stein who speaks first.

"Sisson?" she asks, as though she, too, thought she must have misheard. Sisson is a petite girl but more than capable, and probably one of the quickest, most deadly of all the Hollows. Stein glances at me, with an expression that clearly begs the question—*how is that possible?*

71

"Yes. She was commissioned for a mission to the future, and she has been lost in the time stream."

I frown. Future travel is tricky on a good day, dangerous on a bad one. It's too fluid—too hard to predict how events will unfold. We go, sometimes, but it's rare. This is exactly why.

"She missed her check-in time. Another Rifter caught sight of her in the time stream but couldn't get to her," Gloves continues.

"So do we have to go into the future or the past?" I ask.

"Neither, Lex. She's been trapped in the time stream for the last couple of days from what we can tell. She's running out of Contra and can't rift back to us. We aren't sure why. You need to go into the stream and find her. The Contra I am going to issue you hasn't been programmed with a date to leave the stream, so they won't spit you out. This is important so you can stay in the stream as long as possible to find Sisson. Once you find her, take these to get you all back here. And you need to do it quickly. Claymore's leaking."

What was that supposed to mean?

"Leaking?" I spit out before Stein can beat me to it.

"You know that black liquid in his diver's helmet?"

Stein and I nod. Claymore wears a massive deep-sea diver's helmet made of copper, and he never takes it off. Heck, I don't even know if Claymore *is* a he. The front and side ports are so black and cloudy that I can't tell if there's a living head in there or not. The copper is dented, and there's a pattern of blue-green tarnish all over the helmet that makes it look like a global map from a far-off land.

I mean, the guy can't even talk. According to

Nobel, he's never uttered a word. A huge arrivals and departures board hangs behind the gnarly old desk where he always sits. He sits there, unmoving, with his helmet plugged into his desk. He communicates using the letters that fall into place with loud clicks. The different time zones being displayed by various clocks are mounted at the top of the board. When I first arrived at the Hollows, Claymore had put up on the board, "*Good to have a kid of your caliber amongst us hollows.*"

Nobel fidgets with the Gear Head on the table. "It's called Medulla Serum. That's what keeps him ticking. He can only function when his tank is full."

Gloves explains, "Nobel was able to repair the leak, but he lost a lot of Serum. We sent Sisson to the future to retrieve some more."

"Why the future?" Stein asks. I shoot a glance at Nobel, wondering why he never mentioned it.

"That is the only place to find it," Gloves says.

"Wait, this has happened before?" I ask Nobel.

"It did. Before you got here. He lost about seven milliliters before I could stop the leak."

"Seven milliliters? That isn't that much," I say.

"Seven milliliters doesn't seem like a lot, but it was enough to cripple his ability to monitor the time stream."

"How many milliliters did he lose this time?" Stein asks, concern growing in her voice.

"Too many," Nobel answers, looking up at me for the first time.

"If Claymore loses any more Medulla Serum, he won't be able to make the time stream safe for the Hollows to rift," Gloves adds. "He won't be able to monitor ripples, and no matter how well Stills hides the Tower, without Claymore keeping a finger on everything that happens in the time stream, our location could be compromised."

Staring us down, Gloves adds, "Your whole existence is because of Claymore."

"Let's go get Sisson, then," I say.

* * *

"Let me grab the DNA Detector before we go," Nobel says when we get back to the common room after picking up our Contra. Stein tugs on her long jacket and stuffs a short knife in her boot. Then she gives me a noncommittal shrug that says *better safe than sorry*. I can't agree more.

"I've got it right here," I say, handing the device to him.

Rummaging through the tech bench, Nobel opens a wooden box by breathing onto the lock. Inside the box are dozens of test tubes with blood in them—our blood. DNA samples for such an emergency. He walks his fingers along the corks until he finds Sisson's sample. With a small dropper, he puts a few drops of her blood into the machine, which then beeps to life. I realize I've never rifted and not been spit out somewhere in history. It's going to be strange just mucking around in the time stream without any specific destination. The stream can be disorienting at times, painfully mind-bending. That's why we use the Contra.

We stand in the middle of the common room and swallow the smooth, green pills. The Amber Room mission will have to wait. Priority calls. The Contra that will bring us back is secure in the small hidden pocket inside my vest. All Hollows have one, a secure place to keep our pills.

After Stein takes hers, I hold tight to her hand and smile. Something about Contra creates an almost euphoric effect, and it always makes me happy and tingly inside. As serious as our missions are, some of the side effects are laughing and smiling. We look at each other, and Stein has a huge smile across her face. Nobel smiles behind his surgical mask, his eyes lighting up. I glance down at my hand, interlocked with Stein's, and then at her face as the common room starts to dissolve behind her. Our skin becomes more and more transparent until we are pulled by an invisible rope and stretched into a thin strand, like taffy being pulled.

A rush of wind and a blur of colors replace the common room. Usually at this point, we're spewed out at our destination. This time though, our transparent bodies start to take form. I watch my hand become denser, more solid. Tiny, skin-colored particles start stacking on top of each other until my hand is fully formed. The process repeats itself on Stein and Nobel.

It's like my mouth is full of cotton. "You guys feel okay?"

"Yeah, I'm fine," Stein shouts against the wind.

Nobel gives me a thumbs-up.

Pulling the DNA Detector out of his lab coat, Nobel pushes the button. The gears on the end start to spin and suck up wisps of the time stream. He waves it around until the end dips, letting it pull him toward Sisson.

The DNA Detector pulls Nobel in a zigzag motion through the blur like a Great Dane pulling its master.

He motions for us to follow, and Stein and I move behind him, but our movements are slow without the extra pull of the machine. I push forward as sweat rolls into my eyes. I can't tell if we're actually making progress or not. There's no reference points, no way to tell if we're moving at all. I can't help wondering if the device is really working, or if the DNA Detector is taking us on a wild goose chase. Just wandering like this makes me dizzy. Stein isn't doing well either. A sheen of sweat is forming right above the cupid's bow of her lip.

And Stein never sweats.

* * *

By the time we get to her, Sisson is lying in the time stream flat on her back. Her clothes are ripped, and she's bleeding. She's unconscious. White strands of the time stream have cocooned her, woven into her hair, and are drawing the color from it. Two small robots with glass dome heads are attached to her waist and foot. We hurry over to her and pull her from the invisible hammock. I'm afraid I'm going to pull her arm out of her socket, so instead, I bear hug her and start pulling. Frantically, we work, not knowing what damage the time stream has done to her.

"She's breathing." Nobel shakes his head like he's surprised. "I think the time stream has protected her somehow, kept her alive. That's why she's wrapped in that stringy stuff."

"Can she swallow, though?" I ask.

"I don't know," Nobel replies. "We need to get these Gear Heads off her."

Using my fingernail to pierce the hard gel covering of the Contra pill, I pry Sisson's mouth open and carefully drip the contents under her tongue.

Then I pry the claws of one mechanical creature off her foot as Stein wrestles with the lasso that the other hand has wrapped around her waist. We let them go, and they are blown away. Lost in the time stream.

Good riddance.

I pop the pill into my mouth just as Nobel and Stein do, and we all grab hold of Sisson.

In a blur of motion and color, we are pulled from the time stream. I hold my breath, because returning home always has the sensation of walking under a waterfall without getting drenched. Gloves is already here as we materialize into the common room. Some of the same Hollows who watched us spar are also here, staring with concerned expressions. Low voices whisper to each other around us. Silence sweeps through the room as they see Sisson's limp, bloody body. Moving quickly, I lay Sisson on a tattered Oriental rug in the center of the room. Nobel holds her head, I kneel at her side, and Stein stands behind me with her arms folded.

"This should take care of it," Gloves says, taking a gas mask, with a blender attached to the mouthpiece, from a compartment in his wheelchair.

Nobel must know the routine because he takes the rubber mask and slips it over Sisson's head, securing the leather straps. Gloves turns on the blender and pulls some shimmering, gear-shaped items from his blue conductor's coat pocket. With Sisson's head laid back, he starts tossing the gears into the blender.

"She's inhaled too much of the time stream.

Remaining in it that long isn't good for the lungs. This should help flush her system. These nanites will eat the remaining Contra from her blood," Gloves says over the sound of metal grinding metal.

Sisson convulses, but Gloves puts one white-gloved hand on her forehead and secures the blender with his other.

I see a yellow powder fill the eye ports of the black rubber gas mask. Sisson's chest heaves in and out as she gasps for air. I can feel my pulse quicken, and it takes all my self-control to not knock Gloves over and tear the mask off. Then her breathing normalizes.

"It's done," Gloves says.

I quickly unstrap the mask and watch Sisson's eyes flutter open. She is mumbling. Stein bends down and strokes Sisson's sweat-filled hair out of her eyes.

"You're safe now," Gloves says.

Sisson reaches into her pocket and pulls out a small vial of black liquid. With shaking hands, she presses it into Nobel's palm.

As soon as she lets go, her eyes roll back into her head, and she passes out.

EMBER
Six

The world is on fire

At least, that's how it feels. The heat is unbearable, scorching not only my exposed skin, but also blistering its way into my lungs and throat with every breath I draw. Even though I don't dare open my eyes, I know there is no way to escape the inferno. His room is on the second floor, my brain reminds me.

Even if I can somehow grope my way to the window, there will be no exit there, so I huddle in the farthest corner from the blazing doorway, desperately shielding the person screaming behind me. My new dress is melting into my skin, and the burning lace is blistering my already-red arms.

I don't recall much. Not how the blaze began, not the name of the person behind me, not even my own name. But the lace I remember. How I'd begged for it, complained that the dress was much too plain without it. And, at my insistence, a man with eyes like blue sapphires and a gentle smile had told the frustrated seamstress to add more lace—not the cheap thin kind, but the thick

French lace.

I was happy.

Now, all those things are being consumed in grey smoke and melting silk. I cry out, but the sound never escapes my throat. I choke on it.

For a minute, I'm disconnected from my body—from the pain that's holding me hostage there. I float as if in a dream.

There's a family having dinner at a long table set with massive crystal dishes and fine china. Mother is smiling meekly as my older sister shows her a book she's reading. Papa is leaning to his side, speaking in low tones to a man in a uniform whose name I can't call to mind. Next to me, my little brother is stabbing peas with his fork and feeding them to the dog sitting under the table.

The scene melts away in flames. I'm in another, darker room. A basement. Mother has set up a large blanket on the dirty floor, and we are eating picnic style by the light of flickering oil lamps. Her smile is gone, replaced by deep worry lines around her mouth and eyes. Beside me, my brother's stomach grumbles. I hand him my slice of buttered bread. He smiles up at me and…

"Anya, go fetch your brother. And make sure he's in his fine clothes. The photographers are here," Papa orders, his voice tense and clipped.

"Yes, Papa."

He grabs me by the arm, glancing around at the people beginning to surround us. "He's your responsibility, Anya. Look after him."

His words leave me feeling hollow and confused, but I obey. I turn and head for the bedroom. I'm almost to the stairs when I hear the spray of gunfire.

As quickly as the memory came, it's gone. I can

feel the blood flowing to my brain, searing, boiling inside my head. The pain is unbearable. I'm being carried away from the flames.

"Not without him," I try to say, *but my throat is too scorched to produce sound. I close my eyes and go limp. "I'm sorry, Papa. I'm so sorry. So sorry…"*

Reality crashes to pieces around me, and I begin to heave. Two strong hands grasp me by the shoulders and pull. In the last fragmented pieces of my mind, I'm being ripped from the arms of my brother, who is trying to hold on to me.

The world shifts. When I open my eyes, I'm back in the classroom, clutching my desk so hard my fingers ache. I'm crying, shaking all over. Ethan is holding me, stroking my hair as Kara looks on, her expression worried. With one arm still around me, Ethan reaches over and pries my hands off the desk, one at a time. I pull them into my chest tightly. For a horrible moment, I can still feel the heat of the flames. Lifting me into his arms, he sweeps out of the room and walks briskly down the hall as I fade in and out of consciousness.

Doc lifts my chin so he can shine a light in my eyes. I bat him away, still caught up in the memory for a second before my eyes can fully adjust, allowing me to really see him. He's a kind old man with more white tufts of hair coming out his ears than have probably ever been on his shiny, bald head. He has soft, warm hands and a constant, sincere smile—things that can't be said for most of the other staff in this place. His nurse scares the living crap out of me.

I'm not sure how much of Nurse is human, if any at all. It steps into the room wearing a white lab coat, a full mask of brass and dark glass, and strange leather gloves that stretch up its arms to the elbow. There are sparse tufts of brown hair poking out around the edges of its mask, which only adds to its shocking appearance. None of this is what unnerves me. It's the clockwork implant in the center of its chest, occasionally giving off wisps of steam with a sour hiss, which does it. I hold back a shudder.

I catch Doc shooting Flynn a look I can't quite figure out as he walks in and takes a seat next to me on the gurney. When I peek at him over my shoulder, he smiles—something about the appearance of his chin dimple makes me instantly relax. He nudges me.

"You okay?"

I wince, not because I'm hurt, but because the truth makes me sound like a lunatic. "I, um, kind of freaked out in class today."

"Care to elaborate?" Flynn asks, crossing his legs at the ankles. Just hearing his voice makes the blood rush to my face, burning my cheeks. I hang my head, not wanting him to see me like this. In my mind, I reach back for the memories, but they are splintered and hazy.

"I just… I don't know exactly. I was remembering the day you found me, I guess."

"It's okay, Ember. You went through something extremely traumatic before we found you. It's only natural that pieces of that trauma might float to the surface, especially when you're under so much pressure."

I grab him by the vest, my hands shaking. "What happened to me? I need to know." My voice trembles, though I try to keep it steady. I feel like I'm going crazy. My heart is beating so fast and so hard, I can feel the pulse in my ears. My skin itches everywhere, as if there's something inside me trying to crawl out. I know I shouldn't say more, but it comes spilling out anyway. "I keep getting these bits and pieces. Faces I can't quite place and bits of conversations. I feel like the more I try to remember, the more it fades away." I open my mouth to say more, but Doc Monroe cuts in.

"There's a reason the first trip through the time stream washes away our memories, Ember. It's protecting us, allowing us to be reborn into a new life without the pain of what came before."

"You don't understand!" I'm yelling now, but I can't help it. If I have to sit here a moment longer, I'm going to combust. "I *need* to remember. I've forgotten something really important." I look to Flynn. His face is sympathetic, but sad. My first instinct is to make a run for it. My palms twitch as I release him and ball my hands into fists, ready to fight my way out. Only his kind, familiar voice stops me.

"Ember, you have to know, you were lucky I found you when I did. You almost died in that fire. The recruits have all had to leave their lives, families, friends, and everything else behind to come here. Rifters can't be tied to any specific point in time; we have to be beyond it, above it. There can be nothing holding us back, Ember. It's how we have to operate." He takes my hand, awakening the nest of wasps that apparently lives in my stomach. "We need to keep this from happening again."

"How?" I ask, already knowing the answer.

Doc holds up a pair of intricately made goggles that have clockwork gears where the lenses should be. I tense, and Flynn squeezes my hand. It's all I can do to stay calm, to keep myself from fighting my way out of the room.

"This is a device Tesla created. It isolates specific memories in the brain and builds a sort of mental wall, much the way the time stream itself works. It'll help you forget."

As soon as he says the words, I jerk back, curling up on the gurney.

"Please don't, Flynn. Don't take the memories away. I want them." The words are dripping with desperation. "There's got to be a reason I'm remembering, right? I mean, why am I getting these memories back if they aren't important?"

He takes a deep breath, and I can tell he's considering my words. "Ember, you are one of the strongest Rifters I've ever seen. And maybe I shouldn't tell you this, but you will remember. Eventually, you'll remember everything."

"What do you mean?" I ask, half stunned by his admission.

"I mean, after a while, the abilities of a Rifter fade. You won't always be able to access the time stream. Like Mortimer. Even Catherine is losing her abilities. As you get older, they will burn out. When that happens, your connection to the time stream will be severed and all the things it took from you—all the memories— they will come back."

I have no idea what to say, so I just stare at him, trying to tell if he's being serious. The sad look on his face tells me he is.

"But that means, I mean, weren't you and Catherine trained together?" I ask. "Why can you still rift?"

He exchanges a stern look with Doc before he answers. "Yes. We were trained together. But we aren't all equal. Like you. You are strong, so you'll all be able to rift longer than any of us. It's why Tesla chose you. He chooses only the strongest. You'll probably be rifting years after your team can't anymore."

"The ones who burn out slower," I counter, a strange bitterness swelling inside me.

"Yes. And, as for me, my time is coming. I can feel it winding down. My own memories have been returning for a while now. It won't be long for me."

I reach out, putting my hand on top of his. He looks so young. "How long have you been rifting?" I ask, suddenly curious how much time I have.

"I've been rifting for almost fifty years. I took my first trip through the stream when I was only nineteen."

My eyes must be bugging out of my head, because he chuckles. "Oh, yes. I'm old, Ember. So much older than I look. Tesla thinks it's the traveling. Being in the time stream slows the aging process down. When you stop traveling, the aging speeds back up to normal."

I pull my hand back and clutch the sides of my head. It's so impossible to think straight. "The others should know," I whisper, thinking of Ethan and Kara. Here we are, so close to committing ourselves to Tesla. "They should know what they are signing on for. All of it."

"Tesla won't allow that. He wants the Rifters to have absolute faith in him. If they knew, it might color their reasoning for accepting or declining."

"Then I'll tell them," I say without thinking about the challenge I'm laying down.

Doc puts a hand on my shoulder. "No, Ember. One way or another, you won't. Tesla won't allow it."

I look back to Flynn, who glares at Doc before

turning back to me.

"Ember, I only told you so that you'd realize the memories aren't gone for good. They haven't been erased. One day, when you are older and more able to handle them, you'll remember on your own. But right now, they are dangerous. Please. If this kind of black out were to happen during a rift, we could lose you forever." He pleads with his green eyes, "And you are too important for that. I need you to trust me. I swear I'll never let anything bad happen to you. I'll be here the whole time."

I nod, not trusting my voice to stay steady. I do trust him. Flynn saved my life—brought me here. Besides Ethan and Kara, he's the one person in the world I trust most. Doc slips the goggles onto my head. I can't see anything but a bright green glow, though I hear Nurse's clockwork chest give off a puff of steam. I shudder. Flynn slips off the gurney, and I lie back, still clutching his hand.

* * *

I wake up in my bed. A dense fog hovers over the corners of my mind, making everything fuzzy at first. I sit up, still fully dressed. There is a folded piece of paper, with my name written on it, on my desk. I stand up, wait until I'm steady on my feet, and pick up the note.

Ember,
Report to the rift chamber as soon as you are awake
and have had something to eat.
-Flynn

My stomach growls. No need to tell me twice. Feeling like I've slept for the first time in weeks, I head to the cafeteria.

The small dining area has a counter with a selection of food choices and a cooler of milk and juice. I grab a tray of chicken and vegetables, taking it to an empty table where I proceed to devour the food. But every bite is like throwing a penny in a well. The way my stomach twists is more nerves than real hunger, but it feels the same. I could eat every tray in the room and still want more. Drinking half my milk in one long gulp, I return it to the metal tray with a thud that echoes through the empty room. Suddenly, it feels less like a cafeteria and more like a crypt. The rattle from the air vent is like an ominous breath blowing across my skin. I shake my head.

Ugh. What is wrong with me today? First, I freak out in class, and now I'm jumping at shadows. All because of some stupid nightmares. As I think about them, my mind reaches back for the memories but finds nothing. What happened? My stomach churns again. There is something I wanted to remember. Something important. But, it's gone.

With a grunt, I rise and kick the chair back with one foot. Grabbing my tray, I set it in the dirty dish window. I turn for the door, but, before I can take a step, the room gets hot. Reaching over my head, I wave my hand over the vent. It's thumping, but no air is coming out. I tug at the collar of my grey shirt. It's gotten really hot—like sauna hot. Sweat beads along my hairline as little drops of perspiration roll down the back of my neck.

"What the—?" I walk over to the computer interface. It blinks to life when I touch the flat screen. "Interface, what's wrong with the temperature controls in the cafeteria?"

The voice of Tesla responds with a thick, metallic echo, "All systems functional."

"Interface, run a diagnostic on the environmental control systems."

"All systems functional."

"Then, why is it so hot in here?" I walk over to the door and press the metal plate.

A voice from behind me makes me turn on my heel. "Ember," it says.

There, in the middle of the empty cafeteria, stands… well, me. I feel my mouth drop open the way you only see in cartoons. She—no, *I*—am wearing a black leather corset over a golden tunic and striped pants. Her hair is twisted up in the back with loose strands dangling around her face. But the biggest difference between us is the long, fresh scar on her chin. I don't have a scar there. Not yet, anyway. Before I can compose myself enough to say anything, she takes a step toward me, her hands held out as if to calm me.

"You need to take the first key with you."

My brain freezes. "What?"

I take an involuntary step back, knowing that we shouldn't touch. That would be very bad. Catastrophic. Before I can compose myself enough to ask a more rational question like, "Why *the heck* are we breaking *the* most basic and universal law of time travel?" she steps backward and vanishes.

I blink. She—no, *I*—have just risked destroying time to give myself that message—it must be something urgent. Life or death.

I back up until the door behind me slides open with a whoosh.

Once I'm in the hallway, I can feel the cool breeze of the air conditioning system circulating through the air. I let go of the breath I've been holding. The sudden release of tension nearly brings me to my knees.

Should I tell someone? I dismiss the idea. No need to get myself in trouble for something I haven't even done yet.

"Hey, Ember!" Kara calls, coming down the hall with Ethan beside her. "There you are. We've been looking all over for you. Are you okay? Flynn said you had a panic attack or something."

I hesitate. A panic attack? Is that what that was? It's hazy, but I remember it. Sort of. "Um, yeah. I'm fine. Nerves," I say weakly.

I look back at the cafeteria door, just to verify that she—me—is really gone. Then I turn, smiling at Kara to cover my shock. "I was just getting something to eat before the test."

Ethan catches up with me first. He drapes one arm over my shoulders and runs his free hand through his hair. I let myself relax into him. He smells like saltwater and sunshine. I breathe in the familiar scent, holding my breath until I can't, before releasing it. He's warm and somehow soft and strong at the same time. He feels like home.

"You sure you're okay?" he asks, pulling back to search my eyes.

I nod. "Just nervous."

He narrows his eyes, but he doesn't challenge me. Finally, he releases me. "Nothing to be nervous about. I took my rift test already. It's a breeze."

"Wow. How long was I out?"

"A whole day," Ethan answers.

That explains the hunger.

"He's right," Kara says, taking my hand and giving it a gentle squeeze. "If he can do it, we can do it."

Ethan leans against the wall. "What's that supposed to mean?"

Kara tightens her auburn ponytail. "Just that either of us could beat you with one hand tied behind our backs."

"Really?"

"Oh yes," Kara says, her eyes glinting. "Isn't that right, Ember?"

"Yeah. Sure," I say. I try to sound confident, but my voice is shaky.

Kara turns her back to Ethan and slips her arm through mine. "Come on, I'll walk you."

"I need to go by my room first," I say quickly.

"Why?" Ethan asks, following us down the hall.

I open my mouth, but nothing comes out. What can I say? I'm trying to come up with some excuse, but I'm totally blanking out.

"She got mustard on her shirt, nosy," Kara chimes in. Leaning her head on my shoulder, she whispers, "You sure you're all right?"

"Yeah," I whisper back, kissing her on the head. "Thanks for the save."

"You can pay me back someday."

* * *

They wait outside my door while I run into my room, and, thanks to Kara's cover, throw on a new shirt and brown leather vest. My fingers run over the board where my keys dangle, making them sing like wind chimes. I close my hand around the smallest of them. It's newer than most of the others, its brass not yet showing signs of patina. The end is oval with intricate spiral insets. It's the first key Flynn ever gave me, only days after I arrived at the Institute. I had finally been released from the hospital and Mistress Catherine had just showed me to my room for the first time. Flynn stopped by to check on me, something he did frequently while I had been in the hospital, and gave me the key.

I hope my other self knew what she was doing, telling me to bring it. If I lose it, I'll never forgive myself. Carefully, I tuck it into the pocket of my vest and allow myself a glance around my room. If things go badly tonight, I'll never see it again.

* * *

By the time I reach the rift chamber, I'm hot again, but this time, it has nothing to do with quirky environmental controls. I try to keep my hands tucked into the pockets of my trousers, not just to keep them from shaking uncontrollably, but also to keep my palms from getting sweaty. Behind me, Ethan marches slowly, and Kara is at my side, clutching my arm so hard I can feel my heartbeat in it. She is staring straight ahead, her face stern. Only the lack of arrogance in her eyes betrays her fears. I can't blame her. For all Kara's bluster, this place is her home as much as it is mine. The idea of losing one of my friends, my *family*... well, it scares me even more than the idea of washing out myself, and my first solo rift will be the most dangerous.

"Did Marcia test yet?" I ask. "Did she make it?"

I look at Kara out of the corner of my eye. Her silence is my answer. My stomach flip-flops, but Kara looks impassive. Rifters are taught to be vague—to blend in, to never stand out. We have to be forgettable. Ordinary. I doubt Kara could *ever* accomplish ordinary. She's gorgeous, smart, and one of the best fighters here. She'll make it if I don't. She'll look after Ethan if I can't. I have to let that be enough, because it's all the reassurance I'm going to get.

When we get to the door to the rift chamber, I come to a dead stop, trying to swallow the orange-sized lump in my throat before I bid my friends good-bye. They aren't allowed to go in with me, but they will be allowed to watch from behind the safety glass of the observation room, where Flynn and the other teachers will be. I finally swallow, and it feels like a handful of razor blades slicing me as they slide down my throat.

The technical name for the test is the Trials. There are a series of tests that have to be passed before you reach this point, and I've nailed all of them, but this is the big one. I will have to make my first unassisted rift, hit a specific mark, complete a task, and return to the chamber—all without being lost in the stream or ripping myself apart. That last bit is trickier than it sounds.

So many things could go wrong that I can't even count them. I try not to think about them, but every worst-case scenario is rushing into my brain. Without a Tether or some other way to control the rift, you can end up lost in time. I've heard rumors about kids who rift for the first time accidentally. I shudder, imagining how frightening that must be, just landing in the stream and not knowing how you got there. Even worse, the ones who are lucky enough to find their way out of the stream usually land in some random place in time with few memories of who they were or what they did. It's those lost children the Hollows like to recruit. Strays, Tesla calls them. Mutts.

Kara stops. Throwing her arms around me, she squeezes me tightly. I can feel the tears welling up in my eyes, but I manage to keep them from spilling over. All I can think is—*what if I never see them again?*

So it's a good-bye hug. As usual, Ethan joins in, throwing his arms around both of us. We don't speak. There's nothing to say. Over the large brass door is a floodlight. A chime sounds, and I glance up to see it has turned red. That's my cue.

"All right, get off me, you saps. It's time." I try to laugh, but it just comes out a dry cough. I wave good-bye, and they head up the stairs to the right of the door. Tugging the bottom of my vest, I straighten myself up, run a hand over my braid, and then press my palm to the door pad. It opens with a rickety groan.

The chamber inside is cylindrical, reminding me of a picture I once saw of the Roman Coliseum. But the walls are smooth, grey concrete with metal plates, like windows, hung all around, all the way up to the tall-domed ceiling. In the center of the room is a brass pedestal with two arched handrails. Next to the door is a small wooden table covered with tech.

The months I've spent studying how to use it all evaporates from my mind. As I stare at the familiar objects, my eyes begin to lose focus, softening everything around the edges. I'm breathing too hard, too fast. I grasp the table with both hands and lean over, squeezing my eyes closed. "It's all right, Ember, take your time." Flynn's voice echoes through the chamber. Of course he is watching me. Everyone is watching me. I straighten up, forcing myself to let go of the table. I *will not* fall apart. I *will not* be seen freaking out like this. I *am a Rom—*

The thought explodes like a grenade behind my eyes. I am a *what?*

I try to recall the name that hovers in the back of my mind, just beyond my reach. But it's useless, and I don't have time to deal with my neurosis right now. *Later*, I promise myself.

If I survive this.

Shaking my head, I push it away, all of it, and look back down at the table. The holy trinity of Rifter tech sits on a simple piece of white cloth.

I reach for the Babel Stone ring first. It's cool as I slip it on my finger. Brass is coiled around a tiny round magnet, with one simple, grey stone that looks deceptively like a piece of common gravel set in the side. Such an innocuous-looking thing to give you the ability to speak and understand any language.

Without hesitation, I move to the next object on the table, the Tether, and snap it onto my forearm like an oversized mousetrap. Copper wires and tiny hinges securely hold what looks like a massive watch face.

There is a tiny pin with a spoke at the end that allows me to adjust the current date and time.

I run my fingers over the final piece of hardware before I lift it into my palm. It's the most impressive of the three and the most difficult to conceal. An Earwig. Carefully, I wind the tiny machine over my left ear and pull my long, chestnut hair free of the tight braid I usually keep it in. I run my hands through it and shake it loose so it will hide the tech now attached to my ear. Immediately, the tiny spokes and gears of the Earwig come to life with a series of chirps and clicks. Tesla's thick voice rings in my ear. "Remote Tesla activated. Authorization code?"

I clear my throat before answering, "Marconi is a fraud."

"Authorization code accepted." Apparently, being a computer has not diminished Tesla's heavy Austrian accent or his intense dislike for his former competitor.

I walk on steadier legs to the platform and grab onto the rails, waiting for my assignment. "I'm ready," I say, hoping my voice sounds stronger than I feel.

Above me is the viewing booth, a large glass window where the teachers and other recruits are staring down at me. Below that is a series of ornate clock faces and a ticker board with red lights. A series of numbers flashes across the screen.

"This is your assignment, your final test. Travel to this point and make contact with Flynn at the assigned location," Tesla's computer voice orders.

I look at the screen. I'm going back to 1996. Not very long ago in the grand scheme of things—less than a hundred years. I'm not sure whether I'm relieved or disappointed. I plug the numbers into my Tether and nod.

Closing my eyes, I feel the charge building in the room around me. My hair starts to lift off my head—even the metal buckles on my boots and vest hum. Then I feel a jolt on my arm, the connection to this time being made through the Tether. I breathe out slowly, but inside my head, I feel the heat build until it is unbearable, like melting inside. Taking a deep breath, I hold it, and then let go of the rails.

LEX
Seven

Something isn't right. The room is different somehow. We have been to the Amber Room before, but this time it feels like there is something missing. Not in the room itself, but in the air around us. There is a void in the time stream, like the air in the room is going to implode on itself. I glance into the corner of the room. A crack that was never there before splinters down the wall. Subconsciously, I reach back, taking Stein by the hand. As I watch the crack widen, a small metal leg struggles through, tearing the crack into a small hole. It emerges like a mechanical chick bursting through an egg. I take the brush and shove it in my pocket. When I look back, it's not just one Gear Head, but three of them making their way through the crack.

"Run!" I scream.

Picking up the ornate chair from the vanity table, I chuck it through the window.

"I really hope Gloves doesn't need that," I say, urging Stein out. As I dive out the window behind her, a piece of glass grazes my shoulder. Instantly, blood flows down my arm, soaking my sleeve as I fall. I land next to Stein in a mess of branches.

We land on the main deck of the airship. The wind gusts across the steel bow, forcing us toward the railing. Stein grabs my uninjured arm and tugs me to the back of the ship where long ropes tie it to the rocky cliffs below.

"Why are there Gear Heads?" Stein gasps, leaning forward over the rail. "They weren't here last time."

"I don't know," I answer, shaking my head. It doesn't make any sense. Somehow, they have tracked us to this place, and I have no idea how we are going to get past them.

I swear under my breath. "How could Claymore miss the disturbance in the time stream?"

"I don't know. Maybe the serum didn't fix the problem and he's still not functioning at one hundred percent," Stein suggests, breathing hard. She holds my arm and peeks around my shoulder, looking more freaked out than I've ever seen her.

"We need to move," I say, ushering her forward.

She nods grimly. "I don't see them. Can you see them?"

I'm about to say no, but out the corner of my eye, I see movement. They are coming. And there are so many of them. I can't even count. I look back at Stein; her face is resigned. I nod over the edge to the ropes draped between the giant brass propellers.

"Remind me again how hiding the Amber Room fifty stories above the Grand Canyon was a good idea?" Stein says, climbing over the edge as she speaks.

The Gear Heads are advancing, chewing up the deck with their sharp pincers as they move. Sparks fly off the deck as the little robots rev the saws affixed to their other arms.

"They are going to tear through this thing like a can opener," I say, clinging to the thick lead.

I look to Stein. A Gear Head leaps to the deck inches from where she holds to the other rope. It turns its saw on the cleat holding her rope.

I lurch back onto the rail and swat the machine over the edge. It hits the propeller. Red liquid from its domed head splatters across the bottom of the ship.

Cursing Gloves under our breaths, we coil our legs around the ropes and begin our impromptu descent.

The heavy wind pushes at us as we dangle helplessly. "I don't think this was covered in the orientation manual," I say.

Stein laughs. "There was a manual?"

We land with a puff of dust.

I look up to where the Gear Heads are climbing down the ropes behind us. "I'll cut these tethers. You get the ones over there."

Stein sprints to the cliff's edge to untie the lashes holding the front down, and I tackle the ones right around the base of it.

Untying one of the leads in front of a large outcropping of rocks, I pull the other one free from the sand. Just then, I hear Stein scream.

"Lex, help!"

I look up to see Stein surrounded by more Gear Heads. They are pushing her to the edge of the cliff. "I'm coming!"

Dropping the last rope, I run to her. I don't see it happen, but one of the updrafts from the cliff twists the large rope and it somehow wraps around my ankle.

I trip, sprawling forward onto my face. As I flail to catch myself, I manage to push one of the Gear Heads right off the cliff. I wrap my hand around a chunk of root, which is poking up from the ground, to catch myself from going over. Dazed from smacking my head against the dirt, I look up, focusing on Stein. She loses her foothold as the Gear Heads drive her back again, and she kicks at them, but they are too quick. She tilts off balance, falling backward off the cliff.

Screaming, I lunge forward from my knees to see that she has a one-handed grasp on a jagged rock just over the edge. I reach out, barely able to snatch hold of her before she slides over completely. She reaches up, trying to get a grip on my arm, but it's slick with blood and she slips off, unable to get a firm hold.

"Stein, look at me," I order, clutching her tightly by the wrist as her feet scramble to find purchase on the rocky cliffside. I scream again from the burning pain as my shoulder is ripped out of its socket. She's not that heavy, but the angle is bad, and I can't make my muscles cooperate.

"Lex, please don't let go," Stein begs. She's gone still now, trying to make it easier to keep my grip on her, but I feel her long glove slipping through my fingers. Her silk top hat has long since blown away, leaving her dark hair to blow free. I redouble my precarious hold on the tree root beside me with my good arm. Sliding closer to the edge, I scrape my belly along the loose gravel.

A sharp pain rips into my leg, making me scream.

Looking over my shoulder, I see one of the Gear Heads is trying to saw off my right leg. I look away, not wanting to watch the blood as it spurts out of my calf. I kick and wriggle, but it's no use. The thing has clawed its way into my skin and isn't letting go. Even as the pain shoots up my thigh, I fight to focus on Stein's face. Her grey-blue eyes are wide, her face is pale and marred with dozens of scratches, and her hair is now matted to her forehead with blood and sweat. One of the silver rings that used to loop through her eyebrow has torn free and crimson streaks leak down her face. I start to lose my grip on her.

I will not let you die, I promise inside my head. Somehow, the words don't make it to my mouth, as if saying it aloud is impossible.

"You little—" I look back over my shoulder, giving my leg another quick jerk. I can't move very far anyway, as I'm caught in the net-like tether holding the small zeppelin to the ground. If I had my other hand, I could fight the little metal monster off, but I can't let go of Stein.

I won't.

I kick again, hoping to send the Gear Head over the cliff, but it isn't enough. It has some sort of pincer attached to my calf, and it's slowly eating through the muscle. I turn and look over my shoulder. The blood flow is slowing to a drizzle. There is nothing I can do.

"Pull, Lex... pull," Stein yells, still scrambling to get a grip on me with her free hand.

"I'm trying!"

My arms are getting weaker every second. All my adrenaline is gone and my leg... my leg is on fire, the pain shooting all the way to my brain. I can't concentrate. I can't lift her. This dawns on me just as my vision begins to blur. I feel a frustrated tear roll down my cheek.

I've never felt so weak.

"Don't let go. Don't let go," I chant under my breath to myself, but my mind keeps jumping to that thing on my leg. Stein looks uncertain.

"Don't let go," I repeat. I try to pull, but my whole body is on fire. She knows I can't hold her. I don't know what hurts worse—the look of absolute forgiveness on her face or Tesla's Gear-Faced Pinocchio cutting off my leg.

Can't it go any faster? I wonder with a half laugh, wishing it'd just cut the freaking thing off already. I can't stand the pain anymore. Maybe if it just cuts it off, I can give in to the fog fighting its way into my head. My breathing quickens. Maybe I can just lie here and bleed to death. Anything to numb the agony ravaging my body.

Stein's hand is getting hard to hold onto. I squeeze tighter. It seems the tighter I squeeze, the more she slips—as if I am squeezing her to her death. I start to panic, thrashing my leg with a fleeting hope that the Gear Head will dislodge. It doesn't. My stomach rolls. It's all I can do not vomit from the smell of my own blood and cut flesh.

"Help me!" I scream with the last of my energy. As the words leave my body, I slump, my chin hitting the ground hard. My fingers are losing grip on the root. Maybe we'll both go over.

"Lex, I'm slipping," Stein says, her voice surprisingly calm. "You need to rift out."

I want to look at her, but I can't manage to turn my head that far. "No. I can't leave you."

"Lex, my jacket tore. I lost my Contra. You have to go without me."

The words barely register in my brain. All I want to do is close my eyes and sleep. My mind is shutting off. Did I let go? Is that Stein screaming? I can't tell. I can't lift my arms or my head even though Stein's weight is gone. Turning my head to the side, I puke into the sand.

Lying facedown in my own stomach's contents, I hear a distant explosion. Charred flesh falls and hits me in the side of my cheek. Part of my brain wonders if it's mine—chunks of my hamburger leg. The pain is gone. The screaming is gone. My mind is gone. I don't hear anything. I can't even lift my head to see what's burning. Is it me? I don't care. Smoke slides across the ground, sending wisps into my nose and my throat. I cough. My hand is empty, I realize. As if on pure instinct, I let go of the tree root with my left hand and reach into my pocket to remove the small pill. For a moment, I think I will throw it away, but something stops me short. I place it on my tongue and swallow. My eyes flutter closed.

"Lex," a distant voice calls. "Lex, can you hear me?"

TESLA JOURNAL ENTRY: SEPTEMBER 30TH, 1892

Garrison Tybee arrived today. He seems a clever, good-spirited man for a military sort. His service days are over, but I can see there are still traces of that training to this day. After explaining the process, he agreed to allow me to try to replicate the experiment.
Addendum:
The experiment was a success, but the

103

results were very similar with regards to the memory loss.

Since this does seem a biological ability, (as I have tested now three other men and women all with no success), I plan to do a full genealogical profile on Helena. Perhaps it is there I will find the key to this ability.

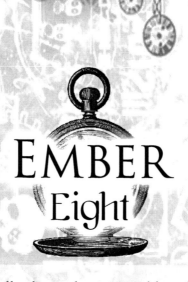

EMBER
Eight

People talk about the stream like it's an actual river, but it's not. It's more like a wind tunnel where everything blasts past you so quickly it's impossible to see anything but the streaks. It looks even more daunting now as I stand outside it alone for the first time. It is beautiful. Terrible. Breathtaking.

The edges of the stream are a sort of thin membrane. It's easy to imagine, as Mortimer says, that the time stream is a living creature. Most of the time, I'm just sort of thrown in when I rift. This is the first time I've ever taken the time to really see it, but now that I do, I can see the subtle pinks and blues of the plasma all around me. I can feel the thrumming harmonies weaving through each gust of wind, whispering to me like lullabies.

Moving purely out of instinct, I step through the outer membrane and into the stream. I'm suspended there as time rushes past me. It's almost like flying.

Thinking only of where and when I want to go, I feel myself being pulled back against the tide whipping past me. The force pulls at my skin. It's tugging my hair from my head with such power I think every strand will be ripped from my scalp. The air is like a million little pinpricks eating away at me. I can't breathe from the pressure coiling around my chest. If one were able to stand in the middle of a tornado, I imagine it would feel something like this.

"Location verified." Tesla speaks in my ear, but I can barely hear him over the rush of the stream.

I reach out, feeling the wind with my fingers. I've never felt so connected—so complete—as I do inside the stream, as if I walk around the rest of my life only half born. I was created for this, my mind confirms. The stream is a piece of me and I of it. The Tether feels heavy on my arm, an anchor dragging me down. For a moment, I wish I could strip free of it and merge with the stream completely—just give myself over to its siren call.

Yes, my mind whispers, *this is the place*. With a regretful heave, I force myself out of the stream, landing on my hands and knees in the soft grass of Central Park. No one seems to notice my abrupt appearance, thank goodness. I've landed off the main path behind a tall oak tree. Standing up, I dust myself off.

Tapping my earpiece, I whisper, "Tesla? Time and date verification."

The voice responds, "Verified. September sixteenth, nineteen ninety-six."

Trying to look nonchalant, I walk around the tree, scanning the park. A few people jog the path cut through the trees, some just walk, and two children play Frisbee with a yellow dog. Then, a flash of light catches my eye. Flynn is sitting casually on a green bench not far from me, his glasses glinting in the bright sunlight. He holds two paper cups in a cardboard container, smiling brightly, with one arm draped over the back of the bench. Bringing his empty hand up, he touches his ear and mumbles something I can't make out.

I'm so excited to see him that I run to his side, feeling like I want to fly. Sitting beside him, I cross my legs and lean back, unable to hide my wide smile. I've done it. I've as good as passed my final test. He hands me a cup without a word. I take a sip. It's dark, thick, and bitter.

"What's this?" I ask, gagging down the hot liquid.

"Coffee. It was very popular in the twentieth-century."

I look down at the cup and make a face. "I can't imagine why."

He chuckles as I sniff the beverage. It smells better than it tastes, that's for sure. "It's an acquired taste."

"So, just out of curiosity, where am I in your time stream?" I hold the cup with both hands and lean forward, resting my elbows on my knees.

"You've been in the Institute for a few weeks, recovering mostly. Doc says you are healing amazingly well. As a matter of fact, I get to show you to your room when I get back." Flynn crosses his legs at the ankle and smiles. "It's actually really good to know you make it this far."

"So you haven't given me my first key yet," I mutter, more to myself than to him.

Why did I need to bring it with me? I take another sip of the horrible liquid.

"What key?" he asks, looking at me from over the top of his glasses. I flush, pulling the key out of my vest.

"This key. You gave it to me the day Doc released me."

"Really?" He plucks it from my fingers, examining it in the light. "Hmmm. Interesting."

"What?"

"I've never seen anything like this, Ember. And I was just about to rift back to the Institute."

"What does that mean?"

He looks at me. "Do you know what a *Fixed Point* is?"

"A point in time that cannot be changed or altered," I recite from one of our lessons, proud to know it stuck.

"Do you know how to create a Fixed Point?"

I shake my head. "I didn't know you *could* create one. I thought they occurred naturally?"

"Some do. But they can also be created." He holds up the key. "To lock—for want of a better term—a point in time, you have to create a *loop*. For example, by giving me this key, you have created a loop in time. This key now only exists from the moment I give it to you until the moment you give it back to me." He slips it into the pocket of his long jacket. "Thus the loop is closed; everything that happens inside that loop is fixed. The timeline between us is permanent. Unchangeable."

"That sounds intense. But where did the key come from then? The first time?"

"It's enough to make your head ache, isn't it?" he asks with a smirk. Then, taking a long drink, he stares off to the horizon before turning back to me.

"Time protects itself like any other living thing. It's very rare for a Rifter to be able to create a Fixed

Point. It's not something that should be done lightly. However, if I don't take this key now, then I won't ever give it to you. I've altered our history. Perhaps not for the better. Do you understand now why we don't deliberately try to create Fixed Points? How dangerous they could be?"

I nod, but I don't know why I needed this to happen. This isn't something Rifters tend to do, especially not on purpose. But my mind flashes back to the cafeteria and I realize, at some point, I *will* do it on purpose, despite Flynn's warning.

I'm not sure whether to be impressed with my future self for figuring out how to pull it off or ticked at myself for doing something so obviously dangerous. If I'd refused and not brought the key, what would've happened? I wouldn't have learned the method for creating a Fixed Point, and Flynn never would have given me the key. How would that have changed my timeline? Would it have, somehow, changed our friendship? My brain is reeling so hard I have to clamp it down before I explode.

"So, does this mean I'm a full-fledged Rifter now?" I ask, trying to keep my tone light. So many things are weighing on me like bricks in my belly—not the least of which is my bizarre future behavior.

His smile falters. "Not quite. There's still something you need to do here. You didn't really think it'd be that easy, did you?"

"What is it?" I ask, my own smile falling around the edges. Yeah. I sort of did. I make a mental note to kick Ethan later.

I hear a burst of static crackling through his Earwig, but there's nothing in mine. Tesla is talking to him, from his own time.

Flynn frowns as he listens but says, "Confirmed."

He motions to the tall building across the street. It's a lovely old hotel, the kind that almost looks like a castle. "In that hotel, there's a wedding today. Lauren Cartwright is marrying Lord Brandon Hunter. But, something goes terribly wrong. Today, the bride and her groom die, the maid of honor goes missing, and the best man has a nervous breakdown."

I try not to let him see the shiver that rolls up my back. "What am I supposed to do?"

He looks at me flatly. "Save whoever you can."

I blink. That means changing history, something we are never, ever supposed to do. "Are you sure?" I ask, not wanting to question him, but not quite sure I heard him right.

He nods. "Better do it fast, too. That wedding begins in an hour."

I drop my coffee and run, cutting through the park and across the street. The inside of the hotel is even more amazing than the outside. The walls are polished marble, and a large crystal chandelier dangles above my head like a glass snowflake. Everywhere, the scent of freesia floats in the air from tufts of the delicate flowers scattered all over the lobby. From the corner of my eye, I spy the concierge.

"Excuse me," I say, trying to look impatient. "Can you please direct me to the bridal suite?"

He blinks, his clean-shaven face making him look no older than ten. His expression sours. "And who, may I ask, is inquiring?"

I look affronted. "Look, you call up that idiot wedding planner and tell her that she better have a *very* good reason for dragging me out of a meeting to rush down here and let out a wedding dress because she couldn't keep the bride away from the petit fours at the rehearsal dinner. This is completely not my problem. You can either direct me up there right now, or you can tell her to kiss my—"

I don't have to finish before he's looking like he just swallowed a lime. "Of course. She's in room seven-fifteen."

I murmur thanks and spin on my heel so hard my hair flips behind me.

"Just a second," he yells, chasing after me. I tense, sure I'm busted. When I turn again, he holds out a small plastic card. "You'll need this to get the elevator to stop on the bridal floor. We secured it to keep out the media."

I take the key and wave my hand. "Of course. Thank you."

Trying not to break out into a sprint, I head for the elevator, stick the card in the slot, and make my way up to the seventh floor.

As soon as the doors slide open, I know I'm in trouble. The floor is teaming with ladies in expensive dresses. Some are in matching pale-pink taffeta dresses that make them look a bit like ballerinas, and others are in an array of designer duds. My brown leather pants and waist cincher are making me stand out like a sore thumb. People are pointing and whispering. I swear under my breath. I need to find a way to blend in, or I'll be kicked out of this group before I can even make contact with the bridal party.

To my left, a door opens and a maid steps out, her arms full of sheets. I catch the door behind her before it closes and step inside.

"Housekeeping," I call out. No response.

Though the room has been recently cleaned, it's still a disaster. Makeup and jewelry are scattered across every available surface, clothes are draped over chairs, and even a few things are hanging from the curtain rod. The room is a small suite, so not the bride's at least. I walk in a little farther. Beside the lounge is a rack of dresses. I walk over, looking at the tags. Designer, for sure, but not anyone I've ever heard of. And from the looks of them, a full four sizes too small. Who in the hell wears a size zero anyway?

I comb through the rack until I find a short, silver number that ties up the back like a corset. It might be my best bet. Grabbing it, I head for the bathroom and make a quick change, stuffing my clothes in an empty trash can and tying up the bag. Thank the heavens I have small feet. I slip on a pair of flat, black shoes from the closet. They are a little big, but they'll have to do. Taking a second to wind my hair up into a bun, I secure it with a few clips, pulling a few pieces out around my face as some of the ballerinas had done. I apply a little lipstick, just for good measure. The whole process takes less than five minutes.

I slip back into the hallway and toss my bag of clothes into the garbage chute. If I have time, I can dumpster dive for it later. If not, well, at least no one will find it.

Following a set of ballerinas, I make my way down the hall. The wallpaper has an antique floral pattern that almost gives the illusion of being outside in a spring garden. Between that and the freesia, I feel like I just stepped into a Martin Johnson Heade painting.

As soon as the thought crosses my mind, I almost laugh out loud, remembering the day we learned about the artist and how Ethan had remarked that we'd never, ever need to know any of that. I make a mental note to tell him.

Following the pink girls into room seven-fifteen, I have to struggle not to look as awestruck as I feel. The room is massive—lots of open spaces and Oriental decor, large antique room dividers and comfy-looking sofas. A few ladies are sharing a bottle of champagne in the main seating area. A man dressed all in white is softly playing the large grand piano in the corner of the room, and a few of the ballerinas are munching on a platter of crudités and chatting. From the back bedroom, another ballerina approaches, only this one is in a warm golden-yellow rather than pink. She glances over, seeing me, and stalks over.

"I have a dress like that," she says. "Freddy Ford, Fall Collection?"

I nod.

She shifts her weight on to one foot and puts her hands on her hips. It's a pose that reminds me a lot of Kara.

"I was told it was one of a kind." She's glaring now, her stare drilling into me.

My mouth twitches. "It's a knockoff," I whisper.

She tilts her head, accepting my answer but not looking happy about it. "It's a good one. Who are you, anyway?"

I hold out my hand. "I'm April. I'm here with the wedding planner."

She looks at my hand, but she doesn't take it. "Uh-huh."

"Have you seen her?" I ask, not having to fake looking nervous.

She turns to the pink girls. "Have any of you seen Diane?"

They shake their heads.

One of the ladies on the lounge speaks up. I can tell from the slur in her voice that it isn't her first glass of the bubbly liquid. "They are doing the bride's pictures down in the rose garden."

The golden ballerina turns back to me. "Shouldn't you know that? I mean, you have one of those headsets." She points at my Earwig. I reach up and touch it gently.

"Yeah, it isn't working. That's why I'm looking for her. To let her know."

She gives me an unimpressed look and walks over to the other bridesmaids. As I turn to leave, I hear one of them chuckle and say, "Greta, you are such a brat."

* * *

The rose garden is actually on the roof, two floors above the bridal floor. After slipping back into the elevator, I hit the button for the roof. The elevator stops on the eighth floor, and a handful of groomsmen pile in. I'm immediately gagging on the heavy smell of cologne and stale beer. They are oblivious to me as they talk.

"This is going to be the best wedding prank ever," the tallest one of the group says with a cocky grin.

"I know. Dude, they will never see it coming."

"Your sister is gonna kill you, man," another jokes.

The tall boy shrugs and tugs at his bowtie. "It's really a gift for Brandon. He's so uptight."

"Well, your gift should loosen up his girdle a little."

They all laugh as the doors slide open.

"Come on, Doug," one of the boys says, motioning to the tall one.

"Doug Cartwright?" I must say the name out loud because one of the groomsmen shoots me a *duh* look.

Before I can follow the groomsmen and ask about this prank, I'm accosted by a short man in a grey tux. He's portly, and judging by the way he's walking and his cute little blue-framed glasses, probably not part of the wedding party.

"Excuse me, who are you? This is a closed floor."

I hold out my hand, which he stares at. What is it with these people and handshakes?

"I'm Heather. I'm with the caterer?" He looks blank, so I sigh. "There's an issue with the cake. Something about too much humidity in the kitchen. The icing is starting to melt."

His little hands actually fly to his face and flutter in front of his mouth. He looks like he's going to cry.

"They told me to get Diane and have her go talk to the kitchen manager about bringing the temperature down a few notches," I finish quickly. His face has gone beet red, and I'm almost feeling bad.

"Oh, yes. Of course. I'll take care of it right away. Tell Rodrigo that Diane is on it," he blurts before scurrying over to a stern-looking woman in a long, powder-blue dress.

I catch a glance of the groomsmen talking as they wait for the bride to finish the photos with her parents. Doug Cartwright makes an exploding gesture with his hands, and a deep ball of dread forms in my gut. An exploding gift. A prank gone wrong. That's what is going to kill the bride and groom. I turn, stepping back into the elevator and pressing the button. The gifts should be in the reception hall. I just need to find the one that's a ticking bomb.

* * *

When I get down to the reception hall, I find the gift table, and a little bit of panic stutters through my heart. It's stacked high with presents. I take a step forward, determined to search every single one if I have to, but a hand closes around my arm, tugging me backward.

"That *is* my dress. And Diane doesn't have an assistant named April. So who are you, *really?*"

I turn, ready to make up whatever lie I have to, but behind her, I see the clock ticking slowly. I've wasted half an hour already. Any minute now, the bride and groom would be saying their vows and then, they'd be here.

"Look," I say, pulling my arm free, "there's a bomb in one of these boxes. And I need to find it."

She looks at me, her blue eyes cold as ice. "Security!"

I grab her by the neck and push her up against the wall. "Look, I don't want to hurt anyone. I'm here to help the bride and groom. Now, Doug Cartwright has rigged one of those boxes to explode as a prank, but something is going to go really, really wrong with that. You can help me find the gift it's hidden in, or I can knock you out and shove you in a closet. Your choice."

She can't talk so she just nods vigorously.

I let go, and she gasps for a second. "That sounds like something Doug would do. Idiot."

Heading over to the massive stack, I start rummaging. "It has to have his name on it, right?"

She looks at me as I toss boxes aside. "And you are sure there's a problem with it—that it'll hurt someone?"

"I am."

"It's not in there. They had bomb dogs in here earlier sniffing for explosives. He was going to bring it down after the ceremony. It's in his room."

I stare at her. Her face has gone pale, making her look even more waif-thin somehow.

She shrugs. "I heard them talking about it. It sounded funny."

I put the gift in my hands back on the table. "Can you take me to his room?"

She nods and motions for me to follow her.

The groom's floor is completely trashed. Tables and chairs overturned in the hallway, room service trays all over the floor. Toilet paper hangs from every possible surface like garland. She leads me to a door and opens her tiny clutch purse, pulling out a key card. I can't help raising my eyebrow at her.

"What?" she says defensively. "It's a wedding. Besides, he just needed someone to talk to. He just lost his offer from FSU, and he doesn't think anyone else is going to pick him up after blowing the playoff game like he did."

I look her over. "How old are you? Fifteen?"

"Sixteen."

"And he's what now, eighteen?"

"Nineteen."

I look at her, but I say nothing. Two years doesn't seem like that big a difference, but something inside me feels almost protective of her. Silly, really. She isn't that much younger than I am. Maybe it's because she looks so frail and wispy.

I shrug. "Whatever."

She unlocks the door, and we go in. This room makes the hallway look downright spotless. What is it about rich kids destroying hotel rooms?

"He completely rock-starred this room, um… what's your name, anyway?" I ask, feeling stupid as she wades through the mess behind me.

"Isabelle Dumont. Izzy for short."

"So, where do you think this thing is hidden?" I ask, rummaging through the closet.

She jerks her head toward the bathroom. "Tub, I think."

I step forward, and the door to the room bursts open. Doug, all six foot three, two hundred twenty pounds of him, is suddenly face to face with me. "What are you doing in my room?" he demands. Then, seeing my partner in crime, his expression softens just a little. "Izzy? What the hell?"

I snap my fingers in his face. "The exploding gift, where is it?"

His face hardens. "I don't know who you think you are, but—"

I cut him off with a knee to the groin. He doubles over in pain. "Don't make me ask again, Doug. The gift. Give it to me, now."

I should expect what happens next, but I don't. His head still down, Doug runs at me, knocking me off my feet and taking me to the ground. Behind me, I hear Izzy scream.

I manage to get my leg up and between us, and I kick him off me, into the wall. The framed painting falls and crashes into his head.

"Doug, how do I disarm the device?" I grab his face in my hand. There's a cut on his forehead. It's small but bleeding like a river. "Doug, tell me."

He cusses and smacks my hand away. Behind me, Izzy is holding the box, her eyes full of tears. "Please," she begs.

He mumbles something rude. I grab his face harder, until he's looking me right in the eye. "Doug Cartwright, you think your career is over now, but I'm here to tell you, in six weeks, you are going to get picked up by UCLA. In four years, you are going to go as the number-one draft pick to one of the greatest football franchises of all time." How many times did I have to listen to Ethan go on and on about this kid either botching or single-handedly saving a game? Too many to count. But now, I was glad I'd half-paid attention. "You will be one of the greatest quarterbacks in the history of the game. *Do not* screw that up by being a *tool* today, do you hear me? I'm opening this box right now. You can either help me do it without hurting anyone, or I swear to you, I will blow us all sky high, get it?"

He closes one eye, smiles, and flips me off. Sighing, I drop him as he passes out. Taking the box from Izzy, I head for the bathroom. Setting it in the tub, I carefully pull off the bow and slowly lift the lid.

The lid blows off the box, and a flash of light blinds me. My ears are ringing. For a second, I can't breathe. Then my vision slowly returns. There's still a ringing in my ears, but I can hear Izzy behind me.

"Are you okay?"

I nod. It was just a flash bang. Not fun, but not

lethal either.

Shaking my head, I use the sink to get to my feet. "That wasn't it. They are still in trouble."

I race past her and down the hall to the elevator.

The reception is outside. We make it to the hallway just before the final pink ballerina walks through the doors into the garden area, where grey clouds have all but blotted out the sunshine.

"Izzy! There you are. I was so worried! Where were you?" the bride demands, her relief quickly replaced by irritation as Izzy scoots out from behind me and takes her place in the lineup. I lean in close. "Izzy, there is still something going to happen here. They aren't safe. I didn't stop anything."

She ignores me and marches forward on cue. I reach out, but she's gone. A large security guard grabs me from behind, holding me back as the music changes and the bride steps out. As soon as she's gone, Diane pulls the headset out of her ear and turns her bitter glare at me.

"Who are you and what are you doing here?" she demands.

What can I say? I struggle, but it's no use. A loud flash of light and a clap of thunder split the air. The guard drops me, and I fall to my feet for only a second before rushing out the door. The bride is lying on the ground, her white dress singed black and melted. The groom has fallen next to her. His eyes are open, lifeless. His short hair has melted to his scalp; his face is red and blistering. Some of the guests are cowering; others are screaming and running. Many are groping blindly and crying. On the ground, a few feet from the bride, Izzy has been blown back against the wall. Her dress is singed, her eyes closed. I move over to her and reach down, feeling for a pulse. Then I catch it, slow and uneven under my fingers.

The maid of honor goes missing, Flynn had said.

Scooping her up, I back through the doors into the main lobby, where people are panicking. No one tries to stop me as I walk her across the street to the park where Flynn waits.

He carefully takes her from me and sets her in the grass at my feet, checking her vitals.

"Is she okay?" I manage, still coughing out the words.

"She'll be fine. You did it, Ember. Well done."

I want to be happy, but all I feel is guilty. Dirty. "You didn't tell me they were struck by lightning! How *exactly* was I supposed to prevent that?"

He doesn't look up from what he's doing. "You weren't."

"But you told me to—"

"I told you to save who you could. And you did. You saved her."

"But the others…" I want to cry. It isn't fair. A wedding is supposed to be the best day of your life, not the last.

Flynn looks up and takes my hand. Pushing up my sleeve, he exposes my scars. "We can't save everyone, Ember. Even when we want to. Even when we try to. You understand this?"

"What about her?"

Flynn looks down. "She's coming with me. She's going to be one of us."

"But I thought she…" I stop myself before the words are even fully formed in my mouth. Of course she goes missing. She's one of us.

He must see the realization worm its way into my brain because he drops my arm.

"She'll have scars, too. Like mine," I say quietly, looking at the angry red burns up her bare arm. "Will I know her, back at the Institute?"

He shakes his head. "She won't remember you, Ember. Or any of this. Her life as it was ends here, and her new life will begin on the other side."

That doesn't really answer my question. I rack my brain, but I can't remember ever seeing her in the Institute.

He stands up, pulling her limp body into his arms. "You still have to make the return trip, Ember. And it's not like when we rift as a group, it's... harder."

"Harder how?"

"That is something you will have to discover for yourself, I'm afraid. But I can say this—no matter what you see or hear, keep focused on the Tether. Just try to block everything else out."

I think about the lure I felt inside the stream. And I'm so tired. Maybe too tired to make it. But I take as deep a breath as I can manage and pull away, standing on my own.

"You should go back to the exact spot you entered from," he advises, readjusting the girl so she's over his shoulder.

"How will I find it?" I glance back to the general area I'd come from.

"You'll find it." He winks at me, and I can't help feeling like I've done something terrible. I could have gotten them both out, I'm sure of it. I could have saved them both.

I let the groom die.

"Thanks." I try to force a smile, but it's raw around the edges.

He reaches over and touches my cheek with just the tips of his fingers. It is like five little points of electricity tingling in my skin. "Ember, you are a very special girl. A princess among commoners. I doubt there's anything you can't do when you put your mind to it. I wish you believed in yourself half as much as I believe in you."

Not sure what to say to that, I just nod, trying to keep a brave face when inside, I'm completely frazzled.

I take two steps toward the tree where I'd arrived before I see it—a thin, nearly invisible ripple suspended in midair. As I get closer, I can feel the Tether tugging on my arm like a magnet being pulled to steel. I inhale sharply and look over my shoulder to the bench where Flynn had been sitting. It's empty. I am on my own.

Reaching out, I touch the ripple and my hand slips through. It isn't a ripple at all. It is a small tear in time, the point I'd come through. It will mostly heal when I go back, but it will leave a weak spot, a scar.

I step through the tear and find myself thrown back into the stream, only this time, something's wrong.

It's a smell, something like sour milk, only it's all over me, coating my skin. I fight back the vomit forcing its way into my mouth. The Tether pulls at my arm like a fishing line trying to reel me in. I struggle to relax, to allow it to pull me, when every instinct in my body is thrashing with the need to escape. Only the pull of the tech and my sheer will prevent me from bailing out of the stream. It isn't the peaceful flow I felt on my first trip. No, the stream is murky now, like a wound left open and untreated. It's festered. Is that my fault? I can't help but wonder as I gasp for breath. The air is being squeezed from my lungs, and I can't breathe except in painful huffs. A familiar feeling beside me makes me force my eyes open. Blinking past the water spilling over my lashes, I focus over my shoulder, and then I slam to a stop.

It feels like I've hit a brick wall. The shock is sudden and makes every muscle in my body tense painfully. I want to cry out, but I manage to muffle my scream by biting into my bottom lip instead. When I can open my eyes again, I see I'm back in the rift chamber, lying facedown on the floor. Pressing my head to the floor, I enjoy the cool hardness of it. I actually have the urge to kiss the ground. Carefully, I wedge my arms underneath me and push up, my muscles screaming in protest as I manage to get to my knees. I want to stand, if only because I know that everyone is watching me from above, judging me, trying to tell if I've been permanently damaged by my time in the stream. I only wish I wasn't so shaky, that I wasn't kneeling on the floor like an idiot.

"Ember, how do you feel?" Mistress Catherine's voice cracks through the ancient speakers.

There's only one way I can think to salvage this. I rack my brain—what would Ethan say?

I look up at the glass where I know they are all watching me, waiting to see if my brain has turned to jelly. Squinting, I cock my head to the side and smile, mustering all the false bravado I can access.

"Can I do that again?"

LEX
Nine

I open my eyes. I can feel my heartbeat in them. They feel like they're going to pop out of their sockets. Without looking in the mirror, I can tell they are bloodshot.

"Hey," Nobel says, leaning over me.

I respond with a faint moan. The sound vibrates in my head, spikes of pain shooting through my skull. My whole body aches. It's all I can do to blink against the bright lights of the lab. He sighs, relieved.

"How long was I out?" I ask hoarsely, sitting up on the rusty, metal table. I wiggle my toes, and electrical currents drive their way up the muscle. Something is wrong. Looking down, I see the problem. One leg is gone. Nobel has given me a prosthetic made of leather and metal, gears and copper.

"About a day," Nobel answers, his voice tight.

I flex the appendage at the knee joint. Steam hisses out of the side. It's almost as bad as a boiling teapot. There's even a little whistle. Groaning again, I flop down onto my back. I open my mouth to ask about

Stein, but I already know where she is—at the bottom of that cliff back in 1905. For a while, I'm paralyzed by the memory of it. Staring up at the peeling plaster ceiling, I replay the mission in my head, looking for the moment where I screwed up, looking for the wrong turn, the bad decision.

Stein is gone.

And it's my fault.

The realization rips its way up my chest, clogging my heart until I'm sure I'm going to die from it. I can't breathe. Doubling over, I gasp and convulse. There are no tears, although I'm sure they will come eventually. Now, it's just hot, unbearable agony.

Nobel tosses a dirty rag over his shoulder and leaves. It's his way of giving me time to mourn. If I want to cry, I can do it now and no one will witness. I've never been so glad to lack an audience. Then I remember how much Stein had hated it—the audience—always being watched and never having enough time alone. I wish I'd been better. Given her more. If I had another day with her, I'd do it right. Tell her how much she meant to me.

The guilt crashes down on me like a giant brick. Every muscle in my body aches with the strain of it. I can even feel it in what's left of my leg.

I tap on the dented brass of my new limb. I should have gone off that cliff with her. It would hurt less, at least. I continue to tap the metal leg as tears roll down my face. The idea of never seeing Stein again cuts me to the bone. It's as if my soul has been torn from my body.

I scream and throw a metal tray full of tools against the wall. They hit the ground with a loud crash. For a

126

while, I just sit there, hitting the leg over and over as if there were a cramp in the muscle. The hollow thuds echo through the room.

How could I let her go? Why couldn't I have held on just a little longer? I stare at the far wall. "Skinard *hearts* Blu" is spray-painted in big red letters. I have never seen it before—in fact, I've never realized how filthy the Tower is. The furniture in this room in particular is being held together by rope and propped up by cinder blocks. Even though this is thought to be our operating and recovery room, nothing is clean or sterile. I can actually smell death hidden in the walls.

My leg lets out a hiss of steam in protest as what's left of my quad spasms. Slipping my other hand in my pocket, I caress the old bottle caps I keep there. The familiar motion helps me focus, helps me push the pain down inside. The tears streak my face even as I realize the obvious.

I've got to get Stein back. Living without her isn't even an option.

I'm a time traveler! What good are my abilities if I can't use them to get her back?

The prosthetic grinds and hisses as I stand, but it holds up. I take a step and fall over, ending up kissing the floor with my face. With renewed purpose, I haul myself upright and limp into the main room.

"It's the best I could do," Nobel says, pointing to the leg. He isn't apologizing, and he doesn't need to. He saved my life, whatever that's worth.

"I know, Nobel." I try not to look sad about it. "Stein is dead, and I have a pressure cooker for a leg."

Nobel begins picking up the tools from the floor and setting them on a brass table. "You made quite a scene when you rifted back. You were lying in a pool of blood—you and your detached leg, with bits of metal embedded in it.

"Gear Head shrapnel," I growl.

"I'm so sorry, Lex."

I can't stand the look of grief on his face, so I put my head in my hands. I can still smell Stein's lotion on them. It's enough to start the tears up again, and I'm glad Nobel is the only one around.

"Has Claymore said anything yet?" I ask, exhausted by the idea. I've been on the receiving end of Claymore's wrath before, but not for anything as serious as this. The last thing I want right now is to get lectured.

"I'm sure he was waiting till you woke up to talk to you."

Great. Usually I go to Gloves for our missions, and then he reports to Claymore. I suspect these missions always come from Claymore, but Gloves is the buffer, the middleman. It's the chain of command. Now, however, I have to go talk to Claymore directly. Something about the thought of sitting in the same room as him makes my skin crawl.

"What happened in there, Lex?" Nobel asks. He tries to look like it isn't a big deal, but I know better.

I shrug, mostly because it's too excruciating to put into words. But I know I'm going to have to. All that thinking, all that playing it over and over in my mind, and I still can't find any mistake on our part. "Did you know it was the third time we went to the Amber Room?"

Nobel's eyes widen and his jaw muscles slacken a little bit. "I didn't know that."

I shake my head. "Exactly. So why risk it?"

"Gloves just has some fascination with the Amber Room. You know it was built in Russia in 1701? Then it just vanished. Poof. But it's still not worth going in three times."

That's how the Gear Heads found us, I realize. They followed the weak spot and came through it. That's why the mission went bust. That's why Stein's dead.

"Did you at least get what you were after?" Nobel asks.

Reaching into my vest pocket, I pull out an old, amber hairbrush. I thought it was beautiful when we lifted it, but now it's the ugliest thing I've ever seen. All I can think is how little it's worth. Not worth Stein. Not worth her life.

I want to chuck the brush across the room, but I don't.

Twisting the beautiful, jewel-studded amber brush in my fingers, I take a deep breath and recount everything that happened up until the moment I let go of Stein's hand. Nobel listens intently.

"I just couldn't hold onto her anymore," I say, failing to blink back tears.

"I'm sorry," Nobel says softly, putting a hand on my shoulder.

I swallow, massaging the handle of the brush with my thumb. I feel sick and sad and pissed all at the same time. "I want to go back and get her," I whisper.

"You can't go back because you're already there. The paradox would be catastrophic, Lex."

He's right. The rational part of me knows that. But the tiny, irrational side is quickly silenced when the memory of her smile floats like a ghost to the front of my mind.

Nobel sits down and slides onto the edge of the trunk. He stares at me thoughtfully, tugging the grimy mask down around his neck. "There might be something. The Institute has a whole vault of tech that Tesla created. I've heard rumors about it."

"What have you heard?" If there is any chance of saving Stein, any at all, I'll gimp through hell itself to get to it.

"Supposedly, there's something there, like a temporal Band-Aid, that can repair a paradox. It might just be a rumor, but…" He trails off with a shrug.

Just the thought of it gives me hope and makes the tension in my chest melt away like a snowflake landing on the surface of one of Nobel's steam machines. I know I'm grinning like an idiot, but I can't help myself.

"If anyone would know, it would be Claymore," Nobel adds finally.

"I'll just have to convince him to let me go get it, then," I say, knowing that when I make my mind up about something, I tend to get my way. And there's nothing I've ever wanted more than this.

"If we can get Gloves to sanction it, then maybe Claymore would be on board," Nobel suggests.

He's right. Gloves is only motivated by tech and expensive, rare objects from the past. Since we don't have tech he doesn't already have access to, we'll have to bribe him with something from the Amber Room.

It dawns on me. "During my first rift to the Amber Room, I took more than just the pendant we were supposed to steal."

I limp to my room with Nobel close at my heels, managing to fall twice before we get there. Reaching under my bed, I pull out a small, brass box.

"This should buy me some leverage," I say, reaching my hand inside.

I place an Egyptian, scarab-shaped brooch in Nobel's hand.

"It looks like it's made of honey," Nobel says, holding it up to the light. "Why will this be a good bribe?"

"Because. Hold it up again and look at the head." I wait while he holds it up to the bare bulb on the ceiling. "That amber has liquid in it. The last time Stewart Stills was here, I asked him to look at it. He said it might be some kind of organic rifting serum. As much as Gloves wants all the stuff from that room, we can't send in another team thanks to the Gear Heads. So I bet he'd do just about anything to get his hands on this."

"Why didn't you turn it over when you took it?"

I stare at the brooch. "Honestly? I'm not sure. Insurance maybe?"

"Kleptomania maybe," he mutters.

I can't help but smirk. When I stand up too quickly, my leg lets out a large burst of steam, and I pitch forward onto my hands and knees.

"Whoa," Nobel says, offering me a hand up. "Are you okay?"

"I guess I'll need a lot of practice," I mutter. I brush off his hand, struggle to one knee, and drag myself toward the old Victorian chair in the corner of the room. When I start to fall again, Nobel comes to my rescue.

He reaches under my armpits and helps me into the chair. The springs are long gone and the seat is worn to threads. I sink in and rest against the once-plush backing of the purple velvet chair.

"Thanks," I say, more bitterly than I mean to.

"You are welcome," Nobel says without hesitation, ignoring my sarcasm. "Wait here for just a minute."

"Okay," I say with a sigh. "Where would I go, anyway?" I don't expect an answer. I sit waiting, watching the steam from the geared hinge moisten the purple chair. *That spot probably hasn't been steam-cleaned in a century.*

* * *

While I wait for him to come back, I start to think about Stein again. How could I just let her go like that? Why couldn't I have been stronger? Why did they send us back there, knowing the risks? My heart is racing, and I almost start to tear up.

"Here, this should help," Nobel says, carrying a cane. "I was hoping you wouldn't need it, but I wanted to be sure I didn't set you up for failure."

"I was hoping I wouldn't need *this*." I point to the booby trap on my leg.

Nobel looks away sadly.

Guilt bites into me. "Dude, I'm sorry. It isn't your fault. You saved my life. It's just…" I point at the leg, and Nobel nods.

"It was the best I could do. I'm working on some other ideas, but for now, you're just going to have to suck it up, Lex," He holds the cane out to me. "Now, let's try this again."

The cane is actually kind of cool. A set of gears underlines the handle, and Nobel has carved some ornate engravings along the shaft.

"I could use this as a weapon," I say, turning it over and over in my hand like a baton.

"You can," he agrees. "It's temporary, but I made some useful modifications. Here." He points to the various gears on the handle. "The oil slick is triggered by the rusty gear. When the shiny gear is spun, it emits a noxious gas."

Suddenly, I love this cane. Then Nobel turns the handle to show me the small gear with one .45 caliber bullet loaded.

"I'm pretty sure I'm going to marry this thing," I say without thinking. Suddenly, the memory of Stein is there again, threatening to crush me. I breathe deeply, trying to focus on the plan. The chugging of Gloves' train chair pulls me from my thoughts.

"What do you want, Gloves?" I ask as he glares, obviously annoyed with me.

He gives me a stern frown. No sympathy from him, I suppose. "Claymore would like you to grace him with your presence."

"Yes, sir. I'll be right there."

Gloves turns his train chair around and chugs off. I try to stand up again. Luckily, Nobel is there to lend me a hand. Once I get to my feet, I keep the cane on my right side. Nobel tells me to swing the cane parallel to each step with my right leg. I take an experimental step with my left leg first, as lifting and stepping requires full concentration. With a hiss, and metal grinding against metal, I take another step. It sounds like a new teenage driver learning how to drive a stick shift. "The grinding sound will go away as you learn to use it," Nobel assures me.

I shrug. The sound doesn't bother me so much.

133

"Well, wish me luck."

Oddly enough, there isn't much pain now that I'm upright. *Hiss, grind, pop. Hiss, grind, pop.* I stop at the threshold and turn around.

"Thanks for the cane," I offer. "I hope I won't have to use it on Claymore." I smile, turn, and hobble down the hallway toward Claymore's office.

* * *

I'm not sure what hits me first—the bitter smell of brass polish or the sound of the arrivals and departures board ticking. Someone is already in Claymore's office.

The office door is slightly ajar when I arrive. I knock. All I can hear is *tick, tick, tick.*

"Come in," a girl's voice calls out to me.

I use my shoulder to open the door, then, without any grace, I stumble in. Fortunately, I stay on my feet just until I can safely fall into one of the office chairs. Sisson breaks into a slight smile, all traces of her near-death incident erased. Small and fox-like, she moves across the room without making the tiniest sound. She's wearing dark goggles and scraps of brown leather wrapped around her body in a makeshift corset. Darting for the door on the very tips of her toes, she looks a bit like an insane ballet dancer. As she passes me, she taps me on the mechanical knee.

"Thanks for the rescue, Lex."

The prosthetic seizes at her touch. "Dang leg," I say, grinding my teeth as I adjust it under me.

Please sit down, Lex, the ticking board spells. I can sense the sarcasm even though I have to read everything Claymore is saying.

134

Claymore rests his hands on his scarred, leather-surfaced desk as if paralyzed from the neck down. I tap my cane on the wooden legs of the desk. The bottoms are so old and mangled it looks like a Gear Head has gnawed at them. Sunlight shines in through the dirty windowpanes, landing on Claymore's canvas overalls.

"I'm sorry," I say. "I'm still getting used to the leg Nobel gave me."

Oh yes, the leg... tick, tick, tick... *Let's talk about the leg. How did your leg become...* tick, tick, tick... *Detached from your body?...* tick, tick, tick... *Or better yet, how did you botch the mission...* tick, tick, tick... *So spectacularly that you lost one of...* tick, tick, tick... *Our best Rifters and one...* tick, tick, tick... *Of your best appendages?*

"So much for small talk," I mumble under my breath. I don't want to recount what happened. I stare at the condensation forming on the brass panel of my leg, knowing Claymore probably already has a pretty good idea what happened.

"Sir." I begin leaning forward with my hands on the arms of the chair. "This mission was a failure from the beginning."

Tick, tick, tick... *What do you mean—a failure?*

Just thinking about what happened to Stein forms a lump the size of a hard-boiled egg in my throat.

"Right when we got there, we could feel a difference in the stream, but we still proceeded as ordered. As soon as the alternate us from the last rift left, we snuck in and retrieved the brush. It wasn't until we actually left the Amber Room that we ran into Gear Heads."

Tick, tick, tick... *Continue.*

I walk him through the mission, not holding back

anything. At least, until I reach the part about Stein going over the cliff. I can't seem to force the words past my throat.

Tick, tick, tick... *Go on.*

I continue to rehash the horrible events while I stare at the front porthole and try to see if there is any emotion sloshing around in Claymore's helmet. No, nothing but blackness.

Tick, tick, tick... *Well, that is very unfortunate for us.* Tick, tick, tick... *Stein was a good Rifter.* Tick, tick, tick... *We will have to recruit a replacement quickly.*

I stiffen in my seat. Replace Stein? Is he smoking crack?

I stare at him, unable to tell what Claymore is feeling. His ticking text doesn't have any emotion in it. I debate telling him about my plan to go back and get her, but I bite down on my tongue instead. If he doesn't approve it, I'll just go without permission. It'll mean exile, but I can live with that. I've already decided. Still, I'll wait until I can get Gloves on my side.

"Can I go now, sir?"

Tick, tick, tick... *Yes, and please get used to that leg.* Tick, tick, tick... *We need you back in the field.*

"Yes, sir." I take that as my dismissal, so I grip my cane and hoist myself up from the chair. Getting this leg to do exactly what I want is a huge chore. In fact, it does the exact opposite of a forward walking movement. Kicking back with a forceful thrust, it knocks over the chair I was just sitting in. I can just imagine the look on Claymore's face—if he even has a face. Not knowing what this leg is going to do next, I don't even try to right the chair on my way out.

136

* * *

The hallway to Gloves' office is in the opposite direction from Claymore's. Walking there is still a huge task to undertake for me. Granted, it has only been three hours since I woke up. Still, I feel like I should be more resilient than this somehow. I shake my head, mentally promising to allow myself a little leeway.

Wardenclyffe Tower's hallways all run off from a central common room like spokes on a bicycle wheel. Hobbling down the hall is more of a chore than I imagined.

As I limp to Gloves' office, the voices from the common room are replaced with the sounds of hissing steam and whistling of trains. Stumbling toward Gloves' door, my leg starts to ache. My hand is already closed around the brooch in my pocket. I rap on the door with the end of my cane. I figure it is appropriate for a man with a cane to use it in every aspect of life. Plus, it makes me smile.

"Enter," Gloves calls to me.

I turn the handle and push open the door. Immediately, I'm hit with a thick wall of smoky steam. Gloves is in the back corner, diligently feeding one of the many small furnaces.

My cane taps on the wooden floor of his office as I stagger toward the back wall.

"What can I do for you?" Gloves asks without even looking up.

"I have something for you." I hold the beetle in my hand, staring at it under the glow of the furnace fire. The light glints off the two emerald eyes set above one-inch, golden pincers. The back is covered with diamonds. Funny that the things that make it valuable are the only things Gloves won't find interesting about it. He turns in his wheelchair and chugs toward me. I hold the scarab steady in the palm of my hand. The presentation is perfect. The liquid in the tail end of the beetle seems to light up like a firefly.

"What might this be?"

"It's a scarab brooch. I picked it from the Amber Room. I think it's some kind of rifting serum. It can be yours for a very small favor." I sound like a game show host, I know.

"Yes. I believe I know what it is, thank you." He holds out his hand. I quickly stuff the beetle back in my pocket and lean on my cane, looking at Gloves. His face is covered in soot and sweat, and his clothes are filthy, except for his gloves. He looks like he's been sleeping in a pile of coal—come to think of it, maybe he has. I can see the indecision playing across his smudged face. Finally, he squints, making his thick eyebrows meet in the middle of his forehead.

"What's the favor?"

"All I need you to do is have Claymore commission two operations for us, and then supply us with the Contra we'll need. I think he'll let it fly if it comes from you." I find a pile of coal and sit down. My new leg is aching and my back is tight from compensating for the limp.

"What's the mission?" he asks, still hesitant.

"We need to break into the Tesla Institute and steal some tech from them. That is the first one. After, we are going to go back to where we lost Stein. I want to save her and use the tech to prevent a paradox."

"Ah. The Dox. I remember it. Untested, as I recall. Very dangerous. Hmm… let me see the brooch again," Gloves says, holding out his white hand. I stand so he knows he won't be able to just take the beetle from me. Slowly, I reach into my pocket. I hesitate, watching the reflection of the furnace fires in Gloves' eyes before I hand it to him.

Using the back of his pristine white gloves, he polishes my oily fingerprints off the beetle. He holds it up to the light and inspects the liquid. As he stares at the brooch, a large smile spreads across his face.

"And you're sure you can get the Dox to work?" he asks, not looking at me, as if he's no longer all that interested in me or my deal anymore.

"I'm sure, sir," I lie. But I'm confident that, between Nobel and me, we'll be able to figure it out.

"Then you have a deal. I'll make your Contra and talk to Claymore later tonight."

"Thank you."

"No, thank you, Lex."

Gloves turns the brooch over and over, letting whatever the strange liquid in the beetle is lap back and forth. With this mission a go, I feel a slight sense of relief. Finally, I can let go of all the sadness and helplessness I've been feeling and just focus on getting her back. Before he can change his mind, I follow the red locomotive toward the exit.

"Wait…" he yells after me. I turn, half expecting him to throw something at me. "Rifting back into the time stream, to a place where you already are, could create a huge paradox. So if you can't get your hands on that tech, the deal is off."

He tucks the beetle into the inside pocket of his

soot-covered jacket and turns back again to his trains. I back slowly out of the room, feeling like I've just gotten off very easy.

EMBER
Ten

The door chime echoes in my room, but I don't get up to answer it. I'm already hunkered down in the corner of my room, a copy of *Persuasion* by Jane Austen in hand.

"Go away," I holler, but the door chimes again. Probably Ethan coming to drag me to the party. I don't want to go. I don't want to celebrate.

What I want is someone to talk to. But that's impossible here.

I want to tell someone about the Trial, about my guilt, and about the terrible thing I did. But I can't.

Because *he's* listening. He's *always* listening.

I'm not sure I even realized it until now.

Ever since the Trial, I've wanted so badly to tell Ethan about what happened in the cafeteria. I want to get his opinion and have him tell me everything is going to be all right, but I don't dare. Somehow, my alternate self managed to get in and out without Tesla becoming aware. It's why the computer was frizzing out. Her visit—her warning—was a blind spot in

Tesla's all-knowing vision. I don't dare reveal the truth now, when I have no idea of the damage it could cause. If only I knew, if only I understood my intentions. Crossing your own timeline is such a risk. And for what? I don't know. I might not know for a very long time.

The chime goes off again, so I climb to my feet and hit the keypad.

The door slides open, and Kara is standing in the hall. Her hair is in a twist on the back of her head and she's wearing one of her prettiest outfits—a simple, green velvet mini-dress and tall, black boots. I sigh.

"I'm not going," I say before she can get a word out.

She steps inside, and the door slides closed behind her. "Of course you are. It's mandatory."

The Time Traveler's Ball is an annual tradition in the Institute. It's where all who didn't die in the Trials get to celebrate the fact that they're still alive and swap stories about their missions. I don't feel like sharing. Or celebrating. Or putting on shoes. I shake my head and slump back into my corner. "I don't care."

Sitting on the side of my bed, she narrows her eyes at me. "You've been acting weird, Ember. First, the thing at the cafeteria. Now this. It isn't like you. What happened?"

I shrug and toss the book on my desk.

She grabs one of my pillows and clutches it to her chest. "Remember that time I snuck out with Crevin, and then rushed here to tell you all about it?"

"Second-Base Crevin?" I laugh. "Yeah. I remember."

She hesitates before she speaks. "I made it up."

"What?" I couldn't have been more surprised if she'd sprouted a third arm.

"It was just, you were new and shy and I really wanted, I dunno, someone I could talk to. A girlfriend. So I made it up as an excuse to spend time with you."

I wasn't sure what to say to that. "So Crevin never got to second base?"

She grins. "Well, yeah, he did, but it was before you came along. So it was a true story, really, just told a little after the fact."

I start laughing, and she joins in. It's so silly. Yet, I can't stop. I'm doubling over, tears rolling down my face before I finally catch my breath.

"It's just..." She shrugs. "It was really lonely here before you came. I mean, I had Ethan, but it's not the same. And then you showed up and you were *nice*. I knew I wanted to have you on Team Kara."

I study her face. "Aw, Kara, that's the nicest thing anyone here has ever done for me. Probably the stupidest thing, to be honest, but nice all the same." The corner of her mouth curves up into a hint of a smile. I push myself up a bit and smile back. "And, for the record, I'm Team Kara. Absolutely. All the way." I crawl forward and rest my head in her lap, letting her stroke my hair.

"I know. Team Kara is the best." She pats me on the head and points to the closet. "Now, what are you going to wear tonight?"

I groan, but she gently pushes me away and stands up, motioning for me to follow her.

"No offense, Ember, but you look like crap. Go wash up. I'll pick something out for you."

"I really don't feel up to going," I whine even as I head for the bathroom.

She peeks out of the closet. "That's exactly why

you should. Dressing up and looking nice always makes me feel better. Besides," she ducks back in the closet, "Riley is going to be there. I think he's into you. Why else would he hang out at the library all the time?"

I groan again. He's so not my type. Not that I have a type, exactly. I think about it as I wash my face. "Maybe he just really likes to read?" I offer.

She snorts. "Yeah, right."

What would I want in a guy? I suppose I've never really thought about it. But now that I am, only one face comes to mind.

* * *

"Best. Party. Ever." Ethan laughs, helping himself to another slice of cake. Okay, it's a gluten-free, reduced sugar, organic, soy-based cake. Still, it's pretty good for being little more than a fiber bomb.

Flynn raises a glass of pineapple juice. "Here's to our newest Rifters!"

Cheers fill the room. I sit in the corner, pushing bits of almost cake around my plate. I should be relieved and excited like the others, but there's a nagging feeling in my gut I just can't shake. Kara kept her word, dressing me up like her own personal Barbie. I'm trying to keep my legs crossed in the short lacy dress, but it's hard because it's so tight. Still, when I saw myself in the mirror, I had to admit I looked really good. Older. Hot, even. I do feel better, or at least I did until I walked into the party and everyone stared at me. Now I'm just feeling uncomfortable.

"What's up, Grumpy Butt?" Ethan asks, nudging me so hard I nearly drop my almost cake.

I sigh, set the plate on the floor by my feet, and readjust myself in the hard wooden chair. "Nothing. I'm just tired, I guess."

I rest my elbows on my knees and hold my chin in my hands. Kara is flirting with a group of boys in the corner. Some of the other kids are huddled near the punch bowl, Riley among them. Mistress Catherine and the others are chatting. No one is paying any attention to us.

I glance back at Ethan. He's waiting patiently for an answer. With each second that passes in silence, however, his expression grows more worried.

"No more classes," I say softly, unable to keep the sadness out of my voice. "No more tests. No more being kids. It's time to grow up."

"You've always been a grown-up," he says, nudging me again.

"Not always. Not yet." I let the words hang between us before continuing. "I guess I've just been thinking about the future a lot lately. About what kind of person I'm going to become."

"Well, that's a depressing thing to be thinking about at a party. For example, right now I'm thinking, I wonder if there's any way to sneak out of here tonight for a swim?"

I feel my eyes light up. That would be perfect. But as quickly at the thought comes, it's crushed. "We still have the Pledge Ceremony."

"So we go after, just you and me."

I want to. I really, really do. But it feels like a bad idea. I shake my head.

"Ember, I'm really worried about you. You've been a little off the past few days."

What can I say? The truth makes me sound like a paranoid lunatic. Even though I'm not looking at him, I can feel his eyes on me. Something in the bottom of my stomach tightens. For a second, I imagine us somewhere else—two normal people, at a party. Maybe we dance and he grabs me by the waist, pulling me close. Eye to eye, he lowers his head, bringing his lips to mine.

The thought shatters inside my head like glass. What's wrong with me? This is Ethan. I mean, *Ethan*. Even so, a warm flush spreads through my whole body. He's still looking at me, and I can barely stand it. I'm about two seconds away from a full-on meltdown. "I've also been thinking about Caesar."

"That's a weird thing to be thinking about. Even for a bookworm like you."

I shake my head. "I mean bridges. Remember the story of Caesar crossing the Rubicon?"

He stares at me blankly.

"I mean, sometimes, you cross a bridge that's so important, you can never go back, you know? Like when he crossed the Rubicon, and then burned it down behind him. No retreat." His brow furrows like he's trying to follow me but can't quite make it. I sigh. "Forget it."

He smirks and touches the side of my face. "Are you asking me to commit arson with you?"

"No."

"Why not? It could be fun." He pauses. "The swimming, that is, not the arson."

I roll my eyes and answer with all the sarcasm I can muster. "Because I don't trust myself alone with you. You, and your awesome brain and your great, big biceps."

I laugh as he pouts and flexes. "But my biceps are awesome, too."

I want to give him a playful nudge or a pat on the back, just some kind, any kind, of physical contact. But there's this little voice in my head telling me it's a bad idea. So I just shift in my seat. "Never mind. It's just—I'm kind of looking for quiet. I need to think and clear my head."

"I can be quiet," he says, and I almost laugh out loud.

Raising an eyebrow, I tilt my head at him.

"Well, I can be quiet-ish. Okay, I'm lying. I suck at quiet. It's my one shortcoming."

I raise my eyebrow again, and he throws his hands in the air.

"Fine, woman. If you really want to be alone, I'll leave you be."

He moves to leave, and I grab his arm so fast he almost falls over. I'm clinging to him, and though I don't know why, I'm pretty sure I'm going to burst into tears any second.

"Can't bear to see me go, I see." He pauses and looks at me seriously. "Ember, I don't know what's gotten under your skin today, but you can't let it eat at you. We can't afford to worry about what might happen in the future. We have our hands full with dealing with the past. Let yourself live in the moment, okay? Let go of the rest."

I sigh, wishing it were that easy. "If we don't worry about the future, who will?"

Holding his hands in the air, he wiggles his fingers. "Here. If it'll make you feel better, I'll look into my crystal ball."

"I don't see a crystal ball."

"Shhh! It's invisible. Yes, here. I see your future and you will be…" He sticks his tongue out the side of his mouth before standing up. "You'll be who you are, who you always were. You'll be Ember."

He grins. I can't help smiling back, even if it's not an entirely happy smile. "And you'll be Ethan." *And things will always be just as they are right now*, I add silently. In my mind, I can see the bridge between us. Do I dare cross it? Ethan is a flirt by nature. What if he doesn't even feel the same? Can I take that risk?

He holds out his hand to me and I take it, letting him tug me to my feet. Wrapping his arms around my shoulders, he kisses the top of my head and mutters, "Always."

The words are enough to blow past my doubt. If there is a bridge separating us, I'm about to burn it to ash. I wrap my arms around his waist and whisper in his ear, "I need to get out of here. Now."

The emotions of the day have come rushing back at me like a tidal wave. My hands shake as he leads me through the crowd, out the door, and down the hall. Behind us, the music fades away. He presses his palm against the next door we come to, and it slides open.

It only takes a second for the lights to sputter to life, but in that instant, I forget how to breathe.

"What do you know, we *do* have a library," Ethan muses, his back to me.

The door grinds shut behind me, and my knees turn to jelly. Somehow, Ethan has his arms around me, helping steady me before I hit the floor. Still, we're a little off-balance, so we fall and stumble back against the door.

"Whoa, Ember. What's wrong?" I can't answer. My throat is swollen closed, or at least that's how it feels. Around me, the room spins. My chest tightens until I'm sure it will crush me. I grab the back of his neck with both hands and pull his face down so our foreheads are touching. Tears roll down my face. Ethan's blue eyes find mine and lock on.

"It's okay. I'm here." Taking my hands, he slides them down just an inch so I can feel the strong rhythm of his pulse under my fingers. "Close your eyes. Focus on my heartbeat, only that and nothing else." He closes the space between us and presses himself against me until I'm not sure where he ends and I begin. "Breathe with me."

I nod and obey. Closing my eyes, I focus on the steady, reliable pattern of his heart beating under my hands. The tightness in my chest starts to relax. When I can breathe again, all I can smell is Ethan. Spicy and warm. Eventually, my pulse matches time with his. I take a deep breath, aware of him in a way I've never been before. Opening my eyes, I find he's still staring at me, only now his eyes aren't so wide and nervous. He is looking at me from beneath his thick blond lashes, and his pupils are so big I think I can see stars in them. His hands are pressed against the door on either side of my waist.

He grins, and I can tell he's about to say something. Knowing Ethan, it will be some ridiculous quip that will make me rethink this. Before he can get a word out, I stretch up and press my lips against his.

He freezes, his heart stuttering under my fingertips. I pull back, sure I've done something wrong—crossed that invisible line. I've never kissed a boy before, not like this. A rush of heat floods to my cheeks, making me almost unbearably hot under his unreadable expression. I open my mouth to apologize.

"I—" He cuts me off by taking my face in his hands and kissing me. I run my fingers through his hair as he moans into my mouth. Everywhere we are touching, my skin burns until I'm sure I'm going to burst into flames. Moving his hands around my waist, he pulls me from the door and lifts me off the ground, carrying me over to an empty study table. He breaks the kiss just long enough to gently set me on it.

"I told you that you couldn't resist me," he jokes, his voice deep and rough.

I sigh. "Well, everyone should get to be right once in their life."

Leaning into me, he touches the tips of his fingers to my bottom lip.

"We belong together. You know that, right?" he says, barely louder than a whisper.

I kiss his fingertips. "Yes," I say breathlessly.

He kisses me again, but this time, the burning urgency is cooled into a slow, almost painful deliberateness. With his arm behind me, supporting me, I let mine wander up his back. He shudders, and I smile against his lips. My heart is pounding so hard I wonder how I don't die from the pressure building inside my chest.

"Sorry to interrupt," Kara's voice calls from the doorway, making me jump. "But it's almost time."

Ethan sighs deeply, not looking at her. "Okay. We'll be right there."

Over his shoulder, I see Kara. She winks, turns,

and struts out of the room, leaving the door open behind her. Ethan presses his forehead against mine, his eyes squeezed closed. Taking a deep breath, I try to calm my racing heart. I nudge him with my nose and he opens his eyes, grinning at me. Not his usual cocky smile, but a smile of satisfaction, almost relief. I understand the feeling. Some part of me has wanted to kiss him since the first day we met.

I kiss him quickly and push him away. He steps back, offering me a hand off the desk. I slide off and straighten my dress, feeling silly and embarrassed but unable to wipe the stupid grin off my face. Only Ethan would cure a panic attack by causing a heart attack.

In the back of my mind, a little voice reminds me that we aren't alone in the library. Tesla, or whatever circuits and gears now make up Tesla, is watching. Listening. Not even that kiss had been ours alone— not really.

The thought wipes the grin off my face as we walk hand in hand back to the ballroom.

* * *

Flynn stands in the center of the room, his glass high in the air. "It's time. If the new Rifters would please join me in the main lab?"

I swallow hard. In all the excitement, I'd almost forgotten about this step, this final initiation. Goose bumps erupt along my arms. Kara moves to Ethan's other side and takes his empty hand. She looks radiant in the glow of success, not a hint of fear or hesitation on her face.

"Relax, Ember. It's like getting a tattoo."

I can't help but raise an eyebrow at her. As if she has any idea.

Ethan chimes in. "Yeah, Ember. Just like a tattoo. Only instead of ink, it's acid. And instead of a cute unicorn skipping across a rainbow, it's Tesla's personal seal of approval. How bad could it possibly be?"

I frown. Just what I need. One more scar. "Well, when you put it like that…"

"Don't be such a whiner, Ember. Suck it up. Everyone does it. It's just a symbol, a reminder of our oath to Tesla," Kara says, tugging Ethan and me forward.

Her tone is joking, but there's an underlying tension, too. Deep down, I bet she's just as nervous as I am.

We drop hands to follow the crowd to Tesla's main lab. It's one of the largest rooms in the facility, which is saying something. About the size of a six-car garage, it holds ten workstations—long tables covered in equipment. As we walk past, I absently reach out, running my fingers over bits of metal. Bad idea. A sharp bit slices into my finger. Blood rises quickly, pooling on the surface of my skin. I swear and bring the wound to my mouth, sucking on it gently before wrapping it in the hem of my dress. Ethan glances over at me, but I shrug. I'll live.

I have to hand it to Tesla—lots of scientists in history have been obsessed with immortality, but he's the only one who's managed it. At least, so far. I can't help wondering if in some dark future there are millions of them, people whose lives have been reduced to brains in jars. As we pass a table of empty holding tanks, I can't help but cringe.

I'd never want to live that way.

I hate this room. It's the same place Tesla chewed me out after my botched mission to the World's Fair, and even with all the extra people in here now, it's still creepy. My eyes are drawn to Tesla's brain floating in the wall. His tank is designed so that, in the event of a breach of the facility, Tesla can be removed and taken to safety. I wonder for a moment whose job that is, removing that tank. Then I blink, bringing myself back to the reason I'm even standing in this room, and the goosebumps reappear. Beside me, Ethan wraps his fingers in mine. Kara takes hold of his other hand, shooting me a glance that isn't nearly as cocky anymore. I can't blame her. This whole place is creepy.

Flynn hits a switch on the wall and holographic Tesla sparks to life. On the ground is a small vent that blows steam upward, giving the hologram a sort of screen to be projected on. The image of Tesla smiles and holds his hands out toward us. He looks so freaking weird like this. Sure, the brain in the jar is pretty bad, but this is worse somehow. His black hair is parted in the middle and slicked down on either side of his head. His features are sharp, his nose is long, and a disturbingly thin mustache rides his upper lip. It's the smile that's bothering me, I realize. It somehow doesn't fit his face—it's too small and too forced to belong there. He speaks, his voice crackling through the speakers in the walls.

"My friends, I am so pleased to welcome you here. You have worked hard and passed all your Trials. Now you stand with the others of your kind, and you will take your place among them." His smile falls away. With a wave of his hand, Nurse appears from the corner of the room. It's holding a brass tray full of metal syringes. Flynn holds up the first and moves to stand in front of the first Rifter, who holds out his left arm and recites the oath. As soon as the words are spoken, Flynn stabs the large needle into his forearm and presses the plunger. The boy doesn't make a sound, but I can see from the immediate sheen of sweat on his face that it isn't pleasant. As soon as Flynn withdraws the needle, the boy shudders. Holding his arm, he walks to stand beside the other Rifters. I stare at him, watching fat tears roll down his cheeks.

The urge to move, to run, is nearly overwhelming. I don't want to do this, I realize. Not that I don't want to be a Rifter—I do—but this all seems too much, too barbaric. Like, Tesla is claiming us as his property, branding us like cattle. It's all I can do to hold still and keep my face impassive. Only Ethan's hand in mine keeps me grounded. Keeps me sane.

The process is repeated until Flynn reaches me. I'm the first of my friends to take the oath. I'm squeezing Ethan's hand so tightly I practically have to pry myself away from him. I step forward, swallowing hard as I hold out my arm, palm up. At first, I'm afraid I won't remember the words, but they tumble out seemingly of their own accord.

"I hereby swear loyalty to Tesla and this Institute," I say, my legs shaking like violent little earthquakes are rippling through the muscles. "I promise to defend the time stream, this place, and Tesla himself to the last breath in my body." I take another step. "I will not falter or hesitate. Willingly do I give my life to this service." I step forward again, sure that my knees will buckle and I'll fall on my face. But I don't. "Freely,

154

do I give my word before these witnesses. This is my binding oath." I'm right in front of Flynn now, and I'm shaking all over. It's not the expectation of pain that's bothering me so much. It's the idea of Tesla on me, inside my skin. I try not to gag. That's the idea. This chemical burn will remind us of our loyalty, the cost of failure, and more importantly, that Tesla is always with us.

The prick of the needle isn't what hurts. But the liquid inside burns like acid, as Ethan predicted it would. My eyes water as it sears through the veins in my arm, and I have to bite down on my lip to keep from crying out. I expect it to continue to spread into my shoulder, but it doesn't. It's contained in the white skin of my forearm. Seconds feel like hours as I fight to breathe through the pain. Soon, the burning sensation begins to swirl and my flesh mounds as if a small creature were burrowing beneath it. It's not a scar, exactly. Neither is it a tattoo. Only a few shades darker than my skin, but raised, it's an inside-out brand. The pain fades, and all that's left is a perfect sun emblem. The symbol of enlightenment—the symbol of Tesla.

When I look up, Flynn is smiling broadly.

I vomit on his shoes.

LEX
Eleven

"This way, guys," I whisper, stuffing the ancient map into my back pocket. I look up, taking inventory of the unfamiliar team. Gloves hadn't just given the green light for the mission into Tesla. He seemed nearly giddy at the idea of breaking into the Institute vault. We have leave to grab whatever tech we can get our hands on. He's wanted to breach the compound for years, but he never had a reason to risk it. I've given him all the reason he needs. The bribe turned out to be just the icing on the cake.

Nobel is here, of course. If Gloves will let us, and if the gods of manipulation grant us with the ability to talk him into doing it, Nobel and I try to commission ourselves on most of the same missions.

"I'm glad you're here, bro," I say.

"You know I wouldn't miss it for the world," Nobel responds.

I'm always glad to have the two security personnel from the Tower with me also—Bruce and Slap Stick. I'm sure Sisson is here so she can report to Claymore about the mission, but I don't mind because she is very good at recon. The last in our party is Journey. I'm not sure how many missions she has been on, but she loves maps and is an expert navigator. Besides, she's the one who figured out the location of the Institute by tracking a couple of Rifters back to it.

"I found the entrance to the old coal mine," Sisson says, not even out of breath despite what must have been a long run through the cramped tunnel.

The mine obviously hasn't been used in a very long time. The bushes and trees have grown over the entrance, concealing it from everyone. The bushes grab at our clothing and equipment. The gears on my fake leg chew at the small twigs as I trudge through the thick undergrowth. The team follows my lead.

Once we get closer to the entrance, I feel cold cave air billowing out from the mouth of the mine. It's moldy, damp, and smells like my hamper back at Wardenclyffe Tower. Sharp crystals poke out of the ground.

"Here you go," Nobel says. He hands me a small flashlight.

"This is too easy," Journey says, tucking a loose patch of her wiry red curls behind her goggles. "Why hasn't anyone found this entrance before?"

"Well, for one thing, it's been blocked off for years. And for another, who would be crazy enough to risk breaking into the Institute itself?" I chuckle, and the team joins me. Good. We need to break up the tension somehow. "Plus, nobody else has had Slap Stick on their side." Slap Stick is the most noticeable of the group, partly because of his enormous height and partly because of the ominous belt of C-4 bricks slung across his body. I slap him on the shoulder not covered in explosives, and he gives me a half-smile. "So Journey, you find the sweet spot, and then Slap Stick will blow a big ol' hole in it."

"Yessir," Slap Stick says, his Texan accent strong as he rubs his hands together. "I really can't wait. I haven't blown up anything for a week now. I'm having major withdrawal."

Pressing a finger to my lips, I lead my team into the dark shaft. At some point, according to the map, it almost connects with a current steam tunnel. There are only a few scant feet of sandy ground separating the two. I know we're getting close because I can hear the growl of electric turbines spinning in the chamber above us.

On my signal, we stop and wait, pressed against the cool mine wall. Roots emerge out of the walls and ceiling like veins on an old lady's arm. As we move deeper into the cave, the growl fades to a hum, and then dies down completely until the only sound left is the light grinding sound of my prosthetic leg and the hiss as a wisp of smoke escapes it. I'm getting used to the sound, and it's a small price to pay for not being bound to a wheelchair for the rest of my life.

"All right, here we go," I say, motioning for them to spread out.

To their credit, not a single member of my team shows fear. In fact, they are oozing excitement, practically vibrating with nervous energy. They drop into place, working more like a well-oiled machine than a group of teenagers on a mission that could conceivably be their last. Each one is a cog in the machine that is the Hollows—all skilled, all prepared, and all full of reckless courage.

"This is so weird," Journey whispers to me as she taps gently on the tunnel wall, looking, I assume, for a thin spot.

"Why?" Slap Stick asks, his hand twitching over a brick of explosives.

"I think this is the first time I've actually done a mission in the field," she answers, pressing her ear to the wall and tapping again.

"Really?" I ask, immediately rethinking the wisdom of having her with us.

I look at her more closely. She might be fourteen, at most, and is still green around the gills. Mentally, I curse. The last thing I need is to get distracted trying to save a rookie.

"Relax, I do stuff like this all the time," Sisson adds from across the room.

I want to say something—something profound and wise that will inspire my team—but nothing comes to mind.

Nobel runs ahead thirty yards and sets down a device that we call Miss Liberty. She has a face made out of gears, and her torch is a small windmill. As the windmill turns with the slight cave breeze, the face gears click, indicating that she is functioning. These gears activate a small projector. The camera lens illuminates the floor with white light. I approach the apparatus and hear Nobel talking to his machine.

"Good girl, that's it, keep going," he whispers.

The white light takes shape into the form of an arrow and points down the mine tunnel.

"And that, ladies and gentlemen, is our compass," Nobel announces with great pride.

"So all we have to do is follow the arrow?" Bruce asks. My metal leg is nothing compared to the overhaul he got after an explosion on a subway a few years back. He was supposed to go in and grab a kid, a Rifter like us, Claymore had located. He got the kid, but neither of them came out completely intact. One arm is made of brass, and half his face is metal burned into skin. A large monocle covers one eye, and his ear is missing on that side. In its place is a tiny transmitter that allows him to hear by echolocation, like a bat.

"Well, sort of," Nobel replies. "The arrow points to Tesla kinda like how a compass points north. So we need to pick the tunnels that head in that direction."

"We've input all the data from my maps into her memory," Journey adds proudly.

At every intersection and fork in the mine tunnel, Nobel sets up Miss Liberty. She keeps our bearings. Finally, we find it—the sweet spot. Miss Liberty's light shines on a section of wall that's partially caved in.

Journey presses her ear against the rock and taps, then gives Slap Stick a thumbs-up. We all run down the dirt tunnel a ways as he sets the charge. He's whistling when he joins us. We crouch and cover our ears. Slap Stick's whistle hits a high note that echoes through the chamber a second before the blast.

* * *

Everything is going smoothly. Too smoothly, I realize. We're creeping silently through the old cargo tunnel. As we turn the next corner, the hair on the back of my neck stands at attention. Journey's earlier words echo again in my head. *Too easy.*

"Guys, stop," Sisson whispers harshly. "Did you hear that?"

As if by unspoken command, we all douse our lights. Bruce nods, and Sisson doesn't hesitate. Her mini Steam Cannon crackles in the darkness as she pulls it from her thigh holster. Donning her night-vision goggles, she takes off down the tunnel to recon, able to navigate her way through the pitch darkness easily.

We hear the sound of her body hitting the ground... and then all hell breaks loose.

The darkness becomes a war zone. A blast of air blows past my face, and I jerk to the side. Rapid puffs fill the tunnel. Then, a sound that is more familiar, tiny metal legs running in our direction, dirt crumbling from the walls around us.

"Lights!" I yell, and the cavern around us illuminates as we reignite our lights.

My mind races. Forward or back? Do we push farther into Tesla or retreat now with my team mostly intact?

"Fall back." I give the order even as Journey is running forward, into the line of fire. Journey is at Sisson's side, pressing two fingers against her neck.

"She's still alive," Journey yells back into the chaos. "She got hit with a tranq dart."

"Get her out of here," I order. "Rift her back to Wardenclyffe!"

Journey complies, dragging Sisson past our line and back into the tunnel. Bruce shoves a Contra into Sisson's mouth.

Journey pulls a Contra from a pocket on her shirt and swallows it quickly. The two girls vanish to safety.

"Take cover!" I order to the remaining team.

Bruce jumps behind a mound of rocks and packed dirt. Slap Stick kneels in the middle of the passageway and holds up a homemade pipe bomb, silently asking permission to light it. I nod as the first wave of Gear Heads crawl up the walls of the dirt cavern.

"Do it!" I yell.

"Good thing we packed the heavy artillery!" Bruce grins, tossing me a telescoping electric baton.

I flick my wrist, and it expands to four feet long. A small ball at the end crackles with electricity. I mouth, "Thanks," just in time to hear Slap Stick cry out.

He slumps to the floor with the unlit explosive still in his hand. I don't have time to think. I quickly slide to where he lies and press my index and middle finger against his neck. He still has a pulse.

Ting, Ting, Ting, Ting. I look down and see what has taken out two members of my team. Four red, feathered darts have hit my machine leg. I pick one up and roll it between my fingers. Gear Heads don't fire darts, I realize, looking up. There are two small turrets mounted in the tunnel, and both are firing rapidly. Without thinking, I grab two bricks of C-4 off Slap Stick's belt and throw them at the turrets. They hit with a wet slap and cover the barrels. That threat is taken care of, but the darts are only part of the problem. There's something a lot bigger than Gear Heads blocking our way. I catch a glimpse of it as it slips behind the next corner.

"Nobel! Bruce!" I yell back to where the others are crouched. "Get over here! And bring Miss Liberty."

They hurry down the tunnel wall and cross over to the intersection where I still kneel.

"Here, give me Miss Liberty," I order, "And take this. Keep the Gear Heads off me."

I hand over the prod as Nobel passes me the sculpture. He and Bruce step forward in the tunnel and continue chopping away at the onslaught of Gear Heads.

I break off the windmill, earning a horrified gasp from Nobel. "Oh man, why did you have to do that?"

"Because we're low on weapons, three members of our team are down, and this mission is circling the toilet in a hurry."

I take the small pipe and scramble over to where the darts fell after hitting my fake leg. Grabbing all four, I crawl back to the intersection, stuffing one of the feathers into the hollow windmill post.

"Now we have a leg up," I say, holding up my makeshift weapon and tossing the unusable body aside.

I see the creature turn and face us. It's carrying a syringe full of clear liquid. It's only sort of a person. It's wearing a long white lab coat and a mask of brass and leather. Bits of thin, brown hair poke out around the edges of the mask, not unlike Bruce's. As a matter of fact, I have to glance over at him to see if he knows the strange creature. The stunned look on his face suggests he doesn't. I leap forward, blowing on the small, hollow rod. *Thup*... I load another... *Thup*... reload... *Thup*. Finally, I load the last dart and wait. A hiss of steam escapes the clockwork gears in the center of its chest as the creature crumples to the ground.

"Wow, nice shot," Bruce says as he steps forward, kicking the creature with the toe of his boot.

"What is it?" I ask.

He shrugs.

Just then, the room shimmers as Journey reappears. "I left Sisson back at Wardenclyffe. Figured you might still need me. So, what now?"

As we wait for Slap Stick to wake up, I try to fix Miss Liberty. Not my best work, we'll have to manually crank it, but believe it or not, it actually works. I hand it to Nobel, hoping his payback won't be as bad now. Bruce hunches over Slap Stick, who is beginning to stir. He then comes to, wildly swinging his fists. Bruce has to dodge a few punches to keep from getting slugged.

"What happened?" Slap Stick asks, bringing one hand to his head. Once Bruce helps him sit up, Slap Stick retrieves a piece of unused blast cord from the floor, wipes it off on his pant leg, and inserts it into the corner of his mouth. He begins to chew on it like it's a straw.

"You got tranqed," Journey says.

"Am I permanently damaged?" Slap Stick says.

"No, I don't think so," I say, clearing away the last of the dead Gear Heads from our path. "You'll probably be woozy for a while, but we have to get into Tesla."

Nobel cranks Miss Liberty, and the arrow shows us which way we need to go at the intersection.

"What do we do about that thing?" Journey asks, pointing to the fallen creature.

Bruce kicks Tesla's Frankenstein again, in the fleshy part. The creature doesn't move.

"Leave it," I decide. "We are in a hurry now. If those things know we're here, someone else might, too."

We navigate as quickly as possible, relying mostly on Journey's memory of the map rather than Miss Liberty. It's risky, but it saves us some time.

"Here it is!" Journey says finally.

We've arrived at a rusted metal grate. When I kick it, it practically disintegrates. We duck through the opening. I know we're inside Tesla now. The walls are smooth metal, polished like steel. There are red floodlights overhead and doors that open up on either side of the long corridor. "Which door is it?" I ask. They all look the same. Each has a small keypad at eye level on the right, but there are no markings.

"Third door on the left, according to the maps," Journey answers with total confidence.

Slap Stick doesn't hesitate. He jogs over and places small bits of clay around the corners of the door. As he works, the blast cord wags back and forth in his mouth.

"Ready?" he asks, jogging back to us as we all crouch down once more. I give him the signal, and the blast echoes through the chamber. After a few heartbeats, the door falls in with a thud.

We file inside, leaving Bruce to guard the door. As the dust settles, the room becomes clearer. The walls are a warm copper color with elaborate designs carved into the metal. Some are just swirls of shapes, but some, I realize, are numbers and signs. Formulas.

"Alchemy," Nobel explains looking at the designs. "An archaic combination of magic and science."

Shelves of dark wood form lines down the middle of the room. It's like a library, only with less books and more tech. In the far corner is an old-fashioned elevator. Even though it's tarnished with large flecks and streaks of green, it's still very elegant. It sits there as a majestic symbol of what once was. Nobel immediately moves to check the functionality of the old machine. The gears haven't turned forever, and the elevator probably hasn't delivered anything to Tesla for over a century.

"It's not here," Journey says, her voice small and confused.

"What do you mean?" I demand.

"It's wrong. I think we are in the wrong place."

Bruce looks in, rolling his eyes. "This is the vault. Look at all this tech. Grab what you can and let's get out of here."

I look at the objects on the shelves. They're pieces, not complete machines.

"No, she's right. This is like a parts room or something."

Trying not to let my frustration show, I set Miss Liberty on the ground and give her a crank. Her beam of light bounces off the ceiling above us.

We all look upward. She has clearly answered our question. We have to go up.

"Then it's a good thing I got this old elevator working." Nobel smirks and hits a button with his elbow, making the ancient machine grind to life. Tesla must know we're here by now. All we can do now is get what we came for before his troops arrive.

We heave the doors open. One by one, we enter the rickety elevator. The old brass cage is going to deliver something to Tesla one last time.

TESLA JOURNAL ENTRY: OCTOBER 2ND, 1892

I have traced Helena's family to a unique fork. A royal bloodline from the earliest rulers of Great Britain. There is record of the royal family suffering from all manner of blood diseases, the most notable of these being hemophilia, a disease that Helena and her brother share to a very mild degree. I cannot help but speculate that this might be the root of their abilities. To confirm the theory, I have enlisted Leonard to help me, in the guise of a family history research center, locate those who might share the same ability.

Also, I have been pondering the method of traveling. The science—ah! The blasted science tells me such a thing is not possible. And yet, I have proof. Perhaps it is unwise to continue using such large currents to trigger the traveling. I plan to create a device that can replicate the results, in a safer way. I believe poor Garrison will be greatly relieved. Just yesterday, we lit his last good jacket on fire.

Furthermore, there is the question of whether it might be possible to travel backward in time. The possibilities, (and potential complications), stagger the mind. The trick would be to find a way to leash them to the present, so that they could travel, forward or back, and return to this same moment from which they left. Perhaps a magnetic anchor of sorts.

Ah! How I wish I could travel with them! To see for my own eyes the stream of wind of which they speak! To stand witness to the discoveries of the future!

EMBER
Twelve

The alarm rips through my bunk like a sonic blast. The air gets heavy and thick as the Institute pressurizes to prevent airborne, viral weapons. Tesla's voice comes bursting through the overhead speakers.

"All Rifters to the armory. Institute breach in progress."

I fling off my blanket as if it's on fire and pull on my vest, pants, and boots. The door to my room slides open and Ethan is standing there, his hair disheveled with lack of sleep. He grabs my hand, and we sprint down to the armory. When we arrive, everyone else is already there. Kara is alert, dressed in black leather and silver chains. Flynn hands her a lash, a sort of electrified whip, and then types furiously into the computer hub.

"We have a verified breach in the lower tunnels, the north steam shaft, and the vault room. Motion sensors are going crazy down there," Flynn says, adjusting his glasses.

Ethan speaks, not looking up from the stunner he's just grabbed, "Tesla, how many are there?"

169

"Five intruders in elevator ten, heading for the vault," Tesla's scratchy voice announces through the intercom closest to us.

Flynn swears and shoots a glance at Mistress Catherine. She grabs a lash and attaches it to a hook on her belt. I step forward, my hand hovering over the last lash on the table when Flynn covers my hand with his.

"It's close quarters in there. Here." He hands me a palm pulse. "Take this. Just hit the button and throw it. It's an EMP grenade."

Ethan lifts his head and looks my way. "Be very careful with that, Ember. It'll disable any active tech in the vicinity, but it'll also knock out Tesla's sensors, too, at least temporarily."

I nod and slip the device into my breast pocket. Hand-to hand-combat it is. I smirk. Good. It will feel really nice to pound on them with my bare knuckles. Maybe I'll be very lucky and get a rematch with the girl who got the jump on me back at the Fair. Ethan picks up a stunner and follows the others to the door.

"Tesla, monitor their position. Let us know if anything changes," Flynn orders the computer, which chirps in response.

Flynn puts his hand on Kara's shoulder and leads her out the door. His face is as hard as I've ever seen it, and I understand why. Our home is under attack. The sensation in my skin is a mixture of rage and violation so strong my hands shake. Looking over my shoulder, I give Ethan what I hope is a reassuring smile. All I can think about is how much I want to make the Hollows pay for this invasion, how much I want to make them *hurt*.

LEX
Thirteen

Sirens wail, cutting through the stillness like a grenade, the sound momentarily freezing each of us in our tracks. They all look to me.

"If they come through that door, you guys swallow your Contra and get out," I order.

Nobel shakes his head. "We aren't leaving without the Dox, Lex. You aren't the only one who wants Stein back."

I nod as they go back to rummaging through the shelves.

EMBER
Fourteen

In a matter of minutes, we are standing outside the door to the vault. I've never actually been inside, but I know there must be something inside that room the Hollows want badly if they're willing to risk their lives for it. That alone means they should never get their hands on it. Every piece of Tesla's experimental tech is behind those doors. For a moment, I'm curious what they might be after. All the weapons that work are in the armory, after all. Maybe it's something else. At the end of the day, though, none of that really matters. What matters is these traitors broke into my home, are stealing from my family, and they're going to try to kill us once we open this door.

Flynn and Catherine flank the door with Kara behind them, and Ethan and I on the other side. Tactically, going through this door is a mistake. My training tells me that much. Funneling us through a doorway will only make it easier to take us out. As Catherine reaches for the door pad, I stop her.

"Wait. Why don't Ethan and I drop in from the air

vents? We can draw their fire away from the door long enough for you to come in safely."

Flynn pauses, considering the idea. Finally, he nods.

"You have two minutes until we breach this door," he says firmly.

"No problem." I motion to Ethan, and we back around the corner and down the hall to the vent duct. He carefully pulls off the cover so we can crawl inside. The space is tight but maneuverable. My blood is singing in my ears. I've never felt so on edge, so ready for a fight. Maybe it's all the pent-up tension, or maybe I'm just having some kind of aftereffects from the branding. I flush, remembering how I let my nerves get the best of me. I made a total fool out of myself in front of everyone. I'm so tired of being the weakest link.

It only takes a few seconds before I can hear the Hollows beneath us. We slide onto our butts and hold our feet over the large square grate. Ethan uses his fingers to count us down from three. In unison, we stomp down on the grate and fall into the middle of the vault. I land, roll to my feet, and lunge forward.

There's someone standing there, facing me. He's not much older than I am, if at all. He has a belt of what looks like explosives hanging across his chest, and his face is caught in a moment of surprise at my appearance. The anger and fear mix inside my head like a chemical reaction, and I lash out, kicking him in the knee so hard he drops to the ground. I kick him again, this time just under the chin, and send him flying backward into a metal file cabinet.

I hear Ethan behind me, but I don't turn. A wiry,

redheaded girl in black goggles comes flying at me. I grab her by the arm and spin so her back is pressed against my chest. Wrapping an arm around her neck, I squeeze until I feel her go limp and let her crumple to my feet. Ethan's lash cracks, and I turn. He's fighting off a boy with a mechanical arm and a face that's scarred and covered in tech.

A pair of arms grabs me from behind and lifts me off the ground.

From behind me, a voice yells, "Drop her, Nobel. Now!"

I freeze. The voice tugs at something in the frayed edges of my mind.

"Why? She's one of them," the boy holding me yells back.

"Because… she's my sister."

My breath leaves my body in a rush as I collide with the floor. In that second, I hear the door whoosh open. The others flood in, immediately joining the fray. My eyes are watering as I roll to my feet and look up into a familiar face.

LEX
Fifteen

I feel her before I see her. Immediately, the feeling of hot flames billows up my neck and my vision blurs.

The room is burning. I can't breathe. Have to hide. My bedroom. Men with guns yell. My clothes are melting into my skin. Anastasia—my Anya—puts out the fire on me with heavy, blue drapes before stuffing the bottle caps in my hand. A flash of light eats the memory.

My heart pounds while I hide behind all the jars of brains on the shelf. Our friend Rasputin tells her that I ran down the hall. He has saved me from losing the hide-and-seek game with her. When Anya can't find me, Rasputin winks, and I laugh. Now I don't have to be "it" for the time being. Another flash.

Anya is gone. I'm not sure where she went, but I'm alone in the flames and I'm crying. My skin hurts from the burning. I see a man in a blue conductor's coat. Am I going to the hospital on the train? I like trains. I crawl onto his back, and the world around me disappears.

I know who I am. I'm Alexei Romanov.

I come to when a sweaty fist hits me square in the jaw, right on my tattooed scar. It might as well have been a target. The Tesla vault is full of my memories. My legs go weak, dropping me to the floor. Someone crashes into my assailant, knocking him into the wall. From my knees, I look up at the girl.

My sister.

"Anya?"

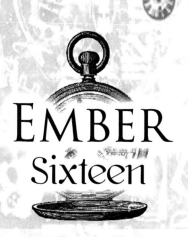

EMBER
Sixteen

I blink once, twice.

My head swims as a flood of memories crashes over me. I can hear my heart pounding in my chest. Alexei kneels in front of me, looking as paralyzed as I am. His eyes are wide, and his mouth is closed in a tight grimace. He opens it and calls out. Not my name, but another name. I can't hear the sound escape his lips, but I can read the familiar shape of it as he speaks it. Something inside me snaps into place. He reaches out, offering me his hand. I reach to take it, but before our fingers connect, the crack of a lash stings past my face, catching him in the arm.

The smell of burning flesh sets me into motion. I jump to my feet, putting the boy behind me, and scream for Ethan. My eyes find him, but he and Flynn are busy grappling with the tall boy. Catherine has the smaller girl pinned into a corner and is slashing away at her. The lash moves through the air like red lightning. The look on Catherine's face is pure rage. She will kill the girl, I'm sure of it.

I don't make the decision to step in—my body just moves of its own accord now. I run at Catherine, shoving her into the wall. She hits her head hard and slides down, leaving a streak of blood on the copper wall. Ethan sees me and freezes. Flynn presses forward and slams the boy into the shelves, knocking a pile of scrap parts to the floor with a clatter. I turn, and the recognition is like a punch in the gut, sudden and painful. I know who he is. He's mine. My little brother. Only he's not so little anymore.

"Alexei?" My voice is a whisper. I'm not sure where the name comes from, but it is smooth and familiar on my tongue. With his back to me, Flynn freezes.

"Anya?" Alexei asks back. I nod even though it's not my name anymore.

With a quick shove, he knocks Flynn out of the way, rushes forward, and wraps his arms around me. Tears well up until they are spilling down my face as I squeeze him back. He was dead, I was sure of it. The fire. I left him behind. I left my brother behind to die.

"I thought you were dead," I say, my heart heavy with guilt.

He pulls back, and I can see the scars on his neck are masked by a beautiful tattoo. He's older too, closer to my age probably. He's a man, an enemy, and a warrior. And he looks so much like our father.

"I thought you were dead, too."

A boy in a grimy surgeon's mask clears his throat. "I hate to interrupt, but we need to go, Lex. Now."

I open my mouth to protest, but as I do, a swarm of Peacekeepers falls from the air vents Ethan and I had come through earlier.

Alexei curses. "Gear Heads. Quick, rift out now."

He grabs my hand, "Come on, Anya."

I pull my hand away. "You can't rift. You don't have a Tether."

"A what?" he asks, confused. "Look, all you need is this."

He reaches over to where his friend is cradling the little redhead in his arms, pulling a green pill from her pocket. As soon as he hands it to me, one of the Peacekeepers leaps into the air and claws it out of my fingers, splitting the pill in half. The green liquid inside drips onto my leg.

The tiny creatures are quickly filling the room. I kick at one as it saws at my boot. I scream. Before I know it, they are crawling up my legs. For a minute, I'm stunned. Peacekeepers aren't supposed to hurt us—they're programmed to only attack Hollows. I glance up and see the Hollows under siege by the deadly robots. It's like being inside a beehive, only instead of stinging us, the Peacekeepers are sawing at us with tiny chainsaw legs. Ethan is trying to get to me. I can see him out the corner of my eye with his arms outstretched, but the swarm is between us, cutting him off from me.

Crying out, I try to shake them off. The others aren't faring any better. As a matter of fact, the Peacekeepers are attacking them even more ferociously. That's when I notice Alexei's leg. It's a prosthetic steam machine. I'm too distracted fighting off the Peacekeepers to ask any questions, but just seeing him like that hurts. And now I remember why.

I was supposed to protect him. Papa told me to find Alexei and take care of him. The realization hits me like a brick. I stumble back, barely keeping myself from falling. I've failed. Whatever this is, whatever he's become, it's my fault. And if he doesn't get out of here soon, the Peacekeepers will kill him.

The emotions override me, like being in the middle of a typhoon. I am being pulled this way and that. The brand on my arm burns as I remember the last order Tesla gave me. His voice floats through my head. "Let the boy die." Inside me, the fighting ends in a snap as the decision is made.

There is no way I am going to let my brother die.

Not again.

"Alexei, do you have what you came here for?" I scream over the chaos.

He holds up what looks like a large, oval lightbulb.

"Then you have to go, now!"

He shakes his head. "Not without you."

I rush at him, throwing my arms around his neck. He smells like sweat, grease, and something underneath that I can't put my finger on. "I can't go with you," I whisper, pushing myself away. His face hardens.

Another wave of Peacekeepers charges us, pulling him away from me. They slice at his arms and face.

"Make sure it's turned off," I yell. He nods, tucking the lightbulb under his arm.

I'm bleeding from where the machines are sawing at my legs, but the pain is nothing, absolutely nothing, compared to what I feel inside right now. Alexei screams something and they all pull out their pills, ready to swallow them.

Pulling the EMP grenade out of my pocket, I look at my little brother as he fights off the metal monsters before putting his own pill on his tongue.

And it's my fault.

If guilt could kill, I'd already be dead on the floor. Pain rolls in my stomach, threatening to force the contents up my throat and out my mouth. Tears roll down my cheeks and into my mouth. They're like bitter saltwater on my tongue. I blink, searching for my brother's face like a lifeline in a storm.

I look at him, catch his eye one last time, and mouth, "I love you."

Flipping the EMP over in my palm, I close my eyes and press the button. A bright light flashes, and then everything goes black.

TESLA JOURNAL ENTRY: DECEMBER 12TH, 1892

We have located two more royal descendants capable of traveling. The first, a young man by the name of Articus Flynn, is a butcher who, thanks to large gambling debts, was quite pleased to participate for the right price. The other is a seamstress by the name of Catherine Crabapple. I doubt that to be her true name, but she is pliable enough. I have asked the doctor to look her over and be sure she is in good health. I have given them both room and board in the hotel Mt. Claire, and they seem only too pleased to be there. Again, the initial experiment seems to have left them quite void of their memories. Although I was hoping this to be an isolated occurrence, I see now that it is part of the process. I can only speculate as to why this occurs, though I imagine the first piercing of this veil of time must be something so traumatic that the mind somehow puts up a wall to protect itself.

LEX
Seventeen

"Claymore would like to debrief you, Lex," Gloves says, glaring at me so hard it's like he's trying to read my mind. Not possible when I'm so tired and confused I can barely see straight.

"Didn't he talk to *you* already?" I ask, my head tucked into the crook of my arm.

The tattered purple lounge chair is really comfortable. I don't want to deal with Claymore at the moment. I don't want to deal with anyone. It feels like all my old scars have been ripped open again, and I am slowly bleeding to death. The feeling is part cold, part numbness. Like tiny crystals of ice swimming through my veins.

I can't get her face out of my mind. I keep trying to match it up—the face of the girl from the vault and the face of my sister. She looks different. Harder, somehow. Her hair is the same, long and brown like our mother's, and her eyes are the color of hot chocolate on a winter's morning. Only the narrow bridge of her nose that slopes into her mouth looks like Father's—

like mine.

"I did," Gloves answers, folding his arms across his chest. "He wants to talk to the leader of the mission. That would be you."

I scratch the scar on my neck and jaw. It's as real and painful as the image of my sister that's now burned into my brain. For the first time, I wish my leg would seize up so that I would have an excuse to stay in the common room staring at the empty half-pipe. The others have given me a wide berth since we got back. That might have something to do with the monumental disaster I made the moment we did. I practically ripped the place apart with my bare hands. I wish I could tap into that fire now, anything to warm myself.

Painfully, I stand and hobble up to Claymore's office, trying not to look at the random faces I pass by. I know they're staring, waiting for me to say something about what happened, waiting to see if I'll fly off the handle again. Honestly, I haven't ruled out the possibility. I kick an abandoned skateboard that has been staring at me from the center of the room. It crashes into the wall, and chunks of plaster fall to the floor. Taking a deep breath, I wait to feel something. But nothing comes.

"Oh, and by the way, I took the liberty of telling Claymore about your sister," Gloves calls after me. It's as if he threw a ball at me without bothering to give me a "think fast." That dude is a sieve. He can't hold information if his life depends on it.

Still, it's probably for the best. If I'd had to see Claymore when we first got back, I probably would've ripped that diver's helmet right off his shoulders. As it is, the first stirrings of returning anger rolls in my gut. My sister, my сестра. My family. Their faces float in and out of my mind like balloons. In the back of my brain, a vague plan is forming. It looks a lot like me going back for Stein, and then going back for my family. Only the *how* is fuzzy.

My geared leg begins to hurt, so I use the cane Nobel gave me to take away some of the pressure. It's tempting to turn around and beat Gloves with it, but I don't want to damage the cane. Nobel tells me that my upgrade is almost ready. The pain should go away with the addition of the new prosthetic.

Walking down the dim hallway, I can almost feel Anya next to me. The link between us is deeper than just being brother and sister. She was my best friend when I was young. We played and talked, and more often than not, she read me stories and tucked me in at night. My lips begin to turn up at the corners as I remember the nursery rhymes she used to recite in her singsong voice. Then another memory invades—the look of shock on her face in the vault. I stop, closing my eyes and reaching forward. As if I think, somehow, I can reach through time and space and touch her. Rifting runs in our blood now. The time stream created us in its womb. We are bound to it and to each other. The air around me feels thin, so very fragile. If I can just reach out…

Breathing in, I can taste the smoke from of the vault from the night before. I can hear her heart beating slowly, like a clock ticking backward. Just a little further and—

I'm thrown from the vision so hard I almost fall forward. Only my cane stops me from spilling face-first onto the floor. Shaking my head, I open my eyes and blink. She felt so close for a second. But whatever it was has passed, and I can't put this off any longer.

Even though the sun is shining outside, the hallway to Claymore's office seems darker than ever. I wonder absently what the Tower looked like back in its heyday. Back when Tesla and his assistants lived and worked here. Back when everything was new and shiny. We have placed it in a time loop created years after the facility was abandoned. Now it's barely standing. Even the radio tower itself is nothing more than a tall, rusty jungle gym.

I hear the ticking before I even enter the room. Not only is Claymore already waiting for me, he has also put something on the arrivals and departures board.

I hobble in to the room without even a courtesy knock. The room remains the same time after time—a butcher-block desk with our mysterious leader sitting behind it.

You were attacked by Gear Heads? Claymore has already posted his message.

"Yes, sir," I reply through gritted teeth. I have so many unanswered questions, and he wants to talk about Gear Heads? What about my sister? What about my age? Did Anya slow down or did I speed up? There is no way she could be more than a year or two older than the day we were taken. And why us? Why were we taken in the first place?

Tick, tick, tick… *Were they the same as…* Tick, tick, tick… *The Gear Heads that took your leg?*

"I have questions," I say flatly. The message board flips furiously.

I am sure you do, but… Tick, tick, tick… *Answer my questions first.*

"Yes, sir," I answer. "But the Gear Heads didn't attack the Tesla Rifters. Well, except for Anya. I—" I swallow, wondering just how much Gloves has shared, and decide to go all in. "I gave her a Contra. The stupid things went after it like flies on crap."

Tick, tick, tick… *That is very interesting.* Tick, tick, tick… *My suspicions were correct.* Tick, tick, tick… *They track the Contra.* Tick, tick, tick… *That is how they…* Tick, tick, tick… *Keep finding us.*

Reaching the end of my patience, I rip off my jester's hat and throw it on Claymore's desk. "Tell me about my sister!"

Claymore doesn't respond at first. Black bubbles form dirty foam around the front view port of the helmet. He sits still, his hands unmoving on the gouged desk.

Tick, tick, tick… *We tried…* Tick, tick, tick… *To save her.*

I pound my cane on the floor. "No you didn't! We are *time travelers.* Yet, you couldn't manage to save both of us? Or what about the rest of my family? You couldn't save them either?"

He tells me about the events surrounding the death of my parents—how when Gloves got to my estate, the flames were already going, and my family was dead, save Anya and me. A man named Flynn had already taken her. Gloves was barely able to save me. As it was, I was so badly injured and traumatized they had to put me in stasis for a while to recover. I was only thirteen when he took me. I've changed so much since then.

"We can go back," I say, on the edge of my seat. "I can go back. I have the Dox. I can go back further and set things right. I can save them all."

Tick, tick, tick… *No. It is a fixed point.*

I shake my head. "There has to be a way. Maybe Nobel can make a copy of the Dox. Then we would have two. I could use one to save Stein and—"

Tick, tick, tick… *No. It is not possible.* Tick, tick, tick… *A fixed point is absolute.* Tick, tick, tick… *The events in that timeline…* Tick, tick, tick… *Will always remain unchanged.* Tick, tick, tick… *They will always happen as…* Tick, tick, tick… *They have already happened.*

Then, in an uncharacteristic gesture, he adds, Tick, tick, tick… *I am sorry, Alexei.*

My mind spins like a hamster in a wheel. There has to be a way. I can't just give up on them. On Anya. Maybe if I can't save them all, I can at least save her. I can go back into Tesla and get her out. I can—

Tick, tick, tick… *You need to focus…* Tick, tick, tick… *On saving Stein.*

I blink, surprised he brought it up.

Tick, tick, tick… *We need her.*

He's right. Stein first. She will know what to do next. Together, we can get my sister out of Tesla. My heart beats double-time in my chest.

Without warning, the ground shudders under my feet, knocking bits of plaster and dust from the walls. I pitch forward out of my seat. From my hands and knees, I see a new message on Claymore's board.

We are under attack.

EMBER
Eighteen

The smell of singed hair is what wakes me. It's too familiar, too ingrained in my mind not to startle me. I think I was dreaming of something nice, and I'm tempted to close my eyes again and summon it back. I can't remember what it was, but the general feeling of comfort from the dream has been replaced with bitter reality.

Blinking up at the white ceiling, I wonder how long I've been out. I try to swallow, but it's like trying to drink sand. Shifting to stretch, I realize I can't move. Panic rushes in. I jerk upright, tugging against the restraints holding my arms to the gurney. They aren't handcuffs. No, handcuffs I could deal with. Two Peacekeepers have linked around each hand, trapping me. I try to pull free, but they click and gears turn, tightening their hold on me until blood trickles into my palms. Nurse lurches into the room, holding a tray full of needles and glass vials. I look down, seeing a large bandage on my left shin. Nurse lifts it and begins to clean it with iodine, making it look even more gruesome. The skin has been eaten away and patched back together.

I scream, kicking out, only to realize my feet are also bound. Nurse grinds to a stop, staring at me through its creepy gas mask. Its only words are the eerie hiss of steam releasing from its mechanisms.

Alexei.

My brother.

I see his face in my mind. My tenuous grasp on reality snaps like a dry twig, and I scream. I scream until my voice is gone and tears run marathons down my face. Until I'm sure I will die from the pressure building inside me. The guilt and anger tear themselves out my throat.

Then, spent, I fall back onto the gurney. Trapped even as my mind unspools inside me.

Alexei is alive.

My family is dead, but Alexei is a Hollow. Somehow, I can't make it feel real. But I saw him. I touched him. My little brother. He looked nothing like the boy I remember. The tattoos, the scars. I swallow again. How could I have forgotten him? Now he is gone again. Not dead, but lost to me. In league with the enemy. My stomach lurches at the thought. No, not my enemy. Alexei will never be my enemy.

The door to the hospital slides open and Flynn steps in, his heavy boots thudding across the tile floor. Nurse turns and walks away, leaving us in silence. I glare at Flynn. To think, not long ago, just seeing his face could make me feel like everything would be all right. Now the sight of him only makes me feel dead inside. The betrayal is sour in my mouth. There are so many things I want to say, but I'm afraid what will come out if I open my mouth, so I just continue to glare as he sits on the edge of my bed and speaks.

"Ember, I know what you must be thinking—"

"That's not my name! My name is Anastasia!" I spit the words out. My decision to stay silent is abandoned in an instant.

"Your name *was* Anastasia. That girl died the night her family was executed. The girl you are now, her name is Ember."

"Вы взяли мою семью от меня." *You took my family from me.* My voice has dropped to a whisper. Some vague, distant part of my brain realizes I'm not speaking English anymore, but Flynn still understands what I'm saying. I can tell by the way his face pales and his eyes drop to the floor.

"I saved your life," he whispers.

I take a moment to make sure the words come out in English again. "Why did you let my family die? Why didn't you save my family? Why let them...?"

He shakes his head. "I couldn't."

I am trembling now, and my voice is unsteady. "Don't lie to me. You could do it right now. Or I could. I could go back and save them all."

He reaches out to touch me, but I flinch away. "No, Ember. You can't. Do you remember your Trial, what I said about Fixed Points in time?"

In my mind, I replay the conversation. "Yes."

"What happened to your family, everything from your birth to the moment we rescued you, it's all fixed. When we failed to get you and your brother, Tesla sent Catherine back further. He wanted to take you both the week before the attack. But she couldn't. Do you understand? She physically couldn't. Sometimes, the time stream fixes points to protect important moments in history. Altering an event like that could unravel the fabric of time itself."

I don't answer that. I'm too busy remembering.

Alexei's obsession with tinkering has made us late for the family portrait. He screams. A fire has broken out in the house. The heat begins to melt the fragile lace of my gown, burning impressions of it into my arms and chest. I push Alexei into a corner and force him to crouch out of the smoke. My mind reels, trying to think of something, anything, that might save us. My mind snaps like a rubber band. There's a dumbwaiter at the end of the hall. If we can get past the flames, I can fit him inside. It won't hold us both. It's too small for that. But I can get him out. And he will have to run into the forest and find a place to hide in there. Surely, some of my father's staff has fled there. They will find him. They will take care of him. I turn my back to the door, trying to explain to my crying brother what I'm going to do. A pair of arms grabs me from behind. I scream and kick. But it isn't a soldier. It's Flynn, taking me away. Leaving my brother alone in that room. I scream to him, telling him to run for the dumbwaiter, but I don't think he can hear me over his own sobs. Flynn drags me from the burning house as rubble collapses around us.

I blink back tears as the memory falls away. Flynn is still talking, but I'm not listening. The memories are flowing over me like water, and I can't stop the tide.

The smoke is thick and dark. Someone else is there, rushing in behind us. The sound of breaking glass erupts around me. A piece of plaster falls from the ceiling. Everything goes dark.

I finally look at Flynn. His face is red.

"Did you hear me?" he asks.

I blink again.

"I said I was sorry, Ember. I never would have left him if…" He trails off, hesitant to speak the final words of his thought.

I'm still whispering, but my words hold a jagged edge. "No. You left him on purpose. You took me and left him. It's all your fault. You let them take my brother."

He balks.

"What I don't understand," I continue, "is why did you take *me*? Alexei was the important one, the one destined to be tsar. Why did you take me and leave him to the Hollows? And how in the hell am I speaking English?"

Flynn clamps his mouth shut. I glare at him until he nods.

"Do you remember when I first met you?" he asks.

"You mean when you ripped me from my brother's arms? Yes, I remember. No thanks to you."

Flynn shakes his head and looks deeply into my eyes. "No, Ember. That wasn't the first time we met. Not even close."

"What are you talking about?" I demand, turning my wrists in my restraints. For a minute, I wonder why I'm strapped down, and then I remember something else. I attacked Catherine. A pang of guilt arises before I can squelch it. But she almost killed that girl. That's why I attacked her. The guilt quickly fades.

"You don't remember because it hasn't happened to you yet. But you asked me to trust you once, and I did. Now I'm asking you to trust me."

I frown, not sure I can trust anything he says right

now.

"I know that when the time comes, Ember, you'll make the right decision. I trust you. And as for the English speaking, Tesla decided it would be best if all the recruits spoke the same language. We implanted it in your head when you got here." He presses his hand over my wrist where the small metal creatures hold me. Instantly my hand is free. "A small thing really, in the overall—"

The slap is so quick he never sees it coming. His face is streaked with my blood as he gets up and turns his back to me.

"Why did you set the Peacekeepers on us?" I demand before he can leave. "You went through such trouble to kidnap me, why try to kill me now?"

He turns. His face, while red and bloody, is unrepentant. "The Peacekeepers are programmed to detect Contra and destroy anyone with it in their system. It's how we've been locating and fighting the Hollows. They detected some on your clothes. That's the only reason they went after you. I didn't know—I couldn't have known—that they would attack you. I honestly thought you'd be safe."

My mouth forms a hard line. "Are you going to wipe my mind again?"

Flynn's face droops. He actually looks like I've hurt his feelings. I pretty much don't care.

"No, Ember. Another memory wipe might do permanent damage. We won't risk it. Unless you give us no other choice."

Before I can say anything else, he's gone, and Nurse is moving forward again. I barely feel the prick of the needle, but as it pushes the clear liquid into my vein, the room fades to black.

When I come to again, my head is throbbing. Next to me, Ethan is sitting cross-legged on the floor. He's reading something on his thin tech board.

"Hey," I manage weakly.

His eyes flick up to me, and he frowns. "It's about time. What, the world goes to crap on crackers and you decide to take a nap?"

I laugh once, and it's dry and painful. One of my arms is free, but the other is still strapped down with half a dozen wires and tubes plunged into my flesh.

"Your skin graft is healing well, according to Flynn," Ethan says.

At the sound of his name, I flinch. "No offense, but I don't trust anything Flynn says anymore. My brother…" I begin to explain what happened. How it wasn't his fault. How Flynn had left him to the mercy of the Hollows.

Ethan takes my hand, pressing something small and round into my bandaged palm. I almost ask what it is, but the look on his face stops me, warns me to wait. I clench my fingers around it and give him a barely noticeable nod before slipping it into my pocket. He turns the board to me, revealing a set of blueprints. "They escaped. With this."

"What is it?"

"It's called a Dox. It's one of Tesla's designs. The purpose was to develop a sort of temporal Band-Aid. Something that could draw enough energy from the stream to contain a paradox."

"In English?"

Ethan chuckles. "That is the English version. If you want the technical response, I'll have to use words like *anthropic directionality* and *corporeal tardyons*, and let's face it, no one wants that. The bottom line is this: If the Hollows need it badly enough to risk breaching the Institute to get it, it's bad. *Chernobyl* bad. Flynn thinks they must be planning to do something that could rip a hole in the stream. Otherwise, why would they need the Dox?"

I nod. The foggy edges of my brain have snapped to attention. "That would be very dangerous."

"Always the queen of understatements, aren't you?"

I flinch again at the word *queen*. "How much did Flynn tell you?"

Ethan sits on the edge of my bed. "Exactly nothing. I figured it out, though. That is, the part about you and your brother and who you were before. I sort of took the little bit of info I managed to hack from your file, and I ran it through the historical database."

I suck in a deep breath.

He reaches out and pushes a stray tangle of hair off my forehead. "Doesn't really matter to us, you know, who you were. We know who you are. The rest is—"

I finish the thought for him. "History."

He smiles and kisses my head before whispering, "Let me know when you're ready to go."

I'm confused, but the look on his face as he sits up is enough to keep me from saying anything. Suddenly, I realize something obvious. They are watching me. Waiting to see what I'm going to do. I smile at Ethan as I realize something else, too. Loosening my grip on the anger inside me, I let it be replaced by the peaceful feeling that comes from knowing you are loved.

* * *

I lie there, slipping in and out of consciousness for a few more hours, before all the tubes are gone, and they release me back to my room. Flynn comes in at some point to talk to me again. I try not to be outright hostile, but I can't quite manage civil. Every time his lips move, I wonder how he might be trying to manipulate me. I think about the stupid, blind devotion I harbored for so long and can't help feeling very disappointed in myself.

Sitting in my room, I absentmindedly rub the small bottle cap Ethan had pressed into my hand. It's Alexei's—I know it. He must have dropped it during the attack. It is my touchstone now, the only thing that feels real. My arm is healed, the broken blood vessels in my eye have cleared, and the skin where the Peacekeepers tore into me has mended, leaving only a faint pink scar. Score one for Tesla medicine. On my own, it would have taken weeks to heal. Now, it's precious time I don't have to waste.

Kicking off the blankets pooled around me, I throw my legs over the side of the bed and slip my feet into my boots. My body is moving before I can fully think through what I'm doing. Raking my fingers through my hair, I twist it into a messy bun at the back of my neck and wind a rubber band around it. Slipping out the door, I walk into the hallway.

I don't know what time it is, but it must be late. The corridor lights have dimmed for the evening and the false windows are dark as I walk past them. No one is wandering the halls. Except for the occasional hiss of steam or sputter of oil from the gas lamps, the Institute is quiet. When I get to Ethan's room, I pause, running my fingers over the cool brass door. I can almost feel him inside. My heart stutters in my chest as I drop my hand and keep walking.

Down three flights of spiral stairs from the Dormitory Floor is Tesla's lab. I stand at the door, wondering how I'm going to open it. Do I knock? Taking a deep breath, I raise my hand to do just that when I hear the gears inside click into place. The whole thing opens just a crack.

He knows I'm here.

Of course he does. Tesla sees everything in this place. Pulling the door open, I slip inside, closing it behind me. As the locks click back into place, a cold spike shoots down the back of my neck. *Should have left it open*, I think before remembering that it's computer-automated. Tesla would have just closed it himself anyway. Behind me, the lights flick on to a full glow. As I make my way slowly through the workstations, I ball up my hands, then relax them over and over. My hands are cold and shaking.

When I get to the main terminal, Tesla's hologram is already there, his flat eyes staring at me.

Part of me wants to sprint back to my room and hide under the covers. But some other part of me, a stronger, braver part, wants answers.

"I have questions," I say, my voice barely a whisper.

Tesla folds his hands in front of him, but he says nothing. He's so pale. I wonder if he was that pale in life. His pallor and his hovering image make him look like a ghost. Maybe that's what he is really—just a ghost in a machine.

"Flynn told me that my life before the Tesla Institute is a Fixed Point. Is that true?"

The grainy computer voice responds, just a second out of sync with the image's moving lips. "That is true."

"Is it common? I was led to believe Fixed Points are rare."

"Five Fixed Points have been discovered in the time stream, including the one you created during your Trial." His tone is flat, but I feel accusation in the words. "That does not mean they are rare. It means they have not been discovered yet."

"How do you find them?"

"There is no way, at this time, to locate Fixed Points other than to accidentally stumble upon them."

"How many Fixed Points have you created?" I ask, not sure where the question came from.

"One. It was by accident that one of my first Rifters created a Fixed Point. Once we realized what she'd done, we were able to study and record the phenomenon."

I swallow, not sure how long he will continue to tolerate my questions. "Why me? I mean, why did you choose me?" I ask, my voice cracking.

For a second, there's no response. I'm sure he's going to shut down. But he finally answers. "You were chosen because of your pedigree."

I shake my head. "I mean, why *me*? Not my mother or my sisters. Alexei and me. Why us?"

"A Fixed Point cannot be altered. It is a universal constant."

"I don't understand why," I say, throwing my hands in the air as I pace past him.

Tesla's image rotates in the fog, following my direction as I walk by. "Imagine, if you will, a fraying rope. To prevent the rope from falling apart, one can tie a knot in it. This is what a Fixed Point does. Should a Fixed Point be untied, for lack of a proper analogy, the time stream would unravel and be destroyed."

"But you said a Fixed Point can't be altered. It can't be untied."

"True. The alteration of a Fixed Point is not in our abilities. I only use this description so you understand how fragile time is and why it creates the Fixed Points. It is protecting itself, as any living organism does."

I lean against the nearest wall, letting that sink in. "Tesla, why are you answering my questions? Why haven't you just mind-wiped me again and sent me on my way?" I ask, dreading the answer. "Not that I'm ungrateful," I add quickly.

"You are valuable to us." His voice crackles through the overhead speakers.

That sounds like a lie, I realize. Even with no emotion on his face, no inflection in his voice, I don't believe him.

"Why am I valuable suddenly? You've wiped my mind before. You sent me on my Trial. I could have died at any point before now."

"Alexei Romanov is alive, and he will come for you," the voice responds.

The blood in my veins turns to ice as I realize what he's saying.

My brother will come for me, and when he does, Tesla will either take him, or kill him.

I'm only of value as bait.

* * *

I've been formulating a plan in my head. I haven't

spoken a word of it to anyone, but I'm sure Ethan knows what's coming. He knows me too well not to suspect something. Outwardly, I've been cool, if not a little detached. I overheard Flynn whispering to Mistress Catherine, something about post-traumatic stress.

Good.

Let them think that. The truth is that since my chat with Tesla, I've never felt more focused. Every sense is on hyper-alert. I can hear footsteps as they pass outside my door. I can smell the meals being served in the cafeteria even from my room three floors up. Of my group, only Kara seems unchanged by the attack. She's been told about my brother, that I know. But she hasn't said anything. I can feel her pulling away even as I do the same.

Ethan and I are playing a game of chess at my desk while Kara is painting my toenails a brilliant, crimson red. No one is talking. Kara finishes, twisting the top back on the contraband bottle of paint, when I finally decide to speak up.

"Hey Ethan, can you go do that voodoo that you do?" I ask, jerking my head toward the computer terminal next to the door.

Without a word, he gets up and walks to the panel. Pulling a pocketknife from his pants, he pops off the plate and starts fiddling with the wires inside. It sparks brightly before Ethan turns back to me with a nod.

"I need to go."

Kara looks at me hopefully. "What? Like to the bathroom?"

I shake my head, but it's Ethan who speaks up. "To get her brother."

His voice is calm, amused, as he walks back over to the table. Like he can't believe it's taken me so long to say something. Kara frowns. She's clearly disappointed, but not surprised.

"Okay. Here's the plan. We know the Peacekeepers can locate the Hollows because of the Contra, right? Well, I've managed to get my hands on a couple. We're going to use them to track your brother down. I'm thinking smash-and-grab. We go in heavy, disable their defenses, grab Alexei, and—"

I cut him off. "I'm not coming back here, Ethan." I can't. I have no idea why Tesla wants Alexei or what he intends to do to him. We'll have to hide, but I've come to accept this. We will run and hide somewhere, and Tesla will never be able to find us. We might have to run forever.

That must surprise him because he pauses, but only for a second. "Fine. Then we land someplace else. The plan is still fundamentally the same."

Kara throws her legs over the bed and stands up. "Forget it. I have no desire to leave my home and go searching for some sketchy, drug-addled Hollow. Even if he *is* Ember's brother."

"What is your problem, Kara?" Ethan asks, his eyebrows raised.

Kara gets to her feet, lifting up the side of her shirt high enough to expose a long, jagged scar across the front of her ribs.

"Your precious little brother did this to me. Let's just say my first time out ended with a three-week stay in the hospital wing." She drops her shirt and points at me. "He would have killed me, Ember. And he still would if he had the chance."

She hurls a bottle of nail polish so hard that it shatters, sending red liquid down my wall. "He's our enemy and always will be, so get that through your thick skull and quit trying to plan a family reunion."

I reach out to her, but she jerks back. She's hurt; I can see it on her face. But she must understand.

"Kara, you know I love you like a sister. I do. But Alexei is my blood. I have to find him before something terrible happens to him. He's my responsibility."

"Then we will help you," Ethan offers, ignoring the nasty look Kara shoots his direction.

I hold my hands up, "No, I have to go alone. It isn't that I don't want you with me." My eyes flicker to Ethan, who looks stunned and a little sad. "But I don't know where I'm going to go or even *when* we are going to go once I get him out. I can't ask you guys to risk that with me. I won't."

Ethan rolls his eyes. "Ember—"

I don't let him finish. "When Tesla realizes what I've done, he will hunt me down. I'm going to have to run far and fast." He opens his mouth to say something else, so I add, "It will be easier to hide out if it's just my brother and me."

Ethan snaps his mouth closed. I can tell he wants to argue, but he can't find the right words. I know how he feels. I don't want to go without him either. There's a pain in my chest, and I really think it might be my heart breaking.

"Kara," he whispers after a moment, "you owe me."

I don't know what he's talking about, but a look crosses between them. She rolls her eyes.

"Fine. If you're determined to do this, I'll at least get you out of here," Kara says tapping her chin. "I think I can create a suitable distraction."

"If anyone can be distracting, it's you," Ethan says, only half-joking.

She bows as if he has paid her a great compliment. "And Ethan, you can hot-wire the rift chamber. Ember just needs to steal a Tether. Can you handle that, Princess?"

"I think she can handle that," Ethan says, looking at me. "But I'm going with you."

He's clenching his hand so hard his knuckles are white from the strain. I put my hand over his and squeeze. Kara glances between us, mutters something under her breath, and steps out the door. As soon as she's gone, I feel the weight of Ethan's stare.

"You can't." There are so many things I want to say. I want to tell him how much he means to me, how I would never risk him—not even for this. But it feels wrong to say those words when I know I'm about to leave him behind. "I need you to run the rift chamber." It's not the whole truth, but it's what I'll have to settle with for now.

After a few moments of reluctance waging war on his features, he sighs. "Fine. But the second you figure out where and when you are going to land, come get me, okay? Don't make me come looking for you."

I promise, wondering how I'm going to pull it off, but determined to try.

Ethan heads back to the computer interface. He pulls a copper disc from his pocket and presses it into a small slot. "I've been saving this for a special occasion." He winks at me. "Started working on it after the break-in. Just in case."

I can't help but be impressed at his forethought.

"What is it?"

"It's a virus. It'll give us a few minutes off Tesla's radar to get to the chamber while he tries to chase it down."

I sweep a gaze across my room. Is there anything I want to take from this place? My hand moves to the cameo at my throat. It's all I want, really. The only memory of this place not tainted with lies is hanging around my neck. Ethan grabs my rucksack and starts stuffing it full of clothes.

"Leave them," I tell him. "I'll get new stuff later."

He doesn't ask why or challenge me. Dropping the sack like it's full of toxic snakes, he doesn't look back. I take his hand, and we slink into the hall. Lights behind us come on as lights in front of us fall dark. Every so often, we enter a new section and the process repeats. "Keep in the dark," Ethan says, pulling me behind him. "It's where the virus is disabling the monitors."

After what feels like forever, we reach the door to the tech locker. The door slides open, and we slip in. Lights blaze to life. For a moment, I can't breathe. Weapons, energy pulse guns, and dormant Peacekeepers line the walls. For a heartbeat, I think I can hear the mechanical creatures grinding to life. I strain to hear better, dropping into a defensive crouch. As soon as I realize they aren't moving, I force myself to relax.

"Breathe, Ember," Ethan says, his tone mocking.

I snort. "Says the guy who wasn't almost eaten by the things."

He reaches up and stuffs a Peacekeeper in his pocket. "Valid point. I will carry the very scary Tinkertoy."

I'm looking for the drawer that holds the other tech. Finally, I graze the correct one, and it glides open to reveal the rifting gear. "Do I need the Tether?" I ask, my fingers hovering above the shiny copper.

"I don't know any other way."

"The earbud?"

But even as I say it, I know the answer. I look over at Ethan, who has come to the same conclusion. "I think you have all you need. Let's go."

He doesn't have to tell me twice. I push the drawer closed, and we're off to the rift chamber.

I half expect to run into someone along the way. Flynn or Mistress Catherine. Mentally, I prepare myself for a fight. Once, during our training, Mistress Catherine had warned us that we might someday have to face one of our own. And for me, today might be that day. She'd been talking about the Hollows, of course. I never could have expected I'd be the rogue. Could I do it? Attack one of them on purpose? As we turn the next corner, the answer is simple. Yes. To save my brother, I could do just about anything. Ethan holds up his fist, motioning for me to stop. For a second, I feel guilty, but not for going rogue or even for breaking up my team. I have put them all in danger. My friends. They are risking themselves for me. Ethan waves, and we continue forward until we are standing outside the rift chamber. The red light flashes and the door grinds open. Kara is already inside.

"Ember, stop!"

I turn just in time to see Flynn running for the door, but he's too late. The door slams closed with Ethan, Kara, and me inside. Ethan turns back to the door and punches a string of numbers into the keypad.

"Locked for now. But it won't take them long to get past it."

As he shoves the Peacekeeper in my pocket, Ethan moves, grabbing me by the arm.

"You're going to have to take this. It's the only way to track the Hollows. Use it like a bloodhound. It'll lead you to them, or at least get you close. "

I open my mouth to protest, but he holds up a finger.

"It's the only way, Ember. Now get ready to go."

Above me, I see Kara watching from the control booth. She presses a hand to the glass and mouths, "Good-bye." Ethan pushes me onto the pad, and I grab the handles. He rushes to the remote console under the large viewing window and pries it open. Pulling on wires, he manages to create a few sparks, and then the device purrs to life. He turns to look at me over his shoulder, and his expression is one of determination.

That's when I realize how much I really love him. I almost can't contain it, as if the words want to crawl out my body. But he just winks and turns away, saying, "Hold on tight."

As soon as he presses the button, the room spins. Blinking, I find myself standing at the edge of the stream. I pull the Peacekeeper from my pocket and carefully hook it to the buckles on my vests. It springs to life. The little legs saw through the air as if it could fly. I move to swat at it, as I don't want it anywhere near me, but I can't bring myself to touch it. It's tugging so hard it's all I can do to hold my ground, but it isn't attacking me, which allows me to let out an anxious breath.

It wriggles like a dog on a leash. I step into the

stream, letting it pull me toward what I hope is my brother. It's already too late when I wonder, *How am I going to turn this thing off when I get there?* A sense of dread turns my blood to ice.

LEX
Nineteen

Hobbling to the window in Claymore's third-story office, I wipe the grime off one of the panes with my sleeve and press my nose against the glass. I can't quite make out what's going on—all I can see is a small fire on the right side of the courtyard.

"Fire!" I say, turning to the desk.

Claymore doesn't move. The board doesn't change. It's as if he's turned to stone.

"There," I mutter, pointing to where Bruce and Slap Stick are ducking behind some thick shrubs. There's movement on the outskirts of the courtyard. Someone is hiding behind the pillar.

From my vantage point, I can't see them well, but from the look of confusion passing between Bruce and Slap Stick, I don't think they can see the intruder at all. But who do I tell? Claymore hasn't said anything since his warning, and I'm beginning to wonder if something shook loose inside him during the explosion. I turn back to the windows, using my cane to shatter the glass. Maybe I can at least call to Bruce and point him in the right direction.

Watching through the broken windows, I try to decide if I will be more helpful here or if I should go help my friends. There's only one intruder I can see, but that doesn't mean there aren't more lurking out there somewhere. Just as I decide to go, my leg groans and seizes up. I smack the metal straps with my palm, trying to get the gears to start turning again. Movement draws my attention back to the window. The intruder hasn't moved, but I notice a small, metal object reflecting sunlight in the middle of the courtyard, weaving through the spray of bullets that Bruce lays down.

"Gear Heads!" I yell through the broken glass window. I am too high up, too far away for them to hear me through the pop of gunfire. I have about a minute and a half to be grateful there is only one before it doubles back, crouches down, and starts spitting out little gears at Bruce from behind. Slap Stick runs to his aid, but the Gear Head lunges, digs into his arm, and sprays what looks like steam in his face.

The Gear Head then generates the rusty old saw I loathe and cuts into his flesh. Slap Stick tears the little creature off his arm before it can move its way up to his face. He throws it aside, motioning for Bruce to take care of it as he advances on the person hiding on the outskirts of the courtyard.

The Gear Head doesn't even miss a step in its pursuit. It's so much faster than the others we've dealt with—it's on Bruce in the blink of an eye. I smack my leg again, harder this time. I need to get out there. The Gear Head backs up, scurrying into a crouched position. I can see where it has taken cover behind a

210

scraggly bush on the other side of the courtyard. It is waiting for a sneak attack. Smart, sneaky little monster.

The only thing I can think to do is to grab my cane and use the oil slick feature. I lift it up to my shoulder like a long rifle, glad I have the gear settings memorized by now so I don't even have to look down to see which one to use.

The cane doesn't kick when I squeeze the small, concealed trigger. Oil starts to ooze out of the end of the cane. The flow is slow, and it drizzles down in spurts.

I slap the side, thinking that maybe it isn't functioning properly.

Then, without warning, the cane gushes with oil like water out of a fire hose. Surprised at how much the skinny cane holds, I rotate my body back and forth like a sprinkler so I can get a good covering of oil in front of the Gear Head. Slap Stick gives me a thumbs-up.

Soon, the path between the Gear Head and its prey is covered, slicked with the shiny substance. The steady stream continues for a long moment. The Gear Head tries to get its balance. But even though it attempts to cut into the ground with its saws and pincers, it is unable to advance on my team. Slap Stick takes advantage of the oil and moves toward the floundering Gear Head. With the stride of a football kicker, he boots the Gear Head over into the far corner of the courtyard. It flails, bounces, and slides under a bush. Sparks fly and the dry tumbleweed bursts into flame. There is no explosion.

From behind the pillar, the intruder puts its hands in the air and shouts, "Will you stop shooting at me, you lunatics? I said I surrender!"

At the sound of the voice, my heartbeat quickens. "Anya!" I yell, smacking my leg once more to get the gears grinding back into motion, and I limp to the main room.

* * *

Nobel and Gloves converge on the courtyard. The other Hollows watch intently while Slap Stick grabs the intruder from her hiding spot and heads to the entrance of the Tower. Grabbing my jester's hat, I head downstairs, desperate to confirm what I hope I heard. As soon as I clear the hallway, my heart leaps into my throat.

"It's okay. Let her go," I order, pushing past Nobel so hard I practically body check him into the wall.

Slap Stick cocks his head, giving me a funny look, but he obeys.

"She's my sister," I say, holding my hand out to Anya. She hesitates, glancing over to where Bruce is giving her a stern glare, and holds up her hands. They are bound with thick brass cuffs. She steps forward, her heavy black boots making the old floorboards creak, but Bruce grabs her tightly by the arm, preventing her from going any farther. She twists away from him, but he grabs out, catching her by the back of her leather vest and tugging her. I'm about to step in, but moving so quickly it's hard to follow, she kicks Bruce. The kick catches him in the side of the knee, and he falls forward. Slap Stick steps between them to stop the fight, but Anya pushes him away, comes up behind Bruce, and slips her arms over his head, using her cuffs to choke him.

"Whoa, what? Really?" Slap Stick asks, surprised by the assault.

"Relax. I come in peace," Anya says, releasing Bruce with a rough shove.

"Anya, you're in hostile territory, about to be tortured, possibly killed, and all you can come up with is 'I come in peace?'" I almost laugh.

"Ember," she corrects me. "My name is Ember now."

I bristle. It must be her nickname, but I don't like it. It just doesn't fit her. "So if you come in peace, why the Gear Head?"

She bites her bottom lip. It's a gesture I remember all too well. "I used it to track you guys through the time stream. It sort of escaped. Sorry about that."

"And the explosion?" I ask, rubbing the back of my neck.

Bruce holds up a geared hand. "That was me. The perimeter sensors went off, so I fired a warning shot. From the cannon." He shrugs unapologetically.

"Idiot," Ember and I mumble at the same time. Then, we look at each other and smirk.

"Okay, girly, that sounds good and all, but if you aren't here to spy on us, then why are you here?" Slap Stick asks, rubbing his neck.

Ember doesn't even blink. "I'm here for my brother." Her face is stern. There is something different about her. Something hard and unfriendly. For the first time, I wonder if my sister is telling the truth.

For a minute, I'm torn. I want to believe my sister, but what if I'm wrong? What if, by letting her in, I put my team in danger? Maybe she's been brainwashed. Or maybe she was sent here to spy on us—or worse.

She must be able to read the doubt on my face because she frowns. Her dark eyebrows pull together as she clamps her mouth shut so tightly the muscles in her jaw twitch.

I step forward so Ember and I are eye to eye. She holds my gaze, unflinching. After a moment of silence, she reaches out and tugs the lapel of my vest, straightening it like she used to when I was a boy. I catch her hands in mine, and she freezes. Her skin is cool and her hands are shaky.

"I would never hurt you," she whispers in Russian.

"I know," I respond in kind.

Bruce and Slap Stick consult Gloves in low voices, with their backs to the group. Finally, they turn around. Bruce pulls a key from his front pocket.

"Okay," he says. Unlocking the manacles, he adds, "If Lex trusts you, well, that's good enough for us. But no funny business."

"No promises," Ember mutters, rubbing her wrists.

I sneak a glance at Anya—no, *Ember,* I remind myself. Her nose is slightly wrinkled. Maybe it's just the smell. Or maybe it's a judgment on our surroundings. I feel a pang of anger blossom in my chest. This place isn't much, but it *is* my home.

Gloves guides us to a couch in the opposite corner of the room. The velvet wall dressings are peeling away. I hit a few of the pieces while we walk, making them fall to the floor like crimson snowflakes. Everyone sits on the worn, tattered furniture and stares awkwardly at each other. I remain standing. We're all waiting for someone else to start the conversation.

When I can't take the staring contest anymore, I

lean forward and rest my hands on the back of the sofa. My head is reeling. My sister is sitting in front of me—alive and well. Flesh and blood. Safe. Away from Tesla. Relief bleeds into my system, but my questions remain. After circling the couch, I squat at her feet.

I look up, staring into her warm brown eyes, and open my mouth to say something. But the words catch in my throat as Ember lunges forward, grabbing me and giving me the hug I never thought I'd have again. We hold each other for a long time. She smells the same as I remember, like warm honey and fresh cream. Finally, she pulls away and just looks at me, tracing my scar with the back of her index finger. A small tear rolls down her face, carving a clean, pink line down her dirt-covered cheek. I'm sure I seem different to her. I'm not the little boy she remembers—I've become something more. More than the little brother who followed her around, begging to play swords. I am the leader our father groomed me to be, though not in the way he imagined. I am a Hollow, and I'm proud of it.

I can almost read the disapproval in her face.

"What happened to your leg?" Ember asks softly.

I don't answer, countering with a question of my own.

"Why did you come here, exactly?" Pulling back, I fold my arms across my chest. I have to maintain my credibility as a leader, though I wish I could just sit and talk to my sister all night without these strangers and their cold eyes.

"I came here to find you," Ember says as if the answer is obvious. "The memories of the fire are still hazy, but they are coming back to me in pieces. I remember the roof collapsing. I remember being dragged away. I think I remember seeing him there, too." She points to Gloves, who is sitting near the couch in his locomotive chair. "Mostly, I just want us to be a family again. I would have come sooner, but something happened and I couldn't remember anything until that day you broke into the Institute. Seeing you there, it sort of broke the dam." She looks away.

"You could have come with us when we left the vault," I say.

She shakes her head, strands of hair falling around her face, "I couldn't. I needed answers." She looks back up at me. "Why did you break into the Institute? Did you come to find me?"

I shake my head. "I didn't remember you either. Nothing. It was all blank. When I saw you, it came rushing back to me." I take her hand again. "If I'd known Tesla had you—that you even existed—nothing would have stopped me from finding you."

"Flynn," she cuts in. "Flynn saved me from the fire. He brought me to the Institute."

"One of our Hollows died during a mission a few days ago. She was my friend—more than. When I heard there might be a piece of tech in the Institute that would allow me to go back and save her, I had to go for it." Ember sits back, silent, so I continue. "Her name is Stein. I know getting her back could create a huge paradox, so I needed something to hold the paradox and the stream together. With the Dox, I can save her."

"The Dox is one of the untested theories we learned about in training," Ember says. "Tesla created it, but he never tested it. It was considered too dangerous to use. If it overloads, it could blow a hole in the universe.

I mean, it could create a black hole in time itself."

I shrug. "It'll work," I say with more confidence than I feel.

"Can I see it?"

"Sure, I guess." I hesitate. Nobel shoots me a look, and I can practically read his mind. Just because I trust her doesn't mean they do. She's a stranger at best and an enemy at worst. The look on Nobel's face tells me he doesn't want her anywhere near the Dox. Still, I nod to him, and he reluctantly leaves the room to retrieve it from his lab. The best way to get the others to trust her is going to be to let her earn it.

Nobel reappears a few tense minutes later with the Dox in hand. It has a clear glass outer shell with an intricate brass machine inside that reminds me of a huge lightbulb. There are gears, spokes, and coils of wire surrounding a main terminal. Small, fragile wires reach out from the center of the machine like veins, and brush the insides of the glass. When Nobel hands it to me, the coils begin to glow a subtle shade of purple.

"That's weird," Nobel says.

"Yeah." I hold it away from my body. Suddenly, it feels less like a lightbulb and more like a ticking bomb. Literally.

"Maybe you activated it," Ember says, holding out her hands for it.

"Yeah, maybe," I say, passing it to Ember. As soon as I'm no longer touching it, the light fades. Around us, everyone looks tense. Everyone, I notice, except for Gloves.

"Guess it doesn't like me," Ember jokes. "I didn't even know the Institute had a working prototype."

She hands it back to me, and I pass it back to Nobel. Ember stares at me, and then glances nervously at the others, who look visibly relieved she didn't spike it and do a touchdown dance.

"Here, why don't I show you around?" I offer. Bruce coughs, but I ignore him, helping Ember to her feet.

"I'm not a spy, you know. My friends risked everything to get me here," she says, looking away. "I hope they are okay." Her voice is almost too soft to hear. I grind my teeth.

Friends. With the enemy. My eye twitches at the thought, but I don't say anything. She runs her hand along the walls, flaking paint off beneath her fingers.

"Alexei—sorry, Lex—can I ask you a question?" she says.

"You just did, but sure."

She pulls me to a stop. "Are you happy here?"

"Yes," I answer quickly. She gives me a look. "I mean, yeah. It's not much, but it's home."

"How long have you been here?" she asks as we continue walking.

I have to think about it for a second. "About five years. Why?"

She looks away again. "You're older. The last time I saw you, you were only thirteen."

Ah. "How old are you now?" I ask. She doesn't look much older, physically, than when I last saw her; she sure doesn't look twenty-two.

"I just turned seventeen. I've only been with Tesla for about a year."

That pulls me up short. "How is that possible? We were taken at the same time."

She shrugs. "We're time travelers. Nothing happens to us in the order it should. From the moment we were taken, we were traveling different paths. Nothing is linear for us."

"This time bubble that Stewart Stills created for Hollows to exist in probably didn't help matters either."

"That's amazing. And only he can do it?"

I shrug. "Or only he knows how to do it. So far, he's the only one who's been able to pull it off. Nuts, right?"

"That's one word for it. If you're in a time bubble, how did I get in?"

That makes me pause. It's a good question. "It must be getting weaker. I'll mention it to Stills and see what he thinks."

She follows me up the stairs and onto the roof. It's almost sunset, and the sky is on fire with reds and oranges. A gust of wind blows her hair into her face. I laugh as she struggles to control it.

"That's why Mother always put your hair in ribbons." I smile at the memory.

"I hated those. They pulled."

I remember. She would sit, whining and squirming, and the second we were out of Mother's sight, she'd tug them out and hide them under the furniture. Absently, my hand goes to my pocket. I clutch the bottle caps between my fingers.

"So," she begins as I walk over to the metal tower. "Stein. She was your friend?"

I bristle and grab the first rung, pulling myself up. "Yes."

Ember follows behind, climbing upward until we're nearly at the top. "More than a friend?" she asks again.

"Yes."

She puckers her mouth.

I sigh, wishing Stein were here now.

"What was she like?" Ember asks, sitting next to me, our legs dangling off the edge of the roof.

I lean back on my elbows. "She is amazing. She's smart and strong. She never lets me get away with anything."

Ember chuckles. "I like her already."

"When she moves, it's like water, you know? And sometimes, when it's just us, she looks at me like I'm the most important thing in the world." I pause and glance over. Ember is staring at me intently. I roll my eyes. "Whatever."

But she isn't about to let it drop. "You love her."

I just nod.

As the sun dips out of sight, a slight reflection of light gleams in the distance. I point to it. "See that?"

She nods.

"That's the bubble. Sometimes, when the light hits it just right, you can see it."

"It's sort of beautiful," she offers.

I watch it until it vanishes.

We talk until the sun vanishes over the mountains, and then we have to climb back down in the dim light of the front door. She tells me about her life in Tesla, which doesn't seem as terrible as I'd imagined, and I tell her about my more glorious missions. Then I tell her about the day Stein died.

I am just finishing my tale as we reach the door to Stein's room. Ember can stay here for now. No one will bother her, and it will make me feel better knowing that that bed isn't empty, even if its rightful owner is still gone.

"I'm going to get her back. I have the Dox. We can pick up the new batch of Contra tomorrow."

She grabs me by the arm. "Lex, if you can't get the Dox to work, you are risking everything for this girl. You could tear time apart."

I look at her flatly. "I know."

She glares at me, as if to be sure I'm not going to change my mind, before she answers. "Fine. Then I'm going with you."

I pull my arm free. "No. I won't risk you. I'll go alone. It's safer that way."

She folds her arms over her chest and shoots me her unimpressed look. It's eerily similar to the one Mother used to give me when I'd bring home boxes of frogs from the creek.

"Safer for whom, exactly?" She was flowing, speaking in perfect Russian again. "If you're stupid enough to risk the whole of existence in order to rescue this girl, then I'm stupid enough to go with you."

I can't help but chuckle. "Fine."

But Stein's voice echoes in my head, ripping the smile off my face as her words come back to haunt me.

It's your funeral.

TESLA JOURNAL ENTRY: JANUARY 1ST, 1893

My group of travelers is working quite well together. Flynn (as he prefers to be called now) has decided that the traveling feels like rifting through an ocean tide. So I have decided to call them 'Rifters'. A silly thing, I suppose, but it seems to please them. They have bonded in a way I did not expect, quickly becoming akin to an extended family unit.

On the more scientific front, we have created a device that assists them in their journeys. I call it a Tether. I dare not file a patent for the device lest that thief Edison get wind and come sniffing around like a dog after scraps. The Tether combines a small charge and a powerful magnet that acts an anchor, tethering them to a specific moment in time. It took several tries to successfully use, but it does work. Next week, I plan to send my Rifters further into the future than they have ever gone. They are going to procure some equipment plans and books that I will need to move forward to my next phase of experimentation.

Also, I was able to successfully send Flynn backward six years into the past and bring him safely back. The time that elapsed while he was gone here was only moments, but he assures me that he was there many hours. In light of his success, I have begun contemplating the consequences for travel to the past and what things we must avoid. The nature of time traveling is still in its infancy. While it affords us great opportunities, it also requires we use it with great wisdom and restraint. I can't help but wonder what might happen should this ability fall into the wrong hands—the kind of damage a person could do.

EMBER
Twenty

Sleeping in a stranger's room is like wearing someone else's clothes. It feels awkward and uncomfortable, even more so considering whose room it is. Stein. Lex's girlfriend. Correction: Lex's dead girlfriend. I stare down. Somewhere in the back of my mind, I'm honestly wondering if my brother has ever been in this bed. Gagging, I tear the pillow off the bed and toss it onto the only clean spot on the floor. Under the pillow, a strip of film flutters. I pick it up. Lex and the girl with the top hat from the World's Fair are smiling and making faces in the four tiny squares.

I can't believe it. She's the same girl who almost killed me. Does that mean he was there too? I can't help but wonder how many times we'd been that close, missing each other by minute tricks of fate. I toss the photos aside.

The room itself looks like a tornado has blown through, depositing scraps of clothing on every possible surface. I have to physically restrain myself from tidying up. When I kick a lone boot under the bed, it hits something with a clunk. Curiosity gets the better of me. I get down on my hands and knees, tugging the metal box free.

My fingers hover hesitantly over the latch on the metal box. There's no lock, just the remnants of a hinge. I know I shouldn't open it. It's obviously private, but I can't help myself. Setting my jaw, I open it slowly to find my brother's face staring up at me. I lift the fragile scrap of paper where a rough sketch of Lex smirks in hard, lead lines. There's another beneath it. This time, it's just his eyes, but it's undeniably him.

I wonder if she drew them. They are really good, I admit reluctantly, biting my lip. I don't want to like her, this girl who has worked her magic on my little brother. I really want to hate her. If not for her, we could have been long gone from here by now.

I toss the pictures aside and dig through the box. Pieces of fabric, drab costume jewelry. Feathers. A set of brass knuckles. I spread the items out around me, trying to use them to somehow piece together a mental picture of her, to see someone other than the girl who served me a major league beat down at the World's Fair.

I don't like what I see.

After I put the items back, I kick the box underneath the bed. I should try to sleep, but the call of curiosity is too strong, so I walk over to the closet. There are maybe three pairs of black leather pants, a couple of black satin corsets, and one black trench coat hanging from a rope strewn wall to wall. I'm about to mumble something nasty when I spy a scrap of pink poking out from the very back. I grab it and pull. The dress in my hand can only be described as "Bubblegum Barbie

Goes to Prom." The laugh that escapes my throat is bordering on hysterical, I realize, and I slap my hand over my mouth.

It's too much. I don't want to be here. Somewhere down the hall, a train whistle blows, and I jump, throwing the dress back in the closet and slamming the door. Curling up in a little ball on the floor, I pull the Tether off my arm and twist my hair under me. My heart is racing.

After tossing and turning for what feels like hours, I crawl out of my makeshift bed and open the door. A random, dark-haired girl in goggles is sitting cross-legged across the hall from my door.

"Hey," I say, feeling awkward as she stares at me. "You my babysitter or something?"

She looks at me quizzically. "No, why? Do you need one?"

I sigh and fold my arms across my chest. The lights are low, but the air is hot and thick. Nothing about this place feels like home to me.

"Then why are you sitting out here?"

The girl shrugs. "It's quiet."

She's petite but really toned. She's wearing a black tank top under scraps of brown leather pieced together to form a sort of corset under her bust. Her grey cargo pants have been haphazardly patched over with what I assume are pieces of the Hollows' common room sofa.

"I'm Ember," I whisper, not wanting to wake anyone else who might still be sleeping.

"Sisson," she answers, pulling at the fraying hem of her pant leg.

"Do you know where my brother's room is?"

She points down the hall. "Around the corner.

226

Third door on the right."

"Thanks."

"But he's not in there," she adds as I move to step away.

I rotate back to her, trying not to be irritated. "Then where is he?"

She jerks her head down the other hall. "Half-pipe."

"Well, thanks again, I guess."

She doesn't say anything else as I walk away, but I can feel her watching me.

Somehow, I manage not to get lost making my way back to the main room. True to her word, I find Lex sitting on top of the half-pipe, his legs hanging over the edge.

"Gimme a hand," I say, taking a run at the wall. I get more than halfway up when he grabs my hand and pulls me the rest of the way.

"You couldn't sleep either?" he asks as I sit beside him.

"Nope."

He pulls a dingy jester's hat off his head and stuffs it in his pocket. "No offense, sis, but I think I'm all talked out."

I lay my head on his shoulder. "Yeah, me too."

We sit like that for a while. Neither of us talks. The room is lit, but there's no one else around. Finally, I straighten, ready to leave him to his thoughts. But when he turns to look at me, his face is red and tears have left trails down his face.

Instantly, I'm crying too. There's no sound, just the gush of emotions too fast and confusing to hold onto. He leans over, laying his head in my lap. I stroke his hair like I used to when we were little.

Our first night in captivity, after the soldiers had taken our family, my sisters and I had to share an old mattress. Alexei was supposed to be sleeping with Mama and Papa, but in the middle of the night, he'd come to me, crying silently so he wouldn't wake them. I'd held him all night, stroking his hair just like this, while a soldier glared at us from the corner of the room.

We never talked about it, and Alexei never let Papa see him cry. But during that long year, we shared many nights just like this.

"Baby, are you asleep?"

"No. And don't call me that. I'm thirteen now," he mumbles with his back to me as we lay across from each other in the dark room. The floor is cold under me, and I'm sure it must be worse for him. I at least have Olga curled next to me. He's all alone under the threadbare old quilt.

"Do you want to come over here with us?"

He's quiet. For a second, I think he's fallen asleep. But just as I'm about to roll over, he stands, wrapping his only blanket over his arm. He folds it out across Olga and me, curling in beside me. "I know you aren't a baby anymore, Alexei. But you'll always be my baby brother. No matter how big you get." Exhaustion rolls over me, and I yawn. "I'll always be here for you. No matter what."

"Promise?" he asks, only a slight tremble in his voice. Down the hall, the sounds of heavy boots march down the stairs. The guards are ending their shift. It'll be morning soon.

"I promise."

It feels so strange now, those memories. I wanted them so badly, but at the same time, part of me wishes

I could forget. How pathetic is that?

* * *

I've just barely closed my eyes and settled in to rest when the gas lamps on the wall flare bright red. The sound of boots stomping past my door makes me jolt upright. I'm not sure how long I've been asleep, but someone has covered me with a scratchy wool blanket, which I immediately toss aside. When I stand, it takes me a full minute to get my bearings. Just as I step forward, the door flies open and Lex pokes his head in.

"Um, Ember? I think you have a guest. Better go claim him before Bruce shoots him with the cannon."

I practically fly down the hall and into the main room, where Ethan is handcuffed to the support rail beside the half-pipe.

"Two intruders in two days," Bruce grumbles. "Did someone put out the welcome mat?"

Beside him, two young boys I don't recognize chuckle. Lex shoots them a stern glare.

"Is he yours?" Lex leans over and whispers.

But I'm already moving. How could I possibly miss someone so much in such a short span of time? I rush him, wrapping my arms around him and squeezing him until he has to tap out.

"Can't. Breathe," he chokes.

His non-cuffed arm wraps around my waist and pulls me tight to his body. Now I'm the one who can't breathe. Pulling back just enough that our foreheads are still pressed together, I inhale the familiar scent of him.

"What are you doing here?" I ask, not really caring.

I'm just so glad he is.

"I told you I'd come for you," he answers, raking his fingers through my hair and sending tingles down my back.

"It's only been a day," I whisper in a weak excuse for protest.

He straightens, adjusting his vest. "As soon as I saw you vanish, I knew I couldn't let you go alone. I left almost right after you did." Grinning guiltily, he adds, "I know I said I'd wait, but I just couldn't."

I should be upset that he didn't do as I asked, but it's really hard to be angry with him looking at me like that.

"Who is he?" one of the Hollows interrupts.

"What does he want?" a girl with frizzy ginger curls asks.

From the hall behind me, Sisson enters the room. "Who's the new guy?"

"Yes, who are you and why are you groping my sister?" Lex calls from the corner of the room, where he's picked up a mean-looking katana.

I roll my eyes, and Ethan clears his throat.

"His name is Ethan," I answer loud enough for the room full of onlookers to hear. "And he's my... he's mine. He's mine." I say the last words with my eyes locked on his, and when they glint in delight, I know I'm right. He's mine.

"Ember, take a step back, please," Lex says, his voice tight as he moves toward us, sword still in hand.

"Relax, Lex. He's with me. He's not a bad guy."

"He's the guy from the pier," Lex says, pointing the katana at Ethan. "The one who nearly killed me. You want what? Us to kiss and make up? I don't think so."

"You mean like how your girlfriend *tried to light me on fire* at the World's Fair?"

"Besides, you aren't really my type. No offense," Ethan chimes in.

"Not helping," I mumble out the corner of my mouth.

Lex mumbles, "She didn't know who you were. To me. She just… I mean, come on. Really not the point."

"But you, knowing who Ethan is to me, would still threaten him?" I glare, folding my arms across my chest. Lex frowns.

"I say we take him downstairs and let some of Nobel's machines have their way with him," Bruce says with a big grin.

I point at him. "I'd like to see you try."

At this point, things get a little out of hand. Some scrawny dude grabs me by the arm and pulls me into the crowd, yelling, "Get him, Lex."

I dart to the side, punch him in the throat, and sweep his legs out from under him. The burly one moves toward me, but before he can take two steps, Ethan leaps onto his back, putting him in a choke hold. His brass cuffs are still dangling from the pipe. I laugh. He's like Houdini but with better hair.

No one moves to the burly one's defense, but Lex throws the sword. It narrowly misses both of them and impales the far wall with a twang. "Get off him," Lex orders, his voice calm but stern. Ethan glances over to me. Then, seeing my nod, he lets go. The burly one drops to his knees, and Ethan kicks him forward.

Ethan glares at Lex with fire in his eyes. "If your friend ever touches Ember like that again, I'll rip his arms off. How's that?"

Lex swings his gaze to the one who grabbed me. "You won't have to."

Ethan tries to step around Lex, moving toward me, but Lex stops him with a backhand to the chest. "I still don't trust you."

At this point, I erupt into Russian. "Lex, leave him alone."

He just stares at me, a tic working in his jaw. Finally, he steps aside. Ethan reaches me in an instant. He takes my hand and pulls it to his mouth, kissing my fingers.

Lex looks like he might vomit but turns away.

"How did you get here, anyway?" I ask.

Ethan reaches into his pocket and pulls out a Peacekeeper. It's wearing a tiny steel collar, and most of its limbs have been removed. Only one little leg is still twitching.

A man in a train-shaped wheelchair rolls into the room. I vaguely remember him from my own arrival. Gloves, I think his name is. Personally, I'd have gone with Wheels.

"I'll take that," he says, holding out his hand. Ethan glances at me, and I nod. He hands it over, and then rakes his hand through his blond hair.

"Might as well put up a sign," Lex mumbles, spreading his hands through the air. "Secret lair—this way." He turns back to me. "You expecting anyone else we should know about?"

Looking at Ethan, I mouth, "Kara?" He frowns but shrugs.

I bite my bottom lip, and Lex throws his hands in the air. Pointing at Ethan and me, he growls. "Great. You two, with me."

Stuffing his hat over his unruly hair, he leads us up to the roof. We spill out into the midday sun.

A feeling of peace washes over me as the light warms my face. At least until Lex spins, his finger inches from Ethan's face.

"Why are you here?"

Ethan frowns, and I can almost read his mind. Lex is gimpy thanks to the fake leg. He's alone. No one can hear us up here. If this were a tactical situation, he'd be toast by now. But Ethan takes a deep breath and points to me.

"I'm here for her. So back off."

Lex snorts and steps back. He pushes his hand into his pocket and pulls out a handful of bottle caps. He rubs them between his fingers and squeezes his eyes shut. I reach into my own pocket, and then walk over to him.

"Here." I hold out my hand. "Ethan found it in the vault. He gave it to me after you left. I've been holding onto it for you."

He laughs dryly, taking the metal disc. "I remember when you gave me these," he says to me. He looks away, over the ledge and toward the woods.

Reaching back in my mind, I try to bring the memory out, but it's blank. I shake my head. "I don't remember. I'm sorry. I wish I did."

He doesn't look at me. "No, you don't. It was the day our family died."

I swallow hard. And here I thought all my memories had been restored. The realization that there are still gaps hits me like a punch in the stomach. "Tesla did something to me. Made me forget."

He looks at me now. "No. It's the stream. None of

us remember back beyond our first rift."

I sigh. "No. I started having these dreams. Memories. They took them away. And I..." I pause, unable to swallow past the lump in my throat, "I let them. Lex, I'm so sorry." I reach out to touch his arm, but he flinches away.

"It's not your fault," he mumbles, climbing down. "Tesla did this." He looks at me, rage cutting canyons between his eyes. "He has to pay."

I take a deep breath. "Lex, Tesla isn't the bad guy here. Sure, his methods are—"

"Are you kidding me? How is Tesla not the bad guy? He took you away from me."

I snap back, "Actually, if he'd had his way, we'd both have ended up in the same place, at the Institute. It was your friends down there that separated us. You wanna blame someone for that, blame them."

He stomps off before turning back to me, pointing to the building under our feet. "Those people are my friends. They have my back."

I take a step toward him, but he cocks his head, glaring at me.

"Lex, they may be your friends, but they aren't the good guys here. Tesla taught us to protect the time stream. All he wants is to keep your friends from doing too much damage. He wants to help people."

The look on his face is stunned disbelief. "Help people? Are you kidding me? The only person Tesla wants to help is himself. You know why there's so many of us and so few of you?"

I don't say anything because I'm not sure where he's going.

He continues. "Because Tesla dumps his cast-offs

in the stream. Alone and scared. He just leaves them to fend for themselves. We are the ones who pick them up. We take them in and give them a home. A safe place."

"All you do is steal things and screw with history."

"Yes, we steal. We steal things no one will miss to keep food on the table and coal in the furnace. And as for screwing with time, yeah, we do. So what? Who says time is better off without being tweaked here and there?"

"Tesla says. He can predict how your actions will affect people and—"

He cuts me off again. "And you trust him why?"

I open my mouth to say something, but I'm honestly not sure how to respond to that. We trust him because we are taught to. Because he tells us he's right. I look to Ethan, who is standing behind me, looking much calmer than I feel.

"What did you do with the plans?"

Lex shakes his head. "What plans?"

"The plans you stole from VonWeitter?"

I look back to Lex. Ethan's calm seems to be rubbing off on him. He pops his neck and waves us over to the back of the building. We look over the edge to see three Hollows in the backyard, assembling something.

"We used them. We needed to build a solar collector that could function inside the time bubble to supplement the coal. It's getting harder and harder to bring enough into the Tower to keep all the rooms warm."

Scooting closer to me, he adds, "Plus, this device was never supposed to be invented."

Now I'm confused. "What do you mean?"

"I mean, this device never existed. However VonWeitter came up with the plans, it wasn't ever supposed to happen. We didn't change anything. Not this time."

"He lied to us," Ethan says softly. He looks at me, his mouth set in a line. "You see, don't you, Ember? It's been a lie. All of it. Tesla's noble mission, our training. All of it was a lie." His face is so sad, so full of regret and disappointment, that I want to close my eyes so I don't have to see it.

Shaking my head, I look back to Lex. "And how do you know what's true? How do you know Gloves isn't the one lying?"

"I trust him," he says hesitantly.

"Well, I trust Tesla," I say just as hesitantly.

With a frustrated groan, he sits on the ledge and chucks the caps into the air.

Ethan steps back from the wall. "Maybe the truth is somewhere in between. I say we get to the bottom of it once and for all."

"After we get Stein." Lex nods.

"After we go get Stein," I agree.

* * *

"This is a really bad idea," Ethan says, sitting on the edge of the half-pipe beside me with our legs dangling over. Lex has gone off to gather the last bits of what we are going to need for the rift. His friend Nobel stripped Ethan of his Tether and Babel Stone ring earlier, and now we are alone.

I swallow and lean back on my palms. He's right.

It's stupid. A suicide mission. The repercussions will be... well, let's say not pretty. Best-case scenario, Lex pulls it off, saves Stein, and we end up with what? Two Lexes? What if he alters everything that happens after her death, including finding me, and it's all erased or, worst case, potentially punches a hole in the fabric of time? All valid points that I've made only to have him dismiss my warnings with one word.

Dox.

I don't realize I'm chewing my bottom lip until Ethan reaches up and pulls it free with his thumb. "I know," is all I can say, because he's absolutely right. And if there were any way to stop him, I'd do it. But there's not. There's no card I can play that he won't trump. "We just have to hope the Dox works."

Ethan doesn't say anything, but I can feel the tension radiating off him. I want to be angry at Lex for the choice he's made, but I can't. Not really. If it were me, if Ethan were the one dead, I'd burn the world to the ground to get him back. It's neither the right choice nor the rational choice. But that's love for you. Leaning over, I rest my head on his shoulder. He wraps an arm around me.

"We could stop him. Steal the Dox," he offers. But I know it's no use.

"He'd find some other way. Or he'd just go. He was never very good with restraint," I say with a faint smile. No one ever told Alexei no, not his whole life. He was the Tsesarevich. He got what he wanted, period. It's a trait he's never outgrown.

"It's just so monumentally stupid."

I let out a deep breath. "It's what I would do."

Ethan snorts. "No. You'd do what's right. You

always do."

"No, if it were me, and it were you, I'd do it just the same."

He tips my chin up so I'm looking into his eyes. Instantly, I'm melting. The room is hot and my stomach is tight. My breath catches as he gazes down at me. Something about the way his eyes droop, the way his cheeks flush with color, makes my heart race. I'm shaking all over. All I want is for him to lower his lips to mine, but it's as if he's frozen. I don't know how long we stay that way, locked in that moment, before I can't take it anymore.

Closing the distance between us is as natural as breathing. His arms are around me, and my fingers are clasped behind his neck. He tastes salty and sweet. At first, he just lets me kiss him, but suddenly, his calm breaks like a dam and he's kissing me back. Desperately, deeply. His hands are everywhere—in my hair, on my face. I can't breathe. I'm drowning in him. Slowly, the urgency wanes, leaving us in a soft embrace. I pull back first, only to gasp for air.

His lips are swollen, and he's looking at me from under his lashes.

"I just had to do that. In case I don't get another chance," I mumble, half apologetically.

He grins wildly. "Oh, you'll get another chance. I'll make sure of that."

He leans forward again but before our lips touch, a train whistle sounds, driving us apart.

"Anastasia?"

It's Gloves in his weird wheelchair.

"It's Ember. And yes?"

"If you have a moment, I'd like to talk to you. In

private." He eyes Ethan, who shrugs.

Ethan presses a quick kiss to my forehead. "I'll go find your brother."

Once the room is clear, I slide down the ramp. Gloves motions to the ratty couch.

"I wanted to talk to you, too," I begin, folding my legs under me as I sit, leaning against the arm of the sofa. His chair blows a column of steam and clicks to a stop as the engine dies. "My brother. Why did you bring him here? Why target us?"

He takes a deep breath, folding his gloved hands in his lap. Oh, I get it. *Gloves.*

"You and Lex are special. Hmm, perhaps we should go to my office so that I might begin at the beginning."

I wave my hand in a "go on" gesture, and then follow him into a smoke-filled room. He motions for me to take a seat on an old bench.

"I would appreciate your discretion with the information I'm about to give you."

I hesitate. The idea of keeping secrets doesn't sit well with me. "I can't promise. But, I'll do my best. I do need you to tell me the truth about Tesla and why you broke off from the Institute." The party line has never sat well with me. They told us it was because they were selfish and wanted to pillage history, but the more I begin to understand Tesla and what he's capable of, the less sure I am about his motives. About any of their motives.

He nods, as if that's good enough. "Tesla had an assistant. The first Rifter. He discovered her abilities after a freak lab accident. Once he realized what she could do, he was like a man obsessed. Long story short, he found us. The originals. There were five. He mapped our family trees, using our genealogy like a map to discover the source of our abilities. And he found a common thread."

He pauses as footsteps pass by, and then he goes on. "A royal thread, as it happened. He began experimenting. Trying to gather as much sample DNA from the line as possible. He also identified people with high potential for the gene. Your family was on the short list."

I shift, bringing my legs up to my chest. "So why Lex? Why not Mother or Father?"

"Tesla convinced a like-minded man to help him. A man from your time. A man with access to you and your family. A man of science."

"Rasputin." The name slithers past my lips like a ghostly snake, sending shivers up my skin. He was my friend. Confidant. The only person I trusted other than my own family. Violent memories crash to the front of my mind. Him taking blood from Lex and me. Trying to cure Lex's hemophilia. The transfusions. Him brushing my hair. Singing folk songs. Bile rises in my throat like acid.

Him being dragged away in chains. Mother ushering us away with tears in our eyes.

"Yes. He was working for Tesla."

I don't know what to say, so I settle for biting down on my lip. "Of your siblings, Tesla felt only you and your brother showed enough potential to warrant training. By this time, I, along with a few of the others—disgusted by his growing obsession—had gone our separate ways. But we had a spy. She told us about his plans for you and your brother. She died getting us that information."

I sit back and let the sofa engulf me. There are too many words, and, at the same time, no words at all that can help any of this make sense to me.

"Ember, we tried to get you both. It was our intent but—"

"But what?" I croak out.

"But you stopped me."

I shake my head, racking my brain for some memory of seeing him that day. "I don't remember that."

He waves his hand, dismissing my claim. "Yet you did. You brought your brother to me. Told me to take him. You called me by name."

He lets those last words hang between us until I can fully absorb them. "Wait. That means I knew you. Me. Not the past me, but *right now* me. I was there."

He stares at me, as if silently challenging me to put the pieces together. It's like with the first key. At some point, I go back to that day, and I make sure Lex is taken by the Hollows. Why would I do that? It doesn't make any sense.

"But it's a Fixed Point. Flynn told me. I can't go back and change what happened."

With the flick of a switch, his train engine growls back to life. He tosses a handful of coal into a chamber under his seat, and it bellows steam from the pipes in the back. "Which can only mean one thing. You aren't changing anything. You will go back again because you always have. Your actions are part of the Fixed Point, so maybe it's not naturally occurring. Maybe, just maybe, you create it."

"But, if that's true, then I can change it. I can make things different this time," I blurt out without really

241

thinking. I would never choose to separate myself from Lex. Not if I could help it. But if I don't, what if he dies? What if Tesla gets us both? Then, none of this—right now—ever happens. A sharp pain explodes behind my eyes as my brain struggles to process everything. All the possibilities and repercussions. A paradox.

"But, what I wanted to say to you is this. I know you don't trust us, and that you probably have every intention of leaving here as soon as possible. But, you are welcome to stay for as long as you like."

"Thanks, I guess."

"And as for changing your past, well, I suppose you can try," Gloves says as he spins and chugs away, quite literally turning his back on me.

The migraine in my head is pounding like a jackhammer, and I feel pure rage bubbling up inside me. In five long strides, I cross the room, and slam the door behind me as I leave. Then, not quite ready to let go of my rant, I stomp off to find my brother.

TESLA JOURNAL ENTRY: APRIL 30TH, 1893

The Tesla Institute is fully functional now. It is my crowning glory. The computer is slower than I would like and not as clever as I am, which sometimes prevents it from reaching its full potential. I have considered using a human interface, but that would mean the loss of one of my travelers, and I am loathe to do that. Two have already been injured to the point they can never again leave this place.

like Rasputin, they have become too disfigured, too much machine to blend in with any time period. They will be my teachers now, help me groom my travelers.

I am sending Flynn to retrieve the Romanov children, one at a time if need be, but I am hoping to get at least the boy tonight. It is a good thing that Rasputin is so unrecognizable, so as not to scare or shock the boy. It was he, after all, who orchestrated the death of the family. He who betrayed them. But that is forgivable, because it was before he truly understood their importance—before he understood the secrets they carried in their blood.

LEX
Twenty-one

Nobel's lab is a mixture of wonder and mess. One time, he got wound around the axel when a group of girls organized his lab for Valentine's Day. His idea of perfect organization is piles. So, from then on, his lab became "by invitation only," like a black-tie event at a prestigious science museum.

I like coming to the lab. It's quiet here and always smells of sulfur and brass. Watching Nobel work on his twisted metal devices helps clear my mind.

"Here, check this out," Nobel says. "The Dox wasn't the only thing taken from the Institute. I also pinched a small bottle of a rare herbs and metals. Its healing potential is out of this world. Lex, this is how I'm going to regrow your leg."

Nobel hands me the bottle. I hold it up to a Bunsen burner that is boiling some red liquid in a glass beaker. The brown glass bottle looks like it holds fine sand.

"How is this going to regrow my leg?" I ask.

Nobel points to the glass on the lab table. "See that petri dish?"

I scan the glassware and find the petri dishes. Most of them have pink gelatin in the bottom. Some have pink gelatin with a dark brown carpet of mold growing on it.

"I think I found it, yeah."

"Great. Now take one with the spores on it to the dissecting microscope and look at it."

I take the petri dish and go to the end of the table to where the microscope sits. "Now what?"

Nobel explains how to use the microscope while he tightens the rivets on one of his brass contraptions. I eventually get it focused. "Describe to me what you see," Nobel says without taking his eyes off his screwdriver.

"Well, I see a field of plant-looking things."

"Okay, good. Follow one stalk all the way up and tell me what's blossomed at the top."

"It looks like a brown daisy or something. There are tons of them."

"What do the petals look like?" Nobel asks.

I adjust the scope to a higher power and focus the knobs again. What I see takes my breath away. It's amazing. "The petals are tiny gears."

"Great! Hand me that one."

I hold the petri dish in my hands like I just captured a dragonfly and pass it to Nobel. He puts down the screwdriver and takes the dish from me. Taking two fingers, he scrapes them into the gel dish.

"Pull up your pant leg," Nobel says. Like peeling the skin off a robot, I lift my pant leg and reveal the brass mechanical prosthetic. Nobel slings the gel spore mixture from his finger onto my fake leg as if he has something nasty on his hand. Immediately, he wipes his hands on his already soiled lab coat. He takes another scoop of the gel to clean out the petri dish and flings it again. I watch where the pink slime lands. He replaces the surgical mask that has been hanging down around his neck and sits on the edge of the lab bench.

The two spots of pink-and-brown goop start to transform.

"What's happening?" I ask.

"Just watch," Nobel says as he folds his arms.

Slowly, the two spots start to bubble before hardening into a skin-like substance. "It worked," Nobel whispers to himself.

I now see what it is. This is the new leg. This is what Nobel was talking about. I now have two pieces of skin fused to the metal on my brass leg.

"The only thing I need to do is take the pressure gauge off and cover it with this stuff. The skin pieces will filter moisture from your blood and create steam to be pushed through the pistons so your leg can work. With it contained as a closed system, you won't need to have the gauge anymore. It will be as close to a new appendage as I can get," Nobel says. And I can see an apology in his eyes. "You still won't have any sensations in the leg."

"I guess it's a good thing I'm hot-blooded," I say. "Thank you, bro."

"I have to synthesize more before we can cover your whole leg," Nobel says, as if he's embarrassed that he hasn't done it already.

I scratch the new patches of skin as if I have hives, but they don't come off. While I'm poking and prodding the skin pieces, I don't see the other Tesla kid come into the lab.

"Hey, guys," Ethan says.

"You weren't invited down here." I don't even look up. He's like a lost puppy. Not one of those cute puppies, though. He's one of those mangy street puppies that follow you home.

"Lex," Nobel says. "It's okay."

"And if you want me to tolerate you, not *like*, I said *tolerate*, then you need to leave."

Ethan steps close—too close—and gets in my face. "What is your problem, man?"

I pick up a screwdriver from the workbench, twirl it in my fingers, and poke him in the chest. "My problem is you. You and your little Tesla buddies kidnapped my sister and kept her from me all this time. So call me crazy, but I don't buy for one second that you are here because you care about her." I toss the screwdriver aside and mutter, "You're probably a Tesla spy."

I feel his hand on my shoulder. It takes everything I have not to punch him in the face as he pushes me slightly.

"Hey, I'm the one who broke her out. And don't you dare give me any crap about keeping her from you. I've been keeping her safe. What have you been doing? Screwing around here and getting tattoos? You couldn't be bothered to come after her, could you?"

His words sting, and anger boils under my skin. He turns his back to me and continues, "She's not here ten minutes, and you have her running all over hell and back trying to defy the laws of nature. Oh, and that's after she risked her life to find you. Some brother you turned out to be."

I lunge for him, but Nobel steps between us.

"You don't know anything, you freaking weasel. Ember is my sister, and I'll take care of her. She'd be better off without you," I growl over Nobel's shoulder. "Where is she, by the way?"

Ethan waves his hand, gesturing to the room around us. "Your buddy wanted to have a private chat with her."

"Play nice," a voice in Russian says from behind us.

"Hey, beautiful," Ethan says.

Ethan looks my way and plants a kiss on my sister's lips, wrapping his lanky arms around her like he's just won a giant teddy bear at a carnival.

"Your boyfriend is about to get the living crap beat out of him," Nobel warns her, though his voice is more amused than I'd like.

Ethan releases Ember and glares at me. "Oh, I'd love to see him try."

That sounds like a pretty good idea to me. "Let's go, then."

"That's enough, boys. I'm going to drown in all the testosterone," Ember says, pinching the bridge of her nose like she has a headache. Instantly, the desire to pummel Ethan fades, and I'm left wondering what Gloves said to her that has made her look so pale.

"You okay, sis?"

She sets her jaw and glares at me. It's a face I know all too well. One that says *don't poke the bear or it'll rip your arms off.* It was a face our mother made sometimes. It used to scare the crap out of me. Still kind of does, actually.

I pull my jester's hat down a little more. "I'm sorry," I say.

She crosses the room, puts her arms around my

neck, and hugs me tightly. "I need you to be nice," she whispers, her voice exhausted.

"I know. But I don't trust him."

She sighs and pulls back. "I know. But I need you to trust me."

I look over her shoulder. Nobel is tinkering with something on the desk, trying to hide a smirk, and Ethan is standing there, looking confused. "Can I hit him, just once?" I whisper.

She grins.

I take that as a maybe.

I head back to my room, grabbing my gear and a spare shirt for Ethan. It's a black T-shirt, nothing as nice as what he has on, but it'll have to do. I'm not sure exactly why he gets under my skin so badly. I ball up the shirt and stuff it under my arm. It might have something to do with the monumental butt kicking he laid on me the last time we met. Or it might be the way he looks at my sister. It's arrogant and possessive. Like she's his. I sigh. It might also be the fact that she looks at him the same way. If she has to choose between us, I can't help but wonder which of us would win out.

Ugh. Now I'm just being stupid. I grab my cane, wishing Nobel could have perfected the gear spores so that we could grow my leg back before the mission. This fake leg will slow me down, and with only half a team, I can't afford anything going wrong. I have to leave some of my best people here in case more unexpected visitors show up.

I argue with myself on the way down to the common room. Should I just leave Ember and Ethan here? Ethan was right about one thing. She came for me. She risked her life and the lives of her friends in order to get here. And as for Ethan, well, he could at least be counted on to protect Ember. I suppose he was right about that, too. It's really just my selfishness that took her up on her offer to help. I can't stand the idea of not having her close.

* * *

When I am done getting my stuff, I head to the common area to meet Ethan and Ember. Most of the Hollows are still asleep. Nobel and Journey are on the half-pipe, saying good-bye it looks like. Ink Spot is doing some rifting stripes for Chernobyl, who rifted back twenty minutes ago. He looks like he got into some gnarly stuff.

"Hey, Chernobyl," I say, walking over to them. "What happened out there?"

"Aw man, it was like a storm out there. It was the first time that anyone had rifted into the American Civil War. We weren't taking anything this time. Gloves wanted us to follow the train that was carrying the Union's payroll, all in gold of course. When we got there, most of the soldiers were gone. In their place were these little dome-headed, geared creatures that tried to take us out."

I look down at my leg. "Those are Gear Heads. One of them sawed off my leg."

"Those guys did that?" Chern asks. "I had no idea, sorry."

Ink Spot slaps him on the neck to indicate that he's done. Chern flinches. "Well, I got to go," he says. "Gotta return this stuff to the lab. I'll catch you later."

"Okay," I mumble, staring at my geared prosthetic.

I walk to where Nobel, Ember, and Ethan are sitting. They are congregated in the same spot we were sitting earlier.

"Hey, something is going on. Chernobyl said he ran into a bunch of Gear Heads during a mission."

"Not a surprise. The Peacekeepers can track Contra. That's how they find you guys in the stream," Ethan says.

"Yeah, but we'd never rifted there before. They predicted where we would be and got there before us. That team walked right into a trap."

Ember puts her hand on my shoulder. "Lex, I don't mean to sound harsh, but has it occurred to you that your friends are stealing? The Peacekeepers were trying to prevent them from taking something that didn't belong to them."

I shrug her hand off. I'm about to say something nasty when Ethan cuts me off.

"I'm worried more about the *how* than the *why* right now. This means they've somehow figured out how to use Tesla's predictive algorithms to predict where the Hollows will strike. This will make it very hard for you and your friends to smash and grab. They could have these things waiting for you anywhere at any time. Always one step ahead."

"True," Nobel agrees. "So our immediate problem is finding a way to disable several Gear Heads at a time. Like some sort of electromagnetic pulse?"

Ethan nods, "That might work. You could try to isolate the correct harmonic resonance to shatter their glass domes—"

"It doesn't matter now," I cut them him off. "We're wasting time. We are going to save Stein."

"All right," Nobel interrupts. "Let's go. Here, take these." He hands each of us a small green pill.

"You got the Dox?" Ember asks, rolling the Contra between her fingers.

"Sure thing," I answer, tapping my pack.

"What are these?" Ethan asks, holding the green pill up to the light like some rare jewel.

"This is how we rift," I answer. "No fancy tech and no practice missions. Take this baby and you'll be hooked on rifting for life."

Ethan looks to Ember, who shrugs. They both remove their Tethers and toss them on the table.

"Okay." She pops the capsule in her mouth. "Let's do this. We just rift from *right here?*"

"Yep. Claymore set the date and time of the mission in these capsules so we can show up at the right time, just before Stein falls. So just pop the pill and hold on tight."

I adjust my jester's hat, put the capsule on the back of my tongue, and swallow.

* * *

Rifting is second nature to me now. I can feel the Contra pumping in my veins, making me lighter than air but also more solid than I could ever be in real life. Colors swirl, and as we approach the spot where Stein dies, I can feel the stream thinning. It's like pressing against tissue paper. I push forward, and the stream shreds around me. I'm spit out onto the sandy ground.

We have come out just behind an outcropping of rocks. I peek over them as the others orient themselves. Ember and Ethan look a little pale, but otherwise fine. I see the blimp overhead, cut ropes flailing in the wind. To the right, I see two Gear Heads, the red liquid sloshing around in their domed-heads as they scramble up the loose rocks in our direction.

"We've got to move," I order.

Everyone follows me as I manage my way down through the boulders where the blimp is still tied. Two Gear Heads have taken position. I see Stein trying to distract them. For a second, the urge to run to her is overwhelming. I am barely able to keep my feet planted.

Then I see myself.

Stein screams. The Gear Heads have pushed her over the edge of the cliff.

My alternate self runs to the cliff. Tripping on the tether, he falls, fighting off Gear Heads while grabbing for Stein. Another crazy little geared-ninja rolls agilely to the side and takes its position on my calf. I wave my hand, giving the others the signal to intervene.

Like a horde of barbarians, we rush the cliff. Ethan and Nobel busy themselves by smashing whatever Gear Heads they can get a hold of. There are more of them than I remember.

"Stein, look at me," the other Lex orders. He screams, and I remember why. I can almost feel the muscles tearing under his skin. As if by reflex, I bring my hand to my own shoulder and squeeze to make sure it isn't happening to *me*.

"Lex, please don't let go," Stein pleads.

Breaking into a sprint, I run as fast as my leg will allow, but neither has seen me, seen us. Ember and Nobel rush past me. Ember lunges for the cliff, grabbing Stein with two hands. Ethan is only half a second behind her, clutching Stein by the back of her shirt. Nobel attacks the Gear Head preoccupied with greedily cutting off my leg. He shoves a screwdriver into the base of its clear dome skull. Sparks fly, and it hisses like a ticked-off snake. Nobel pries the pincers from the other Lex's calf muscle and throws it to the side. It lands, in a heap, against some rocks like a broken toy. Nobel is pulling the other Lex away from the cliff as he flails, confused by what is happening. I dive in beside him, grabbing the hand he only just let go of. Ember, Ethan, and I pull Stein up the rocky cliff face to safety. Stein lies there, breathing heavily, looking to me, then to the other me, and back again. Ember and Ethan stand up. Stepping back, she clutches herself to him. He wraps his arms around her, kissing the top of her head. Nobel makes a quick tourniquet for the other Lex's leg. I lie by Stein, wishing I could hold her like Ethan is holding Ember. But I don't reach out to her. She's looking confused and a little scared, her attention rapt on where the other me is being patched up.

"Stein," I say gently. "Look at me."

Stein slowly turns her head in my direction. Our eyes connect, and she throws her arms around my neck. I breathe in the smell of her and close my eyes.

I take her hand, and we stand. Nobel crouches by the side of the other Lex, putting pressure on the leg wound while that Lex goes in and out of consciousness.

"What's going on?" Stein finally asks. She can do the math. Two strangers, one Nobel, one Stein… and two Lexes.

"We came to save you, Stein," I say, brushing her cheek with my fingertips. "I stole some tech from Tesla so I could come back for you."

Stein looks down at my leg, then back up at me like I'm some kind of freak. She drops my hand and backs away, going to Nobel's side. The shock is fast and hard. It feels like I've just been sucker punched, and it's hard to breathe. I tense, squaring my shoulders and trying to keep my expression neutral.

She bends over the other Lex. "Nobel, would you be so kind as to fill in the blanks for me? I feel like I may have missed some minor details."

"Lex and I came back to save you, just like he said."

Stein frowns, pointing at me. "I'm gonna need more than that."

I walk over to them. My leg hisses at Stein as if it doesn't approve of her.

"You died. You fell off the cliff, and I got my leg sawed off by a Gear Head. But I didn't want to lose you. I couldn't lose you. So I—we—came back to save you."

"Nobel, help me up," the other Lex demands.

Nobel and Stein each hold out a hand and pull him to his feet.

He limps forward, looking me over.

"Oh yeah. This can't be good," he says with a laugh.

It's strange. It's like looking in a mirror, only... not. This can't be good. "Yeah, well, you think that's weird. I never thought I'd see myself with a leg again, albeit a mangled one."

I also never would have thought in a million years that I'd have to compete with myself for my own girlfriend. I shake my head. "I have *got* to think these things through better."

The alternate Lex turns around to look at the

strangers in his periphery.

"Anya?" he asks, stumbling toward her.

"Oh, yeah. I forgot about that. So, our sister is alive, too," I say with a shrug, still staring at my alternate self, half wondering if can just toss him off the cliff.

As if reading my mind, Stein looks at me and glares.

Ember steps between us, blocking me from view.

"But, how are you here? I thought you were dead." The other Lex turns to me. "The tech you used to save Stein, did you use it to save our family as well?"

The hope in his eyes is like a knife in my chest. I shake my head.

Just as the hope dies, Ember reaches him and throws her arms around him, hugging him tightly. But behind his back, her eyes are locked on mine in a silent question.

What now?

"How did you escape the fire?" he asks Ember.

"I was with the Tesla Institute," she tells him.

"Look, we should probably get out of here," the other Lex says, looking at me. "I'm getting a little lightheaded from the blood loss."

"That might be easier said than done," Ember says, pointing beyond the cliff, where the sky is moving like ripples in a pond.

EMBER
Twenty-two

Lex pulls his backpack over one shoulder and fumbles to unzip it while staring at the strange waves. In a flash of white light, the sky splits, tearing open like a burst seam. Inside the gaping wound is darkness and swirling wind. For a moment, we are safe, but then the vortex begins to pull us forward. Dust gathers toward the cyclone, giving it substance. A bolt of lightning crashes to the ground in front of it. Loose dust and small gravel rush past my boots and are eaten by the darkness.

My hair whips into my face. I glance at the others. A tornado of sand and stone taller than a building is sucking us forward. Beside me, Ethan braces himself, grabbing me with one arm and holding the other out for balance. Nobel steps up behind me, pulling me by the shoulders, while Stein wraps herself in the other Lex's arms. Lex pulls the Dox out of his pack, looks up, and sees them.

A look of unexpected pain washes across his face. Maybe no one else sees it, but I catch it, and it makes my heart ache for him. After everything he's gone through to save the girl he loves, he still might end up without her. It doesn't seem fair. I want to comfort him. But, before I can, the vacuum doubles in strength, and we all skid forward in the dirt, leaving tracks behind us. In his hands, the Dox glows faintly.

"Now what?" he asks, looking to me.

I shake my head. "I have no idea. It was never tested, remember?"

The vacuum intensifies again, and I pitch face-first into the dirt. Ethan's not far behind me. I hit the ground so hard my teeth ache from being snapped together. Ethan rolls over, covering me with his body, pinning me to the ground. Something about his weight makes me feel safer, less frantic. But there's something else, too. Another sensation I'm not completely familiar with. It's almost… wonderful, even in the chaos. It feels like, as long as we're together, everything will be all right.

"Whatever you're going to do, do it fast," Ethan orders Lex, who is violently shaking the Dox. It glows for a moment, and then fades like a jar full of dying lightning bugs. Lex is chewing on his bottom lip as perspiration beads on his face. His jester's hat is sucked off his head. He reaches back to catch it, but it's useless. It's gone. Vanishing into the void.

"Maybe we have to get it closer to the tear," Nobel chimes in from where he crouches beside me. I want to slap him. The last thing I want is for Lex to get closer to the black hole. My brother slaps the Dox with the palm of his hand. He looks to me, his eyes full of helpless frustration.

"Maybe we should have stolen the directions, too,"

he jokes uncomfortably.

It's how he hides his fear. Something he learned from our father. He looks like our father to me now. Older. Harder. And with a grim smile that tells me he doesn't expect things to end well.

Stein screams, but the sound is eaten by the split, which is now the size of a house. The other Lex has slipped from her grip and is skidding out of control toward the tear as if being pulled by an invisible rope around his ankles. His arms flail as he gropes for something to hold on to. But there's nothing. Just loose gravel and sand.

I cry out and reach for him, but he skids past me in a cloud of dust that stings my eyes and fills my mouth. Lex leaps forward, the Dox tucked under his arm, and lands on top of his other self. His prosthetic leg emits a puff of smoke and screeches to a stop, seizing up. Losing his balance, he is pulled forward, off the other boy, and they both tumble toward the swirling vortex. Lightning streaks again, so close and so bright I have to close my eyes against the light. I feel the heat of it singe my face. The scent of burnt hair is carried on the wind. When I am finally able to blink, I see Lex holding his other self up. Lightning strikes again, but this time, I force my eyes to remain open. I see the light engulf them both like the sun. For a few seconds, everything is white. When the glow fades, only one Lex remains. I look down and see his metal leg. He looks stunned, shaking his head and pressing his eyes closed with his thumb and forefinger. I can feel the pressure building. Another strike is coming any moment.

"No!" I scream.

I just got my brother back. I can't lose him now.

I turn my head to Ethan, but as usual, I don't need to tell him what I'm thinking. He just looks at me and nods. In a moment of bold desperation, we leap to our feet and lunge for my brother. Ethan grabs him first—using his momentum and the pull of the vortex—swings him around, rolling them both out of the direct path of the suction. As the boys fall, the Dox rolls free of Ethan's hands and is sucked into the air. I lunge for the fragile glass device.

I roll the Dox behind me to Nobel. He covers it with his body. Then I scramble forward, trying to stay as flat against the ground as possible, stretching until I feel the muscles in my shoulders and back tearing. I'm reaching out for Lex, trying to meet him halfway, but the gap between us is too far.

The twister bellows, a thick, hollow drum sound, and we both skid toward the mouth. Behind me, I hear Nobel call my name. Looking over my shoulder, I see he's holding up the Dox, which is glowing faintly. Nobel yells again, and I just barely catch the sound of my name as the words blow past me.

I call out to him. The word rips its way up from the bottom of my stomach and erupts out of my mouth, burning like acid. Between my tears and the hair wildly whipping around my face, I don't see Nobel crawl to my side. Eating Lex's duplicate has not satisfied the time storm. If anything, its power is still growing. I'm breathing too hard, too fast. The air is growing thin as the vacuum sucks the oxygen out from around us. Somewhere in the calmer recesses of my mind, I know it will soon engulf us all. I gasp. My lungs burn. It's like I'm breathing through a straw. No matter how I struggle, I can't get enough air in my lungs.

Nobel pats my hand, and I look over to him. The Dox is still glowing, but the closer we get to the tear, the dimmer the light becomes. Then it dawns on me.

It isn't going to work. The paradox storm is going to eat us alive. Around me, a thick fog is overtaking my vision. I force myself to calm down. Only sheer will is holding me down here. If I faint, the darkness will take me. So my body wars against itself, part wanting to relax into unconsciousness, part struggling to survive.

"I think we have to take it into the tear," Nobel yells. The strange white surgeon's mask that he normally wears has slid down around his neck, so I'm not sure if I'm actually hearing his voice or just reading his lips. Everything is fuzzy.

I nod, beginning to feel a terrifying lightness in my body. I wish I were back at the Institute, surrounded by my friends, playing in the surf with Ethan.

Nobel fights his way to his feet and is immediately pulled off balance, pitching forward onto his knees. The Dox falls from his hands, hitting the ground with a sound that echoes like the crash of lightning. It's the sound that shocks me back to my senses. The glass dome of the Dox splinters, and tiny fractures spread like spiderwebs around the container. The faint glow immediately dies.

"It's no good. We have to get out of here," I yell to Nobel, who is scant inches from the mouth of the vortex. I see him reach into his lab coat pocket, pull out the small Contra pill, and toss it into his mouth. Just before he can be sucked into the darkness, he shimmers and vanishes into the time stream. I glance behind me and see Stein, her face streaked with muddy tears. She opens her mouth to show me the green pill between her teeth.

"I'll get Lex. You get out of here!" I yell.

She hesitates, shooting me a look like, *you better*, then she swallows and is gone too.

I begin the painful crawl to where Lex and Ethan are holding on. Wiping the hair out from my eyes, I see the boys have made a kind of chain. Lex is holding the jagged rock with one arm and holding Ethan with his other hand. Ethan is scooting toward me, his free hand outstretched. In his fingers, he carefully holds a Contra.

My palms and knees are bleeding from the crawl across the stony ground. It's only a few yards, but I might as well be crossing the Sahara. I can feel blood dripping from my chin, but I'm too numb to feel the pain of my injuries. Adrenaline is pushing me forward now—a primal need to survive. I reach Ethan and wrap myself around his arm with both hands. He has to put the Contra in my mouth for me—I can't even let go with one hand for fear of being pulled away. As I draw a breath to swallow, I feel Ethan rising off the ground. Lex manages to take his own pill just before he loses consciousness. Ethan still has a hold of his hand, but we are being scooped up like kites as the vortex engulfs us. I close my eyes and feel the wind change. It's no longer the relentless sucking of the tornado; it's the sharp push of the stream on my skin. Still clinging to Ethan, I let him drag us against the current. With Lex unconscious, we are literally flying blind.

"Where are we going?" I ask, pulling myself closer to Ethan even as the wind tries to force us apart.

He jerks his head. I can just make out Nobel, who is not too far in front of us, cutting through the stream.

He vanishes, so I know we're close. I take a deep breath, preparing to purge myself from the stream just as Ethan stops. With an unspoken signal, we leap out of the stream and fall forward onto the lawn just outside of the Tower.

Nobel is standing with his back to us. I only have a moment to register his tension and the cautious stance of his body before I trip over the first corpse, sprawled lifeless on the ground.

LEX
Twenty-three

When I come to, I find myself in a smoke-filled room that immediately makes me cough. I am facedown, and I must have thrown up from a coughing fit while I was unconscious, because my cheek is wet and covered with my previously half-digested dinner. I quickly wipe off my mouth with my sleeve.

I see the palm of a hand visible through the thick smoke. My senses are coming back. I slowly reach my hand toward the palm. Who does it belong to? Where are we? Did we close the vortex? All I can feel is that something is really wrong. Suddenly, the hand closes around my index and middle fingers, and then a face emerges through the smoke.

"Lex!" Nobel says, sounding tired but relieved.

"Something is wrong," I say, shaking my head. "Where are we?"

Nobel says nothing as he looks me over for injuries.

"We need to find the others," I tell him, trying to urge his focus away from me. I'm fine. It's everyone else I'm worried about.

I sit up and see that we are just inside the door to the Tower. Smoke is billowing past us like dragon's breath.

"Where are Stein and Ember?"

Nobel points into the room. "They must be inside somewhere."

Peeling off my vest, I tie it around my face. We walk through the smoke-filled room with our hands stretched out like a pair of zombies.

We haven't walked very far before I trip over something. I fall forward, landing on a couch. Reaching down, I bring the object closer to my face.

"*Aahh!*" It's half of a Gear Head. I toss it aside like a dead rat. "Ember, Ethan, Stein!" I yell into the smoky room. Have I lost them? This can't be happening. I call out again.

"Over here," Stein calls back. "Ember's sick."

We shuffle in the general direction of her voice. The metal foot of my fake leg clanks against another Gear Head as we walk. The gears still aren't working, so with every step, I have to hobble my leg into position.

"Call out again," Nobel hollers.

"We're over here." It is Ethan this time. I exhale. At least they're all alive.

After what seems like ten minutes of navigating through the dense smoke, we finally make it to the group. Stein is bent over Ember, stroking her hair, and Ethan is looking down at both of them, his face pale and waxy. Ember is breathing, but when she looks up at me, I notice her eyes are bloodshot. She is sweating and clutching her stomach in the fetal position.

"Ember," Ethan soothes, "Lex is here now."

"Lex, I don't think those rifting pills sit well with

me," she says, squeezing her eyes closed.

"It can take some getting used to," Nobel tells her. "Ethan, are you feeling okay?"

"Yeah, I'm fine," Ethan says, but I can tell he's lying. Judging by the shade of green he's turning, he's barely keeping his stomach. I remembered the feeling all too well. Sick as a dog but too proud to let the girl see you sweat.

"Are you going to be able to make it out?"

"I think so," she answers weakly.

I crouch down. The smoke is a lot less dense near the floor. Everyone else follows suit and crouches down. Ethan helps Ember to her knees, holding her around the waist until he's sure she isn't going to fall. We crawl along the floor of the smoke-laden room until we find a wall, then we follow that to a hallway.

"Do you recognize this hallway?" Stein asks, crawling up beside me.

"No, I don't even know where we are."

She reaches up into the smoke cloud that's above us and rips something off the wall.

"Recognize this?"

Stein holds out a piece of the velvet wallpaper that lines the hallway toward Gloves' office. I recognize it. And Nobel recognizes it. We've walked down this hallway many times. I've always traced my finger along the paisley-velvet wallpaper when we're here, trying to connect the lines without removing my finger.

"Are we near Gloves' office?" I ask, already knowing the answer.

"I think we are," Stein answers. "We need to see if there's anyone still alive in there."

"What do you mean?"

Stein and Nobel exchange a glance.

"When we rifted back, there were some… bodies on the lawn. It looked like an attack," Nobel says softly.

I stop, unable to believe my ears. "Who?" I ask, my voice shaking.

"Two of ours and one Ember identified as theirs."

I want to ask more, to demand names, but now isn't the time. If anyone is still alive in here, we need to get them out. Now. We pass by what was Gloves' door. The office has been burned to a crisp. The door is lying off its hinges, and its wood is blackened and blistered, charcoaled beyond belief. But there are no remains.

I turn to Ethan. "We need to get everyone out of here." When he nods, I crawl through the wreckage without hesitation, grab a burnt piece of door wood, and use it to break the window. The old glass shatters on the first blow. I then hack away at the jagged edges so we can crawl out without getting cut.

We are able to scale our way down the side of the old stone building. Most of the rock that was quarried on site to build this tower is now covered in a green carpet of moss.

After carefully navigating each handhold and foothold, we finally jump into the out-of-control Pfitzer juniper that has been unkempt for many years. Fortunately, they provide a soft landing. The hardest part is trying to claw our way out.

Once we orient ourselves, the sight before us is unbelievable. The Tower is no longer erect. The top three-fourths is severed and tumbled back. Flames surround the stump of what remains. It reminds me of a candle left to burn out overnight. To the right of the Tower, there is a massive, armored locomotive that is covered in plants, chunks of earth, and rust. The enormous steel-plated train has clearly moved up an angled track to take down the Tower. I can imagine the train emerging from the ground to bomb the Tower to oblivion.

We run to the front of the Tower where Ethan appeared just a day ago. Stein stands stoic, looking pale and half in shock, and Ember is throwing up in the bushes. Bruce lies dead at the corner of the building. He has a hole blown in his gut. Even being half man, half kettle pot, he couldn't withstand the blast. I walk over, kneel down, and close his one good eye.

Fire has consumed a lot of the dead weeds in the courtyard along with some of the dead bodies. Even though I spent many nights purging my senses of the smell of fiery death, it all comes rushing back so fast that my eyes well up with tears. For a heartbeat, I'm paralyzed by it.

"No, no, no!" I yell, pressing my fists into my ears. "Not again!"

My second chance at a family of any kind has been burned up again. I can't go on. My good leg goes very weak, and I bend over. Am I dying? I'm hyperventilating for sure, and the anxiety has taken hold of my body like a giant Gear Head. My mind is blacking out and my eyes won't seem to open.

I don't want to go. I don't want to pass out. Don't want to die. I will not lose it. Not here. Not today. Today, these people need me. I am the leader. I am a Hollow. A burst of adrenaline surges through my body. My eyes shoot open, and my breathing becomes deep and controlled. I lift my chin to the sky.

I am a *HOLLOW*.

My brows furrow as fury surges through my veins. I stand up and take stock of the situation before me. Big mammoth train over there, dead bodies in the courtyard, and the Tower on fire. My hand slips into my pocket, searching for the bottle caps, but they are gone. My jaw muscles clench and I close my eyes, forcing myself to step back, to observe without emotion. My heart quickens when I see Sisson standing in the distance. She is darting from body to body to see if anyone is alive. A group of Hollows is bent over another body on the side steps of the Tower. I can tell it's Gloves. His train chair lays broken on its side, still chugging and chugging. His body is slumped on the stairs to the Tower. I rush to his side.

"There was a blast and we all came out," Gloves says, trying to tell me what happened despite the small bubbles of blood forming in the corners of his mouth. "Claymore went into hiding so he would be protected. Every Hollow who wasn't on a mission came out to fight. The Tower fell behind us, and then people started to appear on the outskirts of the courtyard."

Gloves eyes fall closed as he coughs up blood. His white beard is already stained crimson from the bloody spittle.

"It was Tesla," he says finally.

"They found us," I say.

Gloves continues. "We weren't ready. That train emerged from under the ground fully loaded. The artillery was too much. We couldn't hold them off. We didn't stand a chance."

"Where is Claymore?" I ask.

"He…" Gloves starts but is interrupted with a fit of bloody coughing. "He went to a safe house. Stills

269

got him out as soon as the fighting started."

Gloves' eyes flutter closed before flinging open.

"Stills!" he growls.

We look around, as we've been so focused on Gloves that we didn't realize that a large man had joined our concerned group. Ember and Ethan gasp. Stewart Stills doesn't have a face. All that sits atop his shoulders is a brass dome with two black portals for eyes. He looks like a bedpost knob with two hollow eye sockets. He doesn't hesitate. After reaching up, he extracts a speaker from the side of his head. Steam hisses out.

Is he going to deflate? I wonder.

The flat speaker is attached to four wires that stay connected to the so-called ear. Like manipulating a toy transformer, he disengages the round speaker into four distinct parts, handing the small pieces to Ember, Gloves, Stein, and me. The small pieces remind me of tiny black bits of tar hooked to wires.

"Hold them…" Gloves says with a rattling wheeze, "up to your ear."

Almost in unison, we take the wedge pieces and hold them to our ears. Stein kneels beside Nobel, sharing her speaker with him.

"Good afternoon," Stills says in a very rich British accent. "I am Stewart Stills. Consider me the property manager of secret loops in the time stream."

"You can respond any time," Gloves says, coughing again. He isn't looking good.

"I rifted back here because we are in quite a quandary. The Tesla Institute has waged war against us. We have lost many good Rifters, and now we are losing Gloves as well."

"Is Claymore with you?" I ask.

"He is at the main safe house in 1986 Los Angeles right now. We are trying to adapt a helmet like mine for him. We require Nobel's assistance."

Gloves coughs again, this time spewing droplets of blood on the side of Stein's face. She doesn't move.

"Lex," Gloves says, looking at me. "It is very important to fix this."

"Me?" Fix this? How could this ever be fixed? How could the world ever be right again?

"Yes, I am going to commission you on one last assignment."

"Okay, Gloves, anything," I say, hoping his plan includes some serious payback.

"The Dox didn't work," he says. I nod. "The tear remains open and chaos has completely consumed the time stream."

He coughs again. His breathing is becoming more labored. His eyes flutter closed for a moment too long.

"Gloves!" Ember yells, and he blinks.

"Lex, you need to rift to Tesla's lab in New York in 1898 and get the original Dox. It is your last chance to set things right. That is your last mission from me." The words rush out in one long, rattling breath. The blood drains from his face.

"No, Gloves, It won't work. We need directions or something. How do we use the Dox?"

"Notes. Tesla will have notes. Find them." He coughs and winces in pain. "They were looking for you. He said—" Gloves coughs again. "Flynn said you'd never get it to work without the key." He opens his hand, his fingers going limp. In his palm is a pile of green pills. The last of the Contra, or rather, whatever

271

didn't burn in the fire. Also in his hand is the Amber Room beetle.

Gloves' eyes close, and his chair slowly stops chugging. I put my head down and fight back the tears. Behind me, Stein rubs my back in slow circles. I grab the pile of Contra and the beetle from Gloves' hand and stand up, wiping the moisture from my eyes before anyone can see it.

Stills kneels down and closes Gloves' eyes. He then taps on the side of his polished brass dome. We respond by putting the small black speakers back up to our ears.

"We need you to complete this last mission," Stills says. "There is a key, a missing piece to making the Dox work properly."

"A key?" Ethan shouts, pulling his hands through his hair. "Are you kidding me? How did you miss that?" He looks at me angrily. I step forward, more than happy to go a few rounds with him right now, but Ember pushes between us.

"What key?" she asks. "What does it look like?"

Stills describes it and Ember turns, putting a hand on Ethan's chest.

"It's my key. First key."

Stills holds out his brass-gloved hand.

"I don't have it. I didn't bring it with me," she responds, biting down on her lip. "But I know where it is. I gave it to Flynn."

She frowns.

"No problem, Ember," Ethan soothes. "We will just go back to the Institute and get it. We can go back the day after the Trials, when everyone is taking the oath. I'll ransack Flynn's room and—"

She cuts him off. "No. It won't be there. I didn't give it to that Flynn. I gave it to a Flynn from a different timeline."

We all stare at her stupidly for a minute. She rolls her eyes. "Oh. This is going to be bad."

I grab her arm. "Do you know where the key is or not?"

She nods. "I used it to create a fixed loop. I don't know if we can get it. Everything inside a fixed loop is sealed."

Stills cuts in. "Has there ever, in your memory, been a time when your key was missing?"

She pauses, tilting her head to the side. "Yeah. A few months ago. I thought I'd lost it, but I found it under my bed a few days later. I figured it fell off the wall somehow."

Stills nods. "That is your window. Take the key during that time and return it when you have used it. It will preserve the Fixed Point."

"Can we do that?" I ask. Following his logic feels a lot like banging my head into a brick wall.

It's Stein who answers. "I guess we'll know soon enough. Either someone already stole the key once and it's part of the Fixed Point, or we'll get our butts bounced back to next Tuesday when we try for it. Either way, it's our only shot."

"Let's do it then," I jump in, ready to go.

"What are the risks?" Ember asks Stills quietly.

"Honestly, it's hard to say. But it still has to happen."

She swallows hard and takes a step back.

"I'll go with you, Ember," Ethan says, holding her hand.

"Um, no, I don't think so," I say. "No offense and

all, but there's no way I'm letting her out of my sight. I'll go with her."

"Really?" Stein adds. "You'll go with *her*? And I'll do what? Stay here and make you a sandwich?"

"She's right. You should go with your girlfriend, keep her safe. I can go with Ember and do the same," Ethan says.

If there was a stupid comment cow pie on the burnt grass of the courtyard, Ethan just stepped in it.

"*Keep me safe?*" Stein challenges.

Ember folds her arms over her chest and moves to Stein's side. "In case you've forgotten, I stabbed you in the leg the first time we sparred, and I wasn't even trying then. You wanna give it a whirl right now? Then we'll see which of us needs protection."

"That's not what I meant. Just that—" Ethan says.

I nudge him. "Shut up."

Stein glares at me. "Why don't we do this, tough guys? Ember shouldn't go back into her own timeline. I think there have been enough potentially world-ending hijinks for one week, don't you? She and I will go together to get the Dox and you boys can go *protect* each other," she says. "Unless, of course, you don't trust us to go without male supervision?"

It's a trap. Some kind of weird secret girl code. Ethan sputters.

"Good job, Ethan," I hiss.

Reluctantly, I hand them their Contra.

"You boys can go get the key, if you think you can handle that?" With that, Stein and Ember hand their speakers back to Stewart Stills and walk away.

Ethan has the dumbest look on his face—like he just had an accident in his pants. Ember turns and shouts to him, "Three months ago, the day I almost broke your leg in sparring practice? That's the day I noticed it missing. It's in my room."

He nods.

I hand my speaker back to Stills and thank him. He reconstructs the earpiece and inserts it back into the socket.

Nobel is in the corner of the courtyard, cradling somebody. I can just make out singed, frizzy red hair. Journey. He sobs into her limp body. I've never seen him show emotion like that before. It's a nightmare. My mind reels. If we can get the other Dox and the key, maybe none of this will ever happen. Maybe everything will be set right. I hold on to the hope.

Ethan and I make our way over to where Stein and Ember are standing by with Nobel. Ember has her hand over her mouth, and Sisson is talking to her. The way she is moving her arms, I can tell she is recounting what happened to Ember, who still looks unnervingly fragile. Normally, I'd ask Nobel to watch my back, especially on this, my last mission for the Hollows, with a guy I'm not sure I trust. But looking at him, I decide to leave Nobel to mourn the girl he secretly loved.

I approach the others.

"We have our missions," I say, holding out my hand. The green pills are soiled with soot from my hands. Ethan grabs his. "Good luck, everybody."

"Lex, maybe you should stay with Nobel," Stein says, leaning in to hug me good-bye. "Ethan can get the key."

It's a tempting idea. But then I remember my outburst after Stein died and how Nobel had been smart enough to give me the one thing I really needed—space to grieve.

I shake my head. "We need to fix this, and I'm not sure I trust Ethan enough to let him go alone. At the rate the vortex is growing, it could chew through a full century in a matter of days. We don't have time to waste."

"I'll stay," Sisson offers, her face smeared with coal dust and tears. I want to reach out to her, to offer some comfort, but I don't. I'm not sure why.

Ethan puts his arm around her small shoulders and offers her a squeeze, earning him somewhat reluctant points from me. When he holds his other hand out for my sister, she takes it without hesitation.

"Who are the other bodies, the ones from your group?" Stein asks.

"Mistress Catherine," Ethan answers. "She was one of our teachers."

Ember shudders and he squeezes her. "And that's Trace and Connor. The other one is Doctor Kevlotrotsky."

"Well," Stein winds her fingers into my empty hand, "what are we waiting for?"

I can't help the feeling of lightness spreading in my chest, even though I know it's not the right time to be feeling it. Something about feeling Stein's hand in mine again makes all the bad stuff seem... survivable.

Nobel stands erect. "Before you go, we need to bury them. They deserve that."

He's right. Time is not on our side, but we can't just leave him and Sisson to do it alone. I look to Ethan, who nods.

Most of the fires have died down or gone out. The

smoke from the burnt tower and the smoldering bodies leave the courtyard shrouded in an eerie haze. It's like a cemetery's had all its bodies dug up and sprawled everywhere.

"Let's make a cemetery in the front corner," Nobel says, pointing to the spot in the courtyard. He wipes his nose and flicks the tears from his face like they are pesky gnats. "We should put the fallen Tesla people in there too," Stein says. She looks over to Ember. "They were all on the same side, once. Whatever bitterness separated them, made them enemies... well, maybe we can put that to rest, too."

I blink. Part of me wants to burn the ones who did this. But looking at Stein, I can see she's trying to heal a rift I didn't realize even existed. The one between Ember and me. We've been pulled apart, drafted to opposite sides in a war that wasn't our own. I can see now that it hurts Ember, having been a part of that for so long. So I agree. Not for them, but for my sister.

EMBER
Twenty-four

Ethan tosses his shovel and comes to my side. Lex and his friends are huddled over the last grave. He's pounding a makeshift cross into the ground. I don't want to be too close to them right now. What right do I have? Tesla did this. Attacked these people. Beyond the soft ache in my heart, there's only shame.

"They need a minute," he says gently.

I nod. "Ethan?"

"Yeah?"

"I have to tell you something." I pause. "It's something I should have told you a while ago, but… I dunno. I suppose there was never time."

He scoots close to me, shoulder to shoulder.

"Okay."

"Right. So back at the Institute, the day of my rift test, you came to get me from the cafeteria, remember?"

He grins. "You were so nervous, you were almost green. How could I forget?"

"Well, I was in the cafeteria and sort of… appeared to myself."

Whatever he expects me to say, it isn't that. His mouth falls agape as he struggles to understand.

"Wait, you mean you rifted back from somewhere and spoke to yourself inside the Institute?"

I nod. "Yeah. It was weird. She told me... well, I guess *I* told me, to take something on my first rift. It was something specific. The thing is, I haven't done that yet."

"Took something on your test or gone back and talked to yourself?"

"Gone back. How will I know when to go do it?"

He sighs, rubbing his hand down his face slowly so he has time to think. Finally, he shrugs. "Well, I would imagine you'd know when. I mean, something will happen, and you'll know it's time to go back. Was there anything different about her? Anything that stood out?"

I think back. "She was dressed differently. And she had..." I reach up and touch the scab under my chin, "a scar right here."

"Did it look old or fresh?" he asks seriously.

"Older, I think. It was healed at least."

He turns his back to the others, blocking my sight. "Then you have some time."

I see something glint on the ground. Kicking it with the toe of my boot, I see it's one of Lex's bottle caps. There's a bunch of them, scattered in the grass. Bending over, I pick them up and stuff them in my pocket.

"If any of it even matters after this," I say, earning a confused look. "I mean, if the Dox works. then... what? It sets time back on track? What does that even mean? Does this still happen? Does Lex ever save

Stein? Or will I wake up in bed like none of this ever happened?" A sudden thought sends sparks of dread through my mind. "What if I don't remember any of this?"

Ethan takes a deep breath, but he says nothing. There's no comfort he can offer. Instead, he pulls me into a tight embrace and kisses the top of my head gently. In the distance, through the smoke and tears of the night, the sun rises. I can't help wondering what tomorrow will bring. I don't think I've ever had so much to lose or so much weight on my shoulders.

A memory slides to the front of my mind. My sisters and I sewing the royal jewels into our corsets to hide them from thieves. I remember not feeling like it was going to happen, like it was a waste of time. But Mama was panicked, so we sewed all night long until our fingers were raw. When I finished mine, Mama held it up to me.

Here, Anya. This will be your armor. It will protect you from the dark things that come for us tomorrow.

I feel a tear slide down my cheek.

She was wrong, my mama. Nothing could have protected me—or any of us—from the dark things that came for us. Just like nothing can protect me now. Now I have to be the armor for Ethan, Lex, and all the people I can still hold onto—all the people I love.

Because I don't think I can survive losing them again.

LEX
Twenty-five

I never thought I'd be crawling on my hands and knees through the Tesla Institute air ducts with my sister's *boyfriend*. I wish I could be crawling behind Stein instead. At least it would be a nice view.

The ducts are cramped and hotter than the tunnels under the Institute. I don't like being the second-in-command, especially to a Tesla Institute student. Stopping at a slatted grate in the floor of the hard metal duct, Ethan says, "Here it is. My room."

Following him, I quietly lower myself onto his desk.

"Lookin' a little green there, buddy," I say. From the other side of the room, Ethan shrugs, leaning against the wall for support. He really does look like he's about to spew chunks.

He leans his head back and closes his eyes. "This is your fault. You and those stupid green pills. Why can't you just use tech to rift like a civilized person?"

I can't help laughing. "Did you just compare me to a civilized person?"

He lowers his head and looks at me. "Good point. What's in those pills anyway?"

"Trust me, you don't want to know. But this batch was stronger. There wasn't a jump date programmed, so it just sort of threw us in. Glad you knew where we were going. Which reminds me. What was Ember saying about breaking your leg?"

He crosses the room and pulls a brass panel cover off the wall, exposing a junction box beneath. "*Almost* breaking my leg. Believe it or not, your sister can pack a serious wallop when she's got half a mind to." He grins before pulling a wire from the wall and stripping the rubber coating off with his teeth. Spitting the remnants on the floor, he adds, "Welcome to my humble abode. *Don't touch anything.*"

I make a point to kick an electronic tablet off the edge of his desk as I jump to the ground. "Sorry."

His room is clean, freakishly so. Nothing is out of place. On the desk is a handheld video game system, a few books that look like they are about to fall apart, and a multi-tool, which I slip into my pocket.

"I mean it, sticky fingers. Hands off my stuff."

Rolling my eyes, I put it back. Then, on a shelf not far away, I see a red velvet bag sticking out from behind a jar of metal scraps. Ethan is busy twisting wires together, so I take a look. Upon dumping the bag upside down, a small necklace falls into my palm.

It's a small, black-and-white pendant shaped like an hourglass. "A little girly for you, isn't it?" I say, holding it by the chain.

Ethan snorts. "It isn't mine."

"Is it my sister's?"

"Yeah. I snuck it out of her room before her rift

test. If things went sideways…" He pauses, his face puckering. "Well, let's just say I wanted to be sure Tesla didn't throw it away. Don't worry; I'll get it back where it belongs without her ever noticing it was gone."

I stuff it back in the bag and toss it aside. "What's the deal with you and my sister?"

He pauses, looking confused. "What? Are you really asking me what my intentions with your sister are? What are you, the key holder to her chastity belt?"

I shrug. "Color me overprotective."

Ethan cracks a grin. "That's a bit of an understatement, isn't it?"

"Hey," I say, crossing the room to level a glare at him. "I'm trying. And considering you and yours have spent the last five years trying to kill me and mine, I think that's pretty good."

He stands, raises his hands into the air, and steps back. "Fair enough, I suppose. Your sister and I have been friends since the day she arrived. She's the first person I've ever known who really sees me. The good parts and bad parts. And she accepts them both." He picks up the bag and dumps the necklace into his palm. Picking it up, he lets it spin in the light before putting it away. "When she found you, I knew she was leaving me to get you back. The thought of not seeing her face again or, even worse, facing her someday as an enemy…"

I roll my head to the side, cracking my neck, and grunt. "I get that."

"So are we good? Can we get this done now? Or should we talk about our feelings some more?" he asks.

"Just waiting on you," I snap.

"Instead of trying to steal my stuff, you could help

me with this panel," Ethan says, putting me back in my place. He's right. I'm wasting time being petty. If we survive this, there will be plenty of time to be petty later.

"In my closet, there is a phonograph with a remote sitting by it," Ethan says.

"Do you want me to get it?" I ask.

Ethan scowls at me and points to the closet. I reluctantly meander over to where the phonograph and remote are stored. I notice his closet is organized by color, short sleeve versus long, and leather versus cotton. What a dork.

The phonograph is surprisingly heavy. I put the remote device in my pocket so I can get both hands on it.

"Thanks for letting me manhandle this thing by myself," I say.

"You are most certainly welcome, good fellow," he says, sarcasm glazing his words. "Just bring it over here."

I slide the vintage record player near the door. "You know how these work?" he asks.

"Are you kidding? We had one on every floor back home. I loved these things."

"Well, this one is special. It works in reverse." He runs his fingers along the edge of the brass horn piece. "You know Tesla invented the radio?"

"No, should I?"

"This one is my own design. Let me see the remote."

Ethan takes the brass button remote box from me and hooks two wires from the freshly dissected wall panel into the back of the phonograph.

"This is going to create radio waves that will jam Tesla. It will disrupt all his active systems on this floor.

I've managed to keep us in his blind spots this far, but it will allow us to move around more freely without being picked up on his scans."

"You know," I say, fiddling with a piece of metal on his desk. "For a guy loyal to Tesla, you sure have a good handle on how to disable him."

Ethan shrugs. "When you spend your life under the constant eye of Big Brother and you want to have any privacy at all, you learn to skirt the rules a little."

He angles the phonograph toward his desk, aims the remote control box back at the horn, and presses a button. Slowly, the machine begins to spin beneath the needle, but no music comes out. Instead, the notes are being fed into the computer.

"Okay. It's activated," he announces, replacing the panel.

"You mean your brain in a bottle, Tesla, is going to be blind and deaf? Cool." A reluctant tingle of pride and excitement makes the hair on my arms stand up.

"We have three minutes until the cameras come back online. Put this on."

He hands me a gas mask from the shelf. The old leather is soft and worn. I slip the straps over my head and adjust the fit. "If everyone is at the initiation, or whatever, why do I have to wear this?" I ask, rubbing the cloudy lenses with my sleeve and taking a deep breath.

"In case I'm wrong and someone is wandering around. Let's go."

The door groans open, and we slip into the hall. It's empty, as he promised it would be. The fact that he hasn't led me straight into a trap bodes well for his continued breathing. We reach another door when he stops, pulling another panel free. Inside, the wires have been crossed and re-crossed. Carefully, he touches one to another and the door slides open. I step inside first.

The room smells like her. I remember. When we were little, I had to share a room with Anya and Maria. Maria always smelled like sticky sweet cakes and honey, but Anya was more like warmth and sunshine.

Her bed is made, but it's still messy, as if she just pulled the blanket up over a tangle of sheets. There are energy bar wrappers balled up on the floor around a trash bin, and, like in Ethan's room, there are piles and piles of books.

She never was a tidy one.

On top of her dresser is a small wooden box with vines carefully carved into the dark surface. Cracking it open, I get a glimpse of what at first reminds me of Mother's jewels. I pick up a smooth, red shard and fiddle with it between my fingers.

"Sea glass," Ethan says, taking the piece from my fingers. "Sometimes when we get free time, they let us go to the beach. She'll spend hours combing the sand for just one little piece. Just sort of slow and patient. It's interesting to watch actually. When she finds a piece, her whole face lights up."

I stare at the box full of rainbow glass. "She always had a soft spot for pretty things, even things other people thought of as trash." I got that from her. My need to collect things. My hand goes to my empty pocket involuntarily.

"Here," Ethan says, putting the box back and pointing across the room. On a Peg-Board near her bed, a dozen keys hang randomly from hooks.

I sigh. "Can't make it easy, can she?"

Ethan shakes his head. "Give me a second. She described it to me. A shiny brass key with an oval at the end, with little spirals inside the oval. I think…" He runs his hands over the keys until it closes on one. "Ah. It's this one."

I make a face, which is stupid since he can't see it under the mask. "Are you sure? Maybe we should take them all, just in case?"

"No, it's this one. I'm sure."

I eye the rest of the keys. "Look, it's not that I don't trust you, but—"

"You don't trust me," he finishes.

"Pretty much, yeah."

He shrugs. "Whatever."

I pocket the remaining keys. No way am I going to risk another botched mission.

Ethan moves toward the door, only to hold up a hand. There are voices on the other side.

"It's fine," I say. "We'll just rift out from here."

Then someone—a girl—screams. I rip off the gas mask. Ethan hits the pad beside the door with his fist and rushes into the hall. I'm close behind. My initial fear is that it's Ember. But it isn't. It's a blonde-haired girl, and she's running toward us. A massive cyclone has appeared in the middle of the hallway, and it's moving in our direction. The girl nearly makes it to Ethan's outstretched hand when she's lifted off the ground and sucked into the heart of the storm. My feet skid forward. Paintings are being ripped off the walls; vases of flowers are hurtling toward the abyss. We stumble backward just as a flock of ravens fly out and over our heads. A split second later, a shaft of lightning strikes, and a lone motorcycle driver in a bedazzled white jumpsuit speeds out, maneuvering between us and down the hallway. I look over at Ethan, who is also struggling to stay on his feet. The things being spit out don't seem to be affected by the storm, only the things being sucked in. Things like us.

"Take the Contra," I yell over the sound of the raging storm. He shakes his head.

"I want to grab some Tethers. This way." He motions for me to follow, and we tear off down the hall. He hits another keypad. We step into a large dome room with metal-covered walls. Above us is a row of windows like an observation area. Next to a platform in the middle of the room is a tray full of tech.

"Here, take this," he says, handing me a contraption that looks like it's going to eat my arm. I take it with two fingers, hoping it doesn't. "Tethers. A much easier way to travel."

Then he moves to the wall and punches a code into the brass keypad. The wall slides up, exposing a cache of the devices. He grabs one, attaches it to his arm, then takes two more, stuffing them under his arm.

He turns to me. "Okay, let's go."

Just then, a hologram appears on the pad beside us. It's an image of a man—tall, greasy hair, and a weird mustache. I know right away who he is even though I've never seen him before.

"Tesla." The name hisses like steam through my teeth. The man who stole my family from me, who has been mercilessly hunting down the Hollows for years. The man who started the time war.

"Identify yourselves," the image demands, making Ethan turn.

"Crap. Go," he commands, plugging the keys on

his Tether.

I shake my head, knowing Ember will kill me if I come back without him. Slipping the Contra in my mouth, I grab him by the arm and we vanish in the time stream. The last thing I see is holographic Tesla, his face contorting with rage as he reaches for us.

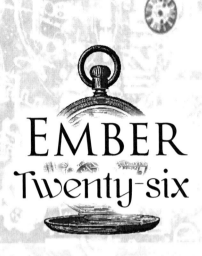

EMBER
Twenty-six

I don't throw up this time, which I consider an improvement, though I'm on my knees and too wobbly to stand just now. My belly is on fire, and I'm weak and sweaty. It's not pain, per se, but a relentless ache that makes you pray for the forgiving arms of death. Stein is unaffected, which doesn't seem fair. She begins to stomp off in the direction of the lab.

"Wait. We can't just go bursting in there," I say, grabbing her by the back of her shirt.

She doesn't shrug me off, but instead offers a hand to help me find my feet. Her tone isn't angry or challenging, just impatient. "Why not?"

"Because if Tesla knows we're here, then Tesla will know that we *were* here. In the future. He'll know he can catch us here. If we alter the timeline here in any way, Tesla from my time will be able to detect it."

Stein nods, so I continue.

"The computer that is Tesla can detect the slightest changes in history. It's part of his elaborate matrix. Our best bet is stealth. We get in and out unseen. We blend in."

"So what's our next move?" she asks, not entirely without sarcasm.

"Recon. We'll go pinch some period clothes and scout the building."

I point above us where strings are tied between the walls of the alley. Freshly laundered clothes hang from wooden clips.

Stein nods and whips a knife from the cuff of her boot. She slices the string where it's tied to a pulley and lets the end fall. The clothes slide free and we're left standing in an alley littered with fallen laundry.

Picking out just a few pieces, we fashion a makeshift bag out of a pillowcase and haul our load out into the street. I'm feeling pretty pleased with myself. My plan is already moving like clockwork. At this rate, we'll have the Dox by nightfall. We step out into the dim New York morning, and I freeze.

We aren't going to need the clothes after all.

"Um, what year is it supposed to be?" Stein asks, putting her top hat back on.

"It should be 1898," I answer slowly.

I step forward onto the corner of Broadway and Houston Street, into the very heart of New York City. A large, hovering police car zips past, nearly taking me out.

"I think somebody got their wires crossed," Stein offers smugly.

For a second, I think she's right. Those stupid pills must have dumped us in the wrong place.

The sound of hooves clopping on cobblestone makes us both turn. A large coach pulled by four brown horses trots by. The driver is dressed in leather skins and a cowboy hat. I'm staring after them when Stein elbows me.

She points down the road. Crossing Houston Street is a young woman from what looks like the 1950s, judging by the poodle skirt and saddle shoes, chatting with an older gentleman whose long, button-down coat and top hat put him in the early 1800s.

"What is going on?" I ask.

"I think it's our fault," Stein whispers. "It's the paradox. It's… leaking time."

She's right. It's as if every moment of time that ever happened in this place is overlapping, the stream touching in places it shouldn't.

"On the upside, at least we don't have to change clothes," Stein says with a smile. She tosses the garments back into the alley.

"The plan is still the same. We recon the building, then go after the Dox."

"Agreed."

"The building should be just up there a block or so," I say, gesturing with my hand.

We move out as casually as possible, passing two robotic street sweepers that remind me of metal trash cans with legs, one lost-looking guy in an old sailor's uniform, and two men having an Old West shootout in the middle of the street. Finally, we stop across the road from the building.

It's tall, at least five stories, with a single entrance at the front. Parked outside the large, arched stairway is a small motorcar. Two men are loading trunks onto the back while another stands guard from the doorway. Even from a distance, I can tell it's a young Flynn. He pulls a pocket watch from his vest and checks the time, saying something to the men before turning to go inside.

I forget to breathe for a second. He can't be much older than me, tall and handsome in a bowler hat and striped pants. I wait for the familiar pang of longing to hit me, but it never comes. He's not a friend. He's an obstacle. Something we must overcome to achieve our mission.

"This is the right time at least—1898—just before Tesla packs up and moves everything to his new lab in Colorado. They must be packing the first of the boxes. The tech will be the last thing to go, since Tesla will want to travel with it," I tell Stein, who is looking around. "The man by the door is Flynn. He was one of the first Rifters Tesla discovered. They move to Colorado so they can more quietly pursue his abilities. If Flynn is here, the other original Rifters may be here, too."

"Do you know who the others are or how many of them we can expect?" she asks.

I shake my head. "No. All I know is that right now, they are all close and very devoted to Tesla. The Hollows don't split off for another few years. Right now, Tesla's lab takes up the entire top floor. I have no idea what's on the lower floors, but there's a private elevator in the back that only Tesla uses."

"Okay, I think they'll be milling around for a few more hours, so let's go up there," Stein says, pointing to the rooftop of the building next to us. "It's a few stories taller. Maybe we can get a line of sight into the windows there. See what we're dealing with."

The building across the street is empty. There's a paper notice on the door announcing the dedication for it next week. It's going to be a luxury hotel. Stein crumples the paper and tosses it into the street. A robot quickly sucks it up just as a dark green 1930s Cadillac blows the corner and crashes into the bot, shredding it to pieces. A man in a hat sticks his head out the car window, producing a tommy gun, and opens fire into a group of people decked out in 1980s ripped leather, lace, and zipped parachute pants. The popping sound is eaten as a hovering fire truck flies down the street with sirens blaring. They all seem completely oblivious to each other, just going their way as if nothing was wrong at all.

"You know, not long before now, this whole area was known as Murderers' Row. Now they are building a fancy hotel here. In the next hundred years, this building will be everything from a doctor's office to a Subway restaurant," I say while I get to work using my small lockpick.

"Allow me," Stein says, gently putting a hand on my shoulder.

Without another word of warning, she spins and lets out a ferocious kick that knocks the door off its hinges and drops it flat into the building with a puff of plaster dust.

"That's how we Hollows do it," she says, stepping into the main room.

The plaster walls are still bare, no paint or decorations, and the lamps are in crates along the floor. The banister up the grand staircase isn't even close to being assembled. It would take even the most dedicated group weeks to finish everything. Of course, with time hemorrhaging all over the place, things like deadlines might be redundant.

I follow Stein up the stairs to the roof access door. By the time we make it to the top, I'm panting and my calves burn. We're seven stories up. The stairs are short and steep, making every step ache. We burst into the open air. I take a deep breath, watching as Stein steps dangerously close to the edge and puts her hands on her hips. Watching her, I totally get why Lex is so crazy about her. She's kind of amazing. He deserves someone amazing. I just never imagined things working out this way.

"You know he loves you, right?" I say into the wind.

"I know. He did rip time apart to save me."

"So why are you giving him the cold shoulder?"

She twists her black hair into a bun and sticks a pin in it to hold it off her face.

"It's just hard to reconcile. The Lex I knew, my Lex, died in that rift."

I understand. He was my brother, too.

"He really is the same person, you know."

"I know that here," she says, pointing to her head. "But it's here that it gets muddled." She moves her hand to her heart. "I almost feel like I'm... betraying his memory."

I have to laugh. Not because I think it's funny, but it's such a silly position we have found ourselves in.

She laughs, too. "I know. It's crazy." Then she pauses. "Also, I'm sorry about before. For trying to kill you and all."

I crack a grin. "Bygones. Besides, I would have beaten you to a pulp if you hadn't run off like that."

Now it's her turn to grin. "You would have tried."

I put my hand on her shoulder. "This whole thing is crazy. But I do think that, if you love him, *this him*, then you have to let go of the past and hold on to right now. If we've learned anything from this, it's that the future isn't written in stone. Especially for us."

Stein and I watch Tesla's lab across the street. I can see most of the top floor through the windows. It's pretty open, not a lot of walls or separation inside. Flynn is carefully boxing up books. I count three other people: the two guys from the street, and one woman who's wearing an elaborate red dress. The front is sort of plain and high-necked, but a large bustle hangs from her lower back. The sleeves are long, ending in black lace cuffs. Her dark hair is coiffed at the top of her head, creating a hat-like bun. I don't recognize her immediately, but when she turns to the side, the silhouette is unmistakable.

"Mistress Catherine," I mumble to myself. Like Flynn, she's young, sixteen at the most. Her face is smooth and unblemished. I've often sat in class and wondered what she looked like when she was whole. Now that I see it, I realize she's stunningly beautiful. She gracefully kneels next to Flynn, putting a hand on his shoulder for balance. It's hard to believe that only hours before, I stood over her grave.

Stein comes over to the ledge and squats down.

"Can't bend at the waist in that corset, can you?" I mumble.

"What's that?" Stein asks.

"Oh." I nod to the building. "Mistress Catherine, the Head Mistress at the Institute, is over there, too."

"Didn't we just—"

I cut her off. "Yeah. We did."

After a minute, Stein confirms what I'd witnessed. "Looks like four inside total."

"All right," I say. "This time, we use the lockpick. Your *break down the door* method won't be the best way to go unnoticed. And don't forget—don't just grab the Dox. We need to find the instructions and copy them down."

"Why don't we just take the original notes?" Stein asks, still watching the lab. "I mean, things are already going to hell in a handbasket. How much worse could things get?"

"Because they need to be able to recreate the design, otherwise the Dox we stole will never exist in our time. It could make the paradox even worse. At this point, caution is the better part of valor," I explain as I double-check that the lockpick is still tucked into the small case strapped to my belt.

"Okay, I think I'm ready. As soon as the coast is clear, we'll head over."

Stein hands me a Contra. "In case we get separated, we meet back at the Tower."

Just the sight of it makes my stomach roll, but I take it anyway, stuffing it in my vest pocket. Night is falling. From this place, I can see the entire dome of the sky above us. In this time, where lamps are still dim and the gross light of civilization has not yet become blinding, I can see the stars.

"It's time," she says, pointing to at the entrance of the building. Four people exit and drive away.

We slink down to the street, completely focused on the task at hand. The street is crawling with men on horseback, cars from various times, and hordes of tourists with cameras snapping photos.

* * *

Unlocking the door takes longer than I expect. Leave it to Tesla to be the only person in 1898 to have a triple dead bolt. Luckily, we don't draw any attention to ourselves and the door finally gives way.

Nothing decorates the tiny room except for some holes in the crumbling plaster walls. No mailboxes or elevator doors exist in this part of the building. There's another door leading to the stairwell, and this one is more easily manipulated.

An old iron and wood staircase is our welcome mat to the mad scientist's lair.

Climbing as fast as we can and fueled by curiosity, we burst into a reception area. No one is here, of course. There's no electricity to speak of, no lights or generators, nothing to make working at this hour possible. We should be alone.

"All right, let's make this quick. We just have to find one Dox and we are out of here," Stein says.

I've already entered the only hallway and found the office. We each grab an oil lamp and light them. The room glows faintly around us.

"It has to be in here." I push on the solid wood door, and it swings open. The office is a mess. Piles of books and papers everywhere. I wonder if it's messy from the move, or if this is Tesla's insane idea of a filing system.

"Piles… a man's way of organization," I mutter from the threshold of the office door.

"Either try to find the Dox or clues to where it might be stored," Stein says.

We slowly start to rummage through the papers and textbooks to see if we can find clues to where the

Dox would be, or maybe even directions on how to use the stupid thing. After a few moments of slow reading and searching, Stein loses her patience and begins to ransack the room like she's robbing the place. I stare at her for a second, trying to decide whether to protest.

"What? He'll just assume the place got robbed. Happens all the time in New York City."

It seems like a solid point, so I pick up the pace, hastily rummaging through the office and throwing papers to the ground. Trashing the place turns up nothing. I stand back to get a good look at the work over we gave Tesla's office.

"We totally rock-starred that room," Stein says as we leave.

I have to kick a couple of books back into the room so I can close the heavy door.

We search the door at the end of the hallway to no avail; it's just a glorified broom closet. The door in between the office and the closet is the last one to check.

"Let's see what's behind door number three," I say, motioning for her to work her larceny. She grins widely and kicks it in.

The door hangs askew on one hinge, welcoming us into the room with the smell of ozone and the crackle of static electricity.

"It sounds like someone's frying a big pan of bacon down there," Stein mumbles. I grunt in agreement, wishing we had more than lamps to use to maneuver in the darkness.

Beneath the grated walkway, we can see sparks. I look over the railing and gasp in astonishment at the size of Tesla's actual lab. It isn't just the top floor as I'd thought. It's the entire building, the fourth floor being the catwalk. Looking from our vantage point, I see three dull grey cylinders in the left corner. Electricity shoots out in all directions from the top of them. This is where all the sound is coming from. No one's home, but someone left the stove on.

Between a control room and a sitting area, there is a conveyor belt with a large robotic arm at the end. It's cocked at the elbow like a cobra ready to strike, but nothing is active.

Under the arm is a trunk full of small cylinders. Sitting on the stalled belt are some of the small glass cylinders that look like the exterior of the Dox. For the first time, I'm excited. It must be here. We must be close.

A large vat full of milky green liquid is next to the bottom of the stairs. Lights from the bottom of the vat illuminate the liquid, giving it an eerie, otherworldly glow.

"That thing has to be two stories tall," Stein says, pointing to the vat.

"Any idea what that it is?"

She shakes her head.

To the far right, there is a carpeted area with a chair. A hefty wooden bookshelf crowns the plush sitting area.

We scan the room one more time to see if there's any activity aside from the loud hissing vases in the far corner. Slowly, we descend the grated stairway to the floor of the lab.

I stare at the enormous vat. The tank wears a bracelet of windows smudged with slime at its base. I press my face up against one.

300

Something slithers through the liquid.

"Whoa!" I yell, jumping back from the window and pointing at it. "There's something swimming around in there."

"Lemme see," Stein says, pushing past me. She cups her hands around her eyes and leans up against the window. "I don't see—" She jumps back, pointing to the tank. "It's like a huge electric eel. Is that his sick idea of a pet?"

I shrug. We exchange an *eww* face before walking over to the sitting area in the far right corner. The ornate Oriental rug is the only thing separating this space from the rest of the lab. The lounge area has two leather chairs and a small table holding a large gas lamp between them. The chairs are so well worn I can see the butt imprint in the seat cushion. Carefully, I light the lamp so we have a better view of the books on the shelves. Some are so old the names have worn off the spines, and others are leather-bound notebooks stuffed haphazardly with papers.

I start on one end, and Stein starts on the other. Carefully, we pull each book out, open it, and stuff it back in place.

"All these are... are boring lab notes," Stein says after a few minutes. "I can't understand even a tenth of what is written in these things."

"Lucky you." I hold the journal up in my hands. "I think I stumbled on the insane ramblings section."

"Nice."

I sigh and shove it back on the shelf, then grab the next book. It pulls the book next to it as well. They both fall to the floor, pages flying everywhere. Stein puts her book back and comes over to help me.

The larger of the two books is a handwritten journal. And it's fallen open to a page with a rough sketch of something that looks a lot like the Dox.

"Wait, this might be it," I say, folding myself into a sitting position as Stein continues cleaning up the mess.

I flip a few more pages. Not what I was hoping for. "This might be the early notes, but the actual Dox designs aren't in here. This looks like something from before, an early draft, maybe."

I look over. Stein is shoving the fallen notebook into the pocket of her leather coat.

"Stein," I say. I'm all set to warn her about stealing from this library, to remind her about the consequences of altering the past, but the look on her face stops me short. She looks paler than usual, and a slight sheen of sweat has broken out across her forehead.

"Are you okay?" I ask.

She shakes her head and stands up, squaring her shoulders. "Nothing a nice frontal lobotomy won't cure. Come on, let's get this finished."

Above us, a door slams. "Hello?" a man calls out in a thick British accent.

LEX
Twenty-seven

Inside the stream, something is churning. Normally, the time stream only moves in one direction—forward—and we are either swimming with it or against it. This is different. I'm rolling helplessly, end over end, as if I'm being beaten against the rocks in a churning sea. I can't get my bearings. There is no backward or forward, just the relentless rolling. My stomach pitches, threatening to lose its contents. It's all I can do to keep it down. I feel something damp rolling down my neck. Reaching up, I touch it, then bring my hand to my ear and open my eyes just long enough to see that the tips of my fingers are covered in blood. I'm bleeding from my ear.

I'm on the verge of hysteria. This *shouldn't be happening*. None of this makes sense. This isn't how it's supposed to be. I scream, but no sound comes out. All I can hear is the wind rushing past my ears.

Something slams into me and I stumble back, landing on a hard, wet surface. I lie there for a while, just trying to breathe. When the dizziness eventually fades, I blink and look up to see Ethan standing over me. He's panting, and sweat has soaked through his shirt. Nobel is on his knees next to me in the grass outside the Tower.

"Lex, can you hear me?"

There is a loud ringing in my ears, but I can just make out the sound of his voice.

"Yeah. Sort of." My hand smacks the side of my head, but it only makes the ringing worse.

"I think you blew an eardrum, but you'll be fine." He looks to Ethan, who, I notice, has a similar trickle of blood leaking from his nose. "What happened?"

Ethan's still panting, so I answer. "There's something really wrong with the stream. Are Ember and Stein back yet?"

Nobel shakes his head. Ethan falls to his knees, closing his eyes as he pulls patches of grass into his fists. I don't know if he's praying or just sick, but I close my eyes and say a prayer. They are going to need all the help they can get.

EMBER
Twenty-eight

"We need to make a decision here. Do we take the person out or hide from them?" I whisper.

"I say we take him out," Stein decides, the smile returning to her face. It's as if hitting something will make her feel better.

"We can't risk being seen by Flynn or Catherine," I remind her gently. "Or alerting Tesla to our presence here."

"Yes, Mom," she agrees, looking only too eager to kick the living crap out of whoever it is.

"We'll take out whoever it is as quickly and quietly as possible. Then we'll stuff them in that broom closet."

We wait behind the large steel vat at the base of the stairs. I'm pretty content to let Stein have her way with the poor guy. Better his face than mine.

Sure enough, a single, unsuspecting grunt lumbers down the stairs. I can tell immediately that it isn't Tesla, Flynn, or Catherine. He's too thick, too tall, and too heavy. Stein steps out calmly.

"Hey, over here."

When he turns, she roundhouse kicks him in the face, knocking him on his back. Not letting up, she kicks out again, catching him in the side and sending him rolling across the wood floor. I leap out, roll him over, and jump onto his back, hog-tying him with a coil of wire I found behind the tank. Stein moves in for the final blow.

"Wait, don't knock him all the way out," I say, a slight tremble in my voice from adrenaline. "Maybe he knows where the Dox is."

We roll the frightened lab assistant onto his back. Stein slaps him in the face until his eyes fly open. He struggles, but the wires hold him tightly. He is easily six foot six, broad-shouldered with dark, straight hair pulled back into a ponytail at the base of his neck and dark brown mutton chops adorning his cheeks, despite the fact he's probably only in his twenties. He's in a brown vest, dark pants, and a dirty lab coat. He could be Nobel's long-lost twin—or a janitor. Whichever.

He stops struggling and sits there with his head down—like a kid who has just been caught with his hand in a cookie jar.

"Hey! Do you know where the Dox is?" Stein demands, slapping him again. I pull her hand away.

"We aren't going to hurt you." I say. "Well, we aren't going to hurt you *anymore*. We just need the Dox. Then we will leave."

Stein throws her hands in the air. "This is nuts. We should just toss him in the vat of electric snakes and find it ourselves."

When she moves, I see his eyes flicker with recognition. Surprise spreads across his face like a light going on. I look at her, then back to him, sure I've never seen this person in my entire life.

Catching her eye, I mouth, "Do you know him?" and nod in his direction.

She shakes her head.

"I think I know where the Dox is," he says finally. "I can show you."

I hesitate, debating Stein's suggestion about dropping him in the eel tank. Part of me thinks she's right, that it might be the smart thing to do, but I can't bring myself to do it. Besides, we need the Dox. Time is running out, and whatever damage we've caused being caught by this guy, well, that's a problem for another day.

"All right, then. Show us," I say. I unwind the coils of wire, but I watch him carefully. He doesn't take his eyes off Stein, which is more than a little unsettling. My muscles are tense. Every nerve in my body is on high alert just waiting for him to try something.

He leads us over to a set of tall electrodes at the far left side of the lab. Without hesitating, he walks between them. A storm of lightning sparks through the room, but he doesn't stop. I cringe. I'm positive I hear Stein gasp, but nothing happens to him. He kneels down on the ground and twists a latch hidden in the floor. With all his might, he heaves a large floor panel open. Holding up the hinged trap door with his knee, he waves us in.

We carefully walk through the veil of lightning bolts emitting from the Tesla coils. They make the hair on my arms and head stand out but never directly strike us. It kind of feels like swimming in a pool of toothless piranhas.

The stranger is the first one to climb down into

the pit while I hold the trap door. When we reach the bottom, he helps me off the ladder by holding out his hand. Stein just glares at him. She doesn't trust him. He doesn't say much. He doesn't have to say much. With a sweep of his arm, he gestures around the room as if to show off his prized possessions. The shelves are wooden and completely makeshift. They hold many items that look intriguing, but I figure since I have no idea how to use the one item we came for, I should probably leave the other tech untouched.

I scan the room. Stein is standing at the bottom of the stairs, her arms folded across her chest, just waiting for the stranger to make a wrong move. Displayed among Tesla's other crazy inventions is the last remaining Dox. Only it isn't the last. There are two. One completely assembled, and one still in pieces. Sitting next to them is a leather-bound lab notebook. Rushing to it like a kid on Christmas morning, I quickly flip through its pages. The directions for using the device are scrawled in Tesla's handwriting. Tearing an empty page from another book, I swiftly scribble the instructions on a scrap of paper, then stuff the book back on the shelf next to the unassembled Dox. I'm about to turn when something else catches my eye. There is a shelf with six rings. Each ring has a small stone affixed to it with copper wire inserted into the stone. I grab one and slip it into my pocket. I'm turning into a Hollow. Stein catches me, grinning.

"What?" I shrug.

Stein slides an identical ring out of her back pocket. "You're not quite the seasoned time thief I am. Found this one upstairs."

I can't hold back the chuckle.

She returns it to her pocket. "I think I'm a bad influence on you."

I smile. "It's a Babel Stone ring. A piece of Tesla tech we use."

"What does it do?"

"It lets the person wearing it speak any language. But mostly, it just reminds me of home." I frown and tap my pocket.

"Well, I just wanted it because it could cause some wicked damage to someone's face in a fight."

"I'm sorry," the strange man says, "I couldn't help but overhear. Are you a Rifter?" He takes a step forward, looking at me for probably the first time.

Stein and I exchange a glance. What am I supposed to say?

"Um, yeah. Something like that," I say, turning away from him so I can shoot Stein a look without him seeing.

"It's all right," he says. "I'm a Rifter myself, you see."

"Great, one of Tesla's devoted minions," Stein grumbles.

I turn back to them just in time to see him staring at her like she'd committed the worst kind of blasphemy.

She shifts her weight and squints at him. "What? Do I owe you money or something?"

He reaches out to grab her, but I'm already moving for them. She's faster, though, and slaps his hand away an instant before nailing him in the face with a right hook that buckles his knees.

"Try to touch me again," she threatens, "and I'll rip your arm off and beat you with your own stump."

"I'm so sorry," he says, surprisingly calm. "It's only,

you remind me of someone."

I stare him down, trying to decide if I should knock him out cold before we leave. My hand twitches. The idea has its merits.

He holds up his hands, looking completely apologetic. "Please. I won't tell anyone I saw you. If anyone asks, I'll tell them I broke the Dox while I was cleaning and threw the pieces away."

Stein narrows her eyes. "Why would you cover for us?"

He looks from her to me, as if the answer was obvious. His brown eyes are sincere when he says, "Because we are Rifters. We are family, are we not?"

I realize he's talking about something more than our common genetic ancestors. It's like being at the Institute or being a Hollow. We've become family. A big, insane, dysfunctional family.

I pass the Dox to Stein and hold my hand out to the stranger, helping him to his feet. "Yeah. I suppose we are. Thanks for your help, whoever you are."

He shakes my hand fervently and says, "My name is Leonard Claymore, and you are very welcome."

Behind me, Stein gasps.

LEX
Twenty-nine

It is raining now, and I can't help but feel like Mother Earth is urinating on the ruins of my home. The charred remains of our beloved Tower sit in a smoky black heap on the lawn. It's only a matter of time before that little game of hide and seek with the paradox ends on a bad note. I am afraid that it will catch up to us soon. The bubble of safety that once engulfed the Hollow Tower has failed. I can see it in the distance. A tall barbed wire fence has gone up around the grounds. Judging by the derelict signs hanging from it, it's been there for some time. I wonder what part of time we have woken up in. Not that it matters now. What's left is nothing but ruins.

Nobel and Sisson are busy trying to board up the remaining windows. They have already scrubbed any trace of our existence from the rooms inside. A wooden crate with a handful of junk in it is all that's left now.

It's hard to focus on anything. My thoughts are jumpy and frayed. I wish the girls would get back already. Knowing they're safe would really go a long way toward making me feel better right now. The idea of losing them now… I can't even let myself dwell on the possibility. Beside me, Ethan is carefully picking up chunks of debris and taking it to the bonfire Nobel has built. The wind blows the smoke across the front of the yard. It looks like something out of a horror movie.

I can't believe the destruction. One of Nobel's glass beakers lays broken in front of me. I stare at myself in the fractured beaker. There's a new scratch on my cheek, and part of my eyebrow is missing. My left eye is black and blue, almost swollen shut. I can't imagine what the rest of me looks like. Not wanting to see myself anymore, I grab a rock and chuck it at the beaker, narrowly missing my target. I look away.

I stare into the nearby flames, letting their movement lull me. Moments later, I hear the glass crack under someone's foot, making me look up.

I am in such a daze for a minute that I think my eyes are playing tricks on me. But Ember and Stein are here, standing right in front of me. Jumping to my feet, I don't know who to hug first, so I grab both the girls I love and squeeze.

"You made it!" I say, unable to keep the relief out of my tone.

"What made you think we wouldn't?" Ember asks, patting at her windblown mess of hair.

"Is it because we're girls?" Stein asks with a smile.

"No, not at all. The time stream is crazy right now and… I was just worried. That's all," I say.

"Well, that's cute," Stein says. "I like it when you worry."

We hug once more. It feels so good to have them

back safe. I almost don't let them go. Ember pulls away to meet Ethan, who is jogging toward us. I let her go but keep Stein tight to my chest.

"Hey," Ethan says, grabbing her and spinning her around.

"Were you worried, too?"

"Nah. I know you can take care of yourself."

She shakes her head. "Liar."

"Yeah, pretty much," he admits with a grin.

Stein takes off her backpack and carefully unwraps the last existing Dox.

We all stare. This oversized lightbulb is going to be what makes things right.

"Hey, you got the instructions!" Ethan exclaims, reaching into her bag to pull out a worn leather journal.

"Hands off!" Stein yells, going zero to ten faster than I've ever seen. "Those aren't the instructions! That's mine!" Ethan lets go of the book and pulls back as if he's trying to dodge a striking snake.

"Uh… okay. Sorry."

I raise my eyebrows and stare at her. What personal stuff? She sees the question in my eyes and looks away, thrusting the unknown book deeper into her bag as if that will make it go away.

She looks at me and shakes her head. I know her well enough not to press, at least not right now. If we survive this, I'll ask her about it later, in private.

"Here are the instructions," Ember says, changing the subject. She holds out a disheveled pile of faded papers with her handwriting on them.

"Okay, great."

"And here is the key," Ethan announces.

"And if that isn't the right one, here are all the other

keys," I say, emptying my pockets onto the steps like I'm trying to find the correct change for a chocolate bar. "Um, we're going to need to put these back eventually. You know, unless the universe explodes. Then, no big deal."

Ember reaches out slowly and takes the key—the one that will lock this paradox down forever—from Ethan's hand.

"I didn't think I would ever see this again," she says.

She holds the key in the palm of her hand, following its ridges with her index finger as if she's in some sort of trance. "The instructions say we have to insert the key into the filament in the middle of the Dox," Ember says, not looking up.

"How is that going to work?" Stein asks. "There's no keyhole."

"I guess we have to break the glass," Ethan says.

"That's the problem," Ember replies. "The instructions have a warning that says it has to be done without breaking the glass."

"That makes no sense," I say. "There has to be a way. Here, let me see the Dox and the key." I take both items carefully. While I examine them, the Dox starts to hum and turn on. When I move the key away from the Dox, it turns off. Frustrated, I put the key right up next to the Dox and watch intently. The humming starts, and the glass ripples like when a stone is thrown into a pond. I hold the key closer, and then the idea slams into my head. With all eyes on me, I slide the key through the ripple on the glass. It's as if the Dox is letting the key inside.

"Don't do it yet!" Ethan yells, half scaring me to death.

"I wasn't going to," I say. I pull the key out, and the glass portion of the Dox turns solid again.

"So that's how we'll get the key through the glass. Just push it through?" Stein asks.

"I guess so."

"Well, there we have it," I say. "The Dox should work this time. Let's go put it in the vortex." I point to the looming clouds in the distance.

"That's the other thing," Ember says. "The guidelines say, in order to have a successful closure of the paradox, we have to set it off at a Fixed Point in time."

"Like the one you created with the key?" Ethan asks.

"Yeah. You think we can go back inside that loop?"

Ethan cringes. "Um, we kind of broke that one, I think."

"The vortex appeared in the Institute," I say, putting the pieces together. "We can't go back inside that loop again. The paradox is already there. I think…" I'm hesitant to say the words aloud. "I think the paradox is *eating* time."

"So, what? Is there another Fixed Point we can use?" Stein asks, looking at Ethan.

"How am I supposed to know?"

"Well, you went to school for this kind of thing, right?" she asks, folding her arms over her chest.

"I know when," Ember says, the color fading from her cheeks. "The only other Fixed Point I know of." She turns to me, putting a hand on my arm. "Lex, we have to go back to Yekaterinburg."

"Yekaterinburg?" Ethan and Stein ask in unison.

I nod. "We have to go back to the night our family was killed."

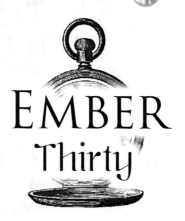

EMBER
Thirty

It's dark when we spill onto the gardens beside Ipatiev House. The tall wooden fence constructed to hold us prisoner blocks out any light from nearby homes. The stale, rotten scent of gunpowder clings to the air, stifling me. In the distance, I hear the cries of battle as the rebels make their way toward us. I hear other things, too. Things I shouldn't hear. The whir of helicopter blades and the boom of cannon fire. For a moment, I can't breathe as panic tightens around me like a vise.

"I still don't like leaving them behind," Lex says, tugging on the strap of the Tether attached to his arm.

Truthfully, I don't either. I'd give just about anything to have Ethan here with me. But the need to protect them is stronger. According to Tesla's notes, the Dox will explode like a bomb when detonated, searing the paradox closed. Neither Lex nor I know what kind of damage it might do to the people setting it off. So we kept it quiet, let the others think we were going to gather supplies, and then snuck out alone.

Hopefully, by the time they notice we've gone, this will all be done and over with.

"I know," I whisper. "But—" I don't want Ethan to see this, I realize, not finishing the thought out loud. Maybe that's the real reason.

The grim visage of the house blurs into view as my eyes adjust to the darkness. It's cold for July, but that's Siberia for you. Even the summer holds a deathly chill. Or maybe it's just this place—being here again. Inside those doors, my family has just been woken from a dead sleep. I remember my older sister Olga being excited. She thought we were finally being moved to safety in exile. But Tatiana was grim as she dressed. I don't think she ever expected to taste freedom again.

Guilt gnaws at me from the inside out. How long has it been since I've thought of my sisters? How long since I cried for them? I can't even remember. From the minute I got my memories back, all I could think of was finding Lex.

"I haven't gone to put flowers on their graves," I whisper. If they even have graves. The thought chokes me.

Lex speaks gently, but his voice is strained and low. "There will be time for that."

I hope he's right.

Only Lex's hand in mine keeps me calm, keeps the despair from pulling me under. I hear boots moving through the grass and pull Lex down so we are hiding beneath the bushes as they pass. The moonlight glints off the steel of their bayonets, and I shudder. Lex squeezes my hand. I almost wish I hadn't left Ethan behind. I could use some of his strength right now. But it's better. I don't want him to see this—see me like this. It's too much.

I can feel my insides trying to shut down, trying to block out the painful memories of the seventy-eight days we were held captive here. But I can't. Over and over, they rush through me, leaving me feeling raw and exposed. Glancing over, I can see Lex is having similar issues. His face is ghostly white, and the muscles in his jaw twitch as he grinds his teeth.

Then I see what he's fixed on. Two soldiers are standing on the porch of the house, smoking. They are laughing. Knowing what is about to happen to our family, they are laughing. I turn away from them, but the image is seared into my brain.

"Lex. We have to do this quickly before—"

I'm cut off by the pop of gunfire. Someone screams. I think it's my mother. I feel Lex tug me forward, but my legs refuse to move. It's as if I've turned to stone. Dropping my hand, Lex rushes for the house, but before he clears the garden, he hits some invisible barrier and bounces off, falling on his back in the dirt.

He groans. "What the—?"

One of the laughing guards has gone inside, but the other hears us and walks over. Something in my brain fires off, and I can move again. Motioning for Lex to stay down, I circle behind the man. He sees Lex and tries to draw his gun, but I've already slipped it from his holster. The guard turns, confused. For a brief minute, I think I'm going to kill him. I can do it. I want to do it. I'm not sure what stops me, but I swing the gun around and slam it into the side of his head, knocking him out cold.

"You should have just shot him." Stein's voice comes from the dark garden, startling me. Stein and

Ethan emerge from behind the bushes. She glares at us, her arms folded across her chest. "You two are so predictable."

Ethan walks over and offers Lex a hand up, then pulls me into his chest.

"Never do that again. We're a team, Ember. You and me. Okay?" he whispers through my hair.

All I can do is nod because I'm crying and my voice won't work properly. I'm just so glad to see him. I want to ask him to take me from this terrible place, to go somewhere the memories can't do me any more harm. As if such a place exists.

But I don't. We have to fix this, here and now. I pull back and wipe my eyes.

Lex moves to hug Stein, but she slaps him across the face. The sound makes me wince.

"You are an idiot," she says, glaring at him.

He holds the side of his face, but he's smiling as if he expected no less.

More gunshots go off, and I tense. Each pop makes me spasm as if the bullet is hitting my body. But I know I'm not in that room with the rest of my family. I don't die with them this night. Maybe that's my fate. Listening to people I love dying over and over again. Unchangeable. But it still hurts like a knife in my heart. Ethan's arms tighten around me again and he leans forward, trying to shield me from the sound with his body.

The family is told the upstairs is no longer safe, that rebels are coming for us. They lead us down to the basement, but Alexei isn't with us, so Father sends me after him. The rest of the household joins the family in the basement. Alexei must have thought, like Olga, that we were being evacuated. He is packing when I find him. Trying to stuff all his trinkets into a tiny pillow like Mother had done with the royal jewels.

In the distance, lightning strikes, bringing me out of the memory. The paradox is moving quickly. It's here now, coming for us, we who tore it asunder. It will eat us to repair itself if we let it. It might eat everything. The whole world destroyed for the life of one girl.

I look at Stein, and I can't say I regret the decision. I can see now why Lex is so fond of her. She deserves to live. She's strong and brave, smart and beautiful. Maybe it's only because of how she was raised—a child of the Hollows. But maybe, just maybe, she's exactly who she was always supposed to be. Maybe we all are.

I think back on what Gloves told me. Can I do it? Can I walk into that house and turn my brother and myself over? Will I? Do I even have a choice? Whatever holds this place fixed in time must still be working because Lex can't get within ten feet of the front door. That's the force field. It's like Flynn said. They physically couldn't pass the barrier.

"Hurry up," Ethan says, holding out his hand for the key.

"I'll do it," I tell him. I don't want him anywhere near this thing when it goes off. I hold my hand out to Lex for the Dox. Lex shakes his head. "We'll do it together."

He holds the Dox. Just as I'm about to insert the key, a sharp pain catches me in the back. I'm kicked from behind hard enough that I fall to my hands and knees, dropping the key in the dark grass.

Looking up, I see Kara standing over me, clad head to toe in black leather. She's wearing a pair of night-vision goggles. Behind her, Flynn holds a lash, and the electric whip buzzes with power. But that isn't the worst part. The worst part is what they brought with them.

LEX
Thirty-one

For a minute, I can't make any sense of what I'm seeing. It's dark, only the light from the moon glowing off the thing moving toward us. From the waist up, it looks like a man—the holographic image of Tesla made of flesh with his pencil-thin mustache and greased black hair. Skin drapes over its shoulders like a caveman's fur. As my eyes focus in, I take an involuntary step back. Large, square bolts pin the pieces of flesh to the metal framework beneath. Pieces of steel and copper peek out in places along its neck and hands. Bright blue currents crawl along the length of its body, through the piece of machinery in the center of its chest that looks like an oversized, metal heart. Bolts of electricity arc from one side to the other. Sparks shower down from the tips of its pincers as the monster snaps its claws together at the dark, smoke-filled sky, and sparks shower down from the tips.

"Kara!" Ethan yells. "You traitor!"

"There are only two traitors I see, and they are standing with a couple of lowlife Hollows," she says, her expression stern and unyielding. From the ground, Ember stares up at her, a mix of disbelief and disappointment on her face.

"That's enough, Kara," the man with the whip says. "Ember, Ethan, we don't have to do this. Hand over the Dox and come back to the Institute with us. No one needs to get hurt here today."

I just grin. The muscles in my legs and arms are coiling for the fight. "My sister isn't going anywhere with you."

"My name is Flynn. I was—am—a friend," Flynn announces, holding the whip idle at his side. Kara rejoins him, standing proud to be on the wrong side of the fight. I shake my head.

"Who invited you to this party, anyway?" I ask, honestly wondering how they found us.

It's Kara who speaks. "You guys, Tesla built that thing." She points to the Dox. "You didn't think he'd know what you'd do with it? You tore the whole world to pieces with your stupidity. Now it's time for you to hand it over and let the grown-ups clean up the mess."

Flynn pushes Kara behind him and reaches a hand out to Ember, who is still lying on the ground. "Ember, I don't want to hurt anyone. But this has to be fixed. Please, let me help you do that."

For a second, I think she's considering his offer. Then he continues, "Time is bleeding, Ember. It's dying. And we can stop it. Here, in this time, we can fix the mistakes of the past. You and your brother can join us. It's where you were always meant to be."

Her face goes rigid, and she slaps his hand away. "What do you think we're trying to do?"

"Enough talk," the Tesla monster orders with a

booming metallic voice. "Keep the Romanov children alive. The others you can dispose of."

The Kara girl rushes our way while Flynn stands back and cracks his whip. Without warning, Stein rushes ahead and tackles Kara. I'm sure she has been waiting for this moment. Payback from the wharf.

The Tesla automaton rears forward, spitting up chunks of dirt. From the waist down, any scrap of humanity is lost. Its front legs are hinged and attached to tank-like caterpillar tracks. Four spindly legs in the back aid the rotating tracks as it moves. Flynn has to slide out of the way. The monster rushes at the two girls and starts pelting Stein with hot white bolts of energy. She keeps throwing punches until she's lifted off the ground by a web of energy. I can smell the burning ozone from the static electricity.

It all happens so fast I don't have time to react. The Tesla machine hurls her through the air, and she crashes into a tree twenty yards away. I watch her fall to the ground, my heart stuck in my throat. As soon as I see her move, I turn back to the fight.

Sprinting as fast as I can, I jump against the time field that surrounds the house. When I ran into it before, I noticed that it had some give, almost like a trampoline. So this time, I use that idea to propel me through the air. I spring off perfectly. Olympic officials would be proud. *Tens across the board.*

Landing, I find myself behind the Tesla automaton. With no weapons and a Dox to protect, I kick out one of the spider legs with my prosthetic. This works brilliantly. The leg I attack breaks off like a dried wishbone on Thanksgiving, and it gives off angry blue sparks. I have to quickly roll out of the way before I get pierced by the other stomping legs. The monster maneuvers itself to where Flynn is standing.

While on the ground, I see Kara approach Ethan. "I don't want to hurt you, Ethan. Just stop this now. Come back to the Institute with me. We are your family. Not them. Come home. Please." She holds out a hand to him.

Ethan slowly approaches, his arm outstretched.

I hesitate where I am, ready to rush him and rip his head off.

"Kara, I'm so sorry if we hurt you, but you have to know that what Tesla's doing is wrong," Ethan says with an outstretched hand. She takes it, and with one quick motion, Ethan wrenches her arm behind her back. She screams in pain. "And I'm really sorry I have to do this."

Not stopping there, he pushes her forward, slowly at first. Right toward me.

I remove Kara's only weapon, some sort of pistol with a tank of red liquid on it and a coil of tarnished copper tubing down the barrel. It looks dangerous. I don't care what it does as long as it stops the fast-approaching Flynn and the Tesla monster. As Ethan pushes Kara to the ground, I see Ember rummaging through the grass between them and us.

Finding the key, Ember says, "Lex, here. Take this."

She tosses it to me, and I pocket the key to the Dox. Leaping to her feet, she puts herself between Tesla and me. I have no shot now, so I can only watch as she dodges a barrage of electrical currents and grabs onto one of the spindly legs. She snaps the leg backward, putting Tesla off-balance. When he dips to the side, she climbs on his back. She reaches around, holding onto his neck with one arm while struggling to get a grip on the tubes running to his artificial heart. The machine lets out a metallic scream and flails from side to side in quick, sharp bursts.

Ethan pushes past me, running for her, but he is too slow. The tube that Ember has a death grip on breaks and starts to flail wildly. Steam and red liquid pour from the exposed ends. Ember falls to the ground. Tesla spins around. With a flick of his hand, a bolt of electricity lifts her up and throws her through the force field and into the building.

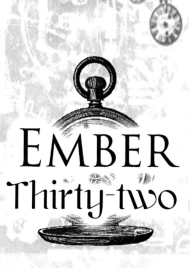

EMBER
Thirty-two

A shrill ring echoes in my ears. I reach back and touch the spot where my head connected with the door. No blood. That's good, at least. Across the distance, Lex looks over, and an expression of surprise is clear on his face for a moment before he turns back to Tesla. It takes me a second to realize why. I'm at the door. Whatever temporal barrier holds the Fixed Point in place has either fallen or let me inside.

Gloves' words drift back to the front of my mind, driving the ringing away. "*You aren't changing anything. You will go back again because you always have. Your actions are part of the Fixed Point.*"

With the help of the doorjamb, I climb to my feet. Ethan is taking on Flynn, and Stein and Kara are going at it like rabid tigers. No one is looking at me. I try to step forward to join them, but I can't. Something is holding me back. Behind me, my hands grasp for the doorknob of their own accord. Opening my mouth, I try to call out, but my voice is frozen. Like a puppet whose strings are being pulled by someone else, I push the door open behind me and step backward into the house.

As I turn to go into the room, two young soldiers stare at me, momentarily confused.

"Get her!" the first screams in Russian. They both lunge for me, guns drawn. I fall to my back and kick out, getting them both in the knee. They each scream in agony as they crumple to the floor. I roll to my feet, spin, and kick the gun out of the first soldier's hand. Then, yanking him up, I pull him in front of me. The soldier on the ground fires a shot, but he hits his buddy instead. I throw him at the armed gunman. While he struggles, I deliver a roundhouse kick to his head, knocking him out cold.

The whole thing happens so quickly it's almost a blur, but I'm still panting as I cross the room toward the stairs. I reach the door as another guard appears. He gets in one good punch to my face, and I stagger back. He pulls a mean-looking blade from his boot. Knocking the knife from his hands, I kick him in the groin. Then I kick him in the head, sending him flying backward. Once he's down, I jump on top of him, pulling the gun from his holster. A sound behind me makes me turn, gun pointed.

"Flynn," I say, surprised. How did he get through the force field?

He cocks his head to the side, staring at me curiously. That's when I realize, he isn't the Flynn from my timeline. He's the *other* Flynn. His clothes are different and his hair is just a bit shorter than the man fighting outside. I lower the gun.

Another guard appears beside him.

"Look out," I shout.

Without even looking—Flynn turns, steps forward, and delivers a blow to the guy's neck. Then another quick punch to his face sends him backward into a small table. An oil lamp rolls off and shatters, setting the drapes ablaze.

"How do you know my name?" Flynn asks, rubbing his hand.

What can I say? "It's a really long story, and not one I have time for right now. Follow me."

I turn the corner and head upstairs. The fire spreads quickly, racing its way up the walls and across the ceiling. Below us, I hear the remaining soldiers panic.

"Get the other children," someone yells.

"But sir, the fire."

"We can't leave them. The Tsar and Tsarina are dead. Their bodies must be moved quickly, before the rebels get here."

"Sir, they are as good as dead up there. There's no way out."

"Fine. You guard these stairs for as long as possible, be sure they don't make it out of this house alive."

* * *

I shiver even through the intense heat. We are almost to the bedroom door when Flynn grabs my arm. Inside my head, time slows down. Every kind smile, every reassuring hug he ever gave me, plays back inside my mind. He was my family. I can change things, maybe. I can try. Take him out of here and let Gloves take us both. But then I never know him, or Ethan, or even Kara. I swallow.

"Who are you?" he demands.

I frown, putting my hand over his and pushing up my sleeve to expose my Tesla mark. His eyes widen.

"I'm the girl behind that door." I point to it. They are worth it, I realize, staring into his eyes. Worth the memory loss and the separation from Alexei. They are worth all of it. And even if I can change it, I won't. "You asked me once to trust you and I didn't. I'm really sorry for that. Very, very sorry. But right now, you have to trust me."

He stares in my eyes before glancing back down to my arm and nodding.

"The room behind that door is about to collapse. You have to go grab her—me—and get us out of here."

"But the boy, Alexei—"

I shake my head. "You can't get them both. You go now, grab the girl, and leave the boy behind. You understand?"

Stepping past me, he rushes into the room. As soon as he disappears, Gloves runs up the stairs, sees me, and freezes. I press my finger to my lips to silence him, waving him to the door across the hallway. He slips inside just as Flynn emerges. The smoke is filling the hall, and I can barely see him. But I can make out my own figure in his arms. She's reaching back and screaming. A loose chunk of plaster falls from the ceiling and hits them. Pushing him in the back, I direct him to the end of the hall. He nods, presses a button on his Tether, and vanishes.

A fit of coughs wracks my body. I run to the door and scream.

"Gloves! Quickly, this way. He's in here."

But he doesn't answer. Holding my arm above

my eyes, I can see that another piece of ceiling has collapsed. He's trapped under it.

I rush to his side. He's conscious, but he's covered in soot and grimacing in pain. "Gloves, are you all right?" I grab the chunk of wood and manage to get it off him. He's facedown on the floor, gasping for air.

"I'm… all right," he says between breaths, "But I can't move my legs."

Tugging my shirt up over my face, I crawl back to the bedroom, trying to stay under the dark cloud of smoke. Alexei rushes into my arms and hugs me.

"Where is Father? I heard gunfire."

I wrap my arms around him, stroking his hair. "It's okay," I soothe. "I'm going to get you out of here. Okay?" When I set him down, he nods, pulling the sword from the sheath at his side.

"You need to leave that behind."

He shakes his head.

"We have to crawl, baby. To stay under the smoke. Can you leave that so you can crawl with me?"

He shakes his head again, and his eyes are wide in terror. Beside him, some burning rubble falls, hitting him in the face. He screams and falls onto his side. When I brush it off, I can see it's already left a nasty red burn on his neck and face.

Think, I command myself.

I reach into my pocket and pull out the handful of bottle caps I retrieved from the ground at Wardenclyffe Tower, the ones Lex threw off the roof in a fit. I'd meant to return them to him. I suppose, in a way, I am.

"Alexei, give me your hand." He obeys, and I carefully tip the metal caps into his palm. "These are special for you. Whenever you are scared or hurt, you just touch these and they will make you brave. Now, can you make it to the hall?" I ask.

He stuffs the bottle caps in his pocket and nods.

Together, we crawl across the hall. I kick a chunk of burning timber out of the way. Looking behind me, I can see Alexei's eyes are watering from the smoke. The side of his face looks worse; it's already swelling and blistering. By the time we reach Gloves, he's nearly unconscious.

"Gloves, the Contra. Where is the Contra?"

He slips his hand in his pocket and pulls out the green pills.

I turn to Alexei. "Alexei. This is my friend, Gloves. He's going to get you out of here, okay?"

Alexei clutches my hand. I give it a tight squeeze.

"Is Father dead?" He coughs, wincing at the pain.

I'm not sure why I lie. Maybe I just can't bear to hurt him anymore; maybe it's just my own wishful thinking. "Father is fine, Alexei. We're all going to be fine. But you need to go now."

Reluctantly, he lets go. Gloves takes him by the hand, offering him the pill.

"You hold on tight, Alexei, and you don't let go, no matter what."

He nods. I lean down to whisper in Gloves' ear. "You take care of him."

I slip the Contra in the side of Gloves' mouth and motion for Alexei to take his. They vanish.

Just as they disappear, a huge chunk of plaster falls from above me, crashing through the floor and taking me with it.

LEX
Thirty-three

Flynn is less than a foot from me, and his lash is drawn back over his head, ready to strike. Leveling Kara's weapon at him, I squeeze the trigger and let loose. Fiery drops of liquid blast out the tip of the weapon. Flynn dodges to the side and rolls out of the way.

There is nothing better than the feeling that we might survive this. The Tesla monster spits sparks and green hydraulic fluid all over the trampled grass.

Flynn looks up, seeing where Ember has landed, and struggles to his feet, abandoning his battle with me to go after her. There is nothing I can do now. I can't get through the force field. He takes a few steps and stops, putting his hand up. At first, I think he's waving to her, but then I know. He can't get through it either. Good. At least one of us is safe.

I turn, firing on Tesla, and though it doesn't look like the weapon is doing much damage, I keep firing. Kara has managed to get free, and Ethan balks as she attacks. Just as I wonder if he has some compunction against hitting a girl, he steps forward, taking her by surprise, and nails her with a right hook. She falls to the ground. I see Kara quickly touch her ear, and then dial something into the tech on her wrist. Immediately, she disappears into nothingness—like vacuum sucking up a plastic trash sack.

We are winning.

"Ethan!" I yell, continuing to fire. "Get Stein up."

It is as if she hears me. She's already struggling to stand when Ethan helps her up and props her against the tree. I keep volleying flaming bullets toward Tesla. They hit, burning holes in the artificial skin. But it's not damaging the metal underneath.

"Come on, guys! A little help here," I yell. Stein staggers over, though she's leaning to the left. It's a sign of broken ribs and a dislocated shoulder.

"You okay?" I ask.

"I'll survive."

Ethan helps support her as we stand huddled together. I hold the strap of the backpack with one hand and keep my other hand clutched around the key in my vest pocket.

"What's our plan?" Stein asks.

That is a very good question.

"You two distract Tesla. I'll activate the Dox," I say just as Tesla shoots an electric bolt in our direction. We dodge it, and I find myself too close to the caterpillar tracks of the creature. Pieces of dirt and damp grass are spit up as the monster tries its best to run me over. Rolling out of the way of the treadmills of death, I find myself on the opposite side of Tesla. Stein and Ethan are standing where the fallen leg lies.

I watch as they jab at the tank tracks. Little by

little, they bend and chip away at them with their newfound weapon.

The wind picks up, lightning striking the tree where Stein once lay. On the perimeter of the burning building, I see the vortex, a giant tornado sucking up time and leaving chaos in its wake. It's moving slowly, but I know we only have a few minutes before we are doomed to the paradox. There's no time. I look over to Ipatiev House, wanting to see my sister one last time, just in case.

I can't believe what I see. Flynn is pulling my sister from the flaming building. He manages to get her through a main floor window before most of the building crumbles in on itself, sending a shower of ash and sparks high into the air. He cradles her in his arms and walks toward me. She's limp. Her arms dangle as he moves, and her eyes are closed.

No, no, no. This isn't happening. I unstrap the backpack and carefully remove the Dox from inside it. Quickly giving it a look over to make sure the thing is still intact, I pull the key from my pocket. With the key in close proximity, the Dox starts to hum. I look up to make sure my team is still okay and realize that the Tesla monster has turned and is heading in my direction. I'm not sure if it's fleeing from the vortex right behind it or if it is attracted to the Dox. Stein lies on her side, and Ethan has been thrown some distance away.

I hold out the Dox as a last resort to stave off the onslaught of Tesla's monster. For some reason, this stops it right in its tracks. The Dox continues to glow as I press the key up against the glass. Holding it in outstretched arms so everyone can see, I insert the key past the glass barrier. It's still a marvel to me how the glass softens just enough for me to put the key in. I don't have to fumble around to find the correct orientation. It's as if the filament recognizes the key and accepts it. As with any good key, all I have to do is turn it. With that simple gesture, I restart the time stream.

Nothing happens at first, but then the base starts to spin. A light brighter than the sun shines from the glass bulb, and the key falls out of the center, back into my hand. Oddly, the Dox isn't hot.

"Lex, give me the Dox!" Flynn yells.

My eyes dart from him to the Tesla monster. There's something about the way that he's looking at me. I can't quite describe it. Not pleading really, but sincere. He gently puts Ember down beside me and holds his hand out.

"Please. Trust me. Just this once."

I hesitate, glancing down at my sister. Ember blinks and lays a hand on my foot. She nods.

Taking a deep breath, I hand it to him. I'm not sure why, but something inside my head is telling me to trust him. Maybe it's just relief that Ember is alive and that we might actually survive this night. Again.

Behind Flynn, the Tesla monster is spinning, its broken track digging a rut it can't escape. With two back legs gone and one track disabled, the monster isn't able to go anywhere. Behind the monster, the vortex looms. I watch as it engulfs the burning house. The flames aren't the problem anymore. Torrential winds rip my parents' tomb from the ground and up into the void.

I watch with awe and curiosity while Flynn tucks

the Dox under his arm and sprints toward the Tesla creature, toward the path of the vortex. He doesn't stop his drive until he comes in contact with the Tesla monster. Bolts of lightning course through his body. I see his eyes roll back, and he jerks with convulsions. Pulling himself up by one arm, Flynn slams the Dox into the creature's chest cavity. He shakes and thrashes, and all his muscles contract around the Tesla coil at the center of the creature. He holds on as the paradox tornado comes at them.

I scramble back without taking my eyes off the scene. Stein and Ethan have crawled to me. We huddle next to Ember, who is awake but limp in my arms.

It's hard to see Flynn now beyond the storm closing in around us. I have no will to run. It's almost like I no longer care if the paradox swallows us. I've got both people I love right here with me. And Ethan's here, too.

We are together. I'm willing to let time take its course. We hold each other, unable and unwilling to move, when the sky rips open like God himself slashed through it with a sword. The last thing I see is an explosion of light that erases everything.

LEX
Thirty-three

Am I dead? I feel like I'm floating. The white light is all around me, but it's not warm like I expect. It's cold. Cold enough to for me to realize something is off. I take a breath and shiver. It's like breathing in ice water. Blinking, I see that it isn't light from the explosion behind my eyes. It's sunlight. Raising my hand, I shield my eyes, and then close one eye and squint. The sun is mid-sky. How is that possible? It was just after midnight a few seconds ago. I jolt upright, looking around.

Next to me, Stein groans. I lean over and give her a shake. She rolls onto her side in the grass, pressing her face against the ground. I can see angry red burns crisscrossing her exposed skin. She's breathing hard, probably trying to get a grip on the pain. A chunk of her hair is melted into a glob just below her chin, but otherwise, she looks all right. A flash goes off and I jump, covering my eyes.

A little old woman in a tan skirt, with her white hair tucked under a pink scarf, holds up a camera and snaps a picture. The flash goes off again. From the steps of the building behind us, an old man yells to her in Russian. She snaps one more picture and wobbles away. A young man is on his cell phone, speaking urgently to someone on the other end. He's calling the police, I realize. He's trying to get us some help. Whatever happened, our landing here in midday must have caused quite a ruckus for these people.

Lex crawls between us, propping himself up on his knees. "You two okay?"

I look down at myself. No major parts missing. Beyond that, I can't tell. I ache everywhere. My ankle might be sprained, and the lump on the back of my head is pounding. The pain in my chest tells me I've probably cracked a rib or two. "Ethan," I say, scanning the area. I don't see him anywhere. "Ethan?"

"Over here," he says with a wave as he stumbles into sight. He's holding one arm at an odd angle, but he's smiling. I struggle to my feet despite the pain and limp over to him. Careful of his injured arm, I hug him, pressing my face into the nape of his neck.

"Where are we?" he asks as Lex and Stein join us.

I nod to the massive building behind him. The elderly woman is talking to a small group of people, one of whom looks like a priest. She's pointing at us and chatting away in Russian.

I walk over to the man on the phone. "Excuse me, sir. My friend and I are lost. Can you tell me where we are?"

He looks at me like I'm crazy, but he lowers the phone. "Yekaterinburg. The Church on the Blood." He pauses. "Where did you come from? You just appeared out of nowhere. And you're hurt. I have called for help."

I mutter a thank you and walk back over to my friends.

"This is bad. We need to go, like now. Before a whole lot of people start asking a whole lot of questions we can't answer."

Ethan nods. "Let's get out of sight so we can rift out."

Together, we walk around to the back of the church. There's no one around.

"So, where to?" Ethan asks, ready to punch the numbers into the Tether.

"We should get Stein back to Nobel so he can take a look at her," Lex chimes in.

She waves him off. "I'm fine. Just sore. And starving. I can't remember the last time I ate anything."

As if agreeing, my stomach rumbles. Ethan laughs. "Someone must have said the magic word."

I slap him playfully, and he winces.

"Ow."

"Oh. Sorry. Yeah. I could eat."

"Me, too. Tacos?" Lex asks, taking Stein by the hand. "I know a little place in Mexico City—"

Ethan cuts him off. "Shouldn't we make sure everything is, I dunno, fixed?"

I look around. "No hover cars or ancient Greek armies. No massive, soul-sucking tornadoes. Not even any *tiny* soul-sucking tornadoes. I think it's safe to say everything is fine."

"And even if it's not, Lex needs a shower. Seriously," Stein says.

I laugh. It hurts, so I clutch my chest.

"Maybe we should go get cleaned up and bandaged first?" Ethan says, pointing to my foot, which I'm holding up gingerly. "Besides, Stein is pushing the no shirt, no shoes, no service policy."

I look over and see that he's right. Her shirt is mostly shredded. Somehow, it still manages to look good on her.

"Just take me somewhere with room service, and I'll be fine," I say, turning to Lex. "Seriously, though. No tacos. How about hot dogs? Just a quick stop on the way home?"

Lex looks at Stein, who shrugs. "Chicago?"

"Why not?" I say. "How about 1965? It was a great year."

EMBER
Thirty-four

"How's Stein?" I call down to Lex as he enters the room. I'm perched on top of the half-pipe, my legs dangling. Ethan is busy working with Nobel, and I'm bored. We've only been back in Hollow Tower a few days, but I'm already itching to get out. It's too noisy here. Too chaotic. I find myself longing for the calm routine of the Institute.

"She's fine. Nobel's salve is a lifesaver. No permanent damage, at least not physically."

He gets a running start and leaps up the pipe, grabbing the lip beside me and pulling himself up.

"She still reading through that journal she stole?"

He sits next to me and nods. "Yeah. I don't know what's in there or why it bothers her so much. She's just been... distant lately. I figure she'll tell me when she's ready."

I nudge him with my shoulder. "She'll be all right. Just give her some time."

He snorts. "I have plenty of that."

The lines around his eyes are deep. I know he's

worried, but there's nothing I can do, so I opt to change the subject. "The new leg looks good."

He runs his hand down his newly repaired leg. "It's not bad. Better than that stupid contraption Nobel built. Still sore. Nobel took a lot of the hardware out to make it lighter and replaced it with that skin stuff. That junk he made in those petri dishes is amazing."

For some reason, that kind of grosses me out. I think Lex can tell.

"Did you know the skin can grow new tendons? He took the main piston out and spread that stuff all over. It works beautifully."

"Speaking of new and better things…" I reach behind me and pull a wad from my back pocket, thrusting it toward him.

Grabbing it, he shakes it out with a jingle, and then stuffs the new jester's hat on his head. He gives it a shake, and the jingle bells rattle. It's red and yellow, with a bright green patch and blue thread stitches.

"It's not much. I had to use scraps of old clothes to sew it together."

He grins from ear to ear. "It's perfect, thanks."

Below us, Gloves chugs through the room, his train chair leaving puffs of black smoke in the air.

Lex shakes his head again, jingling. "I can't believe how well the Dox worked. Everything is back to normal."

I swallow. "Not everything."

The Dox managed to seal off the paradox, repairing the stream from the point it was created forward. Most things went back to normal. No one here remembers the attack. It looks like only those who were in the blast radius remember the paradox at all. Everything that's happened from the point the paradox was created until now has been rewritten, smoothed out, and put back on course.

But Flynn is still dead. The Tesla automaton is gone. I don't know if his brain was in that suit or if it's still tucked away at the Institute. We'll probably have to find out at some point. But the immediate danger is past. Now comes the really scary part.

The future.

"So, what are you going to do now?" Lex asks, looking away as if he's a little scared of what I might say.

"Well, first, I have to go pay my past self a little visit." Absently, I reach up and touch my chin. Nobel's salve has healed it to a faint scar. Soon, even that will fade away. "Then, Sisson and I are going to return all the keys you boys lifted. After that, who knows? Ethan thinks we should stay. Fight alongside the Hollows."

Lex leans back on his palms, "I knew there was a reason I liked that guy."

I roll my eyes. "Yeah. Right. He also wants to take me on vacation. Disneyland or something. Says we need some R and R."

"Also a solid plan."

I pause, taking a breath. "But the thing is, you don't really fight, do you? I mean, you get into fights, but it isn't really the same thing. I want to protect people like us. Maybe the way Tesla did things wasn't perfect, but there has to be a better way to live than as thieves. I mean, we almost exploded the universe, Lex. And for what?"

Lex cocks his head, looking at me thoughtfully. "Them sound like fightin' words, Ember."

I just nod, looking off into the distance. The common room is quiet. It's early. Most of the Hollows are still fast asleep.

"I just mean, it never should have happened. This fight between Tesla and the Hollows, it's doing too much damage. Too many people are getting caught in the crossfire."

Lex juts out his bottom lip. "I still think *brain face* deserves a little payback for what he's done."

"Tesla really hasn't done anything wrong—"

"Except lie to you. And create a giant robot to kill you. And dump dozens of Rifters into the time stream to die."

I shift uncomfortably. He has a point.

He continues, "Let me just ask you one question. What do you think he'd have done to us if we'd handed over the Dox and let him repair the paradox?"

I clench my jaw. "He probably would have killed Stein and Ethan and taken us back to the Institute."

"And then?"

I sigh. The truth is, I have no idea. Brainwash us? Experiment on us? Lock us in a dark room and throw away the key? I can't imagine he just wants to have a tea party, that's for sure.

I stand, putting a hand on his shoulder. "Look, we'll talk about it more when I get back."

"So you are coming back then? For sure?"

"Of course I am. Try not to get into any trouble while I'm gone. And no more stealing. I mean it, Lex."

He shrugs, looking up at me with his jester's hat dangling to the side and a big smile on his face. "No promises."

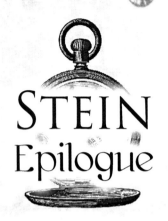

STEIN
Epilogue

TESLA JOURNAL ENTRY: MARCH 23RD, 1894

I have not written here for some time. Things have been exciting and chaotic since the discovery of my travelers—my Rifters. I have written many papers on the phenomenon, only to repeatedly destroy them.

How can I reveal this to the world? A world of liars and thieves with no moral responsibility? I cannot bring myself to do so. Time is such a fragile and precious thing. How can I hand it over to those who would corrupt it for their own ends? No. I will not.

All of this research has been done in secret.

But I wish to reveal the current state of things.

After many months, and with the help of equipment my travelers have brought me from the future, we have created a miracle. A child.

Helena and her husband desperately wanted a child but seemed unable to conceive. After harvesting eggs from the mother, I have taken my own genetic material, as well as genetic material from a second male host—one who shares Helena's unique abilities—and used it to create three viable embryos. Only one survived the process. The birth went smoothly, and the vitals are strong. So far, all my tests show the female infant to be extraordinary. Increased muscle density, sharpened reflexes, and increased respiration. I shall continue to monitor the child until it reaches full maturity, in the hopes that her ability to access the time stream—to navigate it successfully—will surpass that of my other travelers. Perhaps with regular infusions of her blood and marrow, so genetically similar to my own as to prevent my body from rejecting the foreign substance, I myself might obtain the ability to travel as they do.

Closing the journal, I shove it in my hip pouch. With the final entry burning it's revelations into my mind, my hand travels to my naval, involuntarily tracing my small, sun-shaped scar. I know I should share my suspicions with Lex, but first, I want proof—I must be absolutely sure.

And there's only one person who has the answers I need.

***Continue the epic journey in the next novels of the Lost Imperials Saga, **Prodigal & Riven**, now available everywhere books are sold. You can also find exclusive deleted and bonus scenes on the official website, www.thelostimperials.com

Author's Notes

  *Nikola Tesla lived from 1856-1943. He was an inventor, physicist, mechanical engineer, electrical engineer, and futurist. He is best known for his contributions to the modern alternating current (AC) electrical supply system. Tesla's patents and theoretical work helped form the basis of wireless communication and radio.

  His many revolutionary developments in the field of electromagnetism were based on Michael Faraday's theories of electromagnetic technology. His last remaining laboratory, Wardenclyffe Tower, was sold in 1917 when funding ran out for his experiments into wireless energy, which he dreamed he could one day give freely to all humanity. The Tower was sold and eventually demolished. However, today, the laboratory and the foundation of the Tower remain intact. Recently, a non-profit group purchased the property— it plans to turn it into the Tesla Science Museum. It will be the only Tesla Museum in the United States, and it will stand as a tribute to a man who is often overlooked in the records of scientific history.

*The Last Imperial Family of Russia, the Romanovs, have one of the darkest histories of the twentieth century. The family, being forced to abdicate the throne in the early days of Communism, was held prisoner for over a year. The last seventy-eight days of their captivity took place in Yekaterinburg, Russia. It was there, in a place called Ipatiev House in the early hours of July 17, 1918, that the family and their household, eleven people in total, were sent to the basement and brutally murdered by Bolshevik soldiers. The remains were then stripped, mutilated, and buried in a mass grave in a nearby forest.

Many years later, the remains of nine bodies were found and identified as those of the Imperial family and their staff. The two missing bodies were believed to be those of Alexei and Anastasia Romanov.

In 1998, eighty years after their murder, those nine bodies were laid to rest in a state funeral in St. Petersburg. Sometime later, pieces of remains some believe belong to the lost Romanov children were found far from the first gravesite. While they have been tested and found genetically similar, the Greek Orthodox Church and many others have challenged their authenticity.

Today, the remains of the Lost Imperials have not been laid to rest.

*This poem was written by the Grand Duchess Olga Anastasia Romanov and was found among her belongings after their murder.

Give patience, Lord, to us Thy children
In these dark, stormy days to bear
The persecution of our people,
The tortures falling to our share.
Give strength, Just God, to us who need it,
The persecutors to forgive,
Our heavy, painful cross to carry
And Thy great meekness to achieve.
When we are plundered and insulted
In days of mutinous unrest
We turn for help to Thee, Christ-Savior,
That we may stand the bitter test.
Lord of the world, God of Creation,
Give us Thy blessing through our prayer
Give us peace of heart to us, O Master,
This hour of utmost dread to bear.
And on the threshold of the grave
Breathe power divine into our clay
That we, Thy children, may find strength
In meekness for our foes to pray.

CPSIA information can be obtained at www.ICGtesting.com
Printed in the USA
LVOW10s0847310816

502627LV00001B/1/P